RHYTHM AND *Blue Skies*

The Styles of *Love* Trilogy *Malcolm & Sky*

N.D. Jones

KUUMBA
PUBLISHING
CREATIVE MINDS,
PASSIONATE HEARTS

Book Layout © 2014 BookDesignTemplates.com
Cover Design by *Limabean Designs*
Logo Design: Najja Akinwole
Editor: Kathryn Schieber
All art and logo copyright ©2018 by Kuumba Publishing

Rhythm and Blue Skies/ N.D. Jones. – 1st ed.
ISBN: 978-1-7325567-1-3
The Perks of Higher Ed/N.D. Jones ©2018
The Wish of Xmas Present/N.D. Jones ©2018

DEDICATION

For D'Nia and Dee

Thank you for reading *Perks of Higher Ed: An Office Romance* and your desire to want more of Sky and Malcolm's story. Readers can thank the two of you for the Styles of Love Trilogy.

TABLE OF CONTENTS

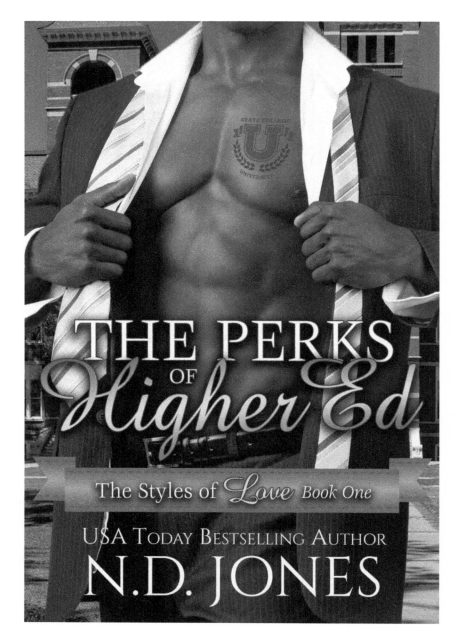

THE PERKS
OF
Higher Ed

The Styles of *Love* Book One

USA Today Bestselling Author
N.D. JONES

STYLES FAMILY

CHAPTER ONE

"No."

"Come on." Malcolm sat across from Angie and Sean in their living room, baffled why his sister was giving him a hard time about his request. "Why not?"

"Did you really just whine those four words at me?"

"Yeah, he did. He's either devolved into a loser of epic proportions or the woman he wants is smokin' hot."

"Okay, two things," Malcolm raised his middle finger at his brother-in-law, Sean, "one, no one says 'smokin' hot' anymore, and the only loser in the family is you. Two," eyes shifted to his older sister, and his index finger joined the middle one, "you owe me a favor."

"For the record, Dr. Styles, that's three things." Sean took hold of Angie's hand, where it rested on the sofa cushion between them, brought it to his lips, and kissed the palm.

His sister's dark-brown eyes no longer shimmered with faith and happiness but flickered with shadows and disappointment when she looked at her husband. Malcolm wouldn't remind Angie why she owed him a favor, not with Sean in the room with them. Some days, he still wanted to go after the guy for what he'd done to Angie. But he'd promised to keep his temper under control and his fists away from Sean's face.

Angie didn't return Sean's smile, but she did reclaim her hand before returning her attention to Malcolm.

"A degree in African American History doesn't mean I'm weak in math." Malcolm's response to Sean's playful jibe came a touch too late for the comeback to sound unforced or to cover the harsh tenor of his voice.

"I know, man. I didn't mean anything by it. I was just... well, you know, playing with you. Like old times."

Yeah, Malcolm knew. Their eighteen years of friendship and Sean's twenty years of marriage were tested and damn near ruined because Sean Franklin, Esquire, couldn't keep his dick out of his former legal assistant. The twenty-something University at Buffalo law graduate thought the father of three would leave his wife and children for her. That kind of relationship had the wrong ingredients for sustainability. For Malcolm, cheating and lying weren't sexy and romantic. They were poorly executed tropes committed by people without creativity but with an inflated sense of entitlement.

Malcolm had no interest in that kind of office romance. People got hurt. People like Angela Styles-Franklin.

"Listen, I came here to talk to my sister."

For uncomfortable seconds, Sean stared at Malcolm, a mixture of guilt, anger, and understanding in his eyes. At six-three, the civil rights attorney oozed confidence and had built his legal career fighting injustice. Until two months ago, Malcolm respected the hell out of the guy as a person and as a professional. Now, he wavered between supporting Sean and Angie as they struggled to rebuild their shattered marriage and beating the big man's ass for breaking Angie's heart.

"Right, right. We don't talk anymore. I get it."

Sean turned to Angie, her five-three frame set in profile to the tall man, and just looked at her. Her skin, rich and dark, like Malcolm's, radiated the same ageless beauty as their mother and aunts. The women in his family were unmatched in intelligence, stubbornness, and loyalty.

Malcolm watched his brother-in-law, who sighed and shook his head when he shifted his gaze back to him. "I know I messed up. With Angie, with the kids, and with you. I'm trying to fix things."

He didn't have a response that wouldn't have Angie snorting her displeasure at him, so Malcolm remained silent and waited to see what his brother-in-law would say or do next.

Sean kissed Angie's cheek, a quick peck. He knew his brother-in-law almost as well as he knew himself. Sean's kiss had been a calculated display of affection. Malcolm got the message. More importantly, so did Angie. Sean Franklin, the cheating bastard he'd turned into, wouldn't give up on his marriage and wife no matter how anyone else felt about his mistakes, including Malcolm.

He itched to punch him. Yet Malcolm couldn't fault the man's spine and fighting spirit. The two attributes kept Sean's law firm busy and high-profile. *U.S. News - Best Lawyers®* ranked Franklin & Associates among the best regional law firms in civil right law in Buffalo, New York.

Pushing to his feet, Sean nodded to Malcolm on his way out of the living room. A couple of minutes later, he heard sounds coming from the kitchen where Sean had turned on the television. From what Malcolm could hear, the Mets were down one run to the Phillies. The second week of the baseball season was in full swing, and he couldn't give a damn about the sport or the early start to the season. He might prefer spring to fall, but football was his sport of choice.

"One of these days, you're going to have to forgive him."

"Have you?"

The house smelled like a flower garden. The sweet fragrance of hyacinth overpowered the clove scent of the dozen red roses on the marble-topped coffee table in front of Angie. His sister liked flowers as much as any woman, but Sean's expensive floral arrangements amounted to slapping a Band-Aid over a gaping wound.

Angie's bare feet lifted to her leather reclining sofa, wide and plush and still in good condition considering the way Angie and Sean's children, fourteen, ten, and four, sprawled over the furniture with no care or understanding of the cost. Malcolm's and Angie's parents, Charles and Kimberly Styles, couldn't afford half the items in either of the siblings' homes. The Styles children, like too many of their east side Buffalo neighbors, had grown up in a household one paycheck from living on the streets.

"I don't want to talk about my marriage. You didn't come here for that, anyway. Let me see the brochure."

Malcolm guessed he wasn't much better than his nephew and nieces with the way he'd plopped onto the ottoman instead of the chair behind it. He handed his sister the brochure and didn't interrupt as she read.

A decade may have separated them, but Angie never treated him like an annoying younger brother, even when he acted like one. No more than she confused the role of a sister with that of a mother.

"SUNY's Summer Leadership Retreat, really?"

"What?"

"You've never shown any interest in higher ed leadership beyond being African American Studies department chair. You don't want to be a chief academic officer or dean, although, if you keep researching, publishing and presenting your papers, you could. And you certainly have no aspiration to claim a presidency."

"One college president in the family is enough. I enjoy teaching too much to ever give it up."

For the briefest moment, Angie's gaze fell away from Malcolm and to her lap. When her focus returned to him, he saw an emotion that didn't suit his sister. Self-doubt.

"I felt that way once."

"This situation isn't your fault. Chasing your dreams isn't an excuse for Sean to chase young, convenient ass. You work long hours. It's the nature of the beast. He's a lawyer who didn't have his law firm handed to him. He damn sure knows what hard work and long hours look like and the impact they have on a marriage."

"I know. It all matters, though. Everything in marriage matters, even the stuff we don't realize or even think about. Enough about me." She waved her hand in front of her face, as if giving the right-of-way to a pedestrian crossing against the light. "Why are you running after a woman who doesn't want to be caught or even chased?"

"She wants both but doesn't know it yet." Angie spoke volumes through her snort, so he added, "I'm not being arrogant or foolish."

"The fact that you chose those words is more telling than if I would've said them."

"I knew you were thinking them. I spared you the time and another snort of disapproval. She likes me... I think."

"You think?"

"She likes the way I look. I'm thirty-six, for God's sake. I know when a woman finds me attractive, and she does."

"She would have to be blind not to. You've always been too handsome for your own good."

"That saying has never made any sense, no matter how many times you've said it to me."

"Oh, it makes plenty of sense. Ask... what's the name of the poor woman you want me to help you stalk?"

"I'm not going to stalk her, and her name is Dr. Sky Ellis. She's the new Director of Diversity & Inclusion at Eastern Bluebird College."

"How do you even know she's going to attend this summer leadership retreat?" Angie shook the trifold brochure at him. "You also don't need me to nominate you. You can self-nominate."

Malcolm pointed to himself. "Chair of an understaffed and struggling department." Angie rolled her eyes, knowing him well enough to anticipate his next words and actions. He pointed at her anyway. "President of Excelsior University. Which nomination would have the greater chance of getting me one of the thirty-five spaces?"

"You want me to use my position to help you get a date." Angie snorted again. "Unbelievable."

"It's not as if I'm not a highly-qualified candidate."

"Highly-qualified, yes, but not highly motivated. You could possibly take someone's spot who wants to be there."

"I do want to be there. Right next to Sky."

"The retreat is intended for institutional leaders who want to improve their leadership skills as they move along their career path. It's not a dating service for the horny and smitten."

"Is that a no?"

"Yes, the same answer I gave you ten minutes ago. There's an ethical line here, M and M, and I won't cross it for something as frivolous as a crush."

He hated when she was right, almost as much as he disliked how much he still loved his nickname.

"I withdraw my other question. I don't want to know how you know she'll be attending the summer leadership retreat. Apply, and see what happens. Or just ask Dr. Ellis out."

"I did. She said getting involved with a colleague wasn't a good idea."

Angie's shrug wasn't reassuring, and neither was her response.

"Well, there you have it then. She doesn't want an office romance, no matter how attractive you think she finds you."

His heart clenched, not from disappointment but with determination. Although Malcolm and Sean were on the outs right now, they'd been close and had a lot in common, beyond their love for Angie and the kids. Tenacity, for one. Charm, for another.

Sky hadn't ever said she wasn't interested in him, only that an office romance was "ill-advised with the potential for awkwardness and embarrassment when it ends."

There, the woman was wrong. She just didn't know it yet.

Malcolm pulled his cell from his pants pocket, found Sky's number, and typed a message.

"We're in the middle of a conversation. Who are you texting?"

"Sky."

"Geesh, you have her cell phone number? You *are* stalking her."

"I'm not. Every member of the Diversity Progress Committee has the cell numbers for the others. I've been a member for years and Sky's new position is the chair of that committee. A committee meeting is how I found out she received an early acceptance to the leadership retreat. I overheard Sky talking to Dr. Mosby about her acceptance letter."

"You mean you eavesdropped on her conversation with a colleague." Angie tsked, an upgrade in judgement from her snort.

"If you want to get all technical and judgmental about it, then yes."

When he'd finished typing the message, Malcolm ended it with a romantic emoji. He'd downloaded the stickers to his phone a few weeks earlier and had waited for the perfect time to begin using them. He didn't want to scare Sky off, so he didn't send anything too forward. But he also wanted to make his intentions clear, so he added an image of two emoji facing each other and sharing a spaghetti noodle. Okay, the noodle did loop, over a dinner plate, in a heart design and two small red hearts were between the smiling male and female emojis.

Tenacious and charming, yes, subtle, not so much.

"Let me see what you wrote."

"Now who's being nosey?" Malcolm joined Angie on the sofa and handed her his phone. He watched her read the short message, waiting for a frown or snort. Neither came, to his surprise. Instead, she smiled.

"This is good."

"Glad you approve. Do you think it'll work?"

"No, but it's a good start." Angie read the message again. "A very good start."

Malcolm took the phone from his sister, reread the text, and then, literally, patted himself on the back. He didn't desire an office romance, although he would take one as a start. At thirty-six, Malcolm wanted to settle down and have everything Sean had taken for granted and nearly thrown away.

What he didn't know, but needed to find out, was whether Sky Ellis wanted the same with him.

Malcolm read his message again.

16% of people met their spouse at work. The celestial sphere, a dome under which the sun, moon, and stars dance and sing in cosmic harmony, is an astrological phenomenon eclipsed only by the limitations of our vision and the gravity of our fears.

"How many square feet?" Sky's father inquired.

"Seven hundred. The same as the last time you asked and the time before that."

"That's one hundred eighty-nine square feet below the national average, one hundred forty-two below New York's average, and one hundred ninety-seven below Maryland's. How much are you allowing yourself to be ripped off in rent? And for what, to have a view of Niagara River? We have rivers in Maryland, you know? You didn't have to go all the way to Buffalo for scenery. What about the weather? They get about twenty-five inches of snow in January. You don't like snow, remember?"

Sky rolled her eyes and plopped onto her bed, her hand clutching the wireless phone the way she wanted to squeeze her father's throat until he shut up. Phones had Caller ID for a reason. Against her better judgment, she'd answered, knowing the obstinate man would keep calling until she did.

Through the speakerphone and a pillow in which she'd buried her face, Sky could hear her father, Retired Captain Robert Joseph Ellis III, spout more pointless stats he no doubt looked up right before calling her. He did this, using data to buttress a dead argument instead of letting it go and moving on. The old man knew all about moving on and letting go, though. He'd done it before.

Sky didn't say that, of course, not that she hadn't in the past. She'd promised herself, after her father's heart attack, to have more of an open mind and less of a closed heart. To forgive, if not forget. She hadn't done either, which they both knew. Like much between them, however, it went unsaid. Well, unsaid on Sky's part. Her father, on the other hand, had turned over an annoying new leaf. His five-hour coronary bypass surgery had left him with more than a physical scar. The man, at seventy-seven, was trying to fill decades of emotional neglect with belated fathering which had long since passed the point of smothering.

"Well? What do you have to say?"

"About what?" Flipping onto her back, Sky glared at the phone, not that her father could see her or had ever been discouraged by her words or frowns. He waded through her anger and tears as if her verbal lashes were passing ocean currents to be endured instead of harsh waves to be avoided. "What do you want to know now?"

"You weren't listening, were you?"

"No, Captain, I wasn't."

After ten minutes of listening to Robert's monologue, crushing silence now bloomed in the distance that separated daughter from father. A distance that had nothing to do with Sky living in Buffalo and Robert in Annapolis.

"I thought you agreed to stop calling me that."

She had. Shit. The looming darkness and her mood had Sky getting out of bed and padding through her one-bedroom loft apartment. Cool hardwood flooring felt good against the heat of her bare feet. Down the hall and into the open living/dining room, she didn't bother turning on the light. Three windows she hadn't taken the time to cover with blinds or curtains blessed her with the waning echoes of sunlight.

Red-and-orange rays glistened off the Niagara River. The sun was a ball of descending fire mirrored in the water below her fifth-floor apartment. She would miss Maryland's Renaissance Festival in September as well as the state's Seafood Festival at Sandy Point State Park. Nitro Circus would return to the city of her birth in July. The Annapolis Crab

Feast would go on without Sky in August unless she decided to take a long weekend and visit Robert. Her father held no fondness for crabs, but the event took place at the Navy-Marine Corps Memorial Stadium, which was all the motivation he'd needed to make the outing an annual event. As she watched jet boats glide through the swift current of the Niagara River and under Peace Bridge, Sky hoped, in time, this city would feel like home.

"Will absence make your heart grow fonder?"

"Why do you do that?"

"Give you an opening as long as the USS *Annapolis*? I don't know. You ran away from home and me, what do you want me to say?"

"Another opening. You don't want me to answer either of those questions. Or maybe you do. Do you want me to say my absence from your life didn't make your heart grow fonder for me? Or do you want to hear that you left me first, so my leaving you proves we have something in common other than my dead mother?"

"Yeah, I knew you had it in you. Feel better?"

No, she didn't. Hurting her father never made Sky feel better, even though he deserved all the venom she'd once spewed.

Sky sat on the white, L-shaped sectional sofa she'd had the movers place under her living room windows. In the morning, sitting there made for excellent reading, the sun at her back and her day ahead of her. Now, as the sun gave way to the moon and darkness encroached, Sky felt trapped by the sureness of her past and the uncertainty of her future.

"Maybe we should stop doing this to each other."

"If you want me out of your life, Sky, just say it."

"Would you respect my wishes if I asked you to stop calling me and to never visit?"

"If it's what you really want. Is it?"

She didn't know. Her father had an annoying way of creating conflicted emotions in her. Sky switched topics, although her question pointed to an ongoing point of contention between them.

"Are you responsible for my invitation to SUNY's Summer Leadership Retreat? I didn't apply, and my president hadn't gotten around to completing the nomination form when I got an early acceptance letter. Do you have any idea how that could've happened?"

"A lie or the truth? Which will make you less angry with me?"

Damn him. When would he learn? When would she?

"You can't make up for not being there when I was a kid by trying to run my adult life. It doesn't work that way. We won't work either if you don't step back and give me room to breathe."

"Okay."

"Okay?"

"Yes, okay. I'll respect whatever boundaries you put up as long as you don't cut me out of your life and you call me once a week. I want to have a real conversation with my daughter. I want to know how your new job is going and if you've met someone special. I might have been a shitty father to you, but I know I'd make one hell of a grandfather to your children."

The man pushed even while pledging to stop his overbearing ways. Robert Ellis was hopeless, and so was Sky. No matter how incensed he made her or how deeply he'd hurt her, Sky didn't think she could stand going back to not having him in her life.

"One call a week. That's it until I say otherwise. The job keeps me busy, but it's great. I don't have time to date, so I don't have a special someone. And that's the closest we'll ever get to having a conversation about my love life."

Not that Sky had a love life, and she had no intention of sharing that with her father either.

"It's Saturday night, and you're smart and beautiful. Too lovely to spend a weekend inside and by yourself."

"If I were out, we wouldn't be having this wonderful conversation now, would we?"

"Sarcasm. You're better than that. Now, who is the young man you don't want to tell me about?"

"There is no young man."

"Of course, there is. I won't believe you if you tell me that, in the two months you've been there, no one has asked you out for drinks or dinner."

She disliked her father, even more, when he saw what she didn't or wouldn't.

The notification alert on her cell prevented Sky from replying to her father right away. She'd heard the beep, which meant the phone had to be… ah, on the kitchen island beside the fruit basket.

"I have another call, Robert, I have to go."

"Robert? Well, I guess that's better than Captain."

"I could call you Bob."

"I hate that name."

"I know."

"Fine, Robert then. I want to meet him."

"Meet who?"

Sky walked the short distance between the sofa and the small, functional kitchen where she'd left her cell. One touch brought the phone to life. Sure enough, she had a text message.

"The man who's calling you at eight-thirty on a Saturday night."

Not a call but definitely a man. Her house phone slipped from her hand and clattered onto the counter, Sky's attention riveted to the text message from the walking temptation that was Dr. Malcolm Styles.

16% of people met their spouse at work. The celestial sphere, a dome under which the sun, moon, and stars dance and sing in cosmic harmony, is an astrological phenomenon eclipsed only by the limitations of our vision and the gravity of our fears.

The African American Studies professor had a way with words. Perhaps he should've chosen the field of English or astronomy because no one, other than astronomers, referred to the sky as a celestial sphere. Men were forever using sky idioms with her, some for seduction, others for humor, but all with the goal of appearing unique and clever.

In her thirty-five years, no one had ever woven such a creative and thoughtful sentiment about her nature name. But the man's arrogance and insight had Sky forgetting her father on the other phone and taking a seat on a barstool at the island to reread the message.

limitations of our vision and the gravity of our fears

Dr. Styles didn't know Sky well enough to make such bold statements. Yet he had, which angered and intrigued her to the point of shooting off a reply text.

You have my number for school-related purposes only. Our next scheduled committee meeting is in two weeks. Be on time.

Before sending the text, Sky searched the net. It didn't take her long to settle on the right article. She pasted the link to the message and sent the text to Dr. Styles.

A grin played about her lips when she picked up her home phone. "Sorry about that. I didn't mean to—"

"What's his name?"

"I'm not telling you."

"So, there is someone. I knew it."

"No, there isn't."

Her cell beeped again, and Sky's smile returned.

'25 Office Romances Gone Horribly, Terribly Wrong', really? I gave you stats, and you send me BuzzFeed Community News. Try again, Dr. Ellis.

He ended his message with another emoji. This one was a chocolate candy with red filling spilling out into a heart design. The image was sweet, the sender sappy.

Sky's smile grew, and her quiet Saturday evening of reading EBC's Strategic Plan for Diversity wouldn't be so dull, thanks to Malcolm Styles.

"I'll call you around this time next week, and we'll talk."

"About him and for a half hour."

"About my job, your health, and for fifteen minutes."

"Ten minutes and you accept the invitation to the retreat."

Sky had thrown Robert's guilt gifts back in his face many times. This gift, however, she'd grabbed with both hands. The opportunity for networking and skill building were too good to allow pride to stand in her way. Sky had no intention of not going, but she would never admit that to her father.

"Make this the last time. Promise me."

"I promise. No more interfering in your life. Personal or professional."

Sky wanted to believe him, wanted to, for once, trust her father to not be exactly what he was—a selfish ass who put his needs and wants before everyone else's.

"Thank you. Goodnight."

"Goodnight, sweetheart."

After a phone call with her father, Sky would normally grab a bottle of wine, a plate of cheese and a bowl of strawberries, then find the bloodiest movie on cable to watch. If she couldn't disembowel Robert Ellis, then she could enjoy senseless violence. Tonight, however, she had a much better alternative to a gore fest.

Snatching up her cell, she walked to the bedroom and jumped onto her bed, propping her back against the headboard. The good professor had sent her another sappy emoji. Two cacti, of all things, embracing with huge smiles on their faces.

Sky raised Malcolm's sappy sticker with an upside-down emoticon with blood running from his eyes.

That's sick. You don't have a romantic bone in your body. We'll have to work on that.

Romance is overrated.

For long minutes, Malcolm didn't respond, but when he did it was with a single image. A pic of him holding a red rose between his plump and very kissable lips.

Damn. The summer retreat couldn't come soon enough for Sky. If she had to spend any more time around Dr. Malcolm Styles, her rule against dating in the workplace might die a painful death at the twin blades of lust and loneliness.

CHAPTER TWO

"President Hicks would like the Diversity Progress Committee's final report before the last day of exams, which is May twenty-third. Due to leadership changes in the committee, that deadline is an extended one for us only. Every other standing committee's report is due a week earlier. If possible, I'd like to meet the same deadline as everyone else."

Half of the fifteen people who sat around the conference table in the suite of the Office of Diversity & Inclusion grumbled, others lowered their eyes and the rest, like Malcolm, did or said nothing to give away their feelings about Sky's statement. The woman wouldn't win fans or friends this way. No one liked more work, especially at the end of the school year.

She steepled long, thin fingers and didn't utter another word until the grousing stopped and she had everyone's attention. Andrew Parker, Chief of Public Safety and Rosalyn Gordon, Director of International Programs, sighed with meaning before finally shutting up.

Malcolm hid a smile. Andy and Ros had given the last chair of the committee hell. Being a devil's advocate to encourage more and better ideas and approaches was one thing, but complaining for the sake of complaining helped no one, least of all students. For many reasons, some valid, others not, the committee had achieved little in the last five years. Hell, in the last decade. Obviously, the new committee chair aimed to change that sad fact.

"Over the last month, we've gathered student cultural proficiency survey results. We need to analyze the data and make recommendations to the senior staff for improving diversity and equity on campus, particularly in the classroom. I anticipate a two-page report, three at most. It's now late April, by the second week of May I'd like to have a final report ready to send to President Hicks."

"But that's earlier than the normal deadline."

"That's the point, Chief Parker. If we want the work we do in this committee to be taken seriously by students, faculty and administrators, and the community, then we must begin with meeting the same deadline as every other committee. Right now, the bar for our work is embarrassingly low. I don't like what I've heard when I've walked the campus and spoken with different constituent groups, especially students. Getting our report to the president before every other committee is smart but also very simple to achieve. An early and high-quality report will be our strategic way of saying we're capable, committed and shouldn't be underestimated or held to a lower standard."

Sky might have a fondness for dark colors, like the black business blouse and skirt she wore today, but the woman burned hot with passion for equity and equality. Hair, in a natural wavy afro that fell to her shoulders, Sky's nostrils flared when she spoke, her eyes sparkled with intensity, and her tone didn't so much challenge as inspire one to moral action.

She nodded to the two student representatives on the committee, a senior and a junior, both female, one African American and the other Korean.

"Everything we do is for them. When our students leave EBC, what do we want them to take away? What will they say about their time with us? More, will we feel proud and humbled by the answers to those two questions or embarrassed and ashamed?"

"Dr. Ellis," Chief Parker began, his dark-blue eyes casting around the conference table before settling back on Sky, "we're here because we want to be here. We're here because we care."

"I know."

"Yeah, I think maybe you do. But we're also not used to..." Chief Parker waved his hands in the air as if the action would help him catch the right words to finish his sentence.

"Expectations?" Sky supplied.

Chief Parker snapped his fingers. "Bingo. Look, this is only our fourth meeting with you as chair. Before that, well, best leave the past in the past. Anyway, we're still in park while you're going a hundred. Slow down so we can catch up."

"Speak for yourself. It's time you got off the shoulder of the road, Andy, and joined the flow of traffic." Dr. Elena Mosby, Vice President for Student Life and Dean of Students, spoke from the opposite end of the rectangular table from Sky. "We have a little over twenty thousand undergraduate students enrolled at EBC, twenty-eight percent of whom are students of color. Yet ninety-five percent of your officers are white."

"When was the last time you hired a diverse candidate, Elena? Don't throw rocks."

Malcolm thought Sky would interject and stop the argument before it escalated, but she didn't. Andy and Elena kept going, then Ros joined in, unhelpful and leveling her own accusations of inequitable practices, from hiring to instruction and assessment.

All the while, Sky watched them with olive hazel eyes of calm steel. Malcolm wondered at her cool exterior almost as much as he wanted to break through her wall to the woman who'd, two weeks ago, surprised the hell out of him by returning his romantic, flirty texts with sarcastic replies that had kept him at Angie's house longer than he'd intended. When Malcolm had snatched one of Sean's guilt roses from the vase, undid the first three buttons of his dress shirt and had asked Angie to take a few pics of him to send to Sky, she'd balked and then bailed, saying something about not taking "nasty sex pics."

If Angie were a cartoon character, the swiftness by which she'd bolted from her living room would've left a white smoke plume in her wake. Being left alone in Angie's living room had been for the best, though. It had given Malcolm an opportunity to examine the wall around Sky, searching for hand and footholds.

Pressing his luck, he'd texted Sky the next day. Thirty minutes after his Sunday morning text, she'd replied with, *EBC has a sexual harassment policy. I've read it. I suggest you do the same.*

He'd ignored the jibe about the sexual harassment policy and came back with, *I've read EBC's policy on dating between coworkers. Have you?*

Section three of the relationship policy addressed romantic relationships at work. While the college would prefer employees to not become romantically involved with each other, especially when the working relationship was that of superior and subordinate, EBC didn't forbid such relationships. It was, however, policy for the dating employees to disclose their relationship to the next level of administrator or to Employee Relations.

Considering how private Sky was, Malcolm couldn't imagine she'd ever be happy having to reveal any aspect of her personal life to a third party.

Malcolm, who'd arrived fifteen minutes early to the meeting so he could snag a seat next to Sky, leaned in and whispered, "How long do you plan on letting this foolishness go on?"

Damn but the woman smelled good. Rose and patchouli clung to Sky's hair and skin, the same way Malcolm's eyes stayed on her when she shifted her cool, beautiful orbs to his.

"From their conflict, I have a half page of recommendations, actionable items that, with a bit of wordsmithing, can be added to our committee report. I don't prefer this processing method, and I will certainly not endorse its continual use, but it's a start."

"You're an only child, aren't you?"

From his experience, only children had a tolerance for bickering in a way people with siblings did not.

Sky paused, blinked, and then stared at Malcolm as if he'd asked her the nuclear equation for fission.

"Not exactly."

He had no idea what her response meant, but her body language, which had been relaxed and inviting, slammed shut. Arms that had been reclined on the conference table, palms down, were now crossed over her chest. Nothing in Sky's facial expression changed, though, not even the eyes that watched him for a reaction to her answer before turning away.

"Mr. Parker and Drs. Mosby and Gordon, thank you for sharing so many excellent recommendations."

The argument, which had waned the longer Sky let it go on, stopped altogether with her statement of appreciation.

"Each of you has just addressed a different but important concern raised by the student survey results. Thank you for taking the time to review the data before today's meeting."

Andy, six feet, short red hair, and all ex-Marine, preened at Sky's calculated, but also genuine, compliment. Elena nodded, and Ros smiled. After that, the meeting ran smoothly with members agreeing on what they needed to submit to Sky's executive administrative assistant for the report. As committee chair, the final responsibility for writing the report fell to Sky.

"Once I have a solid draft, you'll receive an email request for feedback." Sky stood, her frame tall and lean, posture straight and unyielding. "Thank you. I know there's been a lot of leadership change at EBC over the last five years. I also know how hard everyone works to offer high-quality academic experiences for all our students. But academic excellence is that much harder to achieve if we have low social, emotional, and cultural intelligence. Next school year, we'll begin discussing those three big rocks of change."

Increasing the social, emotional and cultural intelligence of faculty, staff, and administrators were lofty and difficult goals for the new Director of Diversity & Inclusion. Eastern Bluebird College was like most other institutions, entrenched in outdated modes of thinking and behaving. He hoped Sky knew what an uphill battle she would have to wage if she thought to change the hearts, minds, and actions of faculty, staff and administrators.

Malcolm had worked at EBC for a decade, only becoming department chair last school year. He'd learned a lot about the college in those ten years. One, people talked a good game about diversity, equity and inclusion, including the president and trustees. Two, when it came to matching action and/or money to words, people often fell short.

Sky's predecessor, twenty years her senior, had resigned. Dr. Mitchell's curriculum vitae spanned an impressive sixteen pages, his articles, books, and presentations comprising the bulk of his CV. Malcolm supposed those sixteen pages also explained the older man's arrogance. Still, Dr. Mitchell, like Sky, had arrived at EBC with fresh ideas and a passion for the work. The man left under a cloud of frustration.

Tender feelings for Sky aside, Malcolm didn't want Dr. Mitchell's fate to also be Sky's. President Hicks had, literally, selected a hire to replace Dr. Mitchell who was his opposite in many of the more obvious ways of defining diversity. Sky was an under-forty, African American female from out of state, private-school educated, articulate and gorgeous. Now she was the face of diversity and inclusion at EBC.

As a member of the Diversity Progress Committee and part of the initial screening team, he'd seen her resume, along with the other applicants'. Her qualifications, while not as extensive as Dr. Mitchell's, were impressive for a thirty-five-year-old. She'd earned the position, for sure, but it galled him that too many people would think Sky an affirmative action hire and nothing more- as if affirmative action meant unqualified. It didn't, but the truth never stopped people from railing against a policy they disagreed with nor did it keep them from judging someone unfairly.

Malcolm took his time gathering meeting handouts and shoving them into his messenger bag with his laptop. He made a show of pushing in vacated chairs and turning off the computer and projector Sky had used to display data tables. Malcolm performed each task with slow deliberateness, going for helpful and not stalker behavior, as Angie now referred to his interactions with Sky.

"I'm sure the cleaning crew will appreciate you saving them a whole three minutes of straightening up after us barbarians. You missed an empty water bottle, by the way."

"That's your water bottle."

"Do you plan on throwing it away for me, Dr. Styles?"

"Why should I? You're standing in front of it, and the trash can is by the door. You can throw it away on your way out."

Sky retrieved her cell phone from beside her water bottle on the table. Malcolm watched her touch the screen a few times.

The cell phone in his pants pocket vibrated.

Sky smiled at him, and Malcolm pulled the phone out. He had a new text message. A very short message. A single image, in fact, of a smiling pumpkin emoji.

"You're terrible at this. That's your comeback to what I just said?"

"Yes, what's wrong with it?"

"It's April. Halloween isn't for six months."

"What's the point of having a creepy-looking pumpkin on my phone if I can't use it whenever I feel like it?"

Malcolm couldn't tell if Sky was serious or joking. Either way, he enjoyed the moments like these when she let her guard down and relaxed.

"I suppose you send Christmas emojis on Thanksgiving."

"Of course. Everyone knows Thanksgiving is just a really early Christmas Eve."

Sky grabbed her blazer from off her chair. A classy red jacket that, when paired with her black outfit, made a bold statement. Sky might love her blacks, blues and dark-grays, but, he'd noticed she spiced up her ensembles with a splash of color. Today, it was her red jacket and a sexy pair of black-and-red heels. With the additional lift, Sky matched his height of five-ten.

Malcolm's mind wandered, seeing Sky wearing those killer heels and nothing else while they had sex from behind. Hand fisted in her thick, wavy hair, the other fondling a breast, Malcolm deep and grinding, Sky wet, moaning, and—

A hand waved in front of his face. "Where did you go?"

"What? What? Oh, nowhere. I'm here."

"You mean you're back." Sky held her jacket in one hand and used the other to grab her soft leather briefcase and the plastic bottle. "I don't know about you, but I have to go. I have another meeting in ninety minutes."

"Perfect. That'll give us enough time to have an early dinner."

"Dinner? As in a date?"

Yes, as in a date, but Malcolm knew the difference between pushing and pulling. If he pushed the issue of dating and an office romance, Sky would pull up stakes and bolt. However, if he went with his plan to cast out a net of friendship, allowing her to take the bait on her terms, pulling Sky in would be the catch of his life.

"Just dinner. On campus, if you like."

Brows furrowed, and hazel eyes bore into him, skeptical and cautious. "Just dinner?"

"Look, you know I want more. But you made your feelings clear about dating a coworker. I may not agree, but that's my problem, not yours."

"Okay, so why the dinner invitation?"

"Everyone needs a friend, Sky. The first time you called the committee together, you spoke about the importance of collaboration, collegiality, and communication. You have a lot on your plate right now and don't know the ins and outs of EBC. I can help you with that. The committee report, too, if you like."

When a single eyebrow winged up, Malcolm knew Sky wouldn't be pulled in any direction she didn't wish to go, any more than she'd swallowed his well-worded bait.

"You're hoping I'll change my mind about dating you."

Malcolm saw no reason to conceal his intention. "Yes. You're so much of what I want in a partner. I think if you let yourself get to know me better, you'll find I'm much of what you want in a man."

"You have no idea what I want in a man or from a relationship. I don't have time for either, anyway."

They stood no more than five feet from each other. Sky's hands were full, posture rigid, and her conviction unwavering. Words wouldn't topple Sky from her pedestal of self-imposed isolation. He had no idea why she chose to live atop it or what in her life had driven her to build it in the first place. One thing Malcolm did know was that if he didn't kiss her now, he might never get another chance.

With one long step, Malcolm closed the distance between them. Sky's eyes, even greener up close, widened at his unexpected nearness. She opened her mouth. Malcolm would never know what she'd been about to say because he touched his lips to hers before the first syllable left her mouth.

Being desperate to have a taste of Sky didn't equate to a hard, rough first kiss. Malcolm's lips pressed into hers, soft and slow, enticing instead of demanding. He breathed her in through his nose, the scent of rose and patchouli, and exhaled her out in their shared kiss.

The hand not holding his messenger bag slipped around Sky's taut waist and pulled her to him. The loose embrace wouldn't hold her if she didn't want to be there. The same way his unforced and unrushed kisses wouldn't prevent her from wrenching her mouth from his.

Sky returned the kiss, an erotic little sigh her acquiescence. She still held her bag and jacket, which meant she couldn't hold him the way Malcolm wanted. That was okay. She could make it up to him the next time they were alone. But their current location, in the conference room, where anyone on the third floor could walk past the open door and catch them kissing, had Malcolm pulling back.

He'd ruined her lipstick, which meant his mouth bore the evidence of his reckless action. But he'd had to taste her, even if it meant her laying him out with her words or fists.

"We shouldn't have done that."

We. He respected her acknowledgment of her role in the kiss. Apparently, Sky took responsibility in every aspect of her life, not just as a professional.

"It's been building since the first day we met. If I waited for you to make the first move, it would've never happened."

"I don't want to do this."

"Kiss me?"

"You know what I'm talking about. Dating and sex between colleagues is a recipe for disaster." Sky found a tissue in her briefcase, wiped her lipstick off him and then reapplied more to her own lips. "If we worked at different schools, I wouldn't have reservations about exploring the attraction we share. As a woman, especially an African American woman, I have to think through every action and how it could be perceived by others."

"You mean misinterpreted."

"Yes. I know you understand my predicament."

He did. His sister waded through the same sexist and racist waters of academia Sky alluded to. Malcolm didn't want to do anything that could mar Sky's image and reputation. At the same time, why must Sky deny herself a chance at romantic happiness by adhering to an unrealistic and biased double standard? Angie's married status insulated her from the potential judgment of a private relationship played out in the public eye of campus life.

"Have dinner with me before your next meeting. I'm starving." A wink and a swipe of tongue over his bottom then upper lip emphasized the double entendre Sky would've caught without the gestures.

She rolled her eyes upward and shook her head. Malcolm wanted to kiss her again—a long, deep kiss with tongue and hands. He glanced at the open door. No one was there, but he could hear people talking in a part of the hallway he couldn't see.

"Dinner and discussion. My offer to help you with the report and give you the inside scoop on all things EBC stands. The offer isn't conditional. We need a strong person to lead the Office of Diversity & Inclusion and this committee."

"You think that's me?"

"I think you can do most anything you set your mind to. If you want it badly enough."

"No wink and lip licking this time?"

"No, you already admitted to wanting me." She hadn't said that exactly, but Sky didn't correct the liberty he'd taken with her words. "But you don't yet want me badly enough to take a risk."

Without a word, Sky slipped around him. When she reached the conference room door, she dropped the plastic bottle into the recycle bin. Her back to him, he couldn't see what she was doing.

A few seconds later, his phone beeped. Smiling, Malcolm reached for it and saw Sky's message. Again, no text but an emoji. A Mr. Grinch smiley face wearing a red-and-white Christmas hat.

He laughed.

She exited the room. But not before saying, "Let's have dinner, Dr. Styles. I'm also very hungry."

CHAPTER THREE

"Dr. Styles is here to see you."

The mere mention of the infuriatingly sexy professor's name sent conflicting waves of heat and cold through Sky. She held her office phone pressed to her ear, knowing Wendy, her executive administrative assistant, awaited her response. Sky had no meeting to rush off to, so she couldn't use that as an excuse to not see Malcolm. Unless, of course, she lied, which she had no intention of doing. She also had nothing on her desk so important she couldn't tear herself away for a few minutes.

While the Susan B. Anthony Hall, where Malcolm's African American Studies office suite and classes were held, wasn't on the other side of campus, the building also wasn't next door. He'd taken time out of his busy schedule to speak with her, and Sky, despite the pounding of her heart at the prospect of seeing him again, wanted to melt into the hardwood floor and disappear under the planks of her attraction and splintering self-control.

"Give me a minute, Wendy, and then send Dr. Styles in."

She hung up the phone and leaned back in her chair, taking slow, deep breaths. Sky hadn't seen Malcolm since they'd had dinner after the committee meeting a week ago. They'd talked the entire hour they spent together, Malcolm keeping the conversation light and about EBC. Sky had found herself enjoying his company, particularly his openness and intelligence.

Dr. Malcolm Styles possessed a kind, sweet nature that must've cost him in the romance department. He displayed his heart openly for the world to see, which should've made him vulnerable to heartache. Yet, the longer the man spoke, the more Sky viewed his tenderheartedness as a strength to be respected instead of a flaw to be criticized.

They viewed the world through different lenses. Yet, they'd ended up at the same college engaged in similar work. Talking to Malcolm felt easy and right, which made her decision to keep their relationship platonic even more important. She couldn't permit herself to get caught up in carnal desires and wishes for happily-ever-afters.

Yet… Sky raised a finger to her lips and recalled the feel of Malcolm's against them. She'd known, when he'd invaded her personal space, what the professor intended to do. Sky had a second to decide if she would allow him to kiss her. It had been the longest second of her life.

When she'd felt Malcolm's warm breath against her face, smelled the fresh, light scent of his aftershave, and tasted the soft, plumpness of his lips, Sky battled the urge to moan into his mouth and deepen the kiss. She'd wanted to know the taste and texture of his tongue, the touch and sensation of his hands on her heated, naked body, and the slide and thrust of his sex into her aching need.

She wanted Malcolm Styles, which meant she could never have him. A man like him, romantic, supportive, flexible, didn't need a woman like Sky, conservative, rigid, stubborn.

A knock came.

"Come in." Sky pushed to her feet the same moment Malcolm opened her office door. Good manners should've had her moving from behind her desk and greeting Malcolm as he entered her office. Instead, she plastered on an awkward smile and didn't comment when he closed the door behind him. "It's good to see you again, Dr. Styles."

"Dr. Styles? I thought we'd moved past titles and last names when we had dinner last week. I'm Malcolm, and you're Sky."

She remembered everything about their dinner, including how spectacular Malcolm looked in his black suit. Styles was a too apt name for the tall, lean man before her. Malcolm dressed the part of an upwardly mobile professional in his well-fitted dark suits. The man even wore vests. Shoes polished to a shine and face clean-shaven, Malcolm Styles looked ready to conquer the corporate world.

But what kept Sky planting herself behind her desk and not daring to venture too close to Malcolm's alluring sun, lest she burn up on contact, were his long dreadlocks. Today, he wore them in a braided style. The locs were pulled up into an intricate knot, revealing his strong jawline and a diamond stud earring.

Damn, Sky wanted too much to suck the stud and the lobe of his ear into her mouth while tugging his hair free so she could run her hands through the thick, heavy texture. How would all that long hair feel between her fingers? More, how would Malcolm, with his wave of black coils spilling over her thighs, look between her legs, his tongue driving into her, Sky's hips meeting his mouth, her hands—

"What are you thinking about? Because you sure as hell weren't listening to me."

Malcolm's overconfident smirk let her know he knew where she'd wandered off to and that he didn't mind her mental journey.

"Why are you here?"

"Am I interrupting?"

"I'm pretty sure you wouldn't care. You didn't make an appointment. And why are you frowning at me like that?"

"Where's today's splash of color?"

"What are you talking about?"

Malcolm continued to stare at her. He moved closer, walking to the side of her desk and taking Sky in from head to toe.

"Your splash of color. You always wear something to contrast with the dark colors you like to wear. Red jacket, purple scarf, bright-blue belt, colorful necklaces and earrings. You know, your splash of color."

He'd invaded her space again, his too-observant gaze roaming her body. She stepped back as far as she could, which wasn't very much considering a wide bookshelf covered much of the wall behind her desk.

A splash of color. She'd never thought of her proclivity to brighten her day by wearing a color she wouldn't ordinarily wear as a "splash of color" in her otherwise monochrome wardrobe. Malcolm saw too much with those dark-brown eyes of his. In her experience, men who saw too much had the tendency to think they knew Sky on a level that left her feeling exposed and vulnerable.

"Here it is." With a broad triumphant grin, Malcolm lifted her leather handbag with a peacock design from the top rail of the chair, looking like a kid who'd won an Easter egg hunt. "I knew it." Malcolm ran a hand over the bag. "This is really nice. Hand painted?"

"Yes."

"Expensive too."

"A little. Are you an expert in handbags, Dr. Styles?"

"Why? Are you angling to charm a gift out of me, Dr. Ellis?"

He batted his eyelashes at her, long, dark, and... shit, those two words had Sky thinking about another part of the sexy professor that was probably also long and dark.

"You know I'm not. And why are you behind my desk and so close?" Her eyes skidded to the door and then back to Malcolm who, if she wasn't mistaken, had moved even closer. "Wendy could walk in. You're too close."

"She won't. She's two parts intimidated by you and one part in awe. I imagine you get that a lot. Competent, no-nonsense sistas normally do. Now, how about lunch? I bet you didn't have breakfast and worked through the entire morning without a break or snack."

She'd done exactly that, which was Sky's routine. Some days, she would manage buttered toast or fruit with her morning glass of orange juice. This morning she'd had a seven-thirty meeting, which didn't leave her much time for breakfast. Unless, of course, she set her clock for an earlier wake-up time, which she didn't do. After the meeting, she'd started in on her "To Do" list. Before she knew it, the morning hours had burned away.

With the mention of food and lunch, Sky's stomach rumbled.

"My next class isn't until three, which leaves me nearly two hours to spend with you. You smell good, by the way. What are you wearing? Lavender oil in your hair and on your skin?"

Before she could process his questions, he'd maneuvered them so that her back was to her desk and Malcolm was in front of her. He leaned in, nose nuzzling her neck and inhaling.

She couldn't breathe, couldn't think, couldn't do anything other than lean against her desk, eyes closed, lips parted, and heart pounding so hard and fast Malcolm had to feel it against the chest he'd pressed to hers.

"Definitely lavender oil. Let me kiss you again."

"You didn't ask the first time."

The breath from his laugh singed her skin. "I know, but I'm asking now. I'm not trying to seduce you."

"I think you are."

He withdrew his lips from her neck to look at her but kept contact with Sky's body. "Maybe a little. I think about you more than I should. I want to call and text you but know it's never a good idea to overwhelm a woman with a man's needs and wants."

"You've cornered me in my office and against my desk. How is that not overwhelming me with your needs and wants?"

Another laugh, in a masculine octave that rumbled through Malcolm's body and into hers. "Sky, if you don't want me to chase you, then you can't look at me as if I'm a juicy cheeseburger you want to sink your teeth into and devour. If I'm wrong, I'll step back and won't cross the line again. Tell me what you want."

Sky knew what she wanted. She'd grown up knowing what she wanted. But she'd learned as a girl that her wants amounted to precious little. She no longer asked for anything. Asking and wishing produced expectations which invariably led to pain and disappointment.

"I don't have a wife or girlfriend if that's what you're thinking. I don't smoke or do drugs. I'm a social drinker, but nothing more. I'm clean. Have the tests to prove it. What else can I tell you about me that will set your mind at ease?"

"I'm not the woman for you. I'm an introvert and moody. I can spend hours by myself and not miss the presence of another person. I live in my head and work too much."

"I've been called over-emotional, mushy, nosy, and smothering. Considering I invaded your work day without the courtesy of a phone call and have damn near pinned you to your desk, I'm sure you'll agree that I may have an issue with smothering those I care about. So, all we've said is that we aren't perfect and that we'll get under each other's skin sometimes. So what?"

So what? Malcolm had no idea how emotionally shut off Sky could be. A nice guy like him didn't deserve an emotional cripple like her. Yet, when she began to frame the words that would send him out of her office and personal life, they wouldn't come.

She tried over and again to open her mouth and tell Malcolm to leave her alone, to not visit, call, or text her again. Sky tried, but only managed to frustrate herself into frightened silence. She didn't want to want Malcolm.

But she did.

For all that Malcolm had said, his talkative nature in contrast to her quiet reserve, he remained silent as Sky processed the pros and cons of getting involved with a coworker. It hadn't worked out for her mother, and she was too practical to think herself an exception to the Ellis rule. From her experience, office romances were doomed to fail.

Yet, for the first time in her organized and structured life, Sky wanted to cast off the shackles of caution and protocol. Taking a leap of fear and faith, she captured Malcolm's lips in a kiss.

They were as full and wonderful as Sky remembered.

Large, gentle hands came to her cheeks and cradled her face. Malcolm's head tilted to the right, and he licked her lips. Back and forth swipes that pressed and coaxed without a hard demand for entry.

Sky opened her mouth, unable to deny herself a deeper, more thorough taste of him. Tongues met, licked, swirled around each other, over teeth, and gums.

She moaned, and Malcolm drove his tongue deeper, stoking the flames and heating her core. They kissed until they needed to come up for air, only to begin again, repeating the cycle of hungry kisses and breathy moans.

Hands went to ass and lifted her to her desk, and lips found neck and sucked.

"Not too hard," she rasped on a shuddering breath.

"I won't give you a hickey. At least nowhere others can see. But that's for another time. When we're really alone and both naked and sweaty."

Damn, there went her imagination again.

Sitting on her desk, she allowed her legs to fall open to accommodate his lean hips and waist. He rocked against her, pressing his center into hers and kissing Sky.

She never acted this way. Technically, Sky and Malcolm hadn't even had their first date. While she might have known him since the beginning of spring semester, those months of acquaintance weren't enough to justify making out with Malcolm in her office, much less encouraging the press of his semi-erection against the crotch of her dress slacks.

But it felt too good for Sky to put a halt to their unprofessional behavior. True, Wendy wouldn't walk in on them. But Wendy had told Sky that members of the Diversity Progress Committee would often stop by the Office of Diversity & Inclusion to speak with the former director, Dr. Mitchell.

Until today, however, no committee member had visited her office.

"Do you want me to stop?"

"Yes. No."

Malcolm chuckled against a throat he lavished with kisses and gentle bites. "Which one is it?"

"Both. We need to stop. We're so beyond inappropriate behavior. But…"

"But?" Head and eyes raised, followed by a lascivious grin. "I've kissed most of your lipstick off. Does the color look good on me?"

Sky laughed. "Light peach isn't your color. For your complexion, I'd go with magenta."

"Hmm, then wear that shade of lipstick tomorrow so I can kiss it off you."

Sky shook her head, another laugh bubbling out of her. "One, presumptuous. Two, magenta only looks good on light brown women if we wear the right outfit. Finding the winning combination is more effort than it's worth."

"Sometimes you sound like my sister. I'll have to introduce the two of you."

"We aren't there yet. I'm a baby stepper."

"Yeah, don't I know it. So, what about lunch? Don't think you can feel me up without also buying me lunch. I'm not a cheap date."

She smacked his shoulder, and he kissed her, shifting from playful to serious in the span of a heartbeat. Under she went again, giving herself over to her repressed needs and denied dreams.

They didn't do more than kiss. Clothes stayed on, and hands didn't seek out intimate territory best left for a more appropriate setting. Malcolm and Sky did, however, move against each other, a clothed mating dance that left them unfulfilled and panting.

A knock sounded at her office door. Malcolm kept kissing her, either ignoring the person on the other side of the door or oblivious to everything except the two of them.

The knock came again, followed by a soft, "Dr. Ellis?"

Not Wendy's husky smoker's voice but the soft, unsure voice of a...

Sky pushed against Malcolm's chest, a solid wall of lean muscle. She bet he had a swimmer's body underneath his suit—pronounced shoulders and large lats. She shoved the thought away.

"There's a student at my door. I need you to move."

As if waking from a coma, Malcolm stared at Sky, confused, before blinking his way to comprehension.

"Shit," he swore under his breath. "Okay."

"Dr. Ellis? Are you in there? Mrs. Steen isn't at her desk."

"Ah, give me a minute."

Sky jumped off her desk, only now seeing the mess she and Malcolm had made. Papers and folders were everywhere, including the floor. When in the hell had they done that and how long were they kissing that Sky had missed Wendy taking her lunch break?

It didn't matter.

Sky grabbed her handbag, plopped it on her now messy desk, and fumbled inside until she found her lipstick and compact. Flicking the compact open, Sky sighed with relief. Thankfully, Malcolm didn't share her hair fetish. Every time she'd reach for his head, wanting to play with his locs, he would pull her hand away with an admonishment to, "Don't mess up my stylist's work."

Sky made sure to keep her voice low. Unless someone standing outside her office spoke loudly, she couldn't hear them behind her closed door. All the same, she didn't want to take any chances the student's youthful ears were keener than hers, so she whispered to Malcolm, "This is why an office romance isn't a good idea. The couple always gets caught."

Malcolm gestured to the lipstick in her hand, then went about picking the papers off her floor. All the while, he grinned at her, not an ounce of shame or regret at almost having a student walk in on them.

Sky reapplied her lipstick and went to the door. Malcolm was on his hands and knees by her desk, which hid his presence in her office. She opened the door and slipped out.

It wasn't unusual for a student to come to see her. For the most part, Sky had an open-door policy. She couldn't get to know students and their concerns if she didn't make herself available to them.

"Hi, Areum. Sorry to keep you waiting. What do you need?"

Areum Jee, a first-generation college student, smiled at Sky and handed her three papers she recognized.

"Thanks for the feedback on the committee report, but you didn't have to hand deliver it to me. An email would've been fine."

"I know, but I needed a break from studying, so I decided to take a walk."

Sky got the impression Areum wanted to do more than take in the fresh, spring air and get a bit of exercise.

"Is there something on your mind?"

A shrug. The junior's non-committal response reminded Sky too much of her teenage self.

"Have you had lunch?"

"Not really."

Which meant she had, but Areum, like most kids her age, were bottomless pits and would scarf down most anything put in front of them.

"Well, I haven't. Give me a minute to grab my bag."

"Um, wait. You want me to join you for lunch?"

"Yes. Unless you don't want to."

"No, well, okay. That's cool, I guess."

"Good. I'll be right back."

She opened the door just enough to squeeze into her office, then she closed it behind her. Which was kind of rude, but Sky had little choice.

"A raincheck on lunch." Malcolm whispered.

"You heard."

"I did. What do you think is really on Areum's mind?"

"That's what I hope to find out over a hot meal." Sky took the handbag Malcolm handed her but he didn't release it. "I have to go."

"I know." He still held on to her bag. "No backtracking, Sky Ellis. No running. No putting up walls. No denying our attraction."

"I don't run or erect walls."

"You also don't lie very well." His hand fell from her handbag. "Call me later. I'd like to take you to dinner. Off-campus, this time."

"A date?"

"Yes, Sky, a date. We've had our tongues in each other's mouths, I'd say we're overdue for a date."

He had a point. Time with Malcolm Styles, away from EBC, sounded like a perfect way to end the work week.

"I'll call you before my last meeting of the day. We can make arrangements then unless you already have a place in mind and want to make reservations in the interim."

"What do you like to put in your mouth?"

Oh, but the man loved his double entendres.

"You're shameless."

He winked.

Sky rushed from her office, but not before Malcolm wrapped his arms around her and kissed her goodbye.

Not on her lips where he'd kiss off her lipstick again, but on her neck, which pulsed with anticipation at seeing him tonight, and many nights afterward, if she were lucky.

CHAPTER FOUR

"How are the kids? Are they excited about summer vacation?" When Malcolm was a boy, he couldn't wait to put his bookbag away and pull out his summer shades and swim trunks. "They only have about a week before the school year ends, right?"

"June twenty-third is the last day of school. SJ finished his Regents Exams last week."

"Big-time freshman took high school exams for the first time. Was he nervous?"

Sean Franklin Jr., taller than his mother by the time he turned twelve, had inherited his father's height and looks but his mother's smile and A-type personality. The fourteen-year-old took life and his future far too seriously. If he didn't learn how to relax and slow down, he'd have a bleeding ulcer before he turned twenty-five.

Malcolm moved Angie out of the way as another runner jogged past them. Bird Island Pier might have a great view of Niagara River, Lake Erie and Peace Bridge, the arch of which they hadn't yet reached, but the running path wasn't the smartest location for a stroll on a Saturday afternoon. In mid-June, the temperature reached a mild seventy degrees, but it felt ten degrees cooler by the water.

"You know your nephew, of course, he was nervous. But he acted like he wasn't. He was fine. The girls are also good. You need to stop by the house more. They don't understand why you rarely come by now."

For the same reason Angie and Sean no longer shared a bedroom. The girls were probably too young to think much about it, but SJ wasn't. He had to have questions. No doubt all the kids picked up on the tension in the house since Sean had come clean to Angie about his affair.

With the bombshell his side action had dropped on him, she'd left Sean with little choice but to confess all.

"How about next weekend? A movie with Uncle Malcolm should square them away for a few hours. You'll get some peace and quiet for a change. Take a nap. Go to the spa. Get a massage. Use that time for yourself, I got you."

Angie's unexpected hug had Malcolm stumbling to a stop. Her head came to his shoulder, her face buried against it.

"Another month or so before we know. Either way, I don't know what I'll do with the truth."

Malcolm kissed the top of his sister's head, wishing, not for the first time, he could take away her pain. When Sean fucked up, he did it royally. How stupid did he have to be to not wear a goddamn condom? Sean could've contracted anything and brought it home to his wife. As it was, Angie had to make an appointment with her doctor for STD and HIV testing after she'd learned the truth.

He'd offered to go with her, but she refused. She had, at least, agreed to have her best friend accompany her. A few days later, Malcolm had introduced his fist to Sean's face. He hadn't cared about the potential repercussions of assaulting a member of the New York Bar. Malcolm had wanted to make Sean hurt, even if it wasn't as deeply as he'd hurt Angie.

"It'll be all right."

"It won't. What if it's his? I don't know what I'll do if it is. I'm trying to not think about it, trying to not let my hurt and anger get the better of me. But it's so hard, especially when I see him with our kids. All I can think about is Sean raising a child with another woman. His time split between our family and his new family. Sean's a good father. He would never abandon his child, and I wouldn't want him to. But I also don't think I could handle the constant reminder of his lies and betrayal."

Malcolm didn't know what to say. Hell, when it came to this, he could never find the right words. Perhaps because there were none. Angie didn't expect him to solve her problems, he knew. All she wanted was a strong shoulder to cry on and a sympathetic ear, which Malcolm was happy to supply. But he wanted to do more. He needed to do more. The fact that he couldn't had him holding his sister tighter and cursing under his breath.

"Don't do something stupid."

"It won't be stupid."

Angie pushed from him, her spine straight and eyes teary flints. "I mean it. No more fighting. It doesn't help. You bloodied Sean's nose and mouth the last time. He had one hell of a time explaining his injuries to the children. He couldn't exactly tell them their uncle had attacked him. Besides, he's your best friend."

"Yeah, in the same way he's still your husband. It doesn't amount to much right now, does it?"

Angie wiped away her tears with the heel of her hand. "No, it doesn't. And, yes, it does. I want to hate him. I've tried to hate him, but I can't. Sean's the father of my children and the man I've loved for more than two decades. You were the one who told me feelings weren't light switches. I can't turn my feelings for him off because they're inconvenient and painful. Trust me, most days I wish I could. You aren't the only one who's wanted to hurt him physically. It's a terrible feeling wanting to do bodily harm to a person you're supposed to love. I get it now, how some spouses snap when they catch their husband or wife in bed with another person. That kind of betrayal cuts deep, Malcolm. So deep."

They began walking again, Malcolm's arm slung over Angie's shoulder.

"Well, I'm glad you didn't go all Lorena Bobbitt on Sean's ass. He may be on my shit list, but only rapists and pedophiles deserve that fate."

Angie laughed, the way he'd hoped she would. "You're terrible."

"So I've been told."

"By whom?"

"By Sky. Actually, she used the word shameless."

"Do I want to know the context?"

"Nope."

They stopped on the path, looking out at the Niagara River. The water rippled, hitting the rock embankment but, otherwise, the river remained a calm expanse of slowly moving blue.

"How are things going with you and her?"

"Slow."

"It's been… what, two months since you began dating? How fast do you want your relationship to move? And don't tell me this is about sex."

"It's not about sex, although that would be nice. What? Don't snort."

"Of course, I'm going to snort. How fast did your other girlfriends put out?"

"I can't believe you asked that." Malcolm shoved his sister with his shoulder. "It's not about sex but trust and intimacy. We talk and laugh. She's whip-smart, as Dad would say, but whole parts of her life are off limits. I talk about you and the kids all the time. I've told her about Mom and Dad, even drove her past the old neighborhood."

"Wait, you didn't introduce her to our parents, did you?"

"Hell, no. I don't think I could've gotten Sky out of the car if I tried something like that." Malcolm leaned against the railing, the hood on his windbreaker blowing in the breeze. "She's private. I knew that from the beginning. I also know that I'm moving way too fast for her. You know how Dad told us the story about meeting Mom and knowing she was the one."

"Of course, every year on their anniversary he tells the same tired but sweet story. Mom smiles and kisses him. You gag and act like you're two, and we all laugh. What's your point?"

"I thought Dad's story was pure BS. That crap doesn't happen. It didn't work like that with you and Sean or anyone else I know."

"Don't tell me, Sky changed your mind. You're such a sap, M and M."

"I know. The first time we kissed, I knew I was done. It's not love, not yet. But it could be, Angie. I can see myself head over heels cliché in love with Dr. Sky Ellis."

"Yeah, you're a big ass sap, just like Dad." Angie lifted onto her tiptoes and kissed his cheek. "Let me see that stalker picture again you took of Sky."

"I told you, I'm not stalk—"

"Just show me the picture already."

Digging his phone from his jacket pocket, Malcolm didn't have to go to his gallery to find a picture of Sky.

"Here."

"God, Malcolm, does she know you use her picture as your wallpaper?"

"Yes."

"And she's still dating you. Maybe you aren't the only one who thinks they've found the one."

"From your mouth to her—"

"Sky's behind you."

"What?"

"Jogging toward us. It's her. Athletic and with one hell of a stride, but definitely the same woman from your stalker pic."

Malcolm turned around, knowing his sister had to be pulling his—Sky Ellis, dressed in black running shoes, racer pink printed tights and a matching short sleeved training top, stopped a few feet from them.

Hands on her hips and breathing hard, she stared at him, as surprised to see Malcolm as he was to see her.

Sean's words came back to him as he gaped at his girlfriend. Smokin' hot, she damn sure was. He'd never seen her dressed down. Even when they went out to the movies, dinner, museum, Sky dressed to impress—fashionable and flawless. But not this Sky. Tendrils of hair fell from her messy ponytail, sweat glistened her face, and her tights fit every luscious curve he hadn't yet had the pleasure of seeing up close and personal.

"Malcolm?"

"Yeah, hey, Sky. I promise I'm not stalking you."

"What are you talking about?"

Behind him, Angie laughed.

"I mean, I'm not following you. I didn't know you would be here."

"It's a public park, and I still have no idea what you're talking about."

"It's my fault." Angie stepped from around Malcolm and toward Sky. "Hi, I'm Angie, Malcolm's sister."

Sky reached into her black, running waist bag, pulled out a small towel and wiped her hands before extending her right one to Angie and shaking.

"Nice to meet you, Dr. Styles-Franklin. I've heard great things about you."

"Call me Angie. You mean great things from my brother?"

"Well, yes, from Malcolm, but I was referring to my dissertation committee chair, Dr. Leslie Gooden."

"Leslie's still at Princeton?"

"No, she retired two years ago. When Dr. Gooden reviewed my dissertation proposal, she suggested one of your books as a reference. I'd already read your dissertation, but I hadn't gotten around to buying your first book."

"Wait, you read Angie's dissertation?"

"Read and cited it in my own. *Culturally Responsive Instruction and Assessment at Three Big 10 Schools*. Groundbreaking research for the time. Her findings helped support the rationale for my own research on cultural intelligence and presidential leadership."

"Close your mouth, M and M. You're embarrassing yourself in front of your very smart girlfriend."

"Oh, so now Sky's your best friend because she read your long-winded dissertation."

"I do love that she has. It gives us something other than you to talk about, which should make you happy. By the way, you're one to talk. Your dissertation was thirty-two pages longer than mine, and it took me five cups of coffee to get through."

Sky laughed.

"Journalist, activist, priest, historian, George Freeman Bragg was an important African American historical figure in the Episcopal Church in Maryland," Malcolm defended in mock outrage.

"Important, maybe, but not interesting."

Sky laughed again.

"Angie isn't funny."

"Except she kind of is. You're adorable, when you're pretending to be offended. What does M and M stand for?"

"That's my cue to leave. You're as smart and beautiful as my brother said. It's nice to meet you. One day, when you're ready, we'll have lunch or dinner. Just us." Angie dug into her purse and pulled out a business card, handing it to Sky who slid the card into her waist bag. "Be good to my brother, he's a little on the sensitive side."

Angie walked away, back down the pier, as if she wasn't his ride home.

"Your sister seems nice. I didn't make the connection with the last name Styles until I saw her. She doesn't look that much different in person than on the back cover of her books. Small world. You really did your dissertation on Bragg?"

"Why? Do you think he's boring too?"

"Not really. You're from New York, why would you select an historical figure from Maryland?"

"Because practically every other doctoral student from New York, in my program, chose a native New Yorker or someone who made this state their home. I didn't want to go the homegrown hero route."

"That makes sense, I guess. May I read your dissertation?"

"It's at my house. Angie picked me up and drove us here, so I don't have a way of getting home."

"Did you leave your wallet there?"

"No."

"Do you not have cash or your ATM card on you?"

"Of course, I do. I should have about thirty bucks in my wallet."

"Good, that's enough to have a taxi or Uber driver take you home."

"That's cold. You can't give a brotha a ride home? Where did you park? Ferry Street Bridge? Unity Island Park?"

"Neither. I live four blocks from here."

"This is your neighborhood? Kind of pricey this close to Niagara River. Being director must pay well. Come here."

"No, I'm stinky and sweaty."

"I don't care. Come here." Sky took three steps forward, and Malcolm pulled her the rest of the way. "I like you like this."

"A sweaty mess?"

"No. I mean without makeup, heels, and dress clothes. You wear them like armor."

He knew Sky didn't like when he spoke like this, seeing sides of her she preferred to keep hidden. Sky stepped out of his embrace, saying nothing but taking his hand in hers. In silence, they walked down the pier, onto Niagara Street, and to Sky's apartment building. One short elevator ride later had them in Sky's apartment.

Sky unlocked the door to her loft, stepping in first and then holding the door for Malcolm. He didn't make it more than three steps into Sky's loft or had more than a few seconds to take in what appeared to be a sunlit room with clean, open space and sparkling hardwood floors before he felt Sky's hand on his jacket sleeve.

"I don't like tracking the outside into my home."

He watched Sky remove her tennis shoes, and then place them in a wooden cabinet with three slatted doors.

"Don't look at me like that. Plenty of people have shoe storage cabinets."

"No one I know." Unwilling to disrespect Sky's house rules and risk her not asking him to return, Malcolm slipped out of his leather loafers and placed them next to Sky's running shoes. He opened the other three doors. "There has to be room for at least twenty-one pairs of shoes."

"The eight shelves can accommodate twenty-five pairs of shoes."

"Twenty-five. Who in the world are you expecting to visit? The Duggars?"

Malcolm closed the doors, neatly concealing the shoes inside. It really was a nice, unobtrusive, espresso-finished cabinet in Sky's entryway, onto which she'd placed a set a four, faux succulent plants instead of family photos the way many people would've. Malcolm guessed he wouldn't learn more about Sky's family that way, a convenient conversation starter if the woman had any pictures on display. A quick survey of her living/dining room proved as picture-less as her entryway.

"Give me a few minutes. I'm going to take a quick shower." Sky pointed to her kitchen area. "There's orange juice and bottled water in the frig, if you're thirsty. There's also fruit in the right bottom drawer and snacks in the cabinet closest to the frig, if you're hungry. I won't be long."

"Take your time," he yelled after her, but she'd already retreated down the hall and out of sight.

Malcolm wasn't hungry or thirsty, at least not for food. So, he walked the length of Sky's loft, being nosey and seeing nothing out of place, not even a dirty cup or plate in the sink.

Being in her apartment, Malcolm hadn't learned much more about Sky than what he already knew or had suspected. She was what some people would call a "neat freak." Sky had expensive and elegant taste. She valued order and simplicity. The light colors and streamlined furnishings of her home were relaxing in a way their jobs as educators were not. If he had to use a single word to describe the energy in Sky's loft, it would be *peaceful*.

The word suited Sky, although Malcolm sensed her life hadn't always been that way.

He moved to the three windows that comprised most of Sky's back wall and gazed out at the panoramic view of Buffalo at midday. Beautiful.

He should find out if Sky had a passport. If she did, which was likely, perhaps they could spend a weekend in Quebec. His French was rusty but not terrible.

"I love that view."

She sounded several feet behind him. He hadn't heard her before she'd spoken, which either said much about her stealth skills or his lack of auditory awareness.

"What's not to love? I can see the Niagara River and Peace Bridge from here. I bet you pay a mortgage payment in rent."

"You sound like my father. By the way, you never told me why Angie calls you M and M."

He should've known she would segue back to his nickname.

"Malcolm Marcus Styles."

"As in Malcolm X and Marcus Garvey?"

"That's right."

"I get it. Your sister is Angela."

"After Angela Davis. I guess you can figure out what life was like in the Styles household."

"A lot different from mine."

"Tell me about it?"

"Later."

Of course, Sky's favorite response when he asked anything about her family. Malcolm shifted from the windows and turned to Sky. It was time they had a little talk about trust.

He opened his mouth, shut it, and then opened it again. Good lord, the woman was stunning and smelled of strawberries. Damp hair clung to her scalp and shoulders, olive hazel eyes watched him with the same lust that was flooding him, and the white, silk robe Sky wore fell to tanned thighs.

Long legs had him striding toward her, thoughts of her emotional barriers forgotten.

"You're not wearing a damn thing under that robe, are you?"

"You're a respected researcher, Dr. Styles. I'm sure you can discover the answer to your question."

Malcolm licked lips that would soon taste every inch of the teasing, sexy siren in front of him.

Grabbing Sky's waist, he pulled her against him and kissed her the way he'd wanted to since seeing her at Bird Island Pier.

Hands fell to ass--hers to his-- and squeezed.

He kissed her more deeply, eating at her mouth and reveling in the feel of her demanding tongue. Mouth slid to neck and hands to the tie of her robe. Licks and kisses and just the gentlest of bites. The primal man that lived inside every male growled at Malcolm to mark his woman with greedy bites of possession.

Malcolm did, sucking hard and drawing a moan from Sky.

"That's going to leave a bruise."

"I know, baby, I couldn't help myself." He did it again, biting and sucking, then laving her skin with swipes of his hot, hungry tongue. "You taste so good. Let me sample more of you."

"I wish you would."

The silk belt came loose in his hands, leaving Sky's robe open. Malcolm stepped back. He had to see her. For two months, they'd kept up appearances at work. Malcolm didn't make a habit of stopping by Sky's office, and she'd never visited him at Susan B. Anthony Hall. He did, however, think Wendy had scoped their game. It wasn't so much what she said, but the way she smiled at him whenever he did spend time with Sky in her office.

The door stayed closed when he dropped by, which probably had a lot to do with her speculation of their involvement.

With the same confidence she displayed at work, Sky removed her robe. Flat stomach, rounded hips, high, full breasts, toned legs, and red painted toenails. Her splash of color against her warm beige skin with red undertones.

"You're gorgeous. So damn hot I'm burning up over here."

"That's because you have too many clothes on. Take them off for me."

Malcolm watched as Sky sashayed that fine ass of hers past him and to her white couch, where she sat, legs crossed and an arm reclined on the back of the couch. So, the woman wanted a show. Malcolm could give her that.

He found his jacket where he'd left his cell phone. Tapping the YouTube icon, Malcolm went to the site and entered his search. After an annoying ad, the song began.

Sky grinned. "_Pony_ by Ginuwine. Good choice."

"Yeah, I knew you'd like it."

Malcolm began to dance, removing his clothing as Ginuwine sang about finding the right partner to take him to the limit. A partner who could jump into the saddle and ride him the way he wanted and needed to be ridden.

He sang along, stripping off shirt, pants, and boxers. Gyrating hips, flexing muscles, even doing the penis shake, which was damn hard to do when fully erect. Each lyric of the song put him closer to a riveted Sky. Malcolm loved the way she watched him, not just with lust but with unconcealed affection and undeniable heat.

"Take your hair down, please."

As he suspected, his lady had a thing for his locs. Sky was forever trying to coax him into undoing them for her. The length could be a nuisance, but he didn't want to cut them, which was why he preferred to keep his hair up and back.

With deft fingers, he uncoiled his hair, letting it tumble over his shoulders and down his back.

Sky's breath hitched, and fingers flexed.

He moved closer, still dancing to the music.

Her heated gaze had him straddling her waist and taking Sky's mouth with his. They kissed, Malcolm's hips swaying to the outro of the song. When the song ended, their kiss didn't.

It went on and on. Sky's hands came to his hair, threading through with exploring fingers and tugging him even closer.

His penis rubbed against and between her heavenly breasts, Malcolm hard and eager to be inside of her, but not yet ready to take her with his length.

He wanted to taste her first.

Sliding down her body and onto the floor, Malcolm licked his lips again. "You want me between your legs, don't you?"

Sky nodded, her eyes so very green with desire.

"Have you daydreamed about my mouth on you, my tongue inside of you?"

"Y-yes."

"Good, so have I. In your dreams, did I make you come, make you scream my name?"

Sky closed her eyes and dropped her head against the couch cushions. "You're driving me crazy, Malcolm. I want your lips on me, filthy the way I know you want to have me. And your tongue. As deep as it can go."

"That's all you had to say, my celestial sphere."

Hooking Sky's long legs over his shoulders, he pulled her to the edge of the sofa and kissed her. With lips and tongue.

He began at the opening to her sex, licking up and down but not entering. Up and down and pressing his tongue against the entrance, teasing and arousing but also learning her body.

Sky's moans rippled through the cool loft on currents of need and want.

Malcolm wasn't surprised when he felt two hands in his hair. She didn't pull him forward or try to dictate how he pleasured her. No, Sky's hands caressed, twirled and fisted his hair.

He dug in, slipping his tongue inside and licking. Over and over, he tasted her, his mouth wet with saliva and her fruity juices. He wanted her to know how delicious she tasted, so Malcolm told her, which did have Sky tugging his hair.

He didn't mind, not when the woman made the most erotic, pleased noises he'd ever heard. Not when she moaned his name between curses. Not when she came with his tongue on her clit and his fingers in her sex. Not when she initiated the kiss that had them sharing her seductive flavoring.

Sky could pull his hair all she liked if it meant she found pleasure in his arms.

"Protection," he whispered against her mouth. "Please, baby, tell me you're on the pill or something."

"I'm not, but I have condoms in my bedroom nightstand drawer."

He scooped her up and walked the short distance down the hall and into her bedroom. Like the rest of the loft, the room was airy, neat and feminine. A queen-sized bed with white comforter and brown-and-white pillows decorated her bed, which he set her down upon.

He opened the top drawer of her white, wooden nightstand and, sure enough, he spotted a purple box of ultrasmooth lubricated condoms.

"Should I be concerned that you have a ten-count box of condoms and this will be the first time we've had sex?"

"They're unopened, if you haven't noticed."

"I noticed. Girl Scout?"

"No, but I assumed we'd get to this point, eventually, and I wanted to be prepared. Do you really think I'd cheat on you?"

She sounded more hurt than offended.

"No. I didn't mean anything by it." Angie and Sean's shit was messing with his head. "I'm sorry. I shouldn't have said that. Can we go back to two minutes ago before I messed everything up?"

"It's fine. I get it. People cheat."

Sky didn't seem fine, and Malcolm knew he'd stepped in something with his stupid question.

He kissed her, not knowing what else in the hell to do to recapture the good time they were having. Thankfully, Sky returned his kiss, tugging him onto the bed with her.

"No more talking."

"Yes, ma'am."

Malcolm made quick work of the condom wrapper, tossing it on the nightstand before rolling the condom on. Like Ginuwine's song, chills went up and down his spine when Sky finally mounted him.

If he'd doubted Sky's word about not cheating, he wouldn't have after she settled on him. The woman was tight. Not virgin tight but tight in a way that women get when they haven't had sex with a man in a while. A good kind of tight that had Malcolm grunting and thrusting. The kind of tight that pulsed liquid heat around his dick and held him deep inside of her. The kind of tight that made a man want to propose because the sex and woman were so good that he would be a fool to let her go.

Sky rode him. Not a pony but an exquisite mare of the finest breeding. Breasts swayed, hips gyrated, and Malcolm was lost.

She kissed him, erect nipples pressed to hard chest.

"I knew you had a swimmer's body. Long and lean with a tight ass and thick…"

Sky's wicked grin had Malcolm rolling them over and trapping her under him. "Say the rest."

"Thick… eyebrows."

"Not that. Say it." He drove into her. Hard strokes angled to hit her clit. "Finish what you started."

"Thick… thighs."

Faster. Harder. Shit, Sky was soaking wet. "Tell me before I come."

He kept moving, pushing into her with everything he had. The bed banged against the wall with the force of his exertion. Sky raised her legs to his shoulders, which had him sinking into her even deeper.

"Fuck, Sky. Tell me."

She rocked against him, her knees to her chest. Sky's eyes closed, and her mouth opened on a perpetual moan.

"Malcolm, oh god, Malcolm."

She came, her walls clenching and pulsing and driving him to the brink of sanity.

Like a great beast of prey, he chased after her. Pumping fast and hard and wild. When Sky yanked his hair, and he opened his eyes to look down at her, two words sent him hurling over the edge.

"Thick... dick."

CHAPTER FIVE

Sky awoke to too many physical demands competing for her attention. One, she had to go to the bathroom. Two, she'd missed her post-jog protein drink, which meant she hadn't eaten since nine this morning. Three, she was on the verge of an orgasm, her sex clenched, Malcolm's fingers ushering her there.

Panting, she thrust her hips into his fingers and then her bare ass against his hard dick. Shit, the man knew how to wake a woman, his fingers a sublime alarm clock.

The heel of his hand rubbed against her clitoris, his mouth on her neck and his right hand in her bed-mussed hair. Sky closed her eyes and bit her lower lip, rolling with the pleasure Malcolm gave her. Reaching back, Sky found his hair. God, she loved Malcolm's dreadlocks. He kept them so nice. The pride he took in his appearance extended to his long, elegant coils.

Crossing her legs and squeezing her thighs tight, Sky rocked against his hand and fingers. The erupting tension of her orgasm rose up and out of her, sending tingling spasms of pleasure through her.

"That's it. Come for me."

She did, jerking her hips hard and fast to wrench every bit of toe-curling sensations from his hand and her stimulated clit. He thumbed the hard nub, flicking it over and again and pressing with the right amount of force to have her screaming and panting and begging Malcolm to not stop.

He slipped inside of her, Sky vaguely realizing Malcolm already wore a condom. But damn, the smoothness of the latex made him feel almost bare inside of her.

Onto her stomach Sky went, Malcolm overtop and driving into her. He wedged his hand between her wet sex and the mattress, finding her clit again and stroking. Yes, between the wonderful weight of him and his relentless thrusts and steady, persistent fingers, it didn't take long for Sky to come again.

Malcolm came with her, doubling their pleasure as he spent himself inside the condom.

Heavy breathing coated her ear and neck. A spent and sated Malcolm Styles felt good atop her, but he wouldn't stay in that position for long. His weight and need to get rid of the condom would have him moving off her sooner than she'd like.

A minute later, Malcolm slipped out of her and off the bed. He wrapped the used condom in a few tissues and tossed it in the waste-basket before climbing back into bed beside her.

She pushed from the bed, still tingling but from a sensation that had nothing to do with the orgasms Malcolm had given her.

"Where are you going?"

"To the bathroom. I prefer to not have sex on a full bladder. The pressure is distracting."

"Not romantic post-sex conversation."

"You asked."

"I did, but you chose to elaborate."

Sky took care of her needs and washed her hands, hoping Malcolm wouldn't call her on her lack of elaboration when he asked her other more personal questions. Thankfully, he didn't, so she padded out to the living room, found her discarded robe and put it on.

"Are you hungry?" she yelled to him. Then thought about Malcolm's tendency toward double entendres and added, "For food? Would you like me to make you something to eat?"

The time on her stove read five after six. How long had they slept? More importantly, how many times had they had sex before collapsing from exhaustion and hedonism?

In nothing but a pair of black, skintight micro-mesh boxers that stopped above his knees, Malcolm joined her in the kitchen. She could do without the distraction of him in underwear that drew her eye, whether coming or going.

"Eyes above the waist."

"They are."

"Unless my waist has dropped to dick level, they aren't." Malcolm chuckled, and Sky rolled her eyes. "I am hungry… for food. What do you have? Would you like for me to help you cook?"

"That would be nice. Thank you. I went grocery shopping after work yesterday, so the kitchen's stocked." Sky opened the fridge. "What about hoisin-glazed salmon with broccoli and sesame rice?"

"Sounds good. Now I'm wondering why we've never done this before."

In ways she didn't like to think about, Malcolm and Robert were alike. They both created openings, or what Sky thought of as traps, to get her to open up about topics best left ignored.

"I also have plenty of ingredients in here for a green salad. You can begin on that while I get the salmon and broccoli ready."

Sky pulled out everything they needed, placing the items on the kitchen island and preheating the oven. In no time, they had broccoli and fish in foil packs in the oven, rice on the stovetop and garden salad tossed and chilling in the fridge. Thanks to Malcolm's ingenuity, he'd turned her French bread into garlic bread.

"How did you learn how to make homemade garlic bread? Your mother?"

"No. I once dated a sous chef. She micromanaged our relationship like it was the kitchen of the restaurant where she worked. I lost one hundred thirty pounds after I broke up with her."

"What?"

"Lighten up, Sky. That's how much Nia weighed. It was my attempt at a joke. Some topics, you lose your sense of humor. So, are exes on the list of things we won't talk about?"

Oven mitts on, Sky removed the foil packs from the oven and placed them on a cooling rack on the counter.

"Do you really want to hear about my past relationships and former lovers?"

She leaned against the counter, arms at her side, and brow arched. Sky had no problem telling Malcolm about the few other men in her life if he truly wanted to know. She wasn't ashamed of those relationships, although she didn't see how they were relevant to what she had and hoped to build with Malcolm.

"Did you actually love any of them?"

"Not enough."

"Not enough for what?"

Not enough to let them inside. Not enough to overcome her fear of commitment. Not enough to place her trust in another person. Not enough, Sky Ellis.

She shook her head. Sky was afraid she'd ruin what she had with Malcolm before she figured out what he could mean to her.

"It doesn't matter. The past is best left there. I don't care about the women who came before me. And the men who came before you are no longer in my life. Will you accept that answer and let it drop?"

Malcolm left little alone, she'd come to learn. He tucked away bits of information like a squirrel preparing for winter. She could see the wheels turning in his brain, through eyes that watched and saw too much. Malcolm may have a kind nature, but a fierce lion dwelled within.

He'd hunted her until she couldn't run anymore, choosing to give in rather than fight her feelings for him. Now that he'd tasted her, pleasured her, hell, marked her, Malcolm wouldn't be easily denied.

"For now. Don't run from me."

"Don't push."

"I'll try not to."

"Thank you. Come on, let's eat before our dinner gets cold."

Malcolm had already cleared off the island and put out place settings so all Sky had to do was put their food on their plates. She turned on the television to a slow jazz cable station, which they listened to while they ate their dinner.

She might have taken even longer to invite Malcolm to her home if she hadn't run into him on the pier today. Sitting there with him, good food and even better conversation, she wished she knew how to build and keep instead of only attract then run off.

There were good brothas out there. Sky had dated her share of them. But good men didn't stick around when a woman couldn't trust their love and intentions.

After dinner, they lounged in bed, one of Sky's favorite horror movies on, Malcolm propped against three pillows and her head on his chest. He smelled of the strawberry body wash he'd used when they took a shower together. Well, they eventually got around to washing after Malcolm fucked her against the shower wall.

"What are you thinking about?"

"Past mistakes. What time is it?"

"Are you trying to get rid of me?"

"No, if I were, I would just tell you to leave." Sky kissed his chest so he'd know she was playing. "Seriously, if there's someplace you need to be or something you need to do, I'll get dressed and drive you home."

"What if I want to stay?"

She lifted her head from his chest to find Malcolm's cool, assessing eyes on her. "You mean stay the night?"

"Yeah, how would you feel about that? Like running?"

A little. Good thing Malcolm couldn't hear her racing heart or he wouldn't believe her when she said, "I don't mind you staying the night."

"Are you sure?"

"I'm sure you're pushing, when you said you wouldn't."

"I am, but you knew I would. Just as I know I'll have to chase you after you decide to bolt when you come face-to-face with whatever prevented you from committing to those other guys. Don't get me wrong, I'm glad you didn't, or I wouldn't be here with you now. Just know, I'm ready to cross that bridge when we get there."

Sky opened her mouth to reply, then decided nothing she could say would matter or change his opinion. He was right, and they both knew it.

She lay down, but not on Malcolm's chest. "I prefer the right side of the bed and don't like a cover hog. I'll also need an hour of quiet time to read and think before I turn in for the night, so don't be offended when I leave you in here and go into the living room."

"How much solitude time do you really need?"

"At least two hours. I was being polite."

"I know how to entertain myself. You have cable, books, Wi-Fi and a laptop, and I saw a fitness center on my way up here. Is it open twenty-four hours?"

She nodded.

"Good. Then I'll be fine while you're in your woman cave. Now come back over here and stop being moody."

Sky didn't budge from her spot, defiant in the face of his arched eyebrow. "What are you going to do if I don't?"

"This." Malcolm pounced, moving so quickly that he took Sky by surprise. He pinned her wrists above her head and to the mattress, his hard body over hers. Malcolm kissed her, rough, wet and sloppy.

"Bossy and independent don't always work in bed. I'm going to fuck that attitude out of you."

He silenced her comeback with another hard kiss. Knees pushed her thighs apart, and his erection rubbed against her opening.

Unable to stop herself, Sky arched into him, suddenly wanton and desperate to feel Malcolm inside her again. But he toyed with her, penetrating her with just the tip of his penis with shallow thrusts. The way his body held her down, she couldn't manage the kind of leverage she needed to lift her legs and hips to force him deeper inside.

"Tell me you want me."

"You know I want you."

"All of me, Sky? Do you want all of me?"

Another damn double entendre. They would be the death of her--or of Malcolm, after she killed him for screwing with her mind and body.

He penetrated Sky another inch but withdrew before she could fully enjoy having him inside her. He did it again. And again.

"M-Malcolm…"

Sky had never begged any man for an orgasm, but she needed him to stop torturing her and let her come. She leaned up and took hold of the ear with the diamond stud earring, sucking, then rimming the lobe with her tongue.

Malcolm's pleased moan had him slipping farther inside her, then all the way when she clamped down on his neck and bit him the way he'd done her earlier. If Malcolm could mark and claim her, Sky could damn sure do the same to him.

The part of her brain not connected to the raw passion that seemed to exist between them since the day they met, knew they were having sex without a condom. Knew and fought hard to remember that bad shit happened when a couple didn't practice safe sex.

"Malcolm," she said against his lips, a moan and a warning.

"I know. I know. I'm going to get one."

With more self-control than she had, Malcolm pulled out, slipped on a condom, and was back inside her in under a minute.

The phone rang. No way would she ask him to stop again. Not that the intrusive sound halted his movements. He kept going, and the phone kept ringing. After five rings and before voicemail picked up, the caller hung up. Then called right back.

Malcolm swore. "If we continue to ignore the phone, will the person keep calling back?"

If the caller was who she thought it was, he would. "It's my father. I'm an hour late with my weekly call. He's very stubborn."

The ringing stopped again but started right back up.

"He can wait. Ignore it. Can you do that?" She kissed Malcolm again, trying to redirect his attention to her and away from the incessant ringing.

After the fifth call, Robert gave up, and Malcolm and Sky rediscovered their rhythm. It didn't take them long to come. Reaching the finish line hadn't been as rewarding as it could've been without the interruption, but it was still damn good.

"Sorry about that." Sky forced herself out of bed and to her dresser. Opening a drawer, she reached inside and pulled out a pair of black lace panties and matching camisole, which she donned while Malcolm watched her from the bed. "I need to call Robert."

"Who's that?"

"My father."

"You call your father by his first name? I tried that once and got a slap upside my head. I'd sooner call my dad Mr. Styles than Charles."

One time, when she'd been young, she had called Robert "Dad" and had gotten a slap from his enraged wife in response. She hadn't told her mother right away, hiding the bruise from her on their ride home. After Sky had escaped to her room, and cried until her head hurt, Sade had come to check on her. Unable to hide the bruise from her mother, she'd told Sade everything. That day had been the first time Sky had seen her mother cry and the last time she'd called Robert "Dad."

The next day, her grandmother came for an unexpected visit and stayed with Sky while her mother went out. As a girl, she hadn't understood her mother's guilt or the rage and sadness that had overcome her and which had sent Sade Page out the next day to confront Robert's wife.

"I don't give a damn what I've done, Mom, Sky's innocent. That bitch had no right to hurt my child." Sky didn't hear her nana's response. She'd scurried back into the den before they could catch her eavesdropping.

Sky shook her head at the memory, feeling exhausted for having drudged it up and dusted it off. It looked the same, sad and depressing, no matter how much time had passed between then and now. "I'm going to go into the living room and call him back," she told Malcolm. "If I don't, he'll start calling my cell phone. I'm surprised he hasn't already."

"I can mute the TV. You don't have to leave."

"I know."

She gave him a swift peck on the cheek and left anyway, snatching up her phone from the nightstand and taking it with her into the living room. Sky felt Malcolm's disapproving eyes on her as she left him alone in the bedroom. She'd been pushed by him enough for one day. He would have to accept a few closed doors in her life if he wanted to be with her. Robert was a non-negotiable.

She was greeted with, "Are you okay?" after the first ring.

Sky slumped onto her couch. "I'm fine. Just because I didn't answer, doesn't mean something's wrong."

"So you deliberately didn't answer when I called."

"I was in the middle of something."

"I called five times. It wouldn't have taken but a minute to answer and let me know you were too busy to talk. I worry, you know."

"Yes, I know. I should've answered. You're right. I apologize."

"You apologize? You've never apologized to me. Now I know something is wrong. Is someone holding you at gunpoint?"

"Ha, ha, very funny."

"Wait, what were you doing when I called?"

"It doesn't matter. How was your week?"

"My week was fine, now answer my question."

Malcolm appeared at the edge of the kitchen, dressed. Her heart raced, and throat tightened. Was he leaving because she'd shut down on him about Robert? He wore his jacket and socks, his loafers in the shoe cabinet in the foyer. Malcolm also held her car keys in his left hand.

"If you don't mind me borrowing your car, I thought I'd run home, pack an overnight bag, and get another box of condoms before coming back here. That should give you plenty of time to talk to your dad without feeling rushed to cut your conversation short because you have company."

"Who's that? Is that a man's voice I hear in the background?"

Sky swallowed, her heart still pounding from the irrational fear of losing Malcolm so soon after having found him.

"Hold on a minute."

Sky dropped her phone onto the couch and ran to Malcolm, who opened his arms and let her crash into him with the weight of her abandonment issues.

"Come back."

"I only live twenty minutes away."

"Just promise me you'll come back."

"I promise."

Sky didn't remember Malcolm leaving, but she was embarrassingly sure he'd had to pry her arms from around him to get out the door.

"Okay, so tell me his name. How long have you known each other? How long have you been dating? When can I meet him? Are you having safe sex?"

Sky hung up on her father, and Robert called right back.

CHAPTER SIX

"I assume you're aware of EBC's policy governing dating in the workplace."

Despite knowing his relationship with Sky couldn't go unnoticed by others forever, the call from Edward Alston, Dean, College of Behavioral & Social Sciences, had still taken Malcolm by surprise. He figured his being away from campus on summer vacation and not visiting Sky at work, he'd have time to solidify his relationship with her before going public at work.

The sixty-one-year-old man's gray eyes, gray suit, and gray personality stared at Malcolm from behind spotless glasses and thin, pursed lips. His salt-and-pepper hair did nothing to add character to the drab man, although his red-and-gray striped tie reminded Malcolm of Sky's splash of color.

He tamped down the smile the thought of Sky evoked, then a frown that had him glancing at the clock on the wall behind Dean Alston.

"Am I keeping you from something, Dr. Styles?"

"I promised to drive a friend to the airport."

"Would that friend be Dr. Ellis? It's my understanding that she's slated to attend SUNY's Summer Leadership Retreat at White Eagle Conference Center."

Until today, Malcolm had had no strong feelings toward Dean Alston. He neither liked nor disliked the man. As a dean and supervisor, he was competent and dedicated, leading with transparency and vision. He also suffered from a case of egoism and an overdeveloped sense of paternalism.

"Impressive for someone so young. Dr. Ellis is a beautiful woman. I can see why—"

"Yes, I've read EBC's relationship policy." He didn't like the path the dean seemed intent on going down and wanted to stop the snowball at the top of the hill. "EBC doesn't forbid dating between colleagues."

They couldn't, not at a public institution. Malcolm handed Dean Alston the envelope he held in his hand. The last-minute meeting request might have been unexpected, but that didn't mean Malcolm had come unprepared.

"What's this?"

"An official letter you can put in my file."

The letter wasn't mandatory under EBC's relationship policy, but Malcolm knew better than to entrust his career and future to words spoken behind closed doors. He'd also asked Sean to draw up the letter. They were still on the outs, and it would be a while before they repaired the dent Sean's affair had put in their friendship. When it came to the law, however, Malcolm trusted no lawyer more than he did his brother-in-law.

"I sent the same letter to President Hicks."

He didn't bother adding that he also intended to forward the letter, signed by both Sky and himself, to the Vice President and General Counsel and to Director, Office of Civil Rights and Sexual Misconduct and Title IX Officer. Among the many lessons his parents had instilled in Malcolm and Angie, thoroughness ranked high on the list. Even private Sky, who Malcolm thought would need convincing to sign the letter of mutual consent to their sexual relationship, had agreed with his plan.

Dean Alston opened the envelope and read the short letter. Malcolm met the gray eyes of his superior and what he saw in their depths reflected Sky's fears about engaging in an office romance. Too smart to voice his thoughts in front of Malcolm, the dean took his time refolding the letter and returning it to the envelope.

There would be talk among the deans and vice presidents before trickling down to other administrators, then faculty and staff. By the opening day of the new school year, Malcolm and Sky's relationship would've made the circuit of EBC's rumor mill.

He hated the idea of people talking behind their backs, of men, like Dean Alston, viewing Sky as a brown-skinned, green-eyed exotic hire.

"I only asked you here today to speak with you. There was no need to involve your lawyer. As you said, EBC doesn't forbid coworkers from engaging in romantic liaisons. It does, however, stipulate that the parties' supervisors must be made aware."

Malcolm pointed to the letter still in Dean Alston's hand. "You've been made aware. I would appreciate your discretion."

"Of course, but this is a college campus. Affairs have a way of getting out."

Malcolm bristled at the use of the word "affair," especially the judgmental tone Alston used. Malcolm and Sky weren't sneaking around on significant others. They didn't have clandestine meetings in hotels. Nor did they hide their relationship from others. They'd spent the entire summer in and around Buffalo, Malcolm playing tour guide.

Juneteenth, Buffalo Niagara Blues Festival, Fourth of July fireworks at the University of Buffalo, Buffalo Bookfest. Hell, they'd even spent a weekend in DC so they could visit the National Museum of African American History & Culture. Sky and Malcolm weren't having a cheap affair. They had an adult relationship.

Malcolm pushed to his feet. "As I said, I'd appreciate your discretion. Is there anything else?"

"No, thank you for coming in during your summer vacation." Dean Alston dropped the envelope onto his heavy, wooden desk, opened his mouth to say something else but met Malcolm's hard gaze.

He closed his mouth.

Good.

"You know the problem with educated men?" his father always asked Malcolm when he got caught doing something he wasn't supposed to do. "They forget that civilizations weren't built and sustained by men of great minds but by the least of our brothers and sisters. Be a smart man, son. Smart men know when to speak up and when to listen. Most importantly, smart men know when to fight and what's worth fighting for."

Of course, it was Malcolm's mother who'd told him the best man of them all was a smart and educated man.

"Enjoy what's left of your summer, Dean Alston."

Once out of Franklin D. Roosevelt Hall and into the sunny July day, he pulled out his phone and dialed Sky. Even if he ran across campus and to his car, then drove like a demon to her loft, he still wouldn't arrive in time to drive her to the airport. They'd assumed this would happen when Dean Alston's administrative assistant called to arrange the meeting. Malcolm had tried to schedule it for another day, but Alston's schedule was tight, and he wanted to meet with Malcolm "sooner rather than later."

He took a seat on the closest bench when Sky answered. Salmon pink and green apple, Alpha Kappa Alpha colors. Malcolm glanced around, not an AKA in sight. Good. Students could be territorial, even about school items they neither owned nor purchased.

"It's fine, Malcolm. I'm almost to the airport."

"I could meet you there."

"By the time you get here and park, I'll be in the air. How did the meeting go?"

"The dean knew, so I gave him our letter. Are you upset?"

"Not really. I don't like him forcing our hand. Our relationship is no one's business, but we also knew it was only a matter of time before it became public knowledge. Are you upset?"

"I'm fine."

"Which means you're upset about something Dean Alston said. Knowing Alston and you, it's something he didn't say. Let it go."

He was trying, but Alston had pissed him off. Professionalism dictated Malcolm swallow his anger, which he'd done. The taste of it, however, was bitter fruit in the pit of stomach.

"I wanted to see you off. He called me in to his office as if we were caught screwing in the quad during freshman orientation. It could've waited until I returned to campus in two weeks."

"It could've, but men like Alston, every now and then, like to remind those who report to him that he's in charge and nothing gets past him."

"I wonder how he found out."

"I have no idea. Someone from school probably saw us out somewhere and passed the information along to the dean. It doesn't matter. I'll deal with any potential blowback when I return. Look, sweetie, I'm about to park."

"Sweetie? That's new."

"I know. It felt weird coming out, so don't get used to it."

"Not one romantic bone, Sky. Not. One."

"Come on, not that again. What do you want from me?"

"Flowers. Candy. A nice card. Hell, you could at least hold my hand longer than two minutes when we're in public."

"I held your hand the entire way home to my apartment that first time."

"Name a time other than that one. You can't, can you?"

"You're such a baby. I guess you expect me to bring you a souvenir from the retreat, too."

"That would be nice."

"I was joking. I'm not going on vacation. It's a working retreat. I'll be back August third."

"I'll pick you up."

"Why? I have my car."

"Because I want to. Why does everything have to make perfect logical sense?"

"Did you call just to whine and start an argument before I got on the plane? Or are you still angry I wouldn't let you join me on the trip?"

"None of the above. Angie is driving to Newark today and I want to speak with her about Sean before she leaves."

He hadn't told Sky everything about Sean's pregnant ex-lover and the pending paternity test. She knew Angie and her husband were going through a rough patch, but Malcolm hadn't gotten around to divulging the details. In truth, whenever they were together, the last thing Malcolm wanted to talk about was a couple who were not them. As it was, Sky still kept huge chunks of her life from him.

They rarely talked about her family. Once, Sky told him about her mother, who he'd learned had died when Sky was twenty. Of a grandmother who lived her entire life in Maryland until she passed away two years ago. But never of her father or the siblings she'd alluded to when he'd asked her, three months ago, if she were an only child and Sky had replied with a cryptic, "Not exactly."

"I have to go. I need both hands to take care of my bags. I'll call you once I check in and again when I arrive. After that, I won't have time to touch base during the day, so I'll call you in the evening. Or you could text me. I like your text messages, but I like hearing your voice more."

"Well, that's the sweetest thing you've ever said to me."

"Sweet? That's all I get. I was going for romantic. Don't laugh."

"I'm sorry. I couldn't help it. It needs work, but you get an A for effort."

"I've always gotten A's. You're not offering me much."

Malcolm laughed again. "I love your arrogance and sass."

"You, ah, umm, yeah. Well, okay, Malcolm. I have my bags out of the trunk now, I have to go."

"I know you do." In for a penny, in for a pound. "I love you, Sky. Be safe and have a wonderful retreat."

He hung up before she could fumble through another inarticulate reply. What in the hell had he done?

"How is Angie?"

Early August in Buffalo, with a seventy-eight-degree high, took a bit of getting used to. Sky liked her summer's hot, not lukewarm. Now, *that* sounded like Robert, which had her slamming her car door, turning on the ignition and blasting her air.

"I can drive to the hospital," she offered, hoping Malcolm would accept.

"No, you've had a busy four days, at the retreat, and you're tired. A hospital visit isn't the way you should spend your first night back in town."

"I'm not too tired, and I don't mind."

The thought occurred to Sky that Malcolm may not want her there. Not only had she not expected his declaration of love, she also had no idea how to react. He'd blown her away and scared the shit out of her. The few times they'd spoken since she'd been away, he hadn't repeated those three words to her and Sky was pretending as if Malcolm hadn't said them.

He loved her? Malcolm couldn't love her. Not enough time had passed since they began dating for him to have developed such strong feelings for her. She needed more processing time.

"If you need me, I'll drive to the hospital to be with you."

"No, that's okay. Mom and Dad are with the kids and Sean is talking to the doctor. Angie's asleep and stable. There's nothing we can do around here but drive ourselves crazy watching her."

He sounded terrible and exhausted. Sky wondered when Malcolm had last slept and eaten. Knowing him, not since getting the call about his sister's car accident.

"Sweetie, drive to me or let me come to you. I can drive to your house, cook dinner and then draw you a hot bath. How does that sound?"

"Nice. But I'll be awful company."

"You're always awful company, but I don't mind."

His halfhearted laugh at her attempt at a joke had Sky driving away from the Long-Term Parking Lot and toward NY-33/Kensington Expressway. Malcolm needed her, even if his male pride kept him from asking.

"All right, if you wouldn't mind coming to me, that would be great."

"I'll drive home first and drop off my things before coming over. Call me when you're on your way home. Do you have food in your house or do you need me to make a grocery or fast food run?"

"No, I'm good. There's soup in the fridge Dad brought over two days ago. Chicken noodle, Mom's recipe, but I haven't eaten any yet."

"That's fine. I'll see you in a bit."

Sky was about to end the call when Malcolm spoke again, voice tinged with uncharacteristic worry and melancholy. "Don't rush. Take your time and drive safely."

She forced herself to not speed. The last thing either of them needed was for her to get into an accident. Malcolm had called two nights ago about Angie's accident. At the time, he had few details about the car crash and his sister's medical situation. Sky had offered to leave the retreat and fly home, but Malcolm had insisted she stay. She did, but her mind and heart were in Buffalo with Malcolm and his family.

An hour later, she was backing her car into Malcolm's driveway and beside his SUV. He lived in a Cape Cod style brick home in Eggertsville, a suburb of Buffalo. The first time he'd brought her there, she hadn't expected a literal house, although he'd used that word. She'd assumed Malcolm rented, as she did. Instead, the professor owned a three-bedroom house with a fenced yard, perfect for family gatherings.

Now, as she did then, Sky couldn't help but think Malcolm had purchased the single-family home with the hope of filling it with a wife, dog, and children.

He opened the door and let Sky in. Wrinkled T-shirt, sagging jeans, bare feet, a day's worth of stubble, and red, weary eyes. This wasn't her Malcolm Styles. Even his locs were pulled back in a haphazard ponytail.

Sky hugged him. She should've gone with her first instinct and returned home early.

"I'm fine."

"You aren't."

"I'm not, but I'm better now that you're here," he admitted with a small smile and a tired slump of his shoulders.

Sky thought about dragging Malcolm into his eat-in kitchen, heating up a bowl of his mother's soup and nagging him until he ate every drop. But from the look of him, food could wait. There were two bedrooms on the first floor and one on the second, both levels with full baths.

"Let's get you into bed."

Malcolm remained silent the short walk down the hall and into the first guest bedroom. He said nothing when Sky sat him on the closed toilet seat, located a grooming kit in the cabinet under the bathroom sink, saving her a trip to the master bathroom upstairs, and shaved his face. He also kept quiet when she finger-combed his hair before forming two neat braids from the locs.

Dark-brown eyes watched as she undressed him. Malcolm allowed himself to be pulled into the shower with her, dried then tucked into bed. Through it all, her tenderhearted, gregarious Malcolm kept quiet, which told her all she needed to know about Angie's condition.

"Go to sleep." Sky kissed Malcolm, a short, heartfelt peck to his lips. "I'll be here when you wake up."

Through thick, dark lashes, he stared up at her, the light on the nightstand behind her a soft glow of illumination.

"It's fine if you aren't ready to say it back. I won't leave you, if you need more time to get to where I am now. That's not how love works for us Styles." A hand reached up, found Sky's nape, and pulled her down for a sweet kiss. "Thank you for coming, for wanting to take care of me. I would've managed, but it's nice to have you here, even better to know that you want to be here."

"I would've come sooner."

"I know. But I was a mess, and I didn't want you to see me lose my shit. She's so little, but Angie has a big personality that makes her seem eight feet tall. When I saw her for the first time after the surgery, broken and in a coma, it felt like punches to my chest, breaking ribs and collapsing lungs. I couldn't breathe, and I hurt everywhere. Sean broke down, crying over Angie's prone form, mumbling apologies and promises."

Sky closed her eyes, fighting back tears and images of her mother after what had proven to be a fatal car crash. A car of teenagers, a nineteen-year-old with a provisional license, beer, and New Year's Eve made for a deadly combination. She hadn't told Malcolm the circumstances of her mother's death, and now wasn't the time to share that scabbed-over wound. Sky prayed Angie's children wouldn't, at such a young age, experience the loss of a mother. The pain hurt like nothing Sky wanted to go through again. Even the passing of her grandmother hadn't gouged her soul the way it had when her mother had died.

Sky burrowed under the covers and pulled Malcolm to her. He came, wrapping long arms around Sky and settling his head beside hers on the pillow.

"You can stay for as long as you want. I'm not going anywhere. I'll always be right here."

She wanted to believe him, wanted to accept his love and lower her walls. Wanted to trust her heart and not fear she'd given it to a man who would one day break it. Wanted to forgive her parents because their mistakes had become an albatross that had plagued her life for too long.

"Goodnight, Malcolm."

"Goodnight, Sky, I love you."

CHAPTER SEVEN

"Thanks for coming with me, but you didn't have to."

"It's fine. I want to be here. I told you that already."

Sky and Malcolm stood outside Angie's recovery room. This morning, he'd awoken to Sky in his arms. Soft and warm, she'd snuggled against him as if his chest and bed were the safest places in the world to be. Malcolm had smiled down at her and then went about awakening Sky with tongue and hands.

On a sleepy moan, Sky had opened her eyes and legs to him, a silent invitation he'd happily accepted. Afterward, they'd shared a shower and breakfast. For the first time since Angie's car crash, Malcolm's heart felt lighter and spirits higher. If he thought Sky would agree, Malcolm would have run out today and had an extra key made for her, moving her in as soon as he could get her packed.

But, asking Sky to move in with him would likely send the woman running back to Maryland. Hell, her complexion had dropped a shade the minute they'd entered the hospital. Malcolm knew better than to ask the reason behind Sky's obvious discomfiture. She might have wanted to support him but she damn sure didn't want to do that by visiting Angie in the hospital.

"Are you going to actually go in with me?"

Sky, dressed in a pretty cream and red, floral wrap dress, glanced over his shoulder to the closed hospital door. The mid-thigh length dress and high strappy sandals accentuated her toned, bare legs. The red in her dress served as her splash of color, as did her red lipstick. The woman was far too pretty to spend her morning playing emotional babysitter to her man.

"Who's in the room with Angie?"

"Sean, definitely. Maybe my parents."

"Your parents?"

"You said that as if my parents are cannibals waiting to add you to their crockpot for Sunday dinner."

Sky's eyes snapped back to Malcolm. "Cannibals? Really? You have an extreme way of putting things. Why are you wearing your hair out today?"

"For you. Why else?"

Hazel eyes glanced from one end of the quiet hallway to the other. Except for a couple of workers at the nurses' station and a man with two bored-looking teens in chairs lining the white wall, no one else was in that part of the hall.

"I assumed, when you didn't put it up earlier, you would at least pull it back into a ponytail when we got to the hospital. You never wear your hair completely out in public."

"What am I missing? You like my hair like this."

"I do. But… It doesn't matter. Forget what I said."

For a second, Malcolm could only stare at her. Was confident, capable, and beautiful Sky Ellis the jealous type? The way she watched Malcolm, her eyes daring him to make fun of her irrational perspective, he thought she just might be. Then he recalled how seriously she'd taken his question about her box of condoms and the unintended accusation of infidelity.

He sobered. Malcolm might have found this jealous side of Sky unexpected and cute, but insecurity, even a mild case, was often grounded in past traumas, failure, or rejection. Sky wasn't the type to fail at much, so that left past traumas and rejection.

"You never bring up anything that doesn't matter to you. You want to talk about it?"

"Not really."

Of course, she didn't. Why did Malcolm bother asking?

"You can't keep every door closed. One of these days you're going to have to start opening them and letting me through."

"Perhaps, but now isn't one of those days." Sky gestured, with her chin, to Angie's room. "My phone is vibrating. Go see your sister. My father met with his cardiologist Friday. I was supposed to call him last night to find out how the appointment went. I'm surprised he's waited this long to call my cell."

Retrieving her phone from her purse and answering, Sky nodded to Angie's room again before walking toward a row of chairs across from the nurses' station and sitting.

Malcolm watched her for a few seconds, long legs crossed, wavy hair piled high on her head, cell phone pressed to her ear. His Sky, sexy, intelligent, complex.

He entered his sister's room. The sight that greeted him squeezed his heart and stilled his legs. Angie appeared as she had yesterday—quiet, small, and fragile. The man sitting in the chair next to the bed looked as if he hadn't slept despite Angie's night nurse forcing them out her room. Sean certainly hadn't shaved since yesterday, although he wore fresh clothes.

If not for Sky taking care of Malcolm, he would've tossed and turned all night before dragging himself back to the hospital, looking no better than his brother-in-law.

Not wanting to interrupt, Malcolm kept quiet and listened as Sean read to his barely-awake wife.

"Lela's bedroom was dark, save for two white candles on each nightstand. The door, slightly ajar, admitted a beam of light from the hallway. A reminder that she wasn't alone in her suite. Thirty minutes ago, she'd left Xavier and Sage in the living room pretending to not watch her for the slightest hint of emotional instability.

Exiting the bathroom, she ignored the haggard image of the woman in the mirror. Lela didn't want to see the full-color details of her appearance. She knew what it would reveal—red, puffy eyes and dry skin. Since reaching the heartrending but no longer avoidable decision to arrange her husband's funeral, she'd lost weight she could ill afford to lose. Yet another reason why Lela cast her eyes from the mocking glass, and why Sage had filled Lela's dinner plate with a volcanic explosion of food. By the time she'd tired of her family's hooded, worried glances and urges to, "Eat as much as you can. It'll make you feel better," she was ready to sink into a black hole and disappear into blessed oblivion.

Lela eased onto her bed, wedging the fluffy, circular pillow under her throbbing head. Her green, sleeveless nightgown felt wonderfully soft against Lela's exhausted body. She was well and truly tired. Yet sleep wouldn't immediately come, nor had it since she'd made the dreaded choice everyone, except Lela, knew she must. Despite it all, her mind now told Lela her decision was a sound one, if not shamefully late in coming. But her heart... well, that delicate organ had yet to be convinced.

Crossing hands over her stomach, she entwined her fingers and rubbed them together. As always, Lela anticipated the familiar sensation of the smooth bands.

Nothing.

She caressed her short, thin fingers again.

Nothing.

She'd given them away—her precious rings, Zion's enduring symbols of his love and faith. They were gone, leaving her hands bare and soul bereft. A wave of morbid dawning threatened to consume her, as did the tears she couldn't seem to stop shedding.

Lela gasped. The violent gulping of air burned her lungs, thick and toxic. Her penance, her sacrifice, her soul that would never be whole again. One, two, three, ten, twenty desperate breaths and then a low shrill of pain held as a prisoner of war in her throat. She refused to submit, not now, not again. The Fates help her, if she broke down again, Lela wasn't sure she'd recover."

"She's asleep." Malcolm moved from where he'd been leaning against the doorframe and went to the side of his sister's bed. He glanced across Angie to Sean. "She nodded off about two minutes ago." Malcolm lowered his mouth to kiss Angie's forehead. She didn't stir. "What are you reading?"

Sean slipped a bookmark into the novel, closed it, and then turned the book toward Malcolm.

"*Bound Souls*. Sci-fi? Fantasy?" His sister enjoyed both genres, especially if they were combined with romance, which this book seemed to be.

"A little bit of both. It's set on another planet about three hundred years in the future, but it also has supernatural elements. It's a new book by an African American female author. When I saw it online, I knew Angie would love it."

Though Sean spoke to Malcolm, his focus stayed on Angie.

"Flowers, candy, jewelry." Sean raised the book again before letting it fall back to his lap. "Books, cards, clothing. All pointless. I can't buy my way out of what I've done and back into her heart. She doesn't trust me anymore. Some days, I don't even think she likes me."

Trinkets wouldn't heal the wounds Sean had inflicted on his wife. The lawyer was too smart to think superficial, even if genuine, gestures of affection would absolve him of his sins and rebuild the bridge between himself and Angie.

"I fucked up."

Sean turned to Malcolm. For the first time, in a long time, Sean wore no artifice. He wasn't acting the cocky lawyer, the jokester friend, or the charming husband. In Sean's weary gaze, Malcolm glimpsed the man behind the swagger and bullshit. There, next to a wife he'd injured long before a car added more damage to an already savaged Angela Styles-Franklin, was the true Sean Franklin.

Guilty. Ashamed. Scared.

"I know you think I don't understand the magnitude of what I've done, but I do. I feel like shit for hurting Angie. SJ is mad at me, although he doesn't know why his Mom hardly talks to me anymore. Funny, how a son jumps to his mother's defense, even against his father."

"Take it as a sign you and Angie raised him right. He's a smart kid. All the children are. They were bound to notice the tension between the two of you."

"I stayed up and read the novel last night. I didn't know what else to do with myself. The kids were asleep by the time I got home. Your parents didn't stay long after I got there, so I had no one to talk to. I considered calling you but assumed you wouldn't want to hear from me. Is Sky back in town yet? Angie and Sky talk on the phone at least once a week. Did you know that?"

Malcolm did know, and he couldn't be happier about the growing friendship between his sister and girlfriend. "I'm glad Angie reached out to Sky. Beyond work, she doesn't know many people here, and she's not the type to go places just to make friends." People like Sky didn't require a lot of friends to make them happy. A few good ones were enough for her. "She's in the hall and on the phone with her dad."

A long conversation, now that Malcolm thought about it. He hoped everything was fine with the older man. For all that she and her father didn't seem close, Malcolm knew Sky would be on the first plane to Maryland if his health were threatened.

"Good. I'm glad you found someone. Sky seems like a good woman. I met her when Angie first had Sky over for lunch at the house." Sean glanced down at the book again, then back to Malcolm, tapping the novel with a finger. "It's about a man who dies, and his soul comes back in the body of a rival love interest for his wife's heart. Zion is still in love with Lela, but she only sees the other man when she looks at him. It's also a story about a woman who struggles to move on with her life after the death of her soul mate. It's the first work of fiction I've read that depicts life after death in a way not defined by any religious belief. It answers questions like, where do we go after we die? Are we conscious and carry our memories with us? What does it mean to have a soul bound to someone else's? It's a good book. Sad and sweet but also moving and thought-provoking."

"What was your takeaway?"

"A lot of hard truths. Lela and Zion loved fiercely but not selflessly. All love, to a certain extent, is selfish. The author wrote about three fates: Purpose, Faith, and Truth. I lied, was unfaithful, and lost sight of the purpose of my life and family. Who knew a sci-fi romance could produce an epiphany in a man as jaded as me?"

Sean laid the book on the side of Angie's bed, on top of the white blankets that covered her broken legs.

"I'm going to do everything in my power to earn her forgiveness, even if Angie decides she wants a divorce. I hope she won't, and I'll fight like hell to win her back, but I won't blame her if she decides to wash her hands of me."

"It sounds like something you need to tell Angie, not me."

"I have, but I also want you to know. I love your sister, despite what I did. And I love you like a brother. I would like your forgiveness, too. I miss our friendship. I want it back. Which means I have a lot of work to do." Sean shrugged. "Nothing worth having is easy."

For long minutes, they exchanged no more words. Malcolm pulled up the second chair in the room and placed it on the side of the bed opposite Sean. The men watched Angie sleep, as if their silence and concern could speed up her recovery.

Cuts and bruises littered her face, neck, and arms. Her sedan was totaled and, if not for her seatbelt and airbag, Angie wouldn't have survived the car crash.

"She has contusions on her back. Burst blood vessels, I was told. I saw the bruises when the doctor examined Angie early this morning. There were black and blue marks up and down her back and across her chest from being jolted forward into the seatbelt then thrown back against the seat. We could've lost her. And, for what? Because some impatient asshole couldn't wait two goddamn minutes at a fucking red light?"

"With your contacts on the police force, you could find out where the bastard lives. If he's out on bail, we can go to his house and beat the shit out of him. How does that sound?"

"Like we would be the ones in jail next." Sean smiled at Malcolm, weak but grateful. "Thanks. I needed that."

"I was only partly joking. If he were here now, you'd have to fight me to get to him first. Whipping that guy's ass wouldn't change Angie's condition or take away her pain, but it'd make me feel a hell of a lot better."

"Yeah, me too. If Angie were awake, she'd snort and roll her eyes at us, saying something about men bonding over violence."

Malcolm didn't know about the bonding part. But he had no problem allying with his brother-in-law against anyone who hurt or threatened their family.

His phone dinged, and Malcolm retrieved it from his pants pocket.

"A text?"

"From Sky." He read the message. Two words were followed by a grim-faced emoji. "I'll be back."

Malcolm hustled to the door and into the hall, his eyes going to where he'd last seen his girlfriend. She no longer sat in the chair against the wall, nor was she alone. The waiting father and his children were gone. In their place, and surrounding a bewildered Sky, was a committee of Styles.

If not for Sky's tall form, he wouldn't have made her out in the center of his fast-talking family. Malcolm's parents were there, as were four aunts and three uncles. They bombarded Sky with questions, talking at the same time and over each other.

He wondered how long she'd attempted to answer their barrage of questions before giving up and texting him her *Help Me!* plea.

Ever polite and professional, Sky smiled and nodded. The woman wasn't shy, not hardly. But she was an introvert, and that many people, vying for her attention and surrounding her, had to be overwhelming.

Malcolm hastened to cross the short distance between himself and his family of vultures.

"Malcolm, there you are." His mother peeled herself from the crowd as soon as she saw him. "You should've told us Sky would be here today."

He leaned down to accept a hug from his mother, who was petite and beautiful like her sisters and daughter. Malcolm wondered if Sky would retreat into her tortoise shell after being bombarded by his family.

His father slapped him on the back. His heavy hand had Malcolm suppressing a wince. At six feet, Charles Styles was taller than Malcolm, and heavier than him by forty pounds.

"What took you so long to bring Sky around to meet the family? Your mother's been asking for weeks."

"How many words did Sky get out before everyone started in on her? I bet she saw you about to bum rush Angie's room, introduced herself and offered a couple of polite comments, because that's how she is, then you guys turned into a committee of ravenous vultures."

His father's meaty hand came crashing down on his shoulder again, considerably harder than the first time.

"How did you convince a nice girl like Sky to go out with you with that smart mouth of yours?"

"She likes my mouth just fine."

The unintended double entendre was out before he realized what he'd said.

Malcolm's mother and aunts tsked, hands going to hips and heads shaking in disapproval. His father and uncles howled, loud and mocking, as if they were at a Bills game instead of in a hospital with recuperating patients. Sky wasn't very fair, but she turned an embarrassed shade of crimson, adding a different splash of color to her ensemble.

"Thanks a lot, Dad." Malcolm stepped past his mother and grabbed Sky's hand, raising it to his lips and kissing it. "Everyone, this is Dr. Sky Ellis. She's kind but not a pushover. Sky is Maryland classy with a sprinkle of New York sassy. She enjoys reading, jogging, and bloody horror movies that would turn any sensible person's stomach. We're colleagues, friends, and she's dating me because I have great hair and taste in clothing, sweet kisses and a good heart. I'm also an entertaining talker and a brilliant thinker. All of which makes me Styles awesome."

"Don't forget humble." Sky smirked. "I've never met a humbler man in my life. Styles awesome? Really, Malcolm? Where do you come up with these things?"

His family laughed, and Malcolm kissed Sky's hand again and winked at her. "Sky, meet the Styles clan. These are my parents, Kimberly and Charles." He winked at Sky again. "They're proof I didn't come from a birch tree, no matter how many times you call me a sap."

CHAPTER EIGHT

"Shit. S-sky. Sky."

Malcolm's thighs tightened, toes curled, and hips lifted. Fuck, Sky's mouth on his dick, warm and wet and as deep as she could take him. In his office and on her knees, she had him gripping the armrests of his chair and praying for thick walls and hard of hearing colleagues.

Fifteen minutes ago, Sky had come charging into his office, full of fire and brimstone. She'd slammed the door and locked it. "Who in the hell does he think he is? I mean, sure, Dr. Hicks is the college president, but still. He had no right to force you to step down from the Diversity Progress Committee."

She wore the red-and-black high heel shoes he loved, which seemed to be matched today by her fiery attitude.

"Dr. Hicks is EBC's president, like you said. It's okay, I kind of expected this. You're not my direct supervisor, so he had nothing on us there. But you're the chair of a committee that I'm a member of… used to be a member of. President Hicks is trying to cover his ass in case someone who doesn't like the work that comes from the committee uses our relationship and supposed lack of neutrality as a point of contention.

It's all about image, Sky, you know how these things work. The truth rarely matters."

"You were on the committee years before I came to EBC. If anyone must leave, it should be me."

"You know why it can't be you. Being chair of the committee is part of your responsibilities as Director of the Office of Diversity & Inclusion. I'm expendable on that committee. You aren't."

"You aren't expendable. I'm tired of the looks and whispers." Anger and lust were in her hazel eyes when she'd approached Malcolm standing behind his desk. "Tired of people thinking every time we meet behind closed doors we're having sex. We've never had sex at work."

More due to Sky's sense of propriety than Malcolm's lack of effort.

Sky had invaded his personal space, just as he'd done to hers the first time he sought her out in her office.

"We might as well make the gossip true." Leaning in, she'd kissed him, her tongue invading his mouth and her hand going to his belt. "Right here, Malcolm. In your office. Sit down for me, sweetie."

Sky used the term of endearment so infrequently that it still surprised him when she did. He hoped, with time and use, Sky would grow more comfortable not only expressing her feelings for him but accepting his love as a fact of life. Malcolm meant every statement he'd made to Sky three weeks ago, including his willingness to wait. He wasn't in a rush. He got it. They hadn't been together long. Most women, even ones not as skittish about commitment as Sky, would think twice about a man proclaiming his love after three months of dating.

"We really shouldn't." Ignoring that token protest from Malcolm, Sky undid his belt and pulled down his pants, then pushed him onto his chair before dropping to her knees.

"You know you want me to. You're already so hard, and I've barely touched you. Lean back and relax. All I could think about after leaving the administration building and walking here was how good you would taste in my mouth and whether I could make you scream my name loud enough for your colleagues to hear."

He'd hissed out her name when she sucked the head of his dick into her mouth and squeezed with her lips. From there, Sky worked Malcolm, licking and sucking and driving him to the brink only to ease him back with slow pumps and shallow sucks.

He had never come in her mouth, but she damn sure was building that orgasm bridge, one deep throat pull at a time.

His Sky didn't like anyone telling her what to do, and she despised having her integrity questioned. Dean Alston had learned as much when he thought to mention their relationship to Sky at the monthly public Board of Trustees meeting. He hadn't heard the story from Sky but from a grinning Dr. Mosby.

"She laid into Alston with such eloquence it was hard to remember they were talking about a sexual relationship. Dr. Ellis didn't raise her voice, although she did raise her fingers as she ticked off each of her points. Then she said something about social critic and novelist, James Baldwin, and not being any man's prize or exotic fantasy."

"Wait, god, baby, wait." With a pop that left Sky's lips wet and his dick cold from losing her warmth, she released him. "I have a condom in my wallet."

For a minute, he thought she would ignore him and take Malcolm with her mouth again. If Sky did, he would be helpless to stop her a second time. Malcolm would come, loudly and shamelessly.

She let him get to his feet, which proved to be a struggle with his pants around his ankles.

Sky was truly in rare form because she hiked up her black dress, pulled down her panties, and placed both hands on his desk, her beautiful bare ass on display and all the invitation Malcolm needed.

"Yes," Sky moaned when he entered her. "Stay close. Yes, like that."

Hands gripped hips and held on tight while Malcolm stayed as close as Sky liked, grinding into her and giving her his full length without sacrificing contact.

Malcolm covered Sky's mouth with a hand and bit on his tie to muffle his grunts. Right now she may not care who heard them, but Sky would when she calmed down. An office romance was one thing, but throwing it in everyone's face by having loud, reckless sex in his office during the day wasn't wise.

She seemed to get the point because Sky leaned onto the desk, face buried in her arms and cries captured by skin and wood.

As irresponsible as they were being, Malcolm refused to rush. He didn't prolong it either, but he did take enough time to bask in the sensation of filling Sky and of having her tight wetness around him.

For two weeks, he hadn't been himself with Angie recuperating in the hospital. The turning points in her recovery began when she'd awakened from her coma followed by a reduction of the swelling around her spine and the return of feeling to her hips and legs.

This week, he felt his life evening out. Despite the hiccup with the committee, the school year had begun smoothly and without as much talk about Sky and Malcolm's relationship as he'd feared. For the most part, people minded their own business. Many couldn't care less. While others, like Dean Alston, acted as if the couple had broken an unwritten ethical code of EBC by becoming involved with each other.

None of that mattered to him, although it did to Sky, who, on this issue, proved far more sensitive than Malcolm. Her current act of rebellion, a prime example.

The rush of having sex in his office, with the department suite occupied by professors during their office hours, made this interlude exciting as hell. The circumstances also necessitated they come more quietly than ever before.

Malcolm slumped onto Sky's back, spent and mouth dry. "We're sprawled over my desk, asses out. When you rebel, you do it in grand fashion. Now I'm wondering about teenage Sky. Were you one of those kids who was a hell-raiser in disguise and never got caught because no one suspected sweet Sky Ellis had a wild side?"

Slipping out of her, Malcolm moved away to take care of the condom and his clothes.

"I didn't have a wild side."

Sky adjusted her clothing, a form-fitting V-neck pencil dress she'd purchased during their weekend trip to DC. Malcolm had assumed, since they were so close to Maryland, that she would arrange to introduce him to her father. She hadn't. He also doubted she'd told Mr. Ellis about their trip south.

"But I was a moody sixteen-year-old. I didn't get into trouble at school, but I did stupid stuff when I got mad."

"Like what?"

"Take Mom's car without permission -- or a license. Throw parties when she went away on business. Ran up her credit card bill. Stupid, childish choices that pissed Mom off and got me grounded."

"Why were you mad at her?"

Sky stiffened. "I wasn't."

Okay, another closed door. Malcolm had two options, ignore the door and back away, which he did every time he slammed into one, or ram into it with his shoulder. Surely, there were more choices than the two he'd laid out for himself?

Tired of Sky's closed doors, he chose option two.

"As good as things are between us, they could be better."

"I assume you have something specific in mind. I also assume, whatever you want to say to me, I'm not going to like it."

"You rarely want to talk about your family. I think we should."

"Every family isn't like yours. I didn't grow up like you and Angie."

"Tell me how you grew up. You've met most of my family. A rowdy bunch, but you survived."

His parents, especially his father, talked about Sky as if she were already his daughter-in-law. Sky accompanying him and even going alone to visit Angie in the hospital, had endeared her to the tightknit Styles clan like nothing else could've.

Leaning on the edge of his desk with arms crossed over her chest, Sky's defensive posture didn't bode well for the conversation they needed to have.

"You want to do this now?"

"Why not? After what we just did, today seems perfect for taking risks."

"You want to *risk* our relationship by trying to force me to talk about something you clearly know I don't want to discuss?"

"No, I'm trying to *save* our relationship by asking you to trust me enough to let down your walls and talk to me about your pain. Because, Sky, you are in pain no matter how much you try to hide it. I mean, just look at you. You're in fight-or-flight mode."

"I wouldn't be if you would stop pushing."

"Pushing is the only way I've gotten anywhere with you. I push, and you give, even if a little. I push, and my nudges give you permission to do what you want to do anyway."

"Permission?"

"You know what I mean. You're scared of not being in control, of letting me in, and of truly trusting someone other than yourself."

"I've never let myself down, Malcolm. Never. I've also never made promises to myself that I couldn't keep."

"That's not true." Malcolm planted himself in front of Sky, his chest to her folded arms and his eyes unwavering in the face of her anger. "You're letting yourself down now by keeping this wall between us. You once told me you'd loved but not enough. This is the reason why, I'd wager. Did those other men who loved you push too much or did they get tired of knocking their heads against your fortified wall and leave? Or did you run when they got too close to the truth?"

Sky held his gaze, granite hard and dark with stubbornness but also with fear.

"You've been at this point before. Maybe those other men gave you an ultimatum, which shows how little they knew and understood you. I'm not going for a powerplay here. I'm not pushing because I want to know your deepest, darkest secrets. I'm pushing because I think we have something great between us that I want to build on and last. You know where I'm headed with this, Sky. I've never said the words, but you know where I want this relationship to go. I think you want it too, but we won't work, not really, if you don't come to terms with whatever happened to you growing up."

"I know."

"You, ah, what?"

"I said I know, now back up. I dislike being cornered as much as I loathe being pushed." He took several steps backward. "You drive me crazy. You and those damn sappy emojis."

Okay, that was random. He'd texted Sky this morning. Malcolm didn't recall adding a romantic emoji, but that didn't mean he hadn't. He was tempted to ask her about the emoji but didn't want to get distracted and lose his small advantage.

"My schedule is open. Nothing pressing. What about you? Do you have time to talk? We could stay in my office or go somewhere else."

"What time is it?"

Malcolm walked around his desk, looked for his cell phone and found it on the floor along with other items that hadn't survived the bumping from their bodies.

He picked it up, saw the time and a missed text from Angie.

"It's a quarter after one. Do you have time?"

"Forty minutes."

"Good, give me a sec to call Angie. I missed her text when you were having your way with me with your wonderful mouth. Not a complaint, by the way. But you could work on your timing and location."

Sky stepped away from his desk, her body, if possible, tenser after agreeing to open up to him. She hadn't bolted or told him to go to hell, which Malcolm acknowledged as a monumental step for Sky and the faith she'd placed in him and their young relationship.

Sky had turned her back to him and was perusing his bookshelf, although he doubted she searched for her next late night read. More likely, the diversion was helping Sky to calm her nerves and gather her thoughts.

"Hey, Angie. I got your text. Are you all right?"

"That's a loaded question. I do feel better being home."

"Is Sean there?"

"Yes, he's working from home so he can take care of me, although I've hired an in-home aide. He needs to return to work instead of being stuck in the house with me all day and acting like a helicopter parent."

"You have two broken legs and a hard head. Let the man hover and take care of his wife."

"Sounds like the two of you made up. That's good."

"I wouldn't go that far, but I saw a man who loves his wife when, for months, all I could see was a guy who hurt my sister."

"He's the same man. I know Sean loves me. It didn't take a near-death experience to know that. For him, I think my accident put certain things into perspective. We have a lot to work on. The car crash didn't change that truth."

"So you've made a decision to give Sean a second chance. I guess the result of the paternity test finally came in."

"It came in a few days after the car crash, but Sean waited until I returned home to tell me. For obvious reasons, he wanted to wait."

"Are you okay? The baby can't be Sean's if you've decided to not throw him out and file for divorce."

"No, he isn't the father."

"Good, I'm glad the kid isn't his."

Sky turned around, and Malcolm smiled and gave her a thumbs up.

"You don't need Sean's ex-lover and child in your life. You have enough to deal with without the constant reminder. I didn't want to say anything earlier, but I was really worried about you. An affair is one thing, but a kid from the deal makes everything worse."

"I know. But the baby is innocent. He didn't ask to be here."

"A boy, good for her and whoever in the hell the father turns out to be."

"You're being mean."

"I'm not. I'm just glad that woman and her baby are once and for all out of your life. What kind of woman screws around with a married man knowing he has a family?"

"Malcolm—"

"I'm just repeating what you've already said." Malcolm tapped the desk with his fingers, anger seeping out as he recalled how upset Angie had been when she'd told him about Sean's affair and Trinity's pregnancy. "Without the curse words. I didn't know you could be so creative. Whore, bitch, slut, homewrecker. Did I miss any?"

"Shut up. I was mad. Women say all kinds of things when we're upset."

"Are you no longer upset?"

"I am. Today, I'm more relieved. For months, all I could think about was the possibility of another woman being pregnant with my husband's baby and how that baby could change my life."

"I know. But the baby is someone else's problem now. A mistake you don't have to deal with. I'm glad you—"

"I have to leave."

"What? Wait, Sky. I thought you said we could talk."

"Sky's there. Tell her I said to call me."

"Yeah, yeah, hold on." Malcolm jumped from his chair, Sky halfway out his door. "Wait, where are you going?"

Shit, people were in the main area of the suite, professors' doors open and the secretary at her desk, doing a poor job pretending to not eavesdrop.

Malcolm lowered his voice. "I thought we were going to talk."

"You've already talked, and now I have to go."

He wanted to reach for her arm and stop Sky from leaving. When he glanced around, however, they had a captive audience.

"I have a meeting to prepare for. Give Angie my best."

With a tight smile, Sky nodded at Malcolm, then left. Half the gazes followed her retreat while the other half stayed on him.

What in the hell had just happened?

Malcolm closed the door, stunned, only to remember Angie.

"Sorry about that." He fell onto his chair, head spinning as if he were a quarterback knocked on his ass by a defensive tackle he hadn't seen coming, much less had time to prepare for before being driven to the ground.

"It's okay. What's wrong? You don't sound good."

"I'm not sure, but I think Sky might have just broken up with me."

Malcolm neither liked the taste of turf, nor the sensation of having the wind knocked out of him. Sky hadn't said the words. Nothing even close. But they were in the pained eyes that fled his office. Sky wouldn't be back.

"Why? What happened?"

"I have no idea. But I damn sure intend to find out."

CHAPTER NINE

"Two weeks. I've given you two damn weeks."

Malcolm's left fist collided with Sky's apartment door again while his right was wrapped around the phone he held to his ear.

"Stop banging on my door before a neighbor calls the police."

"I will when you open up and let me in. I don't appreciate having a personal conversation over the phone while in your hallway."

"That's what happens when you drop by without an invitation. Go home, Malcolm. I don't want to argue."

"Too bad, because I damn well do. Two weeks, Sky. Two. Weeks."

He didn't have to keep repeating himself. Sky knew how long it had been since they'd last spoken and seen each other. She wasn't proud of how she'd handled the situation, but she needed time apart to think. Sky had explained that to Malcolm when he'd called after his conversation with Angie. That had been the last call she'd taken from him. All others, including his texts, had gone unanswered.

But unlike Sky, who'd gone to his office and had sex with him to prove a point that didn't need proving, Malcolm hadn't sought her out at work. A small part of Sky had wished he had while a larger part of her was grateful Malcolm respected her boundaries.

Or he had, until today.

Ending the call, Sky opened the door. An irritated and frowning Malcolm glared at her. She deserved both, so Sky stepped aside and let him in. God, he looked good, dark wash jeans, tan leather loafers, a button-up shirt and a quilted jacket. She closed and locked the door, propping herself against it as she watched Malcolm stalk around her living room like an angry lion.

He wore his hair in a basket weave style, a neat, intricate design that kept his long hair tamed and out of his handsome face. She wanted to kiss those pouty lips of his and take away the pain she'd put in the eyes that lifted and met hers. Sky had missed him more than she'd thought possible when she'd left his office two weeks ago.

"We need to talk."

"I know."

"You said that the last time, then you disappeared from my life."

"I'm sorry. I needed time to think. I couldn't do that if you were around."

"I knew you would run. I thought I was prepared for it to happen. I wasn't. I have no idea what I did or said that day to set you off."

Dark-brown eyes traveled her body. Taking in, for the first time, her clothing. She'd missed her Saturday morning run, so she'd thrown on a pair of leggings and a sports bra, intending to get her workout in at the fitness center downstairs. Ten more minutes, she would've had on her T-shirt and tennis shoes and been out of the apartment when Malcolm arrived.

"Going somewhere?"

"Not anymore."

"You look really good in that outfit. I want to kiss you."

Her eyes lowered to Malcolm's lips, full and plump like always, then back up to eyes that saw straight into her.

Sky didn't remember moving, although she must've, as did Malcolm, because the next thing she knew they were in each other's arms and kissing. Tongues fought. Teeth clashed. Lips sucked and hands roamed.

The wireless phone dropped from her hand.

Back against couch cushions Sky went, Malcolm on top of her and between her parted thighs.

Trembling hands pushed Malcolm's jacket off and fumbled with the buttons of his shirt until she had them undone and was able to slide her hands over a layer of delicious mocha skin and ribbed stomach muscles.

Malcolm pushed up her sports bra, holding the material out of the way for his luscious tongue and predatory mouth. Nipples hardened on contact, tingling and aching for the attention she'd denied them for fourteen interminable days.

Sex throbbed, and Sky squirmed, opening her legs wider to feel Malcolm's erection through his jeans. He pressed and thrust. Lips left her nipples to reclaim her mouth, and hands found breasts and kneaded with a roughness that blurred the line between pleasure and pain.

No words were spoken as they all but mauled each other on Sky's couch. Clothes were yanked off. Skin was scratched and bitten. Hairstyles were ruined. A condom was almost forgotten. The minute he slipped into Sky, hard, bare skin against her soft, wet walls, they stopped and stared at each other.

Malcolm thrust a few times before withdrawing and sheathing. Sky closed her eyes, loving having him inside of her again. The reassuring weight of Malcolm on top of her. The fresh, masculine scent of him around her. The strength of his arms keeping her close, and the taste of his lips nibbling hers. Everything about Malcolm Styles appealed to Sky, and she'd almost thrown this and him away.

She began to cry.

"It's never a good sign when your woman cries in the middle of sex. What's wrong? Do you want me to stop?"

Hugging him to her, Sky wrapped her legs around his waist. "Don't stop. I need you to make love to me."

Despite having confessed his love weeks ago, neither Malcolm nor Sky ever referred to their sexual acts as making love. Hadn't that been what they were doing, though? If not before Malcolm's declaration, then surely after Sky returned from her retreat and began spending most of her nights at Malcolm's house and sharing his bed.

So he did make love to Sky, slow, sweet and erotic as sin. Malcolm had an inventive mind, and Sky was flexible. The combination had them on the floor, against a wall, on top of her kitchen island, and in a barstool chair.

By the time they finished, all movable pieces of furniture in her kitchen and living room were in a different place and the remaining condoms in her nightstand drawer used. Now, they lounged in Sky's bed. Ironically, one of the few pieces of furniture they hadn't made love on.

The night was still young and neither of them exhausted.

"This isn't what I thought would happen when I came over here." A big hand rubbed up and down Sky's back, half her naked body draped across Malcolm's. "Honestly, I didn't think you would let me in."

"What would you have done if I hadn't?"

The hand on her back stilled. "Licked my wounds and gone home. It doesn't feel good to be ignored."

She knew the truth of that better than most. Sky kissed his chest, then rolled out of bed to put on a nightgown. As nice as being in Malcolm's arms felt she needed a layer of clothing if she intended to bare her soul.

Malcolm sat up in bed, sheets pooled at his waist, a pillow behind his back and against the headboard. "Is this when we talk?"

"Yes." Sky perched on the edge of the messy bed, as nervous about telling Malcolm the truth as she'd been the day in his office. A deep inhalation then a slow exhale. "Did you mean everything you said to Angie about Sean's former lover and the woman's baby?"

"Oh, did I offend you when I called the woman a bitch and whore? Listen, I don't normally say stuff like that. I mean, I've used those words before, but I've never called a woman any of them to her face."

"It's not that. Well, it is, but not in the way you mean. It's just," Sky rubbed her eyes with the heel of her hands, an image of her mother's defiant face sparking behind them, "my mother used to be called names like that. Rarely to her face, although I witnessed a few times. It wasn't pretty. I don't think my mother ever regretted a single mistake in her life. So, when someone came at her with their hateful, judgmental words, she gave as good as she got without lowering herself to their level. Her venom didn't need curse words, which made what she had to say more poisonous and hurtful."

Her father received the brunt of her mother's tongue-lashing, which he deserved probably more than Sky knew.

The loft had great acoustics and thick walls. She heard nothing but the sound of her heavy breathing and rampaging heart. Malcolm remained silent, although his worried, tender eyes spoke the words he wouldn't until she finished. The man might enjoy speaking, but he also listened better than anyone she knew.

"My father is Robert Joseph Ellis III."

She waited for Malcolm to put the pieces together. The professor not only possessed a history degree, but he'd also studied Maryland politics and history as part of his research on George Bragg. She'd read his dissertation as well as two of his scholarly articles on politics in Maryland. Her father would've come up in his research. Not only because he'd garnered an unprecedented percentage of the African American vote but because of rumors of his affair with an African American campaign staffer.

"Your father is Governor Ellis?"

"He hasn't been Maryland's governor for a long time. Nowadays, he's chairman of the United States Naval Academy Foundation. My mother worked on his first gubernatorial run. She was his campaign manager. He courted the African American vote, which my mother helped him win. Baltimore City and County, Prince George's County, Maryland regions with significant populations of African Americans. His navy background and wealthy Annapolis roots did the rest."

"They had an affair."

It wasn't a question but a vocalization of the unstated but implied fact.

"Like Sean and his legal assistant. An older man, a younger woman, and a surprise, inconvenient pregnancy."

"Shit, I didn't mean…" Malcolm started for her, but Sky raised her hand to stop his progress and protest.

"You meant what you said. Do I think, if you'd known the circumstances surrounding my conception and birth, you would've popped off the way you did in front of me, I don't. But that doesn't change what you think or how you feel about men like my father and women like my mother. The spouses they hurt, the families they ruin, and the bastard children they create."

"Sky, come on. I was angry on my sister's behalf. I wasn't talking about you and your parents."

"You were. You just didn't know it." She waved him away again when Malcolm started for her. "You didn't say anything I haven't heard before and it's what most people think. I can't help being a product of an adulterous affair. I'm not guilty of anything, but that never stopped the stares or judgment." She laughed, low and mirthless. "I don't even know why Mom gave me his last name, Robert didn't openly acknowledge me as his child until after his political career ended, his wife divorced him, and his other children were grown. I was eighteen, when he decided to stop pretending the rumors were lies. Annapolis isn't that big, and people talked, even if behind closed doors."

"Sky, I—"

"Mom took me to see him once. I was seven and had never been in a waterfront home. I can still see the wide staircase my father walked down, his eyes wide, green and mad as hell at my mother for bringing me there. We went to his office. They argued. I cried, but they were too engrossed in their disagreement to notice, blaming each other for things no child needed to hear. So I left."

"What do you mean you left?"

"Just that. I slipped from Robert's office and ran as far away from my parents as I could. I ended up in a library where I hid until a woman found me. I asked if my dad was mad at me for running away. The woman turned out to be Mrs. Ellis." Sky pointed to her face. "She took one look at me and said, 'You have her face but his eyes.'"

Sky spared herself Malcolm's pity by omitting the part where her father's wife had slapped her after she'd called her father "Daddy." That had been Mrs. Ellis's way of striking out at an unfaithful spouse and a woman who'd stolen parts of her marriage and husband.

Sade couldn't force Robert to be a dad to Sky. Frustrated and angry at Robert's dismissal of his responsibility to Sky, her mother might have been, but driving to the home he shared with his wife wasn't a moment Sade could look back on with pride. When it came to Robert Ellis, however, every choice her mother had made flew in the face of her intelligence and common sense.

"I don't know if Robert told his wife or whether she suspected the truth. I do know Mrs. Ellis met my mother during the campaign and she knew Robert and Sade spent a lot of time together. I never wanted to know the details of their affair. The result was clear enough. I was born. Robert Ellis was a name on my birth certificate only, and he paid child support."

Not that Sade needed financial support to take care of Sky. Being a political consultant paid well. So well, Sade deposited every child support check she'd received into a Money Market Account for Sky. By the time she'd reached the age of majority and Sade had turned the account over to her, Sky had one hell of a nest egg for an eighteen-year-old. Between the money and property bequeathed to Sky in her mother's will and the insurance payment from Sade's death, Sky still hadn't touched a penny of Robert's money.

"Robert was never my father. He never even tried to be, except when he called on birthdays and sent Christmas presents. By the time I came around, he had two sons and two daughters by his wife. He didn't need a little biracial kid messing up his pristine life."

Malcolm scrambled to Sky's side. His arms went around her, and he nestled her head on his shoulder. She didn't want his pity. Sky wasn't an abused child. Plenty of women raised children on their own. Her mother loved and cared for Sky. She taught her the value of an education, hard work, and persistence. Sade Page had slept with a man who could never give her what she needed or wanted. For Robert to have done so, he would've disrupted his entire life and that of his family.

He should've known better. They both should've made better and different decisions.

"You know why your mother didn't regret her affair with your father." Malcolm lifted her chin and made Sky look at him. "Because it gave her you."

Sade said the same, every time Sky threw away one of Robert's guilt gifts and cried about wishing she'd never been born. Sky hadn't meant it, of course, but the words had come from a place of rejection and anger. Malcolm was right. Sky had grown up mad at not only her father but her mother as well.

"I'm sorry about what I said. I'm sorry I hurt you. I didn't mean to."

"You didn't know because I didn't tell you. I don't like talking about my family. I don't even like thinking about the secondary reason my father didn't want his affair with my mother to come out and to acknowledge me as his daughter."

"Don't say that."

"Why not? We're both too smart to not think it. Hell, you wrote about white liberalism in your dissertation. Their liberal ideals didn't miraculously free them from racist thoughts and actions."

"He's your father."

"I know. Most days I even believe he loves me. But it's hard to ignore the role race plays in all our lives. A white man who sleeps with an African American woman doesn't necessarily make him any less a product of the racist society that birthed and raised him."

"Have you talked to him about this?"

"It's not exactly the kind of conversation either of us wants to have. What would he say? What would I say? It's there between us, and the truth would change nothing. He wants to be a father to me, and I'm trying to let him. Nothing between us will ever be normal, but our relationship isn't as bad as when he'd first tried to insinuate himself into my life. At that point, I damn near hated Robert."

"And now?"

"He's my father, as you said. I want to be able to trust him, to think the best of him, although Robert makes it hard, sometimes. I do love him. I hadn't realized I did until his heart attack. I can't bring myself to think of his other children as my siblings, except for Carrie. She's the only sibling who reached out and befriended me. On my mother's side, the Page family is pretty small. I have an uncle, an aunt, and cousins."

"You now have the Styles and me."

She shook a head that pounded from the ache of opening an old vault of pain. Malcolm's expression couldn't have been sincerer. "No, what I have is your sympathy and guilt. I don't want either. I've never told anyone my story."

"Then why did you tell me?"

Sky knew why, but the words stuck in her throat. If she told Malcolm, she would have nothing left.

He kissed her. Sky's forehead, nose, cheek, lips. "Why me, Sky? Why bare your heart after what I said?"

"I don't want to talk anymore, Malcolm. I'm tired."

"You mean emotionally drained."

"Same difference."

"Do you want me to leave?"

"No, but I'll understand if you want to go."

He frowned. "That's more than a little insulting. You aren't a mistake, and I hate that you've felt that you were. You also aren't your parents. And, Sky, I don't care how you came into the world, only that you're here." He kissed her face, cheeks wet with tears she hadn't known she'd shed. "I love you. I know you believe me because you trusted me with your pain."

Sky hadn't trusted anyone this much since her mother and grandmother had died. Revealing so much of herself to another person, even Malcolm, left her feeling self-conscious and raw.

She crawled to the top of the bed and under the covers. Malcolm followed, spooning behind Sky, a hand on her hip, a leg wedged between hers. She shifted onto her back, and her hand went to Malcolm's face.

"When I first met you, you scared the hell out of me."

"Why?"

Her hand traveled to his hair, locs a waterfall of strength and beauty. Like Malcolm.

"You were insanely handsome but also intelligent, funny, and sensitive. For the first time, I wanted something I'd never had and thought, deep down, I might not deserve."

"What's that?" Malcolm turned and kissed the palm of the hand that had returned to his face.

"A man who would love me enough to put me first. I don't mean that selfishly. I mean—"

"I know what you mean. Your father put his career, wife, other children, even his public image before his care and responsibility to you. For a long time, he abandoned you. Children need more than money and material goods from their parents. I get it. I know you don't mean that you want me to put you first in everything I do. No more than I can expect that of you. But you want to be of equal value to other people in my life. Not to supplant them in my heart, but for me to make room for you in there beside them."

Sky closed her eyes and fought the tears Malcolm's words evoked. He'd looked into her heart with his perceptive mind and kind nature.

Like tea leaves at the bottom of a cup, Malcolm had divined the pattern of her soul.

"I love you, Malcolm." She could feel his smile against her hand on his face. Sky opened watery eyes, her heart overflowing with love and affection for the man grinning down at her. "I love you."

"I know. My father used to tell me that anything worth having is also worth fighting for." His laughter made her smile. "But it was Mom who told me that any person worth having is also worth waiting for. It took thirty-six years for the woman worth having to walk into my life. Now that you're here, Sky Ellis, I'm never letting you go."

"Promise?" Heart fluttered, lips trembled, and tears fell.

Happy tears.

"I do. I'll repeat the same, but louder and with a romantic poem I've written, on the day of our wedding. How does that sound?"

"Like you're pushing."

He nudged her thigh with an interested penis. "I thought you enjoyed my pushing."

Sky refrained from rolling her eyes but couldn't contain her sigh. "Another double entendre."

"You better get used to them because you're stuck with me."

She rolled him over and straddled his hips. Her hands went to the hair that spread across his broad chest and wrapped the locs around her fingers. "I don't mind being stuck with these."

"I think you only want me around so you can play with my locs."

"Maybe I'm jealous. Your hair is prettier and longer than mine."

Sky began to move against him, teasing them both. They'd used the last of her condoms.

"Did you bring—"

"In my wallet. Two. I'll go out tomorrow and get more. Unless…" Hips thrust, sliding Malcolm's tempting offer between her lips.

Unless she wanted to go without. Yes, very tempting.

The phone rang. Dammit, she should've known.

Sky swore.

"What's wrong?"

"You're not the only male in my life I haven't spoken to in two weeks. Robert's going to burn my ears if I answer the phone."

"Then let me answer."

"Uh, no."

"Why not?"

The ringing stopped. Thirty seconds later it resumed, and Sky swore again.

"I'm not ready for this." Reaching toward the nightstand, Sky plucked the house phone from the cradle and handed it to Malcolm. "Too much, too soon. Don't smile, Malcolm, I'm serious. I'm not ready for any of this."

Still giving her a self-satisfied grin, Malcolm took the phone from Sky's hand. He hit the talk button after she slid from his lap and buried herself under the comforter.

She cringed when she heard her father's worried voice. Why in the hell had Malcolm also pushed the speakerphone button? Sky should take a shower and leave the men to talk. Instead, she found herself listening to their conversation.

"Oh, you finally decided to take pity on your father and answer the phone. Lucky for you because my next move was to book a flight to Buffalo. Buffalo, Sky, really? The only thing that city is known for are its wings. You can't possibly prefer Buffalo wings to Maryland crabs."

"Actually, I do. I like classic Buffalo wings without the extras. Crunchy and well sauced. Maryland crab soup is okay, if you like mixing meat and vegetables into one dish."

Her father didn't even like crabs, but he would take offense to Malcolm's playful banter. No one loved their state more than Robert Ellis.

"I'll have you know, Maryland crab soup is a hearty meal, a perfect blend of seasonings."

"Seasonings? What spices are in that soup other than Old Bay?"

Sky peeked her head from under the comforter, looking up at Malcolm. He still wore a smile plastered on his face, while she was sure her father was frowning on the other end of the line.

"It's nine in the evening, and you answered my daughter's phone. I assume you're the man she refuses to tell me about. Are you the reason she hasn't spoken to me in two weeks?"

"My name is Malcolm Styles, and I'm pretty sure *you're* the reason she hasn't spoken to *me* in two weeks."

He did not just say that. Sky sat up in bed and reached for the phone, but Malcolm batted her hand away.

"You're in her apartment, and she allowed you to answer her phone, knowing it was her father calling, I'd say those two weeks of silent treatment didn't put a dent in your relationship with Sky. Care to reveal your secret to getting around my daughter's wall and into her heart?"

Malcolm's eyes, dark with lust, scanned Sky's face before lowering to nipples that hardened under his lascivious gaze.

"You'll have to figure out your own strategy, Mr. Ellis. It's nice to finally meet you, by the way."

"It's good to meet you, too, Mr. Styles. Where's my daughter?"

Sky leaned close to Malcolm's hand holding the phone and projected her voice when she spoke. "Right here. How are you feeling, Robert?"

"Better now that I've heard your voice and met your young man. We need to talk about the last two weeks."

"I know. I promise to call you tomorrow."

"There's something I've wanted to speak with you about. Since Malcolm is there with you, I'd like to extend my invitation to you both."

Sky was already shaking her head at Malcolm, who was nodding at her, his smile even larger.

"Listen, I was hoping you'd come for a visit. I know you're busy with the new job and probably don't have much time off accrued. But, with winter break in a few months, I thought you'd like to spend part of it with me. Christmas with my youngest daughter would be wonderful.

Don't answer now. If you do, you'll reject the invitation on principle alone. Mull it over. December is months away, which gives me more time to chip away at your walls and wiggle my way into your good graces. Are you still there, Malcolm?"

"Yes, sir."

"Do you love my daughter?"

Sky reached for the phone again, but Malcolm's long, strong arm kept her at bay.

"Yes, sir."

"Great. That makes me happier than you could possibly know. I would love to meet you face-to-face. No pressure, for either of you. Just give my invitation serious thought."

"We will."

Robert laughed. "Take it from an old man, Malcolm, never answer for an independent-minded woman unless you're one hundred percent certain she agrees with you. The fact that you're still breathing and I'm not listening to a dial tone tells me all I need to know about Sky's feelings for you. That makes me want to meet you even more. Sky…?"

"Yes?"

"Christmas in Annapolis with your Ellis family."

"What do you mean my Ellis family?" This time, when Sky grabbed for the phone, Malcolm gave it to her. "What do you mean?"

"Your Ellis family."

"I don't have an Ellis family."

"You do, and it's past time you joined it. I would like all my children here for the holiday. I know it's my fault that never happened. Apologies never worked on you so I won't offer another one. Just know, I want you with us. I value and love you as much as I do your siblings. For good reason, I'm sure you don't believe me, but it's true."

"I can't do that. I can't…" Sky dropped the phone, overcome with emotion. Thirty-five years too late. No longer a little girl crying for daddy and his love, Sky couldn't reconcile her unwanted need for familial acceptance and her self-preservation instinct. She couldn't allow Robert to draw her into his web of lies and hope.

Malcolm picked up the phone with one hand and hugged her to him with the other.

"You've laid a lot on Sky tonight."

"I know."

"I'm not sure if you really do, but it's not my place to get into that with you. But know this, wherever Sky decides to spend Christmas, that's where I'll be."

"Fair enough. I hope to see you both in December. Goodnight."

Sky curled in on herself, listening as Malcolm returned the phone to the base.

"Don't shut down on me again." Malcolm's warm, comforting body spooned hers, his right arm around her waist and his lips pressed to her shoulder.

"I'm trying not to. I don't want to push you away again. You didn't deserve it, and I had no right to punish you for issues I should've resolved years ago. I'm sorry."

"I hated it, but I now understand why you asked for distance. I don't mind giving you space. I just need to know, when I do, you'll always come back to me. I don't want to wonder if I've lost you because I don't know what's going on in your head."

"You won't lose me." Sky shifted onto her back to look up at Malcolm. "You won't lose me."

He didn't smile the way she'd hoped he would. Malcolm stared down at her, expression serious and heart in his eyes. Unlike Sky, who hid her emotions behind silences and professionalism, Malcolm wore his like a crown of gold.

"Don't take this the wrong way, but I can't lose what I don't fully have. I have bits and pieces of you. Probably more of Sky Ellis than you've given to any other man you've dated, which I appreciate. But there's more of you, and that's the woman I want to marry-- the entire Sky."

Closing her eyes, Sky sucked in a deep breath and then opened them again. As she knew they would, Malcolm's eyes were still on her, steadfast and earnest.

"I won't pop the question until you're ready."

"How will you know when I am?" *What if I'm never ready? Will you stay or leave?*

"I'll know. Styles men always do. So, about your father's Christmas invitation. What do you want to do? Annapolis with the Ellises or Buffalo with the Styles clan?"

Sky groaned. "December is four months from now."

"Which only means you have four months to brood about a decision you could make today or tomorrow."

"You're pushing again."

"I know. It's a bad habit, when it comes to you. What about birth control pills, implant, IUD, vaginal ring?"

"What? You're giving me whiplash. We weren't talking about birth control, and you know far too much about female contraceptives."

Malcolm's hand slid under her nightgown and up to a breast. A finger began to play with her nipple, and lips lowered to her neck, kissing and licking.

Sky squirmed against him, her legs opening to accept his thick, strong thigh between them.

"We're spending a fortune on condoms. We're both disease-free." Thigh pressed into her mound, a hard friction that had Sky rutting against him. If he kept that up, she'd come. "If you were on the pill, I would slip inside you right now. Tease you with the head of my dick, shallow thrusts before giving you every hard inch of me."

Malcolm put action to words. Kind of. On his hands and knees and between her legs, Malcolm glided his wonderfully stiff dick between her lips and over her clit.

"Shit, Malcolm"

"Feels good, doesn't it? My skin against yours. Nothing between us but love and lust." Leaning down, Malcolm's hips pressed even more into hers, increasing the friction they produced. "Tear down another wall for me. Trust me with your heart and your body."

Sky had never had sex with a man without making sure he wore a condom. Twice already, with Malcolm, she'd broken her rule, if only for a couple of minutes. He was pushing again, and not in the way she enjoyed.

Holding his face between her hands, Sky kissed him as she rode out the pleasure of his body taking hers to another orgasm. Her clit enlarged, sensitive, and pulsing with stomach-clenching desire and release.

She reached down between their bodies, taking hold of Malcolm's erection. He rolled onto his back, and Sky went with him, her hand still wrapped around his magnificent length.

"You want too much. Ask for too much and push too damn hard."

Malcolm thrust into her hand, a devilish grin his response. Then he closed his eyes, tucked his hands behind his head and luxuriated in Sky's hand job. She mixed up pressure and speed, guided by Malcolm's moans and breathing.

Her left hand moved between his thighs and to his perineum, her pointer and middle fingers gently massaging the sensitive stretch of skin. Knees fell to the sides, hands gripped sheets, and Malcolm came with bear grunts and a lion's roar.

Pleased with herself, Sky rolled out of bed and went to the bathroom. Five minutes later, Malcolm joined her in the shower. Twenty minutes after that, they were back in her bed, lights off, and wrapped around each other. The emotional weight of the day had Sky's eyelids closing, head resting on Malcolm's solid chest and hand over his heart.

"What am I going to do with my cloudy Sky?"

Love me and never let me go. "Have faith in me. In us."

"I do because behind every dark cloud is a rainbow."

"Now I'm a dark cloud?"

"You know that's not what I meant."

She did.

"Angie and Sean's marriage is a dark cloud, right now. Stormy with rain, thunder, and lightning. It wasn't always like that. But life isn't perpetual sunshine and rainbows, and neither are relationships. To appreciate our good fortune and the blessings we sometimes take for granted, we have to also experience cloudy days and chilly nights."

"Those were a lot of sky and weather references."

Malcolm chuckled. "Yeah, I know, and I wasn't even going for them." Arms held her tighter and lips found her forehead and kissed. "I hope Angie and Sean can rediscover their rainbow."

"That kind of betrayal won't be easy to get past."

"I know. But, like you said, faith. They both have to want to get to the other side of hurt, anger, and guilt."

"You're also talking about Robert and me, aren't you?"

"You're a smart woman, and I'm a romantic man who believes in an arrow-shooting Cupid, Santeria love spells, and pixie dust of protection and enchantment. As I told you once before, the celestial sphere, a dome under which the sun, moon, and stars dance and sing in cosmic harmony, is an astrological phenomenon eclipsed only by the limitations of our vision and the gravity of our fears."

Vision and fears. Malcolm's vision. Sky's fears.

Point taken.

"You really want to spend Christmas in Annapolis with the Ellises?"

"No. I'd like to spend Christmas in my house with you. What I want, however, is for you to cast off the shackles of the past and step into the future with me as an emancipated woman. If it takes going to Maryland and meeting your father and siblings to make that happen, then I'm all in."

All in. Their relationship had turned out to be much more than a shallow office romance.

Sky hadn't decided whether she would spend her Christmas with Robert and his family. But she liked the idea of taking Malcolm home and showing him where she grew up and her favorite places, much as he'd done for her in Buffalo.

"I love you, Malcolm. You're my best birthday, Christmas, and Valentine's presents rolled into one tasty Tootsie Roll."

"A Tootsie Roll? You do know that candy is neither chocolate nor a taffy. I do like that it also comes in a lollipop you put in your mouth and suck until you find the chewy center. Please don't tell me that was another one of your attempts at being romantic."

"Fine, I won't."

"You've got to be kidding me." Malcolm pushed to his elbows, displacing Sky from his chest. "Comparing an African American man to a fake piece of chocolate candy is not romantic."

"So, if I bought you chocolate candy for Valentine's Day, you wouldn't eat it?"

"Hell, yes, I'd eat it. Chocolate is delicious, and I have a sweet tooth. But that's not the point."

"If you'd eat the box of chocolates -- I will get you, by the way -- I fail to see your point. And we're not having an African American Studies debate about the appropriateness of me referring to you as chocolate candy. If you knew how many times I've thought of you as—"

Sky slammed her mouth shut.

"As what?"

"Nothing, let's go to sleep. I'm exhausted."

"You're going to tell me."

Sky pulled the comforter up to her shoulders and closed her eyes. "I can feel you glaring at me, go to sleep."

The bed shifted, and then Malcolm had Sky in his arms, her head back on his chest and her hand over his heart.

"Hot as jalapeno peppers? Thick as cucumbers? Sweet as cinnamon-sugar popcorn? Filling as three-bean soup? Tell me."

"I'll tell you in the morning."

"No, you won't. You're going to send me one of your ridiculous emojis, aren't you? Probably a weird avocado one I've seen all over social media lately." Malcolm swatted her bottom. "On second thought, send me one that's cut in half."

What in the hell was an avocado emoji? "Cut in half? Why?" An image popped into her mind of a sliced avocado. "You're terrible. I'm not sending you that."

"What about a red-hot chili pepper or grapefruit?"

"No."

"You're no fun."

"I'm plenty of fun. I'm just not going to send you an emoji that looks like a vagina or penis. Even I know that's not romantic."

"It doesn't have to be romantic. I'd love it because it came from you. I'm tired."

"You should be. And thirsty, for as much as you talk."

"I'll make you pay for that tomorrow. Right now, I just want to hold you while I sleep."

Being in his embrace was a perfect way to end Sky's day and her two-week Malcolm drought.

"Goodnight, sweetie."

"You're getting better at that. I love the way the endearment flows effortlessly from your mouth now. It makes a man feel all warm and gooey inside like a caramel-filled brownie."

"That was terrible, and you're an unrepentant sap."

"I am. Goodnight."

Sky closed her eyes, relaxed, and began to drift off to sleep. Somewhere, in the murky space between sleep and consciousness, she heard Malcolm mumble, "Move in with me."

Sky's eyes popped open.

The End of Part 1

MERRY CHRISTMAS

THE WISH OF Xmas Present

The Styles of *Love* Book Two

USA Today Bestselling Author

N.D. JONES

PAGE FAMILY

ELLIS FAMILY

Dr. Sky ELLIS

ROBERT (FATHER) · GARRETT (BROTHER) · AARON (BROTHER) · OLIVIA (SISTER) · CARRIE (SISTER)

CHAPTER TEN

"No."

Malcolm didn't like his sister's response any more than he appreciated the put-upon huff that followed. "Come on. Why not?"

"Did you really just whine those four words at me?" Angie asked.

"Yeah, he did. Wait." Sean, Malcolm's brother-in-law, looked from Malcolm to Angie, and then back to Malcolm. "Didn't we have this conversation already? I swear I remember you sitting on that ottoman in our living room about six months ago."

Angie nodded. "It was the beginning of baseball season, and you came over here desperate about a female colleague who wouldn't give you the time of day."

Angie's laughter bubbled out of her, and Malcolm's heart clenched with relief and joy at his sister's good humor. Even if it was at his expense. Ever since Angie had learned of Sean's affair with his legal assistant, little in life, save her three children, made her smile.

Sean wanted a second chance with his wife. Angie had decided to give him one. However, the couple didn't seem to be any closer to reconciliation than they were a month ago when Sean brought Angie home from the hospital.

"I wasn't desperate. I just needed help from my older sister."

"Sounds like revisionist history to me," Sean said, grinning at Malcolm from his perch on the end of the sofa. He sat as near to Angie as her wheelchair and two broken legs would allow. "You wanted Angie to use her position as President of Excelsior University to get you into a leadership retreat Sky was slated to attend. Does she know that story?"

Malcolm hadn't forgiven Sean for cheating on Angie, and neither had she. It would take a while before he and Sean mended their relationship and returned to being best friends. Yet, each time he visited his sister, one thing was obvious. Sean was putting in the work.

Later, Malcolm thought, he would have a private word with Angie to see how she was dealing with everything. The Styles might be a big family, with aunts, uncles, and cousins galore, but Malcolm and Angie's parents, unlike their siblings, only had two children. Even though they were ten years apart in age, Malcolm and Angie were close. When she hurt, so did he. But when she laughed, the way she did now, he basked in the angelic beauty of Angela Styles-Franklin.

"Look at your face, M and M. It's clear you didn't tell Sky you planned on stalking her at SUNY's summer leadership retreat because you couldn't figure out another way to get close to her."

Funny that, even though there were three people in the room and talking about the same topic, Angie hadn't directed a single sentence to Sean. Okay, maybe he didn't need to speak privately with her to know how things were going between the couple. For Sean's part, he seemed unfazed by Angie's subtle snub. Sean's large hand, that went to Angie's dark-brown hair, sweeping bangs out of her eyes and behind an ear, told the silent tale of their emotional war.

Angie had once told Malcolm that everything in marriage mattered. The longer he and Sky were together, the more his sister's words of wisdom proved true.

Malcolm hadn't told Sky about his ridiculous plan from six months ago and Angie's refusal to aid and abet him. He didn't know why he hadn't. Perhaps he feared she'd view him as not only a romantic sap but as manipulative as her father. Or maybe she would think his idiotic plan a sign of desperation, as his sister had joked.

Sitting there, in Angie and Sean's living room, he felt the same sense of anxiety and desperation as he had six months ago when he'd driven there with what he thought was a surefire plan to win Sky over. He'd needed Sky not to think about dating him as an off-limits office romance. For that to happen, Malcolm reasoned, he required neutral territory, which he wouldn't get if Sky's only interactions with him were at Eastern Bluebird College where they worked.

"We were just ribbing you, man. No need to get down in the dumps about it. Zuri's your niece. If you want her to spend time with you and Sky, I have no problem with that."

For the first time since Malcolm's arrival, Angie addressed Sean directly. "Well, I do. I won't allow Malcolm to use our five-year-old child to lure Sky into a marriage she may not be ready for."

"But Zuri is the perfect talisman. She's a pixie-cherub mix. Magical, adorable, and with the chubbiest cheeks that make you want to take a bite."

"A pixie-cherub? That's not even a thing."

"My only point is that Zuri is perfect for the job. All Malcolm wants is for Sky to see what her life could be like if she married him and they had a family of their own. Zuri looks more like you than me, which, by the way, is going to be hell when she wants to date. I'm telling you right now, Angie, I'm not going to be able to deal with boys sniffing around my daughters." Sean balled his right hand and punched the palm of his left. "It's bad enough that Kayla is beginning to develop breasts."

"Maybe you should've married and had children with an unattractive woman," Malcolm baited Sean. "That way, you wouldn't have as many boys coming around to date your beautiful daughters."

Angie's derisive snort could've cut Malcolm's tongue out his mouth.

"That's an awful, sexist comment. Both of you are ridiculous. We won't permit our child to be used to manipulate anyone, least of all a friend of the family."

We? Interesting how a woman chose to speak for a man, even when he disagreed with her. Malcolm had witnessed his mother, aunts, and female cousins take the same approach with their husbands.

"Zuri isn't a pixie or cherub anything," Angie said to Sean. "I don't even know where you got that from. As far as Kayla's development, don't you dare say anything to embarrass her. She gets that enough at school. She's only ten, and it's no fun being the first girl in her class to develop breasts."

Throughout Angie's gentle scold, Sean nodded, a twinkle in his eyes. While Malcolm thought he'd been the one to bait Sean, it had been the civil rights lawyer who'd baited his wife into speaking to him. Sean and Angie's children were the one topic Angie wouldn't remain silent about, even if it meant engaging Sean in conversation.

Considering the couple's rocky relationship, Malcolm didn't see the benefit of Sean riling Angie and starting what could turn into an argument.

"Now, for you." Angie narrowed her gaze on Malcolm, reminding him of their mother whenever he got into trouble and Kimberly Styles was about to lay into him. "You're better than cheap tricks. Sky's a smart woman with a good heart. Just as you're a smart man with a sensitive soul. Do you think Sky doesn't see you for the amazing person you are? Trust me, she does. She may not say all the flowery words you want to hear, but I've seen the two of you together. Sky loves you."

"I know."

"Then what's the problem? Why do you think you need Zuri to help you seal the deal?"

Malcolm pushed from the ottoman and onto the leather chair behind it. "Insecurity, I guess."

"I don't get it. Why are you insecure? Has Sky given you a reason to think she doesn't want more out of your relationship? I mean, let's keep this in perspective. The two of you have only dated for six months. Exclusively, sure, but still only half a year."

How could he answer his sister's question without revealing Sky's family background and emotional scars? He couldn't, not without violating her trust, so he tossed Angie and Sean the same meaty bone he'd been gnawing on for weeks.

"I asked Sky to move in with me."

Malcolm's sister and brother-in-law wore twin expressions of disbelief followed by sympathy. He thought Sean would say something when he slid to the edge of the leather sofa, forearms resting on his legs and lips parting, but he closed his mouth without uttering a syllable or sound.

Good, Malcolm didn't want relationship advice from Sean, despite having sought it many times over the course of their eighteen years of friendship.

While Sean may have decided against commenting, Angie wasn't holding back. "Geesh, Malcolm, are you trying to scare Sky off?"

"Of course not. But she's either at my house, or I'm at her loft. Why wouldn't I ask her to move in with me? We practically live together already."

"Do you have personal items at Sky's apartment?" Angie asked.

"An extra grooming kit, a few shirts and pants, two pairs of shoes, T-shirts, boxers, stuff like that."

"What does she keep at your house?"

"She brings an overnight bag whenever she stays the night and takes everything back home when she leaves."

"That's what I thought. Sky's not ready, but I'm sure you surmised the same. You want everything yesterday. If you don't slow down, M and M, you're going to smother Sky to the point of making her want to get away from you, so she can breathe. You don't want to be *that* guy. She's with you, in love with you. Let that be enough. Just because Sky's thirty-five, that doesn't mean she hears her biological clock ticking, or is even concerned about becoming a wife and mother yet."

"I don't know why I came over here."

"Yes, you do. You hoped I would be the voice of reason because you know when you're thinking with your heart and emotions instead of with your brain. Finding the right partner and falling in love is only part of the equation, Malcolm Marcus Styles."

Malcolm X and Marcus Garvey-- Charles and Kimberly Styles, in naming him after those great men had set the bar high for their only son. Angie, named after political activist and educator Angela Davis, rarely used his full name in conversation. He may have liked her nickname for him, M and M, but not the way she'd said his full name, with a sprinkle of empathy and a touch of judgment.

"Many people haven't even gotten that lucky. It took you a while, but you're there now. You want the rest. Trust me, I get it. I'm sure Sky wants it too. You'll know when she's ready, even if she doesn't tell you."

"I told Sky the same thing. I told her I would know when she was ready for me to propose. That was a month ago, and the same night I asked her to move in with me."

Sean opened his mouth, but he quickly closed it again without saying a word. Malcolm wished Sean would either speak his piece or stop imitating a fish.

"Sky said no?"

"Not in so many words. Sky accused me of pushing then went to sleep. We haven't talked about it since."

"Turnabout is fair play," Angie said.

"What is that supposed to mean?"

Sean laughed but didn't offer more than a mocking grin for Malcolm and a wink and an air kiss for Angie, who ignored her husband's antics.

"As romantic and sappy as you are, and as many intelligent and beautiful women as you've dated, you have disappointed more marriage-minded females than you have dreadlocks on your head."

Sean laughed. "Angie's not wrong. You broke up with Nia. Who breaks up with a woman who not only enjoys cooking but who can actually burn in the kitchen?"

Angie looked as if she wanted to laugh at Sean's weak-ass joke but shrugged when Malcolm glared at her.

"Nia was a micromanaging control freak of a sous chef."

"What about Tammy?" Sean asked.

"The biggest complainer I've ever met. She even complained about other complainers."

"Miesha?"

"A jealous streak as deep as an ocean. I couldn't even talk to my sister without Miesha having something to say about how long we were on the phone."

"Dariel?"

Malcolm threw up his hands. "I don't remember, but it was *something*."

He honestly couldn't recall. Malcolm had had a damn good reason for ending his relationship with Dariel, but for the life of him, he couldn't remember why he'd broken things off with her.

"Sean's point, if you're too stubborn to grasp it, is that you have a pattern of dating women who are at a stage in their lives where they want to find a husband, settle down, and have children. When they got involved with you, they thought you were the man who would make their dreams come true."

"Are you trying to say I have a fear of commitment? Because that's damn sure not true."

"No, I'm saying you're picky as hell, and I can't believe you dumped four smart women before they dumped you first."

"Not five minutes ago you said I was a great catch."

"You are. For Sky. But not for your last four girlfriends. They were ready, but you weren't. Now that you're ready, you're with a woman who isn't." Angie shrugged. "As I said, turnabout is fair play."

Malcolm's focus shifted to Sean, waiting for his brother-in-law's mocking laughter or another stupid joke. What he was met with was Sean's rugged profile. Sean had turned to face Angie, his voice low and gruff when he asked, "Do you really believe turnabout is fair play?"

"This conversation is about Malcolm and Sky. Don't make leaps and apply to our situation what I'm saying to my brother."

"You didn't answer my question. It requires a simple yes or no. You have a doctorate, so I know my question didn't stump you."

Not only did Angie fail to respond to Sean, but she also refused to look his way, although he was drilling holes in her with his eyes.

Malcolm wondered if this argument Sean and Angie weren't quite having had something to do with the Provost and Executive Vice President of Academic Affairs at Excelsior University. He'd visited Angie at the hospital after her car crash. No match for Sean's height and physique, Dr. Murphy would still be considered an attractive man. If nothing else, he and Angie had a lot in common.

Angie wasn't the type of woman to cheat. Then again, until Sean's confession, Malcolm hadn't thought the lawyer the unfaithful type either. Apparently, Malcolm hadn't been the only one to notice Dr. Murphy's attraction to Angie.

"I would think a provost would be too busy to drop everything just to hand-deliver papers for your signature. I'm sure that could've been handled electronically and by your executive assistant."

"If you haven't noticed, I'm confined to a wheelchair. Are you accusing me of something?"

"You know I'm not. I just… shit, I don't know."

"Let's not do this now. We're making Malcolm uncomfortable."

Sean turned to Malcolm. "Yeah, yeah, sorry, bro. We're supposed to be helping you with Sky."

They couldn't help him with Sky. Hell, Sean and Angie couldn't help themselves out of a maze with glowing red arrows showing them the way to the exit.

Angie glanced down at the baby video monitor stored in the side pocket of her wheelchair. Pulling it out, she examined the image on the screen.

Before the older couple started arguing again, Malcolm decided to get the hell out of there. "It's getting late."

"Don't leave yet, M and M. Sean has some man thing to tell you he doesn't want me to hear." She looked at the baby monitor screen again and frowned. "Zuri's awake. It looks like she had a bad dream. I need to go to her."

Angie's gaze moved from the baby monitor to Sean, and her put-upon sigh had Malcolm hiding a smile. Even as a kid, his sister was the worst patient when she was sick. She rarely complained, but she hated depending on anyone.

"You need to stop firing my aides," Angie told Sean.

"I can take care of you. Four more weeks, then the doctor will see about taking off your casts. Until then, call me Nurse Sean."

"You're neither funny nor cute. Malcolm, once I'm upstairs I won't be back down, so make sure you come up and say goodbye before you leave."

"I will."

Sean stood from the sofa and, with a huge smile and gentle hands, he lifted his wife into his arms. For several seconds, Sean didn't move, his grip on Angie tight, their faces inches apart.

A look of love and longing passed Sean's eyes before Angie lowered her gaze. Then they filled with disappointment but also with determination.

A small part of Malcolm felt sorry for Sean. Angie may have agreed to work on their marriage, but it seemed clear she hadn't made an ounce of effort beyond her resolution not to seek a divorce. What they needed was a good marriage counselor. If that didn't work, then maybe they should consider parting ways. It would be hell on the kids but living in a house with parents who no longer knew how to communicate couldn't be healthy either.

"I'm going to get Angie into bed, and then take Zuri to her mother, which is the only way she'll fall back asleep if she's had a nightmare. Give me a few minutes, Malcolm, and I'll be back so we can talk."

Malcolm had no interest in talking about Sky with Sean, but it would be rude if he left while the man was upstairs with his wife and youngest child.

He pulled his cell phone from his pants pocket and sent Sky an emoji of a woman with a pink bow on her head, bright-red heart-shaped lips pursed for a kiss, long curling lashes, sparkling blue eyes, and huge breasts. It wasn't totally tasteless. The emoji did wear a pink bra to cover nonexistent nipples.

His phone dinged with a text message notification almost immediately. His lady's feminism never disappointed, neither did her lack of romanticism.

You're shameless, Dr. Styles. Her breasts are nearly as big as her head.

She ended her message with an orange President's Day emoji of Donald Trump holding a cell phone and tweeting: #notfakenews #mydayoff.

President's Day? It's September. At least send me a Hispanic Heritage Month emoji.

Of course, being Sky, she sent Malcolm a meditating, self-awareness emoji because, who knew, September was also Self-Improvement Month. She also included a link to a self-improvement blog for men who suffered from "romantic fanaticism."

Malcolm started his reply message but stopped when he heard Sean reenter the living room, which was for the best. When they got started, Malcolm and Sky could waste a lot of time exchanging silly text messages.

"How come you aren't with Sky tonight? It's Friday. Even SJ and Kayla are out."

"I know. Mom told me they were going to the movies with a couple of the older cousins. What did they go see?"

Sean sank onto the sofa, his six-three frame dropping as if exhausted. "I have no idea. Probably a PG-13 movie. Kayla's almost eleven, and Angie is fine with her watching that rating of movie, so I'm good with it too."

For awkward seconds, they sat across from each other, Malcolm unsure what kind of relationship they had. They weren't buddies anymore, but they also weren't enemies. That left a huge gray area between the men that silence couldn't fill.

"Sky's having dinner with Elena Mosby. Elena is Vice President for Student Life and Dean of Students. She's also on the Diversity Progress Committee, which is where she and Sky struck up a friendship."

"That's the committee Sky is the chair of?"

"Yeah. It's also the one I used to be a member of until EBC's president found out about me dating Sky."

"I hadn't heard. Sorry about that. Listen, I know I'm the last person to give anyone relationship advice." Sean ran a hand over his clean-shaven but weary-looking face. "I'm a selfish asshole, Malcolm. I keep firing Angie's aides because, if they're here, she won't give me the time of day. Sure, we talk about inconsequential things. And she normally won't outright ignore me if I ask her something. But that's all small talk or pretend when the kids are around."

"Maybe Angie's like Sky. She wants more but isn't ready to take the ultimate leap of faith."

"You're saying Angie's not ready to truly deal with our marriage although she was the one to make the decision to stay together. That sounds about right. She won't be in those casts forever. In another month or so, she'll be back at work and my time with her limited."

"Back at work with Dr. Murphy, you mean?"

"That guy has a thing for my wife."

"It doesn't matter. Who else looks or is interested never matters. It only matters when we allow it to."

"Is that your way of asking me why I cheated on my wife?"

"No. That's my way of saying you should've ignored your legal assistant's interest in you. I'm saying if you were attracted to the young woman you should've fired her ass instead of fucking her. I'm saying I don't think my sister is heartbroken or vengeful enough to screw around with Murphy or any other man to get back at you. Let's be real here, Sean, if Angie had fucked some guy after she'd learned about your affair, your ass would never know. Men get caught. Women rarely do, unless they just don't give a damn."

"That's kind of harsh coming from you."

"Maybe, but I'm right. Do you really think Angie had no idea you were messing around before you confessed?"

"Is that what she told you?"

"No. Even though we're close, Angie doesn't tell me everything. But I know her, and I know women. I'm sure she at least suspected."

"If she suspected I was creeping around on her, why didn't she say anything? I damn sure would've."

"Because to admit, even to yourself, that your husband is cheating, means you must decide to do something, even if that something is to ignore all the awful signs of infidelity. Men, on the other hand, we want to break shit and beat the hell out of the guy fucking our woman because we're possessive and revert to our primal state when it comes to the woman who owns our heart."

Another silence lapsed between them. Angie was right, he'd gone to their house because he knew his sister would see through his lame plan and get to the core of his concern. Until tonight, he hadn't realized, consciously, the power imbalance in his previous relationships. Malcolm had known his last four girlfriends hoped to get an engagement ring out of their time with him. But he hadn't played them.

How did a guy, however, explain to his girlfriend that he did want to marry and have kids but, when he dreamed, she wasn't the bride he saw standing opposite him at the altar? No one, except an insensitive ass, would do something like that. Malcolm had never lied to his former girlfriends or made them promises he didn't intend to keep. Those truths hadn't prevented his guilt after each breakup, though.

Sean slid to the edge of the sofa. This time, however, when he opened his mouth, he spoke. "Have you ever heard the expression why buy the cow when you can get the milk for free?"

"Who hasn't?"

"Fair enough. Well, you're the cow."

"I'm the what?"

"In your relationship with Sky, you're the cow. I'm not limiting this to sex. I'm talking about the whole thing. You already treat Sky as if she's your wife."

"What you're saying is nonsense. I'm not a damn cow."

Malcolm's phone dinged. Instinctively, he looked at it to read the new text message.

You asked me to remind you to buy eggs and milk. Consider this your reminder. Free of charge, but I wouldn't say no to a small token of appreciation.

A winking emoji followed Sky's text. No explanation was needed because Malcolm knew what Sky wanted as a "token of appreciation." Another lap dance, which he loved giving her.

"You should see yourself. Just looking at you, I know the text is from Sky."

"You sound jealous."

"I am. But I'm also not. This is what you must understand, Malcolm, as screwed up as my marriage is right now, and as much as my wife may hate my guts, we're still here. Twenty years later and we're still here. We don't have that new love glow like you and Sky. We don't send sweet texts and cute pics to each other. We don't snuggle in bed on a Saturday and listen to the rain. While sexy and sweet, probably even romantic, that shit isn't why marriages endure."

"Okay, so tell me, man-who-sleeps-in-the-guest-room-of-his-own-home, what's the secret to a long, happy marriage?"

Malcolm moved back to the ottoman, shoulders tense and jaw tight. Sean had no damn moral standing to offer Malcolm a goddamn bit of advice. A cow? ... please.

"I may have messed up, but I know the difference between sex with a younger woman who stroked an older man's ego and my wife. Don't get it twisted, Malcolm, I never got the two confused. A wife is entitled to a hell of a lot. A girlfriend less so, and a sex partner even less. That kind of outlook may make me sexist, as Angie accused us of being earlier, but it's true for me. I may have slipped, but my wife deserves everything I have to give her."

"That's the big secret? I must've missed it between you explaining how you prioritize your women."

"Okay, I deserved that. But check it. You may be thirty-six, but you don't know shit about being a husband. No man does until he becomes one, even though we think we got it under control when we take those life-changing vows. Marriage is what happens after the new car smell fades. It's the broken car radio, the scratched finish, the stained seat cushions, and the dirty floor mats. It's the car you get into every day, in need of new tires, an oil change, and windshield wipers. When you sit behind the wheel, though, and turn on the engine, the feel of the car coming to life makes you smile because you know how the car came to have every imperfection. Even better, you know every mile put on that car because you helped put it there. Cars that endure the test of time are called classics for a reason."

"I doubt Angie would like you comparing your marriage to a broken-down car."

"Not a broken-down car, a classic. There's a huge difference. One is a trip to divorce court, while the other has you sleeping in the guest room in your house with your wife and children. Love, grit, and hard work. That's why some marriages last and others fail. Trust is also important. That's what I'm working on rebuilding and re-earning."

"You didn't mention sex."

Sean laughed, a low sound that didn't go beyond the living room. "I know you probably think my affair was about sex, but it wasn't. I haven't had sex since the day I told Angie about Trinity. That was mid-January and the forecast for sex, anytime soon, is overcast and gloomy." Sean chuckled again, self-deprecating and sad. "Angie won't let me touch her in that way, and I don't want the feel of any woman but her. So, here we are. In our classic car and driving down the highway of love, grit, and hard work. Are you sure you want this?"

"I want it all if it's with Sky."

"Okay, then back to my cow analogy."

"Forget the damn analogy."

"It's a really good one, so shut up for a minute and let me finish. My point is that Sky isn't your wife yet, but you act as if she is. What's her incentive to move you from the boyfriend column to the husband column? From where I'm sitting, none. She gets all the milk she wants for free. Sky doesn't have to put in any work. And guess what, that's your fault, not hers."

"On that less than philosophical note, we're done." Getting to his feet, Malcolm shoved his cell into his pants pocket. "I'm going to run upstairs and kiss Angie and Zuri goodnight."

"You're making a mistake."

"I'm not taking your advice."

Sean also got to his feet, taller than Malcolm's five-ten. "I'm not suggesting you show Sky any less love and affection. I'm just saying you may want to let her come to you, sometimes, like she did when Angie was in the hospital. You needed her, and Sky was there. How many other opportunities have you given her to take the lead in the relationship? Sky can be lazy in that area because she's never had to work to get what she wants from you."

"You don't know what you're talking about."

"Fine, don't believe me. You know, Malcolm, a mistake in one area doesn't make me wrong about every damn thing. Sky won't marry you, not because she doesn't love you, but because you've given her no reason to want the upgrade. She gets most of the benefits of having a husband without the legal entanglement or having to move in with you and give up her woman's cave."

Malcolm was done listening to Sean. He turned away from him and walked toward the threshold of the living room, which led to the hallway and the stairs. The sooner he said his goodbyes, the sooner he could get the hell out of this house.

"You know I'm right," Sean yelled at his retreating back. "If you don't trust me, then trust your gut."

Halfway up the stairs, Malcolm's phone dinged.

Stop by after your visit with Angie. We can snuggle under the covers and watch the new horror movie I bought. :)

I'll be there in 30.

Perfect, don't forget to bring popcorn.

CHAPTER ELEVEN

Annapolis, Maryland
Thirty-Five Years Earlier

"Sorry I'm late. It's difficult to leave the Government House without an entourage, especially when I'm going to a meeting that isn't on my official calendar."

Sade's gaze fell away from Robert Ellis and his excuses and to their sleeping daughter in her crib. Sky's small frame was curled under a pink-and-white blanket. The only part of Sade's bundle of joy that was visible was Sky's dark-brown hair, a riot of curls locked in a daily battle against stubborn waves. Only time would tell which one would win the war.

"Leave Sky's nightlight on when you come out. She doesn't like the dark."

Sade wouldn't argue with Robert. Well, she would, just not in Sky's bedroom.

Several long strides took Robert from the threshold of Sky's bedroom, where he'd been lurking, to stand next to Sade beside Sky's crib. "You're going to let me visit?"

She always did. If Robert could see beyond his selfish needs or view Sade as more than a campaign manager turned lover, he'd understand the mother of his youngest child and why she granted him parental privileges even when he didn't deserve them.

"Look but don't touch. Sky's a light sleeper. I have a meeting in the morning, so I don't need an eleven-month-old up this time of night. I'm going downstairs. If you don't have anything different to say to me than what you've been saying since I told you I was pregnant, then you should leave after your visit. I don't want to hear any more of your tired excuses and lies."

Sade looked from Robert to Sky, shaking her head at her stupidity. What in the hell had she been thinking to involve herself with a married man? A rich, white, married politician at that. She shook her head again, leaving Robert alone with their daughter. A daughter who, except for the times he visited Sky in Sade's home, he pretended wasn't his.

Sky's birth certificate claimed Robert as Sky's father, regardless of the public face he donned for his family and constituents. To assuage his guilt, no doubt, Robert sent Sade monthly child support payments, which she neither asked for nor needed. What she wanted was for him to be a real father to Sky. These late-night visits weren't enough. But Sade feared, if she pushed for more, Robert would withdraw completely from Sky's life.

Sade made herself a cup of decaffeinated lemon citrus green tea. She would've preferred a strong, steaming cup of the Australian, arabica coffee beans she'd purchased two days ago but, as she'd told Robert, she had to work tomorrow. She had an appointment in Baltimore with the city's mayor. Sade didn't see his Republican challenger as a serious threat to unseating him, which she'd told Mayor Jennings on the phone. He still wanted to meet with her, so she'd agreed. Sade made it clear, however, if he hired her as his campaign manager, she wouldn't begin until the New Year. She wasn't ready to re-enter the political game and leave Sky with a nanny.

Hot teacup in hand, Sade sat in a loveseat across from the sparkling Christmas tree. No other lights were needed in the living room. If Sky were down there, Sade would watch her olive hazel eyes light up as she stared, with joy and awe, at the multicolored lights. She would also have to stay vigilant. Sky loved the gold-and-red garland, which invariably ended up in her mouth.

"Why don't you have decorations at the bottom of the tree?"

Robert stood in the doorway of the living room, tall, broad-shouldered, and fit. She knew his forty-two-year-old body as well as his wife did. Robert should be hers. But he never truly had been, not even when he'd been inside of her, whispering his love and lies of devotion.

"Sky can't walk yet, but she's big enough to reach the lower branches of the tree when on her knees."

He smiled. "That's right. I forgot."

Robert meant he'd forgotten that little fact from when his other children were Sky's age. Sade didn't need the reminder of how little time he spent with Sky that he no longer remembered what precautions a parent had to take with a child nearing the first year of life.

Sade continued to watch the play of Christmas lights. This year, she'd added more blinking bulbs than normal, thinking Sky would enjoy the show.

"That tea smells good. May I have a cup?"

Robert knew where everything was in her house. If he wanted tea, he could damn well get it himself.

"Okay, I'll take that as a no."

Sade didn't quite slam the teacup down, but she'd placed it none-too-gently on the side table.

"You're mad." Robert, never cowed by her temper, came fully into the room. "It's complicated."

"It's not."

"That's not true, and you know it."

She did, which only made her feel more like a fool. At thirty-one, she knew the repercussions of taking a married, white man as her lover.

Robert may be a blue tie-wearing Democrat, but Annapolis was red, through-and-through. It wasn't that white Annapolis men didn't sleep with black women. They did. Interracial relationships weren't unheard of or even rare. But such unions were uncommon among the political, social, and economic elite of the city.

It simply "isn't done," as Sade's mother had told her when she'd learned of her affair with Governor Robert Ellis III.

"You never intended to leave your wife for me or even for yourself. My brain knew you fed me lie after lie. But my ego and heart wouldn't listen. When it comes to love and men, sometimes smart women drop a few points on the IQ scale. I have my Sky, so I can't regret our time together."

Robert sank to his knees in front of Sade, his eyes, in the dim light, appearing browner than the mix of green-and-brown she knew them to be. Sade adored his eyes, and she saw them every day staring at her from the innocent face of their daughter. Hazel, many people called eyes like Robert's and Sky's. But hazel eyes could also be a mix of brown-and-blue. Daughter matched father, and no blue for either of them. Depending on the lighting or their mood, however, green or brown predominated.

"I love you, Sade. I never lied about my feelings for you. I also love Sky. I want to spend time with her. She'll turn one in two weeks, and I'd like to spend her birthday with her. Will you allow me to visit Sky on her special day?"

"Despite your lies and broken promises, I've never denied you access to Sky. She's as much your daughter as she's mine. But understand, Robert, I won't permit you to hurt her the way I've allowed myself to be hurt by you. For god's sake, she's never seen you during daylight hours. What kind of relationship do you hope to build with her, if you keep Sky relegated to the darkest corner of your life? She's not like our affair, with the lies and sneaking around. Sky's a person with feelings. She deserves a father who doesn't view her as a political and social liability. She's *not* a mistake."

"I've never said she was."

"You have. Every time you deny paternity rumors. Every time you come here at night, wearing dark suits, sunglasses, and a baseball cap. Every time Sky calls you Da-da, and you flush red. She's too young to understand this crazy, racist world we've brought her into. But she won't always be."

Sade would never tell Robert, or anyone, her fear of Sky one day looking at her with judgment, perhaps even disgust, for her affair with Robert. Worse, how would Sky view herself when she learned the truth of her parentage? Sade had years before she would have to face that tough conversation or deal with Sky's reaction, but not as many years as she wished. Never wasn't an option.

Sade Page didn't regret having Sky. Her baby wasn't a mistake. Having an affair with Robert was. But one was the price for the other.

Robert's large hands took hold of hers, bringing them to his lips and kissing. "I'll figure something out. I want us to be together as a family. I want Sky to know me, and I want to get to know her. I'll be here on her birthday. It's Christmas, after all. There's no other place I'd rather be than here with the two of you."

"Don't make promises you can't keep."

He kissed her hands again. "I'll be here. Trust me. I'll be right there beside you on the loveseat, watching our daughter celebrate her first birthday and Christmas."

Sade wanted to trust Robert. When he smiled at her, handsome with his sexy, boyish grin, she could almost believe him.

Almost.

From where Sky sat on her bed, she glanced over at Malcolm, who lounged beside her. "You're quiet tonight."

"We're watching a movie, and you dislike when I talk during one of your nasty horror flicks." Malcolm shoved a handful of buttered popcorn into his mouth. "What? Why are you looking at me like that?"

Malcolm had arrived an hour ago, carrying plastic bags, one with two bags of popcorn and a bottle of sparkling apple cider and the other with milk and eggs from the grocery store down the street from Sky's apartment. He'd eaten an entire bag of popcorn himself, while Sky drank the cider.

When Malcolm had arrived, he'd removed his coat and shoes, and then had given Sky a short peck to the lips. She'd taken the grocery bags from him, put the milk and eggs in the frig, grabbed two glasses with ice, a large bowl for the popcorn, and led the way into her bedroom.

While she'd opened the cider and poured them a glass, Malcolm finished undressing. She'd cleared a drawer for his use, as well as space in her closet and bathroom for the personal items he left at her apartment.

Besides her mother and grandmother, she'd only lived with someone else once during freshman and sophomore years of college. Junior and senior years, she'd rented an apartment not far from Harvard's main campus. So, Sky didn't have much experience sharing living space with anyone, least of all a man.

They sat propped against the headboard of her bed, pillows behind their backs and ceiling light off. Sky paused the movie just as the killer's arm appeared from the shadows, the sharp blade in his hand poised to claim another victim.

"You always talk during our movie date nights. You're more considerate in public, whispering comments and questions so you won't disturb others, but when you're here, or I'm at your place, you don't hold back. Tonight, you're quiet. Did something happen at work?"

"No. Work was good. Students in my Introduction to Race and Ethnicity in the United States class presented their oral reports. They did an amazing job for their first group assignment."

"Dammit, I got so busy today I forgot to drop by. That's your Monday, Wednesday, Friday class. Did all groups present today?"

"No, there are still two groups who'll present on Monday. If you have time, I'm sure the students would love to have the Director of Diversity and Inclusion observe their presentation. If you can't fit us into your Monday schedule, no big deal. I've had a student record the presentations, which I'll post to the class's Blackboard site. You can watch the presentations whenever you have time. My African American Resistance Seminar class has individual presentations during the first week of October if that's a better fit for your schedule."

From his tone, Malcolm wasn't upset about Sky missing his students' presentations, not that she thought he would be. Being a teaching department chair, his schedule was more fixed than Sky's. She, on the other hand, spent too much time in meetings that ran over. Too many academicians liked the sound of their own voice. But those same educators often had too little to say when asked to show impact data.

Malcolm grabbed more popcorn, eating the salty food as if he were starving.

"So not work. Are Angie and Sean's children okay?"

He nodded, crunching and dropping popcorn bits onto his dark-gray T-shirt.

"What about Sean and Angie? How are things between them?"

"Sean fired another one of Angie's in-house aides. She wasn't happy about it. She doesn't like depending on Sean to get her up and down the stairs and into and out of her wheelchair."

"You do know that's not the reason why Angie keeps hiring an aide, don't you?"

"What are you talking about?" Malcolm lifted the bowl of popcorn to Sky. "Do you want some? It's almost gone."

"No, you can have the rest." Not that there was much left. "It's not as simple as carrying Angie up and down the stairs. She needs help with everything she used to take for granted. Getting dressed. Washing her body. Every intimate part of her life is now filled by her husband. It makes Angie vulnerable in a way she's not ready to be with Sean again."

The hand reaching for more popcorn stilled, then Malcolm swore. "How in the hell did I miss that? I know for a fact Sean isn't thinking that way. He only wants to prove his worth to Angie and doesn't know the best way to do it. Do you think I should talk to him? Or maybe you could speak with Angie?"

"I think we should stay out of it, unless they ask us to get involved, which I can't see them doing. What do we know about married life? For the last ten minutes, I've been trying to get you to tell me what's bothering you. I run away when I get upset. Apparently, when you're upset, you turn into a junk food junkie searching for a date with high blood pressure."

"I'm not upset," Malcolm answered quickly and defensively, two signs Sky's assessment was correct. "I just have a couple of things on my mind." He glanced down at his crumb-covered shirt and grimaced. "That's not sexy. Forget you saw me inhale almost two bags of popcorn. That's not the image I want you to have of me."

"I'm sure you didn't become a junk food junkie tonight. The longer we spend time together, the more we'll see the less flattering sides of each other."

"Are you ready for that?"

"I think it's you who's not ready. I don't expect perfection from anyone, least of all from myself. I know the parts of me that are jagged shards and dull blades. If nothing else, I'm painfully honest with myself. So much of my life was an ugly lie and one painful truth."

Sky had shared her family's secrets with Malcolm, a painful but necessary process of honesty and faith, if they were to move forward and grow in their relationship.

"You think I'm lying to you?"

"No, I think you're lying to yourself. About what, I can only guess. If it's about me, then tell me. If it's not about me and you want an ear, then you have mine. If you want to keep it inside and bury it under popcorn that's also your choice. Just don't pretend everything is fine when it clearly isn't."

He nodded, short and nearly imperceptible. "Okay then. Why don't you keep any of your things at my house? You're there as much as you're here."

When Malcolm hadn't mentioned moving in with him again, Sky had assumed his silence was the calm before his oversensitive storm. The walking heart that was her boyfriend lasted longer than she thought he would, today's gorge fest and sulking six weeks in the making.

Sky removed the bowl of popcorn from Malcolm's greedy hands, placed it on the nightstand next to her, and then straddled Malcolm's hips.

"What are you doing?"

"Making sure I have your full attention."

"You always do."

Tonight, she hadn't, but that was fine. Sky kissed Malcolm, the way she should've when he'd arrived. Long, deep, and with her tongue in his mouth and her hands on his head.

Tempted to remove his locs from the updo style he wore it in, Sky tamped down her desire to see his long hair out of its confines and onto the muscular chest that was hidden by his T-shirt. Then there was Malcolm's diamond stud earring. If Sky sucked on the lobe of Malcolm's ear, she would want to put something else of his into her mouth. That would come later. Right now, she needed her tongue for talking.

"We're going to do this right, Malcolm."

Sky's eyes closed on a moan of pleasure. Malcolm's right hand had skated under her satin nightgown, sought out a breast and teased her nipple while his left hand massaged the nape of her neck.

"We always do it right."

"Not that. I mean us. Our present and future. I want to do it right."

The hand on her breast lowered to her hip. "What do you mean?"

She opened her eyes. "I'm not running anymore, but you're racing, headlong, into the biggest commitment of our lives. I don't need a test run."

"That's not what living together is."

"I disagree. It's a test run for marriage. I don't need or want that. When or if we decide to marry, I want to do it right. I'm not old-fashioned, but I don't want to live with a man who's not my husband."

"But you'll have sex with one."

"Obviously," she said, with a smile, instead of getting mad and climbing off him. "Believe it or not, in some respects, living with a man is more intimate than sleeping with him."

"You're afraid of having that level of intimacy with me?"

"No. You aren't listening. I want to know the joy of anticipating moving in together as husband and wife. I don't care if we live in your house or if we decide to buy a home we choose together." She lifted her hands, palm-up, and shrugged. "Maybe I am old-fashioned. My mother never married. So, I not only never had my biological father as a constant in my life, but I also didn't have a stepfather. I think, after what happened between Mom and Robert, she didn't want to expose me to another man who could possibly disappoint me."

As an adult, Sky could see a secondary reason for Sade's seeming lack of interest in marriage. It was for Sky's sake, but also for her own. Sade had trust issues that began with her own father and continued through her relationship with Robert. Beautiful and intelligent, Sade never wanted for male attention. She'd dated, but Sade hadn't trusted any of her companions enough to carve out a place for them in her life and heart.

"My gut tells me moving in together would be a mistake."

"We've already blurred that line."

"We have, but blurring it and outright eliminating the line aren't the same. You know I love you. You also know I love spending time with you. I have no plans on leaving Eastern Bluebird College, Buffalo, or you."

"This really is my issue, isn't it?"

"No, it's both of ours." She kissed him again, a quick, teasing peck that ended with, "But, yes, more your issue than mine. You're impatient, pushy, and soft-hearted. You want everything your way, and at your pace. Which is fast and faster. Slow down, sweetie, there's no rush."

There were layers to her Malcolm, which Sky was only beginning to fully unearth. He'd once told her she hid behind professionalism and silence. For Malcolm, his shield of choice was his easy-going personality, laughter, and gregarious nature. But a shield was a shield, no matter the form.

Fortunately for Malcolm and their relationship, Sky would never begrudge him his growth areas. But she would support and challenge him to be better, the same way he would for her. Thinking of them and their future had Sky concluding now was the perfect time to mention her idea. "Your birthday is next month. Unless you have other plans, I'd like to take you away for the weekend."

"You're going to plan a birthday weekend getaway?"

"Don't sound so surprised. Or was that horror I detected in your voice?" Her eyes narrowed. "Wait, you think I'm incapable of planning and executing a romantic birthday getaway."

"Have you ever done anything like that before?"

"I don't appreciate your dubious tone."

"I'm just saying. We both know romance isn't your forte. You should leave it to the experts."

"By expert, you mean you?"

"Of course, I mean me. But I'll appreciate anything you do for me, you know that."

"Oh, how magnanimous of you, Dr. Styles. What would I ever do without your appreciation for my meager, unromantic efforts?"

Malcolm ignored her sarcasm and asked her, "Where are you taking me?"

"Tupelo, Mississippi."

He smacked her bottom instead of calling her a smartass.

"It's a surprise. You'll need to take Thursday and Friday off. I've already put in for leave."

"You're serious. You've actually planned something special for my birthday."

"That's what we've been talking about for the last few minutes. I know your brain may be a little dehydrated from your high salt intake but try to keep up. We're going away for a long weekend for your birthday. You don't have class on Thursdays, so you'll only need coverage for your Friday morning class. I'll have you back in time for class on Monday. Unless you'd rather stay here with your family. I don't want to impose if that's what you normally do for your birthday."

"No, no, well, yeah, it is what I normally do. But…"

"But what?" Sky pulled off Malcolm's T-shirt and tossed it over her shoulder. The man really did have one fine body. His shoulders alone made her mouth water. "But what?" she whispered against his ear, her mouth taking hold of the earlobe with the diamond stud and sucking. "You taste good. You'd taste even better in my shower and wet."

Sky jumped from the bed. On her way to the bathroom, she turned off the television and slipped out of her nightgown and panties.

Naked and standing in the open door of her bathroom, she turned to face Malcolm. One step backward had her in the bathroom. Two licks of her lips had Malcolm out of bed and crossing the bedroom in quick, long strides.

He reached her just as Sky turned on the spray of water. She had no idea when he'd shed his underwear, not that she cared. Malcolm's hard, lean body felt too good for Sky to waste time contemplating inconsequential details.

Sky stepped into the shower, a frameless glass design that gave the space an open, airy feel. Malcolm followed her in, taking time to grab a condom from the medicine cabinet first and slipping it on.

Snaking an arm around her waist, Malcolm pulled Sky flush against him. "How do you know my birthday is next month?"

"I have my ways."

"Angie or Mom told you."

"Pretty much."

"Which one?"

"Both. Your father too. And your Aunt Debbie and Uncle Curtis."

He shifted them until they were under the water, the spray set to massage. The water was hot and stimulating but not as luxurious as Malcolm's body rubbing against hers.

They kissed, lips giving and receiving.

Hands touched, stroking and squeezing.

Water cascaded over their heated bodies, saturating skin and increasing the sensual pleasure of the shared shower.

Sky loved Malcolm's kisses. Adored the time he took, the skill of his tongue, and the way he held her close to him. When they kissed, Sky tasted Malcolm's heart, so much did he give of himself when their lips met. Desire and love seeped from Malcolm and into Sky, inviting her to return what he happily gave.

She did, no entreaty required.

His hand drifted from her waist, over her ass, and toward her sex. One finger, then two slipped inside Sky -- long, slow strokes meant to arouse and prepare her for his entry.

No additional prep work was needed, though.

"I'm ready."

"I can tell. You're so responsive."

"For you. God, Malcolm, I've never been like this with anyone else. You're addictive."

His fingers worked her, and Sky slumped against the seashell mosaic wall tiles, riding his thick digits. Sex was so good between them. Sky couldn't imagine it being better. Yet, every time they made love, she fell that much deeper in love with Malcolm Styles, which made the sex between them better still.

The thought of moving in with Malcolm was frightening yet tempting. But not so tempting she would risk their future by moving too quickly with their present. Sade had taught Sky how to take care of what mattered most in her life. For Sade that was Sky. For Sky, it was Malcolm.

She raised her leg to his hip, and Malcolm joined them. Yes, sooo good. Eyes slipped closed as Malcolm lifted her off her feet and pressed Sky against the warm, wet tiles.

Blindly, she searched for his mouth, finding chin and cheek before Malcolm's seeking lips found hers. She held on tight, ankles locked at his back, arms around his shoulders, breasts crushed against his chest, slick and throbbing.

"So close," he groaned, "but you haven't come yet."

"That's fine, I'm—"

Swifter than she thought possible in a wet shower, Malcolm set her on her feet, turned off the water, and dropped to his knees. Then his mouth was on Sky, kissing her and opening her for his tongue.

She cried out when his tongue found her clit. Malcolm lifted one of Sky's legs onto his shoulder, the angle opening her more to him. In went two fingers, fucking her while he sucked on her clit.

Sky swore, loud and with shuddering breaths.

He lapped at her release, silky-smooth tongue and wicked fingers bringing her a second and then a third time.

Weak-kneed, Sky slumped in Malcolm's embrace when he turned her to face the tile wall. He was inside of her again, even harder than before and thrusting his way to his own loud completion, his grunts primal and self-satisfied.

Sky might not have the most romantic birthday getaway planned, but she'd built in plenty of time for toe-curling, hair-pulling, and voice-losing sex.

CHAPTER TWELVE

"In their work, *From Slavery to Freedom: A History of African Americans*, historians John Hope Franklin and Evelyn Higginbotham discuss the emergence as well as the social, political and cultural impact of the Black Power Movement in America. The authors trace the latent origins of Black Power to the militancy and black nationalist sensibilities of nineteenth-century freedom fighters, such as Henry McNeal Turner and the alleged father of black nationalism in America, Martin R. Delaney."

Jerome Exum, a junior, advanced to the next slide in his PowerPoint presentation. A familiar black-and-white picture of Martin Robinson Delaney, in his Union Army uniform, replaced the image of a raised Black Power fist every student had used in their presentation. Jerome, however, had taken his Black Power oral report a step further than the other students by wearing a black, leather jacket, a black beret cocked to the side, a pair of black jeans, and a red-and-black T-shirt that read: The Revolution Will Not Be Televised.

"Interestingly, the authors not only trace the trajectory of this ideology to the early twentieth century Pan Africanist Marcus Mosiah Garvey but to his ideological adversary, A. Philip Randolph and his purported March on Washington in 1941."

An animated three-grid display slid in front of the image of Delaney. A picture of Garvey's round, full face filled the left grid, while the slim figure of Randolph occupied the third grid. In the center were the words: Pan-Afrikanist vs. Socialist.

Malcolm forced himself to pay attention to his student's oral report. On any other day, focusing wouldn't have been an issue, despite having sat through a dozen of these reports, all a variation on the unit's theme of Black Power.

At this point in the semester, his African American Resistance Seminar students were used to Malcolm's preferred style of assessment—individual, pair, and group oral reports. He differentiated instruction, as much as he could, making sure to combine lecture with student-led discussions and Socratic Seminars. He assigned the occasional paper and gave an obligatory midterm and final exam.

Part of EBC's mission was to prepare students for life, not just for a job. To that end, Malcolm believed students should be given the opportunity to cultivate many skills, two being public speaking and critical thinking.

Sky shifted beside him, the scent from her sweet cinnamon body butter driving him crazy. Why in the hell had he purchased the lotion for her? Worse, why did she pick today to wear it for the first time?

"The basis for Randolph's inclusion in the nascent lineage of Black Power ideologues was his desire that the March on Washington be solely composed of black men, thus excluding white participation."

They stood in the back of the lecture hall, Malcolm's preferred spot when his students presented. When he sat closer to the front and in easy view of his students, they tended to speak to him instead of to their peers.

"I'm glad I could make it today," Sky whispered. "I can't stay for the entire class, though."

A waist-high wall separated the last row of seats in the lecture hall from the landing, behind which Malcolm and Sky watched Jerome progress through his report and PowerPoint slides.

"Is that the theme song to *Shaft*?"

It damn sure was. Malcolm made a notation on the Word document on his phone where the criteria for success for this presentation was located. Jerome knew better. The young man enjoyed playing to the crowd and females in the class too much for Malcolm to view the error as a lack of content knowledge and comprehension.

Sky leaned forward, her elbows going to the wall and resting. Without thinking, Malcolm's eyes slipped to Sky's ass, which now poked out enticingly. She wore a Greystone flyaway jacket, lace-up skirt, and black high heeled shoes-- a classy business suit she spiced up with a splash of color. Today it was a bright-pink, asymmetrical ruffled V-neck blouse and pear-shaped, pink sapphire drop earrings.

Like the body butter, the earrings were a gift from Malcolm. Considerably more expensive than the lotion, Malcolm couldn't resist buying the earrings for Sky. He'd gone into the jewelry store looking for a birthday gift for his mother. They shared the month, with Kimberly's birthday at the beginning and his at the end. Sean and Angie's oldest daughter Kayla's birthday was between her uncle and grandmother, on October twelfth.

Malcolm had made a beeline for a case of rings. Jewelry Kimberly Styles could wear to church was always a winning gift for his mother. Last year, it was a rose gold, angel cross pendant. This year, Malcolm had purchased and personalized a white gold, devotion cross, birthstone ring. For the soon-to-be eleven-year-old Kayla, Malcolm bought a pink, leather bracelet with six charms. Angie would tell him he'd spent too much for a girl Kayla's age, but it was in his job description as Uncle Malcolm to spoil his nieces and nephew. When he and Sky married and had children, cross fingers, Angie could spoil his kids all she liked.

After his two purchases, Malcolm had shifted to a case of engagement rings. The same saleswoman who'd helped him before, plastered on an even larger smile when she saw Malcolm eyeing diamond engagement rings.

Nothing in the first case screamed Sky, so Malcolm had moved on to the next one, and then the next. By the third case, credit card fisted in his hand, Malcolm had taken a deep breath and made a phone call.

"I'm halfway out the door," Sean had said, sounding hurried and pissed. "Make it quick."

"Could you sound more like an asshole?"

"Probably. Angie hired another damn in-house aide, which means I don't have a convenient excuse to stay home and not go in to the office. This one's a guy. A big ass linebacker-looking MOFO with no damn neck."

"Which means Angie took away your only real argument against her hiring an aide to take care of her instead of using you."

"Yeah, a slick lawyer's move I didn't see coming. What's up, man? I don't have long to talk."

"I'm in the jewelry store at the mall."

"Which one?"

"The expensive one. I have a saleswoman breathing down my neck for her next commission, and I'm torn between a Princess-cut and a Round-cut diamond. Then there's white gold, yellow gold, two-tone gold, and rose gold. I really like the rose gold," Malcolm had told Sean. "Sky has long, thin pianist fingers and—"

"Breathe and shut up for a minute. Damn, you need to get the hell out of there."

"I can't leave. I tried. I haven't gotten more than two steps away from the cases before being pulled back."

"Okay, okay, relax. Have you asked to see any of the engagement rings?"

"No. But I *really* want to. Did you snag one of Angie's rings to get her size when you bought her engagement ring or did you—"

"Stop talking and focus on my voice. Don't agree to see any of the rings, no matter how many times the saleswoman asks. I'm telling you, Malcolm, if you buy a ring and propose, Sky will say no. It's still too soon."

"What if I buy it and hold on to the ring until the time is right? That way, I'm prepared."

"You're fooling yourself if you think you're capable of anything close to that. We both know the minute you see Sky you'll be down on one knee and pouring out your pathetic heart. You'll shove an expensive ring in her face and pray she'll accept your sappy ass as her husband."

"You're right. What should I do?"

"Get the hell out of there."

"I can't, not without buying Sky something."

"Fine, then buy her a just-because trinket. Not a ring and nothing expensive. A bracelet or a pair of earrings. A gift that says I'm whipped, so please give me back my dick."

"You're an asshole."

"We already established that. Bracelet or earrings, then get the hell out of there and don't look back. I mean it. The next time, I may not be able to talk you off the ledge."

"Bracelet or earrings and nothing too expensive. Got it. Thanks."

The saleswoman hadn't hidden her disappointment well when Malcolm had walked away from the engagement rings. But she'd rallied after he'd strolled back to the case of sapphires, his eyes going to a row of pink sapphire earrings.

"Nevertheless, it was Stokely Carmichael, later renamed Kwame Toure, who coined the term "Black Power" in 1966…"

Damn, he'd missed a good chunk of Jerome's presentation. Malcolm erased the minus five points for Jerome's *Shaft* reference, typed in a perfect score at the bottom of the document and, making sure all students were facing the speaker, slipped behind Sky.

With all eyes on Jerome and the wall hiding half of their bodies, no one saw when Malcolm pressed himself against Sky's very nice ass.

She stiffened at the contact but didn't move away or whisper a reprimand. Compared to Sky initiating a blowjob in his office, three months ago, Malcolm's slow grind amounted to a peck on the lips.

Well, not exactly. If a student turned around and saw them, it wouldn't take much to figure out what was happening behind the wall.

But Malcolm's students were being good little active listeners. More than halfway through his assigned chapter, Jerome's presentation would soon end, which meant Malcolm had to work fast.

He couldn't afford to get a hard-on, so he eased his hips away from Sky. At her soft moan of protest, he ran his hand under her skirt and up to her panties, where he slipped inside.

The contact had her moaning again, softer than before. She rocked into his hand. They were dead wrong for doing this there and then. Which didn't stop them from doing it anyway. Malcolm's hand covered Sky's mound and he rubbed his heel over her lips and clit.

"Black Power also culminated in the emergence of the Black Panther Party for Self Defense in Oakland, California. This bold..."

Malcolm rubbed faster, pressed harder, and Sky's fingernails dug into the side of his right leg.

"Unlike some black nationalist organizations considered cultural nationalists by some, who emphasized a purely racial analysis, the Panthers emphasized a racial and class analysis to black oppression..."

Wetness coated fingers that were welcomed by Sky's clenching sex.

Sky's breath hitched then squeaked, and Malcolm drove his fingers deeper, her arousal headier than the body butter she wore.

"Many of the student activists of Black Power also promulgated the aesthetic symbols of Black Power as many donned afros and African clothing, which to many symbolized blackness..."

Sky hunched in on herself, her head lowered to her chest, her release quiet and her panties soaked.

Malcolm's fingers were gloriously sticky.

"Many black students desired the infusion of black cultural curriculum into the European educational framework. This development spawned Africana and Black Studies and facilitated the hiring of African American professors to teach such subject matter ..."

Since Sky and Angie had become friends, she'd visited the older woman's home several times. With the types of jobs Angie and Sean had and three growing children, the couple had need of and could afford a spacious home. Tonight, however, every bit of space was taken up by a Styles either through birth or marriage. Sky had met a few of Malcolm's relatives, but far from all of them. Thank goodness they weren't all there or Sky might have opted to stay home tonight. As it was, fifteen minutes earlier Malcolm had run off with his nephew, leaving Sky but promising to send someone to help her traverse the landscape that was his plentiful and boisterous family.

Sean Junior, as tall as Sky's five-eight height and a smaller version of his father, had grinned at her with a mischievous twinkle in his eyes, when he'd retrieved Malcolm. She'd had no clue what the look meant, but Malcolm had worn a matching grin. Sky had once heard Angie tell Malcolm he was "too handsome for his own good." Sky agreed, but the same could be said of SJ and every other Styles male she'd met. How could one family have so many good-looking men? All of whom, unsurprisingly, was married to equally attractive women.

Music pumped and pulsed through the house, an odd mix of kid-friendly tunes, classic Motown grooves, and smooth R&B. People talked, danced, and laughed. No one drank anything stronger than fruit punch spiked with Ginger ale. This wasn't that kind of party. The Styles didn't need alcohol to have fun. They possessed a natural high Sky found equal parts enjoyable and overwhelming.

She wondered if Malcolm would be offended if she stepped outside to get away from the crowd and trapped heat. The thought of October's cool night air on her face and a few minutes of much-needed quiet had Sky stepping backward and up against a big body.

"Excuse me, I—"

"Trying to run away?"

Sky recognized the baritone voice, with its undertone of humor. "No."

"I think you are. You look like a mouse caught when a light is turned on."

"You can't see my face."

"I don't have to. I know the feeling. I was you once." Sean grabbed Sky's hand. "Come here, Minnie Mouse. I have the perfect spot. Malcolm asked me to reserve it for you, which is damn hard to do with a bunch of mouthy Styles ripping through my house as if they pay my mortgage."

Sky allowed herself to be led through the crowded living room. With Sean's six-three frame in front of her, everyone the tall man encountered moved out of his way. When he stopped, they were on the other side of the room.

"Good, Sean found you." Angie, Sean's physical opposite, used the cane beside her to stand. She hugged Sky, who had to bend down to embrace the shorter woman. "I'm glad you came. You're either brave or love my brother more than he deserves. The Styles love an excuse to party, and the end-of-year holidays, combined with birthdays, are all the reason we need to get together."

"Wait until Thanksgiving, Sky," Sean said. "Don't get between a Styles and Thanksgiving football. It can get downright murderous. Charles is the worst, though. The biggest Buffalo Bills fan you'll find."

"Thanks for the warning," she laughed.

"Don't listen to him. We aren't that bad."

Sean mocked whispered. "I won't call my wife a fibber in front of our child." Sean pointed to his left. "By the way, the chair over there is for you. Prime real estate for the festivities. I could've been Oprah rich if I'd sold that chair to the highest Styles bidder. But Malcolm would've pitched a fit if I didn't turn that chair into your throne for the evening."

The chair, with ottoman, Sean had pointed to was placed in an alcove of the living room. All the furniture in the room had been shifted to accommodate the mass of people. The sofa, where Angie and her youngest daughter, Zuri, sat, was pushed close to the alcove. The loveseat and second sofa were moved closer to the walls. Folding chairs were propped against a wall, although few people used them, milling about instead of planting themselves in one spot.

"How are you feeling?" Sean asked Angie.

Sky's gaze fell to Angie's cane. She knew the doctor had removed Angie's casts, but this was the first time she'd seen her without them since the car crash.

"Don't spend the evening worrying about me."

Sean looked as if he would argue, but he only smiled down at his wife before telling their daughter, "Take care of Mommy for me."

"I will, Daddy."

"Good, that's my big girl."

Zuri beamed at her father, her eyes big, brown pools of happy sweetness. Every inch of her adorable face glowed when she smiled. Hair in spiraled box braids in the front, simple cornrows in the back and twisted up in a ballerina bun, Zuri was walking cuteness.

"SJ is helping Malcolm and Charles get ready. I need to rejoin them, but I want to make sure you're fine first. I know you brought your pain medicine downstairs. If your legs hurt, take a pill before it gets too bad."

"Here, Mommy." Zuri handed Angie a white studio pouch from beside her on the sofa, which, Sky assumed, contained Angie's painkillers.

"Thank you, sweetie." Holding firmly to her cane, Angie retook her seat. "I'm seated and have my medicine. You put Zuri in charge, so you know I'm in good hands. Sky is also here if I need anything."

"You're basically telling me to go away."

"I am."

"You're a force of nature Angela Styles. It's what I love about you. I get all four seasons in one indomitable woman. You're winter now. But after winter is spring."

"You're waiting for me to thaw, huh?"

"I would've used the word melt. Summer is my favorite Angie season."

Sky couldn't tell if they were flirting with each other or politely arguing. Maybe a little of both.

Sean winked at Angie. "Abloom, ablaze, active, blazing, blistering."

"Stop, do not go through an entire alphabet of words related to summer."

Undeterred, Sean continued. "Burning, cheerful, clear."

"Stop at the C's, Sean. I'm serious."

"Clammy, clear, cloudless."

Sky couldn't help it, she laughed.

"Don't encourage him."

"Your husband doesn't need encouragement."

"See, Sky finds me funny."

"She's dating my brother. Of course, Sky has a sense of humor. Go away, Sean, and take your summer list with you."

"Fine. I'm leaving, Mrs. Winter. I'll wait for the thaw. Sky, make sure you vote for me. My wife never does. She's partial to her brother. But I trust you know true talent when you see it." Sean leaned down and kissed Zuri on the cheek. "You always vote for me. You're the best."

Zuri wrapped her arms around her father's neck and held on with the full weight of her small body, which had Sean kissing and tickling his daughter until she laughed and let him go.

He shifted his attention to Angie and whispered something in her ear that had the woman dropping her eyes and not coming back with a quick-witted quip. She wondered what Sean had said, but, of course, would never ask.

Sky was about to retreat to the chair in the alcove, but Angie reached for her hand.

"Don't sit all the way over there. Share the sofa with Zuri and me. Mom can sit there."

"All the way over there? The chair is three feet from the sofa."

"That's not the point. I'll have to raise my voice for us to talk if you sit over there."

"You're raising your voice now. The music is loud."

"Oh my god, I see what Malcolm means. I honestly can't tell if you're joking or serious."

"I'm kidding. I assume you don't want to sit next to your mother because she'll use it as an opportunity to ask you questions you don't want to answer."

Angie looked at Zuri, who played with two female superhero action figures, then back to Sky. "Your statement was wonderfully vague. Did you get that trick from your mother?"

"Yes. She and my grandmother had indecipherable conversations when I was a young girl. Nana used to say, 'Little ears,' before they launched into spy speak."

Sky sat, sitting on the opposite side of Zuri, who, to her surprise, crawled into her lap. Ah, what was she supposed to do with her? Sky might have years of experience handling college-age students, but she couldn't recall the last time she'd touched, much less held a child.

"She's not a bomb who's going to explode in your lap. Relax. Zuri won't detonate or break. Will you, baby?"

Zuri shook her head.

"Does she know what detonate means?"

Angie's smile was as polite as ever, still managing to y scream that Sky was clueless about children. "She's five, and you probably spent too much time with adults when you were growing up."

Angie had tossed out the statement with such certainty, Sky wanted to contradict her. Not because Angie was incorrect, but because she was just as maddeningly perceptive as Malcolm.

"That's kind of rude to say."

"True, but I'm probably right." Angie looked out at the assembled crowd, enjoying themselves in her home. "Is this too much for you? Do you need a break?"

"I'm fine."

"Of course, you are. Just as my legs are fine and I don't need to take my pain relievers."

"Take your pill, Mommy. You want water?"

"Yes, please. Go into the kitchen and ask someone to give you a bottle of water."

Zuri slid from Sky's lap and darted through the crowd with the speed and exuberance that came with youth and perfect health.

"She's adorable."

Sky smiled after the little girl. She could pass as Malcolm's daughter, so much did she favor her uncle and mother. Sky couldn't help but wonder who their children would resemble if she and Malcolm were fortunate enough to have them. She wouldn't mind having a child as even-tempered and huggable as Zuri. She'd never given much thought to motherhood before but—

"Malcolm was right. So was Sean, damn him. A pixie-cherub mix, of all things."

"A pixie what?" She returned her attention to Angie.

"Nothing." Angie waved a hand in front of her, as if she could wipe away Sky's question and confusion. "Thanks for coming. It means a lot to Malcolm. Since Mom's, Kayla's, and Malcolm's birthdays are all in October, whenever possible, we celebrate them on the same day. We're doing it a little earlier this year because Malcolm won't be in town on his birthday."

"I apologize if I messed up your family tradition. That wasn't my intention."

"No, it's fine. If that came off as bitchy or sounded like a complaint or judgment, that's not how I meant it. The day we celebrate is inconsequential. With a family as big as ours, there isn't a month that goes by without at least one birthday. Before Uncle Lester died, we had two Styles men with Halloween birthdays. Malcolm loves that his birthday falls on that day. It gives him a reason to show his ass, which he loves to do."

An image of said fine ass popped into Sky's mind, and she smiled. "He hates when I send him holiday emojis on the wrong day."

"I bet you do it intentionally."

"Not at first, but I do now."

"When's your birthday?"

Zuri came barreling through the crowd, her face triumphant. She handed her mother an eight-ounce bottle of water.

"Thank you."

"You're welcome, Mommy." Zuri stood in front of Sky's knees. "May I sit on your lap, Aunt Sky?"

She gaped at the little girl, having no idea what to do or to say.

"Out of the mouths of babes," Angie said. "I promise, no one put her up to that, least of all Malcolm. She's just never seen her uncle with a woman before. So, you know, kid assumptions. She's five."

"You keep saying that."

Sky helped Zuri onto her lap, unsure how she felt about the title of aunt. She wasn't upset, exactly. Being in Malcolm's sister's home and surrounded by his family, she couldn't help but feel the uncomfortable weight of marital expectation.

Zuri reclined her back against Sky's chest, quiet as she played with her superheroine action figures.

"It's way past her bedtime. She's struggling to stay awake. Aren't you, sweetie?"

"Daddy's going to sing and dance for Kayla."

"He is, and you don't want to miss it. Do you?"

"Nope."

"Sing and dance?" Sky asked, having no idea what Angie and Zuri were talking about.

"Malcolm didn't tell you?"

"No."

"He must've wanted it to be a surprise. I won't ruin his fun by spoiling it. You're in for a Styles family treat, Sky."

"I think that should worry me."

Angie laughed, white, pretty teeth and flawless skin. "No, you're safe. If you do become Aunt Sky, though, not so much."

Sky let that go. She'd once told Malcolm he wanted too much too soon. Every Styles she'd met of Malcolm's generation were married and had at least one child. The pattern was clear. Styles married in their twenties, became parents, and then stayed married through sickness and in health. And, according to Sean, stayed married through all four seasons, the sunshine and warmth of spring to the frost and chill of winter.

"When's your birthday, Sky?"

"I don't want to tell you."

"Umm, that's an odd answer. Why not?"

"Because you'll tell your brother, and he'll become a pain in my backside."

"Oh, wait, it must be in February. Valentine's Day or close to it. He would love that."

"Not February. I'm not an Aquarius."

"No, that would be me."

Sky couldn't help it, she laughed, disturbing the nodding-off Zuri. "Malcolm's Halloween and you're Valentine's Day. That's the cutest and oddest sibling... I don't know what you'd call that. But it's charming. I wonder if there's an emoji for that."

"You said all of that to avoid telling me your birthday, which means it's worse than Halloween and Valentine's Day. There's only one holiday Malcolm adores just as much as Valentine's Day, and that's Christmas. Are you a Christmas baby, Sky Ellis?"

She sighed. "Unfortunately. Do *not* tell Malcolm."

"You're dating. My brother is going to find out. I'm surprised he hasn't already asked. Beyond the fact that Malcolm will make a big deal about it, why don't you want him to know?"

"When did Sean propose to you?"

"Valentine's Day. I get your point."

"The birthday-holiday combo will be too much sappy for Malcolm to resist."

"Would it be so bad if he proposes? When you envision your future, do you not see Malcolm sharing it with you?"

"I see him sharing everything with me. But we haven't had a fight yet."

Angie's perfectly arched eyebrows lifted. "You want to fight with my brother?"

"No. What I want is for Malcolm to be his full self around me. When he is, we'll fight because disagreeing, even loudly, is part of loving and living. I don't want him to be careful around me, more concerned about showing me this perfect, romantic Malcolm Styles than being himself."

"One day, you'll wish for days when you and he didn't argue. You're romanticizing it."

"I'm not. Trust me, I've had my share of family disagreements. They aren't fun and are as painful as passing a kidney stone." Zuri shifted on her lap, turning to the side and resting her head on Sky's shoulder. "Fighting with me isn't the point I'm making. That's just an example of my larger point."

"Which is?"

"When we began dating, Malcolm accused me of hiding parts of myself behind walls. He was right. But he has his own walls."

"Have you talked to him?"

"I tried. Malcolm is stubborn, which I already knew."

"You don't seem concerned."

Sky was about to shrug before remembering she held a sleeping Zuri to her chest and shoulder. "I'm not concerned. Malcolm will figure it out. It may take a while, but he'll work it out on his own."

"I was wrong. I thought you were the one who's not ready for marriage, but it's still Malcolm."

"What do you mean by 'still'?"

"Never mind. Forget I said that."

Angie waved that away too. Between her pixie statement and the last one, Sky felt as if she was getting snippets of a conversation the older woman had had about Sky but didn't want to tell her about. She could push for an explanation, but she would rather learn what she needed to know about Malcolm from the man himself.

Kimberly Styles, lovely in a navy-blue embroidered swing dress with scoop neck and half sleeves, gray-and-black hair in a classic layered bob cut, appeared, as if in a puff of magic, before Sky and Angie.

"How does that feel?"

Sky hadn't seen the woman in the hour since she'd arrived at the party, and the first words she'd spoken to her made no sense.

"Don't start, Mom."

"I just asked the girl a question. Zuri may be kind-hearted, but she's smart enough not to take to everyone. But look at my sweet grandbaby, asleep on Sky as peaceful as she wants to be. So, how does it feel?"

Sky had no idea how to answer Malcolm's mother, so she said the only thing that came to mind. "She's five."

Angie laughed, and Kim shook her head.

"Yes, Zuri's my third grandchild, I know her age. I think, with more practice, holding a child will grow on you. You're doing all right now, but I can see the telltale signs of a woman not yet comfortable with little children or the prospect of becoming a mother."

"Mom, give Sky a break." Angie pointed to the chair in the alcove. "It's your birthday party, have a seat. The show is about to begin."

"I love how you grow up and think to boss me around." Kim moved closer and kissed Angie's cheek. "You look good, my dear girl. I'm here if you want to talk."

"I know, Mom. Thank you."

Kim kissed Angie again, the love between mother-and-daughter beautiful and heart-aching, as was this night for Sky. It was a reminder of what she'd lost when her mother and grandmother passed away, as well as all she'd never had growing up.

Sky looked away, her eyes falling to the sleeping child in her arms. She rubbed Zuri's back, her nose going to the top of her head and inhaling shea oil, a light nutty fragrance.

"Zuri is a special kind of Styles," Kim told Sky. "We need more of her type in this family." The grandmother of three lifted Zuri's chubby hand and kissed her fingers, so gently the little girl didn't stir. "You're also special, Sky. If you weren't, Malcolm wouldn't have invited you to our little get-together. Our family can also become your family if you want us to be. I'll tell you the same as I've told Angie. I'm here when you want to talk. We Styles don't bite." She kissed Sky's forehead. "Much."

"Mom, you're terrible."

"No, I'm seventy, and ready to be serenaded by my husband. I think I'll have that seat now. By the way, don't think I didn't notice how you've strategically placed Sky next to you and me in the chair in the corner. Kayla can have the ottoman, although she'll probably squeeze her skinny behind between you and Sky. You spoil your kids."

"Said the kettle to the teapot." Angie leaned close to whisper in Sky's ear. "Mom's harmless. She's really a sweetheart. It's Dad you must watch out for. He's a shit starter."

Children of all ages filed into the living room as if a school bell had sounded and teachers had dismissed their classes.

"Um, Angie, where did all the kids come from?"

"The basement. Sean built a rec room for the kids down there. It takes up ninety percent of the basement, which leaves me a corner for laundry and a treadmill I don't use enough but a punching bag I love."

Sky had never taken a self-defense class, although it was a wise course of action for women, particularly for someone as petite as Angie. Sky may not have the fighting skills to thwart an attacker but if one wanted to do her harm, he'd have to catch her first.

"Come walking with me on Saturdays."

Those perfectly arched eyebrows of Angie's went skyward again, and she snorted at Sky. "I've seen you, and nothing you do could be considered walking. You run like a demon." Angie fingered the sturdy handle of her cane. "I can barely manage the stairs without help. I would only slow you down."

"I'll pick you up the first Saturday after Malcolm and I get back from our trip. Around ten. We can go back to my apartment building. There's an onsite fitness center we can use. Are you in physical therapy?"

"Once a week."

Sky figured as much. Physical therapists were good, but little lifted the spirits of dealing with pain and the fear of not being as you once were like working out with a friend who expected nothing from you.

"When you're with me, we can work on whatever part of your body you want. You don't have to focus on your legs if you don't want to."

"You're kind, and I'm forty-seven."

What did her age have to do with anything?

Sky followed Angie's gaze, which wasn't on her when she'd made that nonsensical statement. They were on her handsome husband, who'd entered the living room behind her father, Charles, her son, SJ, and her brother, Malcolm.

Music no longer played, and people no longer talked and danced. Everyone had shifted from the center of the room and now lined the walls. The children sat on the floor, cross-legged and chattering low and with anticipation. Folded chairs now held Styles. Those who couldn't fit into the room stood in the threshold, eyes on the four impeccably dressed males.

All of them, including Angie's son, were dressed in three-piece, black suits with orange vests, handkerchiefs, and bowties. The crowd clapped for the men, who formed a horizontal line, their heads down, each wearing a black fedora.

"Dapper," Kim said with more than a touch of pride and love in the single word.

Angie's "forty-seven" made sense to Sky now. Sean's affair had been with a woman twenty years Angie's junior. Even for a woman as attractive and as confident as Angie, the age difference would be hard to ignore. Self-doubt plagued everyone, sometimes. Youth wasn't something anyone could recapture, no matter how well they ate or how often they exercised.

Music began again, and the crowd clapped louder when Kayla, thin and pretty, entered behind the men. She wore an orange ball gown with sweetheart neckline, beaded bodice with tulle accents, and an A-line tulle skirt.

Zuri, roused awake by all the noise, shifted on Sky's lap to take everything in. As soon as she saw her father, she squealed and yelled, "Daddy, Daddy."

Sean lifted his head and blew Zuri a kiss.

Malcolm's gorgeous locs fell from under his fedora and down his back. God, he'd taken his hair down since arriving, and it looked so damn sexy with his Halloween-inspired ensemble. Now she knew what had been in the garment bag he'd brought with him. He'd refused to tell her when she'd asked.

All the men were sharp, but Sky only had eyes for Malcolm. When she looked to Angie again, she wasn't surprised to still find her gaze locked on her husband. Sean was a handsome man. But good looks weren't enough to have a woman like Angie choosing to stay with a man after an affair.

Love did that and so did children.

At one point, Robert must've had this with his wife. She'd loved him, probably as much as Angie still loved Sean. Years of marriage had bound Robert and Lois, as had their four children. Sade and Sky had come between Robert and his family. The truth of the role Sade and Sky played in the dismantling of Robert's marriage became clear as she watched Angie's emotional conflict play out in the dark-brown eyes that couldn't contain or hide her feelings for Sean.

Being there brought up too many unwanted emotions. Sky wished she could slink away. But she'd promised herself to stop running, which included emotional flights when childhood memories crashed over her in heavy waves of rejection and sadness.

The music stopped and then started again, with Kayla lip-syncing Gladys Knight's _Love Overboard_.

Kayla's brother, father, uncle, and grandfather danced in the background, doing an admirable imitation of The Pips. They were good, including fifteen-year-old SJ, who moved with a grace outmatched only by his uncle.

Sky's heart thudded. The way Malcolm moved was almost sensual. She'd seen him dance before, knew how well he worked his hips. Compared to what he could do behind closed doors, this performance was downright mild, but it was still lip-licking hot.

"Here, it looks like you need this more than I do."

Angie's cold bottle of water. Yes, Sky needed a drink because Malcolm always left her thirsty.

CHAPTER THIRTEEN

Angie's Bedroom
Earlier

"Don't think you're going to upstage me this year."

Malcolm scoffed at Sean and adjusted his bowtie. "I'm better than you. After all this time, you need to face facts."

"You're delusional. Your sister takes pity on you every year and throws you a sympathy vote. It's pathetic."

Making sure SJ wasn't watching, Malcolm flipped Sean the bird.

"Neither of you have a chance of outperforming me."

Sean and Malcolm, standing in front of the full-length mirror in the master bedroom, turned to face Charles, whose tie dangled in his hand.

"You can't even tie your bowtie, and you think you're going to beat us." Malcolm took the silk tie from his father's hand. "Arthritis acting up again?"

"A little. I could've managed, but thanks for the help. You need me to sit on the bed?"

"In what universe is five-ten short? You're only six feet, Dad, I got this."

"Five-ten is average for a man, Uncle Malcolm."

"Thank you, buddy."

"What are you thanking SJ for?" Sean asked. "He called you average. You'll never convince Sky to marry you if you're just average."

"Oh, good, a sex conversation." SJ planted himself next to his father.

"What makes you think we're talking about sex?"

"Please, Dad, give me some credit. I turned fifteen over the summer."

"So, what do you think you know about sex?"

"We've had the talk. I know about sex. I'm just saying. You made an average joke, and you're talking about Dr. Sky. That was a joke about Uncle Malcolm having an average-size dick, right?"

"Don't say dick. For god's sake, Sean, is this how you're raising my grandson?"

"You've got to be kidding me. I've heard you say far worse than that around SJ."

"Come on. I'm not a kid," SJ grumbled. "It's just us men in here. We can say stuff like—"

"We're men." Sean pointed to himself then to Malcolm and Charles. Finally, he pointed to SJ. "You're fifteen, like you said, and in your mother's bedroom. Have more respect, even when she's not around. Angie wouldn't want you talking like that."

"Respect?" SJ's face morphed from happy and humorous to hurt and angry. "You haven't slept in here in almost a year. You think I don't hear the two of you? You think I'm too young or stupid to know what you did? Is that what respect looks like?"

Malcolm finished his father's bowtie. He and Charles should leave. They may be family, but this dispute was between Sean and his son. Charles, apparently, didn't feel the same way.

"Come here, SJ."

The teen sulked around his father and to his grandfather.

"At your age, we all thought we knew everything. It's not until you get older and look back on your teenage years that you realize you didn't know shit. You're full of piss and vinegar, right now. I get it. But what happens between your parents is grown folk business you couldn't possibly understand. This is what you do understand, though-- your father hasn't gone anywhere. He's here. Not perfect. Not faultless. But still here because that's what responsible men do. When you've made a few fuck-ups of your own, you'll find out what it means to be a man and whether you are one."

"Are you saying, I don't have a right to be upset?"

"You have every right. What you don't have a right to do is to allow your attitude to spoil everyone's good time. Tonight isn't about you or your dad but about your Uncle Malcolm. It's also about your sister and your grandmother. Tomorrow will come, and you'll still be mad at your dad, which is your right. Did you hear me when I said he's still here?"

"Yes."

"Good. Do you know what that means?"

"That Dad and Mom aren't getting a divorce?"

"It means as long as your dad's around you can mend the rift between you. It means you get to see the worth of a man, not through his accomplishments, but in how he handles his mistakes. Do you understand me?"

"Yes, sir."

Charles slapped SJ on the shoulder before pulling him in for a hug. "For the record, Styles men don't have average-size dicks, no matter how short your uncle is. When we sit on the toilet, our dicks get a drink of water. That's how well-hung we are."

SJ laughed and stepped back from his grandfather.

"Dad, come on with that."

"What? This is real talk. The boy needs to know what he can look forward to. By the way, when are you going to pop the question and get started on your own family? You'll be thirty-seven in almost two weeks. It's time for you to release those little swimmers and add to the Styles clan."

"We aren't there yet. Stop pushing." Shit, he sounded like Sky. "We're taking things slow. I'll propose when the time is right, and not a day before. I don't want to screw this up. Sky means too much to me to rush into anything and not get it right."

Last month, Sky had told him the same, explaining why she wouldn't move in with him. Her reasoning hadn't boosted his confidence in a shared future. He'd taken to spending fewer nights at her loft, deciding it best to give her space. Malcolm had also stopped asking her to stay the night at his place. She hadn't commented on the change. Either Sky hadn't noticed, or she didn't mind the distance he'd put between them. He minded, though, his bed no longer as comfortable without Sky sharing it with him. Malcolm's house was also emptier and colder without her laughter and sweet scent.

"I didn't see you as the slow starter type. By now, I thought you would've been married for a decade. You got the house, what's taking you so long to fill it with a wife and kids?"

Malcolm tossed everyone their fedora. Now that the teenage angst that was Sean Franklin Jr. had calmed, they could refocus on the entertainment they would supply and the freshly minted eleven-year-old getting dressed down the hall.

Not even Angie knew what they'd planned. Without help from any Styles female, Sean had taken his oldest daughter shopping. When Malcolm had seen Kayla later that day, her broad grin told him all he needed to know about the father-daughter outing. Sean had taken one look at Malcolm and said, "I now know more about bras for tweens than any father should. Tweens? Why is that even a real word?"

"I'm not a slow starter. Just because you and Mom had your first kid at twenty-three, doesn't mean I had to. I do things at my own pace."

"A snail's pace. Okay, I get why you didn't marry one of your other girlfriends. They weren't right for you. But Sky is."

"She's hot," SJ blurted.

"Watch your mouth," the three men said in unison.

"Sorry. Too soon for me to add to the conversation again?"

"If there's a fifteen-year-old girl at school you want to talk about," Sean said, "share away. Sky's going to be your aunt. You can't find your aunt hot."

"Even if she is?"

"Especially if she is. You can't crush on your uncle's girlfriend. She's Aunt Sky. That's what I told Zuri to call her."

"You what?" Malcolm snapped. "Why in the hell would you do that?"

"I thought you wanted the pixie-cherub's help. I saw Zuri in the kitchen getting Angie a bottle of water, so I slipped her a couple of chocolate eyeballs in exchange for her calling Sky Aunt."

"You bribed your kindergartner with Halloween candy. Angie's going to kill you if she finds out."

"Snitches get stitches, Uncle Malcolm."

"I'm going to kick your wannabe thug ass."

"What? I can't say that either?" SJ sighed, dropped onto the bed before jumping up almost instantly. "Hey, why didn't you ask me? I like chocolate eyeballs."

Charles reached around Sean and smacked SJ upside his head. "Because your father has a brain. If you called her Aunt Sky, it would've come off as a teen boy's wet dream. All creepy and with a pubescent hard-on to boot. Zuri has that angelic darling thing going for her. I bet she gobbled up her bribe before going back to Angie, all sweet as pie innocent. That girl has everyone fooled."

"All right, all right, that's enough." They were giving Malcolm a damn headache. "One last wardrobe check then we get Cinderella."

The four of them stood in front of the mirror. If Malcolm had to say so himself, they looked damn good.

When Malcolm and the others finally made it downstairs and into the living room, he realized he didn't look nearly as good as Sky did. Hell, did she have any idea of the way she watched him when he danced backup to Kayla, as he mimicked the moves of Merald "Bubba" Knight Jr., Gladys Knight's older brother? Or how maternal she appeared with a clapping Zuri in her lap? He'd never wanted Sky as his wife and mother of his children more than he did tonight. She sat next to Angie and among his family, smiling and clapping along with the Styles. Not an ounce of introversion showing. He knew it was there, though. She was just repressing it for his sake, enjoying herself in a sea of rowdy Styles.

Malcolm's cousin Rodney, the DJ for the evening, lowered the music as planned. Normally, Charles would showcase his celebratory talent first, followed by Sean and then Malcolm. This year, however, with Kayla choosing to participate in her own birthday celebration with her father, Malcolm and Charles opted to let Sean go first. After what could've been a disaster with SJ, the man deserved a happy moment with one of his children.

"Quiet it down. Quiet it down," Sean yelled over the den of people. Then riled them up again with, "How did you like our opening act?" As if choreographed, Kayla and the men hit a synchronized dab move, dropping their heads into the bent crook of an upwardly angled arm, while the other arm lifted in a straight parallel direction. "Okay, okay," Sean laughed at the raucous crowd. "Now that we've got the party started right, let's show some love for our birthday VIPs." Everyone clapped. "That's right, give it up for Momma Styles, Malcolm, and Kayla."

His family exploded in hoots and loud applause. Kim stood and waved at the crowd. Kayla bowed and giggled, and Malcolm winked at a still-staring Sky. If sultry looks could produce children, Malcolm and Sky would have a baker's dozen.

Present

"Three special people share the same birthday month," Sean continued when the group settled down. "You know how we do this time of year. October and Halloween kick off the holiday season. There will be a vote at the end of the night for the best performance. Are you ready, Styles?"

"Yeah!" the crowd cheered.

"All right then. Up first is Kayla Franklin. She's my lovely princess this evening, glowing and beautiful in her ballgown."

"Yay, Kayla," Zuri shouted, her little hands clapping, chubby cheeks in a full-on grin.

Malcolm, SJ, and Charles stepped back, leaving the center of the living room to Sean and Kayla.

When Sean bowed to his daughter, that was Rodney's cue. Instrumental music echoed through the suddenly quiet living room.

Hair pulled back in a banded bun with a black-and-orange silk ribbon embellishment, Kayla bowed in return, her birthday dress falling over black ballerina slippers.

For this performance, Sean didn't require lyrics. He never did because, damn the man, he could sing, which he took too much pleasure rubbing in Malcolm's face every year.

Sean crooned to Kayla the opening line of Stevie Wonder's song, _Isn't She Lovely,_ as she began her ballet routine. Stevie Wonder wrote the 1977 song for his oldest daughter and first child.

Kayla performed her self-choreographed dance with confidence and grace. Malcolm had sat through enough of her school ballet performances to know the eleven-year-old possessed real talent. Whether she would turn her passion for dancing into a career was anyone's guess. Not that it mattered. If ballet continued to bring her joy, her family would support her.

Kayla danced, and Sean sang, changing the name Aisha in the song, Stevie Wonder's oldest daughter's name, to Kayla, and the name Londie, Aisha's mother, to Angie. Father and daughter melded in perfect harmony, and the Styles were mesmerized by the duet.

Malcolm glanced in Sky's direction again. Her eyes were glued to the pair, arms wrapped around Zuri's waist. When she raised a hand and wiped at an eye, he wondered if she were crying. Angie certainly was, as were many of the Styles, his mother included.

Kayla's straddle split leap brought down the house. Everyone jumped to their feet, their cheers and applause drowning out the last words of the song. Kayla hopped into Sean's arms, who swung her around, kissing her cheeks and whispering words meant only for his daughter.

Malcolm was man enough to admit the sweet moment made him a little misty and a lot envious. He looked to Sky once more, and it was obvious now that she was wiping tears from her eyes. A horrible thought struck him, and he could've smacked himself upside the head. He'd been so eager to share this day with Sky and to introduce her to more of his family, it hadn't occurred to him how uncomfortable tonight could be for her.

Sure, Malcolm had taken into consideration Sky's introversion, which was why he'd asked Sean to seat her in the alcove, so she'd have space and relative privacy. How his mother came to be sitting there, he didn't know. What he'd failed to consider, however, was how being around his family would remind Sky of the loss of her mother, as well as her rocky relationship with her father.

There was no help for it now, unfortunately. Malcolm couldn't even rescue Sky by leading her out of the living room and to a quiet spot in the house. Malcolm wouldn't make a scene by going to her now. She would hate being the center of attention and treated as if she were fragile and couldn't take care of herself.

Tamping down the need to protect Sky from unintended harm, Malcolm stayed put.

SJ, ever the showman, pulled Kayla in for a hug and dipped her the way his father had taught him, with much hooting and hollering from the Styles.

Sister Sledge's *We Are Family* came on the minute SJ lifted his sister and spun her around. SJ sang along with the song, dancing around Kayla and playing up the crowd. He made his way to where his mother and youngest sister sat, dancing all the way.

Plucking Zuri from Sky's lap, SJ planted kisses all over her face, Sister Sledge singing in the background. Spinning Zuri around and making the little girl scream her excitement, he placed her next to Kayla.

The Franklin children danced, with SJ lip-synching the 1979 song to both of his sisters. When Sister Sledge urged people to join them in dance and song, so did SJ. The Styles didn't need any encouragement, though. Half of them were on their feet the second they recognized the song, singing and dancing along.

Malcolm also went to Angie and swept her up into a dance. He had to be careful, which he was.

Sky nodded her approval, olive hazel eyes wet from tears. Of joy, he hoped.

Sean strutted past Malcolm and Angie, his hand of invitation going out to Sky when he reached her. After only a second of hesitation, Sky accepted, and Sean pulled her to her feet.

His brother-in-law may have cheated, but Malcolm trusted Sean with Sky. They were working on rebuilding their friendship, but Sean's kindness toward Sky had nothing to do with Malcolm. Sean was just a good guy who'd taken a liking to Sky as a person and as a friend of his wife.

After the song ended, Malcolm returned a laughing Angie to the sofa. He stole a quick kiss from Sky, which earned him raucous hoots from the Styles men. He wanted to kiss her again but knew better than to tempt his luck with another PDA.

"Excuse me, Uncle Malcolm." SJ elbowed his way past him and onto the sofa next to Sky. "Hey, Dr. Sky, did you see my moves out there?"

Malcolm grunted a laugh at his nephew's cute attempt at flirting with an older woman.

"I did. You were very good."

"What about me?" asked Kayla eagerly, while managing to squeeze between her mother and the arm of the sofa.

"You were amazing. I didn't know you could dance so well."

"I've taken ballet classes since I was Zuri's age."

"It shows. Maybe you could teach me how to do a proper split. I think your uncle would love for me to learn how to do that." Sky looked from Kayla and to him. "Wouldn't you, Malcolm?"

He choked on his response and the heat in Sky's eyes.

Angie sputtered on her water, a plastic bottle pressed to her open mouth. "You're bad in a way I didn't foresee. She's time enough for you, M and M. I had no idea."

Holding Zuri, Sean used his foot to push the ottoman away from Kim's chair and toward the sofa with his wife and children. Of course, he placed it as close to Angie as he could in the crowded room.

"It looks like a Franklin clown car," Malcolm's mother complained. "Angie's not going anywhere. All of you huddled around her are going to smother the poor woman."

"Smother, Mommy, smother Mommy." An enthusiastic Zuri jumped from Sean and toward Angie, landing hard with her knees on her mother's thighs.

Angie didn't protest, but Zuri had clearly hurt her, spurring Sean into action. He grabbed Zuri off Angie, quick but gentle.

"You, okay, Mom?" SJ asked.

Kayla slid from the sofa and onto the floor, her eyes filled with the same worry as her brother and father.

Charles's song for his wife began to play, and the old charmer escorted Kim onto the makeshift dancefloor. Unlike the earlier performances, which were meant to hype the crowd, Charles's strategy involved subtly and romance. Holding his wife close to him, he swayed from side-to-side to Percy Sledge's *When a Man Loves a Woman*.

Charles whispered the song in Kim's ear, the way he did every year. But, as in time's past, Malcolm questioned if his father sang the song or spent the time saying all the dirty things he knew his father capable of uttering. Charles Styles may be a sap and a charmer, but he'd heard his mother playfully refer to her husband as a *rascal*. Like SJ, when

Malcolm was a teen, he knew when his parents were talking about sex, even when they didn't use any of the obvious words.

SJ moved to the floor so Sean could sit beside Angie, who had yet to speak. Sky had taken Zuri from Sean, which freed him to check on Angie, whose eyes were closed and face scrunched in pain.

"Where does it hurt?" Sean asked.

"Give me a minute, and I'll be fine. Zuri took me by surprise."

"You don't look fine. Let me take you upstairs and to bed. Everyone will understand."

Angie opened eyes, which revealed the depth of her pain and the lie. "I'm fine. Don't look at me like that."

"You're one stubborn woman."

"I know. I don't want to upset Zuri. Sky's holding her?"

"Yes."

"That's good. Zuri likes Sky, which means she'll be asleep in less than five minutes, even with the music and laughter." Angie raised her eyes to Malcolm. "When Zuri falls asleep, will you and Sky take her upstairs and put her to bed?"

"Of course."

"Make sure to turn on the camera and bring down the baby video monitor."

"I can take both of you upstairs," Sean offered.

"I won't lie, my legs do hurt, but not as much as you seem to believe. As I said, I'll be fine. But I won't stay down here much longer if that'll put your mind at ease. I want to watch my parents dance and see Malcolm's tribute to Mom. After those two things, I'll submit to you babying me."

"Submit?" Sean cupped Angie's cheek and stroked with his thumb. "You don't know the meaning of that word, but I'll accept the compromise."

"Thank you."

"You'll have to come up with a better payment than your thanks. I have a few ideas if you're interested."

"I'm not."

"I think you are, but don't want to admit to that either."

Malcolm had no interest in finding out whether Angie agreed with Sean, so he was happy when she didn't respond. He was happier still when Zuri fell asleep and he had an excuse to get away from Sean and Angie and the strange mix of emotions flowing between them.

He followed Sky out of the living room, down the hall and up the stairs.

"Where's her room? I've never been up here before."

"Right here." Malcolm opened the door across the hall from the guest room where Sean slept.

"Nightclothes?"

"I'm not sure."

"Look in her dresser. Try the second and third drawers first."

Sky settled a dead to the world Zuri on her bed and stripped her down to her undershirt and panties.

"Here." Malcolm handed Sky a pink, yellow, and blue princess nightgown, which she put on Zuri after removing her undershirt.

"Don't forget the baby monitor and video," Sky reminded him. "If Zuri's anything like me when I was her age, she's afraid of the dark. We should dim the ceiling light when we leave."

"Good idea. I didn't like the dark when I was a kid either."

Malcolm watched Sky tuck Zuri in, fuss over the sheets longer than was necessary and then, with a tenderness typical of her, kissed Zuri's cheek.

Sky blushed when she caught Malcolm watching her.

"It's how my mother used to put me to sleep. I don't know much about being a mother, but I remember how warm and safe I felt when Mom kissed me goodnight. Sean and Angie have a beautiful family, and they love each other. I hope it proves to be enough."

So did he.

Malcolm set the camera and grabbed the video monitor, leaving dimming of the light to Sky, who also pulled Zuri's door partially closed.

He stopped her before they reached the top of the stairs. Knowing he shouldn't, but doing it anyway, Malcolm backed Sky against the wall and kissed her. He couldn't resist her lips a second longer. When together, they were two flints capable of creating fire.

Sky opened her mouth to him, no hesitancy in her return kiss and tight embrace.

"You look so good in that suit and hat. When we get back to your house, I want to see you in the fedora, hair down and butt naked."

"You're coming home with me?"

"If you keep touching me there, I'll come right here."

"Tempting." Malcolm removed his hand from under her sweater dress and from between Sky's legs. There would be more time for that later, especially if Sky intended to stay the night.

"You have lipstick on you."

"I don't care. Besides, we've been up here too long for my family not to know we've been fooling around."

Sky used his handkerchief to remove her lipstick from him.

"There's thinking you know, and then there's evidence proving you right. Now, let's get back to the party before someone comes looking for us."

"It's about time," Charles bellowed the second Malcolm and Sky reentered the living room.

Everyone's eyes were on them, and he had no idea why.

Malcolm saw Angie shaking her head at him, as if in warning. He was pretty sure it was too late to avoid whatever was about to happen.

Sky stiffened at his side, and Malcolm knew she'd drawn the same conclusion.

Someone took the baby video monitor from his hand. Malcolm watched the impromptu assembly line of Styles pass the monitor from one person to the next until it reached Sean and Angie.

"On October thirty-first, my only son will turn thirty-seven. Since Malcolm was SJ's age, he's participated in this annual Halloween-birthday celebration. Normally, he celebrates his mother's birthday with some sweet, grand gesture that melts her heart. When Kayla came along, we began celebrating her October birthday too. Sean sings or dances and raises the bar for any man who'll want to marry our Kayla in the future. Malcolm is no different. He showers his niece with the same affection he has for all the females he loves."

Malcolm had no idea where his father was going with his speech, and was growing anxious despite the seeming compliment he'd paid him. Angie's continuous warning shake kept Malcolm on alert. Even Sean wore a concerned look he didn't think had anything to do with Angie's legs.

"Not once, since Malcolm became an adult, have our October birthday celebrations honored him. Our tradition is simple, parents celebrate their young children, children celebrate their parents, spouses celebrate spouses, and children can celebrate the birthday of their sibling if they choose to."

"Stop," he whispered to his father.

"Every year Malcolm comes to his birthday party alone."

A chorus of, "Poor Malcolm" went around the room, followed by laughter. Not mean-spirited, but he didn't like it because he now knew where his father was headed.

"Stop, Dad."

"But not this year. Our Malcolm has finally brought a woman to his birthday celebration, and I couldn't be happier for him." Charles stepped between Malcolm and Sky, wrapping his long, beefy arms around their shoulders. "This is Dr. Sky Ellis, for those of you who haven't met her yet. She's my future daughter-in-law, and I couldn't be happier. She's smart and beautiful and will provide the final birthday celebration entertainment for the evening in honor of my only son."

The roars from his family were deafening, and Malcolm wanted to commit patricide. What in the hell was wrong with his father? Malcolm had told him. Dammit, he'd told both of his parents Sky wasn't an extrovert. She didn't seek the spotlight or enjoy being the center of attention in social situations. Sky loved deeply but displayed her affections privately, quietly.

Sky also had a passive-aggressive type of temper. She'd told him enough about her relationship with her parents to know this as fact, despite having never experienced her anger firsthand. She was also one of the most self-disciplined people Malcolm knew. She had the best poker-face, which meant someone like his father would never know he'd pissed her the hell off until he felt her claws in his neck, ripping out his throat.

"Dad, Sky didn't come here for this. I didn't invite her here for you to put her on the spot in front of the family."

"What are you talking about? You said Sky's the one. She's here, which means she agrees. I don't hear the lady complaining, just you."

"She's not complaining because—"

"It's fine, Malcolm."

"It isn't. Dad is wrong, and I'm sorry about this."

"I'm not wrong. Sky's part of the family, and this is your birthday party. I'm sure Sky is smart enough to come up with something for your birthday. It's all in fun, Malcolm, lighten up."

It wasn't fun. It was presumptuous and insensitive.

Charles raised his voice again, speaking to the crowd. "Let Sky know how much we appreciate her joining us today. Let her know how much we love Malcolm and will grow to love her."

When it came to being loud and supportive, his family never disappointed.

Sky didn't dance or sing. She also wasn't a musician. If Sky could juggle or pull a rabbit from Malcolm's fedora, he didn't know it. To his knowledge, Sky didn't possess a talent the Styles were used to seeing and performing during one of their holiday-birthday celebrations. This wasn't *Apollo Live*, although the Styles put on a good imitation of the talent show, without the booing and Sandman, of course.

Sky shrugged from under Charles's arm, a move his father wouldn't interpret as anger but should. She took hold of Malcolm's hand and walked backward and away from Charles. Sky stopped when they were in the center of the living room, which, to his surprise, had quieted with their movement.

With the poker-face she wore that kept him from knowing if Sky was serious or joking, she held on to his other hand and began to speak.

"'It's all a farce,—these tales they tell
    About the breezes sighing,
And moans astir o'er field and dell,
    Because the year is dying.

Such principles are most absurd,—
    I care not who first taught 'em;
There's nothing known to beast or bird
    To make a solemn autumn.

In solemn times, when grief holds sway
    With countenance distressing,
You'll note the more of black and gray
    Will then be used in dressing.

Now purple tints are all around;
    The sky is blue and mellow;
And e'en the grasses turn the ground
    From modest green to yellow.

The seed burrs all with laughter crack
    On featherweed and jimson;
And leaves that should be dressed in black
    Are all decked out in crimson.

A butterfly goes winging by;

A singing bird comes after;
And Nature, all from earth to sky,
Is bubbling o'er with laughter.

The ripples wimple on the rills,
Like sparkling little lasses;
The sunlight runs along the hills,
And laughs among the grasses.

The earth is just so full of fun
It really can't contain it;
And streams of mirth so freely run
The heavens seem to rain it.

Don't talk to me of solemn days
In autumn's time of splendor,
Because the sun shows fewer rays,
And these grow slant and slender.

Why, it's the climax of the year,—
The highest time of living!—
Till naturally its bursting cheer
Just melts into thanksgiving.'
Paul Laurence Dunbar, *Merry Autumn*, 1896."

"Thanksgiving," his cousin, Damon, crowed before laughing up a storm. "Sky skipped right over Halloween and went straight to Thanksgiving. That's some serious shade your girl threw your way, Malcolm."

Charles's deep rumble of a laugh preceded the ripple of amusement that cascaded through the room before erupting into full-blown hilarity.

"I thought you were mad."

"Oh, I damn sure am. Just not at you. Happy Thanksgiving, sweetie."

186 · N.D. JONES

"Halloween," he groaned. "For once, get the holiday right."

"So, you'd rather have candy corn and caramel apples than the sweet potato pie and triple layer chocolate cake I made you?"

"You made me what?"

"You heard me."

"Where are they?"

"In your refrigerator."

"How did you get them in there?"

"I used the spare key you left at my apartment."

"You little... I don't care. Let's go."

"Don't you have a performance... or something to do for your mother?"

"I bet Dad played the video I had made for Mom when we were upstairs making out."

"But, what about ...?"

Malcolm all but dragged a muttering Sky behind him, uncaring he was being less than his usual polite, charming self. Neither did he care about missing the voting portion of the evening nor did he give a damn about the whistles and approving cheers when Rodney blasted Maxwell's *Til the Cops Come Knocking*.

CHAPTER FOURTEEN

Annapolis, Maryland
Twenty-Eight Years Earlier

"Why would you take her there? Hell, why did you go there?"

Sade sat at her kitchen table, across from her mother, Gloria Page. Light streamed in from the window, brightening the room but not Sade's heart. "You know why."

"You should've never—"

"Never what, Mom? Had an affair with a married man? Given birth to his child?"

"I never suggested an abortion. But, no, you shouldn't have had an affair with a married man. I raised you better than that." Gloria, hair still short from her chemotherapy, took another sip of coffee before placing the cup on the kitchen table. "At least I thought I raised you better than that."

"I don't need the added guilt today. You've made your feelings about my affair with Robert crystal clear."

"You don't see anything wrong with what you did? How would you feel if you were his wife?"

"Don't you think I know? You sit there, like you always do, ashamed and angry at your whore of a daughter."

"I've never called you a—"

"Your friends have. Your church-going, God-fearing, holier-than-thou friends."

"Don't be disrespectful."

"I'm not." Sade leaned forward in her chair, elbows going to the spotless wooden table, eyes glued to Gloria. "I'm neither a villain nor a saint. I also don't throw stones at others. I know I embarrassed and disappointed you, and I'm sorry. Having an affair with Robert wasn't the right action to take, but that doesn't make me a bad person."

"I never said you were a bad person, but your thoughtless, selfish behaviors hurt people. They are *still* hurting people."

Gloria meant Sky. But she also meant herself. Sade and Gloria rarely spoke about Sade's father, Isaac Page. Yet, his abandonment of his wife and two children for another woman had ravaged Gloria's soul more than the tumors had her breasts. She'd survived cancer, but still suffered from the sickness of Isaac's betrayal and the virus of a broken heart.

Relaxing, Sade unhunched stiff shoulders. Her eyes traveled past her mother to the window behind Gloria. Annapolis was beautiful in December, especially when it snowed, the way it had last night. Her Sky didn't like snow, not even the first fall that draped the ground, trees, and houses in a fluffy powder of white.

When Sade gazed out of her kitchen window, the midday sun high in the sky and the snow the sun's losing opponent, she felt like the melting slush. Everything in nature changed. Not always for the better, but certainly not all for the worse. In her opinion, people were like gray skies. They didn't shine every day. They weren't always at their best. Most days, it was all they could do to show up and keep going.

Sade wouldn't allow her affair with Robert and the people who judged her, including her mother, to cloud every day of her life and make her feel worthless. She owed them nothing. The only person Sade owed anything to was the seven-year-old girl who watched television in the den.

"I know Robert hasn't been a good father to Sky. I also know he makes promises and breaks them, which hurts you and my grandbaby. Despite that, you had no right to go to Robert's home. And you certainly shouldn't have taken Sky."

"I don't give a damn what I've done, Mom, Sky is innocent. That bitch had no right to hurt my child."

Gloria's suddenly balled fist and deep breaths had Sade biting back more angry words. Her mother had seen Sky's face when she'd arrived, although Sky had tried to conceal the bruise by pulling her turtleneck up as far as it would go.

True, Sade shouldn't have gone to Robert's home. His second gubernatorial term would end at the beginning of next year, so he was transitioning from the Government House to his Annapolis home. Sade hadn't thought his wife would be there. Like the governor, her schedule was a matter of public record, and Mrs. Ellis was supposed to be at a charity event.

She hadn't gone there to argue with Robert. At least, that's what she'd told herself on the drive to his house. For the first four years of Sky's life, Robert had made an effort to see Sky, minimal though it was. He'd even managed to spend her birthdays with her. The fifth year, however, he hadn't arrived on Christmas. Sky had waited all day for him. The FedEx delivery of presents on Christmas Eve couldn't compensate for the lack of a phone call or a visit from Robert.

The sixth and seventh years were the same, with Robert promising Sky the world but delivering less than crumbs. Each year, Sky would wait for her father to fit her in to his Christmas plans, and each year she would cry herself to sleep when the day ended without sight or word from Robert. No child should have to spend their birthday and Christmas like that, praying for a morsel of attention from a father who'd turned his back on them.

Angry and hurt on her daughter's behalf, Sade had bundled Sky up, put her in the car, and had driven to Robert's house. She didn't want this year to be a repeat of the last three. Sade going to Robert's home had been, as her mother said, a mistake. Taking Sky with her, as a visual reminder of Robert's responsibility, had been an even worse misstep.

When in the hell would she learn? When Isaac had left Gloria, Sade, and her brother, Kenneth, he'd never looked back. Some men weren't worth a dime, and the Page women seemed to be magnets for the wrong kind of man. Sade hoped when Sky grew to womanhood she would find a man worthy of her tender heart. A man better than her father and grandfather.

"I may understand Robert's wife's pain at his betrayal and her anger toward you, but she laid hands on my sweet, little Sky." Gloria's fisted hand unfurled, and she wrapped it around her coffee cup. "What kind of woman, a mother at that, smacks a child in the face?"

Growing up, Sade and Kenneth got into their fair share of trouble. No more than the average kid, but enough to give their mother a migraine and ample reason to spank them. She never did, though. Gloria didn't believe in the proverb 'spare the rod and spoil the child'. She did, on occasion, look as if she wanted to shake the holy hell out of her children.

"I need you to watch Sky, while I go out. I won't be long."

Raising the coffee cup to her mouth, Gloria's head shake neither surprised Sade nor dissuaded her.

"I wouldn't have come if I'd known why you wanted me to watch Sky. You don't need to go back there. Mrs. Ellis could have you arrested."

Sade scowled. "She assaulted my child. I have pictures of her bruised face. She's lucky I haven't had her arrested."

The thought of Lois Ellis's handprint on Sky's face turned Sade's stomach. After arriving at Robert's home, he'd rushed Sky and her into his office. They'd argued, which they did all the time now. She'd accused him of choosing his white children over his black child. He'd accused her of getting pregnant to trap him into leaving his wife for her. The accusation had stung, not just because it was untrue but because Robert was leveling the same sexist and racist judgment as everyone else who was quick to paint Sade as the seductress and Robert as her victim.

Few knew of their affair and Sky's true paternity. Of those who did, they'd blamed Sade more than Robert.

Sade and Robert had argued, hurling cruel insults meant to hurt the other person, forgetting their daughter was in the room and listening to every mean and nasty word they exchanged.

Engrossed in blaming each other for their affair, Robert and Sade hadn't noticed when Sky slipped from the room. Fear had tightened her heart when Sade came back to her senses and realized her daughter was missing. Her heart clenched tighter when she found Sky outside in the frigid December air, sitting on the cold ground and leaning against the side of their car.

When Sade and Robert had rushed to Sky, she had her coat pulled up to her chin and her winter hat low on her forehead. She'd refused to look at either of them and had said nothing when Sade unlocked the back door for her. Sky had climbed into the car, strapped herself in, and then yanked her hood up over her head, effectively concealing most of her face.

Sky didn't speak the entire drive home and had bolted up the stairs and into her bedroom the minute Sade had unlocked and opened the front door. She'd given Sky an hour of privacy before going after her.

"She said, 'Captain Ellis's wife hit me,' when I finally saw her face and asked what had happened. 'Captain Ellis' -- that's how Sky refers to her father now after her violent run-in with his wife. I don't need you to say it again, Mom. I know it's my fault. Most days, I can accept being the only parent in Sky's life. But it's so damn hard during this time of the year. They have an annual dad-daughter Christmas dance at her school, and she never attends, although I know she wants to. Last year, I asked Kenneth to take Sky, but she refused to go with her uncle. I know what it's like to go through that, to see other kids with their dads and know yours barely acknowledges your existence."

Gloria drank from her coffee cup, her judgment, for once, silent.

"I didn't mean to do this to my daughter. Not having a father isn't the end of the world or the worst thing that can happen to a person. But when you're a kid it feels like you were given a raw deal. Which, in a way, you were. I'm trying to be enough for Sky."

"Was I enough for you and Kenneth?"

An easy question to answer, but a painful response to voice aloud.

"Not always," Sade replied with gentle honesty. "We missed Dad almost as much as we grew to resent his absence. You were a good mother to us. You're still a good mother. We don't tell you that enough."

Sade stood from the chair and joined her mother on her side of the nook. Sliding in beside Gloria, she hugged the older woman and kissed her cheek.

"I don't regret having Sky. I never could. I won't ever apologize for her. I never want my child to feel unwanted by me, no matter how she came to be in this world. She is my sky, a reminder of the endless possibilities of life and the beauty that can come from a shameful beginning."

Gloria returned the embrace, and Sade hugged her mother with a fierceness that came with having almost lost her to breast cancer.

"Be careful, and make it sting."

Sade laughed. Her mother had never been the turn the other cheek kind of Christian. At least not when it came to her children and grandchildren.

"As I said, I won't be long."

Sade left her mother in the kitchen sipping on what had to be cold coffee. When she reached the den, Sky lay sprawled on the carpeted floor, television on but her face buried in a book.

"I'm going out for a little while. Nana will watch you until I get back."

Sky turned a page in her book but didn't respond. Okay, her daughter's silent treatment was still in effect. Sade supposed she deserved the little girl's attitude, not that she liked Sky withdrawing into her tortoiseshell.

"How about we make Nana's triple layer chocolate cake when I return? You've been begging me to show you how to make it since Thanksgiving."

Lowering her paperback, Sky glanced over her shoulder. "You said I was too young to use the oven."

"You are. But you're not too young to help me mix the ingredients and to spread on the frosting."

Book dropped from long-fingered hands, and Sky moved from her belly onto her bottom, now interested in what Sade had to say. "From scratch, not a box."

"What do you know about making a cake from scratch?" Sade moved into the den and knelt in front of her daughter. "You've been talking to Nana, haven't yet?"

Sky's nod had her wavy, light-brown hair falling into her eyes. She'd removed the three ponytails with double strand twists Sade had put her hair in this morning. It had taken her thirty minutes to get it just right and Sky far less time than that to undo her hard work. Now, it was a riot of waves in the back with remnants of her curly baby hair in the front.

"Come here, sweetie."

Sky came, and Sade sat fully on the floor, cradling Sky in her lap as if she were still her chubby toddler instead of a second grader who would turn eight in a couple of weeks.

"I'm sorry." A kiss to her unbruised cheek couldn't express the depth of Sade's guilt. "I'll never do anything to hurt you again. I promise, baby."

Far more sensitive than either Robert and Sade and also far less talkative than them both, Sky buried her face against Sade's chest and wept. This harsh world would force Sky to toughen up or risk being devoured by sharks. Sade would do everything in her power to stand between Sky and all harm, which included a selfish father and a hot-tempered mother.

"I'll buy the ingredients while I'm out. From now on, you'll help me make sweet potato pie and triple layer chocolate cake every Thanksgiving and Christmas. How does that sound?"

"Good."

"You have the expressive vocabulary of a twelve-year-old, can you not do better than 'good'?"

Sade tickled Sky, and her little girl squirmed off her lap, trying to get away. Sade was having none of it. She went for her stomach and sides again, digging her fingers in and tickling.

"You're above grade-level in reading, and all I can get out of you is a lousy four-letter word."

Sky squirmed even more, but she'd also stopped crying and was laughing. God, Sade loved that sound. Sky's laughter was the best sound in the world, second only to when she called Sade Mommy.

Sky laughed and laughed, and Sade felt sorry for Robert. He would never know this Sky -- this intelligent, sensitive, and playful little girl whose heart was as pure as freshly fallen snow. Right now, Sky could only see her lack of a father. But it was Robert who was missing out on more than he'd ever know.

Children were precious jewels to be loved and valued, even if, at times, their parents were not.

Sky lunged at Sade, taking her by surprise and knocking her onto her back.

They laughed, Sky on top of her and not a tear in sight.

With a straight face and an unreadable expression, Sky looked down at Sade. "Very good. Is that better, Mommy?"

Before Sade could process whether her seven-year-old had mocked her or was serious, Sky jumped off her and ran from the den screaming, "Nana, Mommy and I are going to make pie and cake for Christmas. Yaaay."

CHAPTER FIFTEEN

"Oh my god. So good, Sky. So damn good." Malcolm moaned, licking out his tongue and rimming his lips. "So good, baby."

He moaned again and again.

Sky smiled. How could she not with Malcolm's passionate reaction? "Come here, you're a mess."

She reached for Malcolm, but he intercepted the hand going to his face. "Not with the paper towel. Use your tongue."

"My tongue?"

"Yeah, I want you to taste yourself on me."

"You mean taste my cooking on you."

"No, baby, I said what I meant. If you want to remove the chocolate frosting from my lips, use that long, sexy tongue of yours."

Heat and desire flooded Sky's system, fueling the low buzz of need that watching Malcolm savor her triple layer chocolate cake had created within her.

He ate another piece, fork going to his mouth. Lips parted, tongue peeked out and tasted before Malcolm consumed the moist, rich chocolate. "If you want to clean me up do it properly, Dr. Ellis."

Oh, Sky damn sure wanted to lick him clean. When Malcolm had made a show of dragging her from his sister's house, with the intent of driving them back to his home to eat the cake and pie Sky had made for his birthday, she'd assumed, like everyone else, it was all for show, and they would have sex as soon as they reached his house. But no, being a true junk food junkie, Malcolm had gone straight to his refrigerator, found the desserts and pulled them out. He didn't even bother with the ice cream Sky had stored in his freezer when she'd put away the sweet potato pie and triple layer chocolate cake.

They sat beside each other, a half-eaten pie across the table and a fist-high slice of cake on a saucer in front of Malcolm. He'd consumed a tall glass of milk after his third slice of chocolate cake. How he wasn't full and his suit not bursting from the seams, she didn't know.

Sky scooted her chair around, so they faced each other. "You're a messy eater."

Dark-brown eyes lowered to sensual slits. "You knew that about me already."

Malcolm's erotic voice conjured a ghost-like feel of his head between her thighs, mouth and tongue eating his fill of her.

Sky kissed him. If she didn't, Malcolm wouldn't stop his sexual teasing until he had her dripping wet and begging him to take her on the kitchen floor.

Double chocolate, Sky would say, if her tongue wasn't otherwise engaged. As much as she enjoyed the rich flavor of the chocolate frosting, the creamy confection paled in deliciousness to the organic taste of Malcolm Styles.

Sky licked Malcolm's lips, slow back and forth swipes of her tongue, while she shifted from her chair and onto his lap. While she sucked and licked every speck of frosting and cake from his face, one of his hands settled at her waist and the other in her hair, holding her close. Sky performed the task a second time, ensuring she missed nothing, including the sweetness she found inside Malcolm's mouth and on his tongue.

"You're the best kind of pastry chef." The hand on her waist fell to a hip and massaged, and the one at her nape kept their faces delectably close. "The very best kind."

"What kind is that?"

"The kind that tastes their scrumptious creations to make sure they got it right." More massaging of her hip and a nip to her lower lip. "Trust me, you got it *juuust* right. How does your cooking taste to you?"

Sky kissed Malcolm again. Her hands went to his face and her breasts against his chest. Her entire body was draped over his, as they consumed each other, hungry gulps of need and possession.

She was lifted from Malcolm's lap and onto the sturdy, wooden kitchen table.

Up went Sky's sweater dress and off came her panties. Out came a condom and down went Malcolm's pants and boxers.

Sky wrapped her legs around Malcolm's waist when he pulled her to the edge of the table. God, she never got enough of this, of him. Malcolm's body kept her coming back for more. But it was his kind nature and good heart that made Sky want to stay with him forever.

"Do you know how many times I've fantasized about fucking you on this table?"

She also loved his mouth, imagination, and the raw appetite he had for her.

"Mmm, tell me."

"I'd rather show you. I also want to eat icing off your body, beginning with your nipples and working my way down. Or maybe whipped cream. Did you sneak that into my house, too?"

Malcolm kept talking while making love to Sky. He talked and thrust. Talked and kissed. Talked and talked, his words dirty, his voice orgasmic, and his tempo fast.

She loved it all.

"Since you didn't bring any whipped cream, buy some for my birthday trip. Butterscotch, caramel, orange, or lemon. Chocolate, salted peanut butter, and brown sugar cinnamon would be redundant. I got those already taken care of."

Sky's eyes snapped open and stared at Malcolm. "You did not just say that."

"You know I'm right. Chocolate, salted peanut butter, and brown sugar cinnamon, you're getting all three now." He pulled Sky even closer and whispered in her ear. "You love it. It's okay to admit being a Malcolm Styles junk food junkie. I'm the best kind of food addiction, and you get a work out when you have me. A win-win."

A win-win. The arrogant man damn sure was.

Sky grabbed a fistful of Malcolm's gorgeous dreadlocks. They hung over his shoulders and down his back. Once they finished, she'd find his fedora, undress him, cash in on her lap dance, and then make love to him again. She doubted he would have a problem with her plans for the night, if she left time for more pie and cake eating.

"You're terrible," she told him.

"I wasn't before I met you."

Laughter had Sky losing her rhythm. "I don't believe that for a minute. Don't forget, I met your family. Except for sweet Zuri, you're all terrible."

"Shows how much you know. Zuri is the Styles type you never see coming. She's ninja Styles."

Sky started to laugh again, but Malcolm's fingers on her clit had her moaning and grinding against his hand instead.

They stopped talking. Well, their mouths did. Their bodies, however, continued with a different, more table-shaking, sweat-inducing, and body-clenching conversation.

Ninety minutes later, they'd done everything on Sky's sex list. They'd also retreated to Malcolm's bedroom, his bed one she hadn't slept on in weeks. When he'd stopped staying over at her loft, Sky hadn't argued or even complained. She'd viewed his actions as relationship growing pains and had given him even more space by not sleeping over at his house. Now, however, she wondered if she'd taken the right tactic with Malcolm. Whereas Sky needed physical distance when an issue weighed on her mind and heart, Malcolm, it seemed, required the opposite. He didn't need space but reassurance and closeness. The same things she once craved from her father.

"Dating you, I have no choice but to keep my gym membership." A wicked smile followed Malcolm's statement. "Between your cooking and athleticism, a man has to be able to keep up or risk turning to flab."

Sky reached across the short distance and pinched Malcolm's side, not an inch of flab on him. He was all hard body and mouthwatering abs.

"I'm like this now. But I wasn't always." Malcolm's eyes raked over Sky's nude body. "I bet you never had a weight problem."

"You did?"

"I told you I had a sweet tooth. I just didn't tell you how much I enjoyed sugary and salty foods."

Sky remembered him putting away nearly two bags of popcorn and her joking about high blood pressure. High blood pressure was too prevalent in the African American community, which didn't make it funny at all.

Sky watched Malcolm hook the comforter with a toe and use his foot to pull the bedspread up far enough for him to grab it with his hand. He covered their naked bodies, which was how they would sleep unless they got up to put on night clothes. The lights were already out, Malcolm having turned them off when he'd rejoined her in the bedroom after taking a shower.

She turned on the nightstand lamp on her side of the bed.

Malcolm blinked at her and frowned. "Why did you do that?"

"I want to see your face when we talk."

"Don't worry. You won't wake up one day to a roly-poly or a bed full of cookie crumbs if you decide to marry me."

"A roly what? What are you talking about?"

Malcolm's gaze moved from Sky and to the ceiling.

On her side, cheek in her hand, she watched him in silence. Sky knew there were layers to her Malcolm Styles, far more than the triple layer chocolate cake he'd scarfed down.

"I was overweight as a kid. I ate a lot of sweets and greasy foods. Even when Mom laid down restrictions and changed how and what she cooked for the family, I still managed to get what I wanted. I would stop by the corner store on my way to school every day and buy a bag of candy. After school, I would grab a couple of slices of pizza or a hamburger and fries and eat them before I got home."

"Why? What was going on at school that made you want to eat like that?"

"What makes you think my overeating was school-related?"

"Oh, please. My mother made me join my high school's cross-country track team because I ran away from everything. I mean, I literally ran, Malcolm. I would jog around my neighborhood, whenever someone or something pissed me off, mainly one of my parents. If I heard them arguing on the phone, I'd throw on my tennis shoes and slam the door behind me on my way out. When my father sent me roses and chocolates on Valentine's Day or tickets to musicals and sporting events but wouldn't spend more than five minutes on the phone with me, I'd run myself to exhaustion. Running helped me clear my head but did nothing for my heart."

Malcolm nodded. "You know, Sky, colorism is an awful practice in the black community. 'He's cute for a dark boy'. Do you know how many times I heard something like that? Or was called Shaka Zulu, Kunte Kinte, blue-black, dark as midnight? Children can be creative when they want to be."

"Cruel and mean."

"Those too. I ate and gained weight, which didn't help my situation. I went from You so black to You so fat jokes. Some days, it was both. 'You so black you were marked absent at night school.' 'You so black you blend in with the chalkboard.' Stupid, mean shit like that."

"Mulatto, high yellow, house negro, oreo, light bright, damn near white. 'You must be mixed because you got good hair.' 'Just because you have those fake-ass green eyes don't make you better than me'. 'You're bougie.' "

Malcolm's eyes found hers again, a dark cavern of understanding and sadness. He shifted onto his side, so they faced each other.

"Malcolm, colorism runs the gambit of our skin tones. The psychological effects of racial oppression are real and painful. Trust me, I get it."

"I should've known you would. You're darker than friends of mine who have two African American parents, and they've been called the same names you were. Sometimes light-skinned African Americans think they're better or more attractive than darker complexioned African Americans. Other times, darker-skinned brothas and sistas treat those with lighter skin as if they aren't truly 'black,' " he said, using air quotes, "or 'down for the cause.' That's how messed up we are because of the psychological effects of racial oppression."

"Do you want to talk about the rest of it?" Malcolm was chair of EBC's African American Studies Department. He would know what she meant.

"The darker the berry, the sweeter the juice. In college, some girls wanted to find out, both white and black. Are you searching for your authentic blackness by dating a brotha as dark as I am?"

"Are you dating a biracial woman because you really want a white female but don't want to go that far and risk losing your racial credibility?"

They stared at each other, no anger in the questions posed but a revelation of past experiences and pain.

"I do love your dark complexion and dreadlocks," Sky said into the silence. "I've never made a secret of that, and yes, I did go through what my mother called my 'black militant' phase. She used to tell me to hold my head high and not to allow others to define me. 'Love yourself. Be yourself,' Mom would tell me whenever I questioned where I fit in."

It was Sade's mantra, too, and she needed the cloak of self-affirmation more than Sky understood as a girl. As an experienced woman, Sky felt oddly more in-tune with her mother than she had when Sade was alive. If Sade had lived, their relationship would've grown as Sky matured, her eyes now open in a way they weren't when she was younger and her mother alive. Back then, Sky was too consumed with finding her identity and judging her mother's actions with Robert to see the complex woman that was Sade Page.

"I'm not trying to find my so-called authentic blackness by dating you. No more than I was when I dated other African American men. I don't need anyone's stamp of racial group approval. I define myself as biracial but also as African American. That's my choice. I'm not ashamed to have a white father any more than I'm ashamed to have been raised by a black, single mother. If anyone has a problem with that, it's their hang-up, not mine."

Again, there was no heat in her voice. No matter how much Malcolm might want to marry Sky, their marriage wouldn't last if they weren't willing to grapple with tough issues like racism and the deleterious effects on the psyches of African Americans, including their own.

It wasn't as if they didn't already talk about race and racism, which made sense considering what they did for a living and who they were as so-called people of color. But they'd never spoken about race and colorism in regards to their relationship with each other.

"Even when I was going through my 'black militant' phase, Malcolm, I was never so shallow as to be interested in a dark-skinned guy because of his complexion. You're too intelligent and perceptive not to know when a woman wants you for that reason. I don't. I never have, and I never will."

Malcolm propped on his elbow, leaned forward and kissed her. "You know I adore your olive hazel eyes. In college, I dated a couple of white girls, so I'm not looking for that in you. I know what you mean, though. Some brothas go crazy over a light-skinned woman, especially ones with eyes like yours. I bet you had all kinds of guys in your face when you were growing up. Hell, I see it now, with a few of my colleagues. I hate it because I know what they are thinking. They act as if you being biracial is an upgrade from any other brown-skinned woman I've dated. It's an insult to me, you, and black women." He kissed her again. "Being biracial isn't what makes you an upgrade from my previous girlfriends, my sweet, sexy Sky."

"It's you who's sweet and sexy. You're also a junk food junkie."

Malcolm flopped onto his back. "I know. I know. Don't hate me because I'm greedy. There's nothing suave or charming about a man willing and able to wolf down half a cake in one sitting."

"Or two bags of popcorn."

"Don't remind me," he groaned.

"I don't mind."

"You say that now. If I let myself go, I bet you'd change your tune."

She wouldn't, not that she didn't appreciate the tantalizing effect of Malcolm's faithful weight training and kickboxing classes on his luscious body.

"We'll help each other stay in shape and eat right."

"Does 'eating right' mean you're going to stop baking me sweets?" He sounded like a spoiled, disappointed child. "If it does, I think I'm going to show you another side of me."

"What side?"

"My crybaby side."

She laughed. "Did Angie call you a crybaby when you were a kid?"

"Of course she did, but she was the one who made me cry. A tiny bully. Dad said she had a Napoleon Complex. I think he was right. I mean, come on, she's five-three and married a man a full foot taller than herself."

"That doesn't make your sister a bully. I'll still cook you desserts when I feel up to it and have time."

When Malcolm lifted his arm, Sky snuggled against him, her breasts pressing to his side and her leg thrown across both of his.

"Did your mother teach you how to cook?"

"Mom taught me everything Nana taught her. They were both excellent cooks, although Mom had a heavier seasoning hand than Nana."

"Yum, I think I would've liked your mother's cooking."

She would've liked you. You're the kind of man Mom hoped I would find and marry.

"Are you still upset about tonight?"

"Except for your father putting me on the spot, I enjoyed myself."

"I'm sorry about that."

He didn't need to be. Sky knew Malcolm would never do anything to embarrass her, just as she knew the performance request had been Charles's way of testing his son's choice of a potential wife. Life was full of challenges, all of which she faced in the same way, with stubbornness and grit.

"It's fine. I'll pay Charles back."

"You're going to what?" Malcolm laughed but sobered when she didn't join him. "You're serious?"

"Didn't I sound serious?"

"Yeah, but you always sound like that, even when you're joking. I honestly can't tell the difference. But you can't get my father back."

"Why not? I'm not going to do anything to hurt him if that's what you're thinking."

"It wasn't. It's just… just… well, no one gets Dad back for anything he says or does. Mom complains, and Angie ignores him, but no one does anything about his behavior. Not even his sisters, who, I'm convinced, were happy to turn him over to my mother when they married."

"Is that your way of telling me you'd be upset if I did something to pay your father back for deliberately putting me on the spot?"

Malcolm whistled and clapped his hands, startling her. "Hell no, someone should've put the old man in his place a long time ago. I can't wait to see it. Front row seats, Sky. That's where I'll be."

"You're terrible."

"Look who's talking. You're the one plotting my father's downfall."

"And dramatic."

"That's right." He clapped again, loud and more awake than he should be at one-thirty in the morning. "You're going to do something at Thanksgiving dinner, aren't you?"

"Maybe."

He smacked her behind. "Don't 'maybe' me. You agreed to be my date, and it's the next time most of the family will be together. Which makes Thanksgiving perfect for your wicked Ellis payback."

"Not Ellis, Page. I have no idea what the Ellises do when someone messes with them and they decide to push back. I do know about Page payback. My mother and uncle were masters."

"And you have the nerve to call me terrible. My father will never see your payback coming."

Malcolm raised his arms to clap again, but Sky grabbed one and pulled it down. "You're loud and hyped up on sugar. Calm down and go to sleep."

"I will, as soon as you tell me how you pulled off that Paul Laurence Dunbar poem. You couldn't have known what Dad had planned. But you were prepared."

Sky wasn't prepared, at least not in the way Malcolm meant. She'd intended to recite Dunbar's poem to him during his weekend birthday getaway. Sky had already memorized the poem. Thanks to Charles, she'd been forced to change her plans, turning a private joke into a public gag.

"We'll talk tomorrow." Sky yawned, hoping Malcolm would take the hint and stop talking.

"Technically, it is tomorrow."

"Come on, I want to sleep." Damn, that had come out as the worst kind of girlie whine

"You turn grumpy when you're tired. I didn't want to say anything before. However, since we're being so honest tonight, I thought I'd let you know."

Sky slapped Malcolm's chest, then rolled away and toward the nightstand. She clicked the light off and burrowed under the covers.

"Yup, grumpy. You're no good after midnight."

"Be. Quiet." Sky threw her pillow in the direction of the sound of Malcolm's laughing face. He didn't stop laughing, so she supposed she missed.

"You were in theatre, weren't you?"

"Yes, now be quiet and go to sleep."

"Really? I was kidding. Who knew my introverted Sky was a thespian. What plays did you star in? *A Midsummer's Night Dream*? *Alice in Wonderland*? *You Can't Take It with You*? *A Raisin in the Sun*?"

"Yes, no, no, yes. Go to sleep, Malcolm, or so help me I'm going to get dressed, take your car keys and drive myself home."

"Okay, okay. Damn, you'd think I'd get better treatment on my birthday."

"It's *not* your birthday yet, you big Halloween *baby*," she yelled. "If you don't let me sleep you won't make it to October thirty-first."

Sky considered getting out of bed and dragging herself to one of Malcolm's other bedrooms. The thought of a quiet space tempted more than it should've. She may have enjoyed herself with his family, but the Styles, in large numbers, were exhausting.

"Come back over here, and I'll stop talking and let you sleep. You really do need your woman's cave sometimes, don't you?"

Sky had no idea what Malcolm was talking about but wasted no time moving back to his side of the bed. She would do almost anything if it meant Malcolm would shut up and go to sleep.

He hugged her to him when she laid her head on his chest. Malcolm did have a wonderful family. A family she wouldn't mind joining. Her Ellis family, on the other hand, were a complete unknown. Sky still hadn't accepted her father's invitation to spend Christmas in Annapolis with him and his other children... her siblings. She also hadn't rejected his offer.

"By the way, when's your birthday?"

Sky snored and pretended to be asleep.

CHAPTER SIXTEEN

In the time they'd spent traveling from Buffalo, New York to Newport, Rhode Island, Malcolm had learned several facts about Sky. One, she packed thoroughly but lightly. Two, she preferred reading to talking on the plane. Three, she read reverse harem novels, a genre of romance he'd never heard of before. Paperback, not eBook. When he'd seen four guys and one woman on the cover, he'd quirked an eyebrow. "You're into books about group sex?"

"It's not about group sex but a mutually respective polygamous relationship between the heroine and the men she loves and who love her."

"That's a very nice, overly intellectual way of justifying reading about a woman getting it on the regular from four men. Sometimes one or two at a time, other times with all of them at the same time, I bet. It doesn't matter how in love you claim they are. One woman and four guys, that's a mini orgy. A sex fantasy of yours, Dr. Ellis?"

Sky had rolled her eyes at Malcolm and resumed reading. He'd stewed for a full five minutes. To his way of thinking, she'd chosen a smutty novel over his company. Reverse harem his ass. Was this what feminism had devolved into, women having the right to have as many sexual partners as they wanted and without any moral and social stigma attached?

Four, he'd learned that Sky could go into business as an event planner. Her level of detail was both admirable and intimidating. From the flight, to the car rental, to the lodging, she'd organized it all, and they were only a few hours into their weekend getaway.

Five, his Sky had expensive taste. He'd already concluded as much from her clothing, car, and loft, so her choice of a luxury car rental and beachfront cottage shouldn't have surprised him. But they had.

"What's wrong?"

Malcolm stood beside a queen-sized bed, a small sitting area to his right, a motionless fan above him and heated floors below. The French doors across the room were closed, but he could see they opened onto a private deck that overlooked the ocean.

"This cottage is on sand dunes." He pointed to the quiet, empty beach beyond the French doors. "Is that a private beach?"

Sky stepped away from the white armoire, the two doors open and one of Sky's dresses already on a hanger. "Yes, Neptune Coast."

"Roman god of the sea. Not very creative."

Turning back to her suitcase, Sky took her time placing her items in the armoire and dresser drawers. "What would you have named the beach?"

"Something like Ethereal Cove, Fluorescent Shore, Coral Coastline."

"Not Sandfoot Cove or The Sandy Shore?" She plopped onto the bungalow bed, relaxed-looking in skinny jeans, black crepe jacket, and a gold, sleeveless, tank top with a sequined front. Her gold chandelier earrings and two-tier, gold necklace matched her top, pulling her splash of color together into a comfy-chic style that was all Sky Ellis.

"With uninventive names like that, you might as well call it The Beach and be done with it."

Malcolm moved to the French doors and opened them. Cool Newport air ran the length of his body, swirling around him and sending aromas of salt marsh and wetness up his nostrils. Albatrosses flew over the rippling water, their large wingspans and narrow wings distinct, the marine bird one of several taking advantage of the sixty-degree weather and sunshine.

Arms wrapped around his waist and a chin pressed to his shoulder. "What's wrong? You were quiet the half hour drive from the airport and haven't said much since you brought our luggage inside."

"I don't talk that much."

"You do, which is why it's easy for me to know when something is on your mind."

Malcolm had no good reason to be upset. Sky had planned an entire weekend for him. She'd taken off work and had gone to a lot of effort to give him a special birthday. He knew whatever she'd scheduled for them to do in the seaside city would be wonderful because Sky, while not the most romantic person, was a thoughtful one.

As Malcolm soaked in the oceanfront view and fresh air, he had to reevaluate his position on Sky's level of romanticism. The Neptune Coast and beach cottage were Styles-level romantic. Hell, even the name of the retreat, Snowy Dream Paradise, conjured romantic images of a couple strolling on the beach, sipping wine on a hillside, visiting boutiques and touring elegant mansions. No matter how he put what was on his mind, he would sound like an ungrateful jerk.

Sky held him tighter and kissed the lobe of his ear. "Tell me what's going on in that brooding head of yours."

He shifted to face her, her arms still around him. Malcolm might not like the direction his thoughts had taken, but he wasn't a coward who couldn't face the woman he loved, even though he felt groundless in his irritation.

"You spent too much."

Sky blinked up at him. "On what?"

"Everything. The plane tickets, car, cottage, and whatever else you have planned for this weekend. I didn't expect all of this. You shouldn't have spent so much money on me."

Malcolm was about to offer to pay Sky back, but she released him and walked out the French doors and onto the wraparound deck.

He followed.

Sky sat on a wicker lounge chair facing the beach, the breeze blowing strands of hair into her impassive face.

Malcolm couldn't tell if she was mad, hurt, or offended. She had a right to be all three. He should've kept his big mouth shut, but since their talk on colorism and his former weight problem he'd pledged to show Sky all sides of him, even the hard-to-love ones.

Hearing his mother's voice in his head about "heating the outside," he closed the doors and joined Sky on the deck. Instead of taking a seat in the chair beside Sky, Malcolm walked over to the railing, right in front of her. He leaned against the wood, arms crossed over his chest.

Sky's eyes never left the panoramic view behind him-- not even when she spoke. "Mom told me the best education doesn't take place behind a desk and in a school but through exploration and exposure to different people, places, and cultures. When I wasn't in school and Mom working, we went on trips. Some were day trips to parks, museums, eateries. Other trips took us out of the state and country. Those vacations were taken during spring, winter, and summer breaks when I had more time out of school. The year before Mom died, she brought me here. We didn't stay in a cottage or beach house because they were booked. She reserved us a suite in the main resort building and promised to bring me back the following summer. I may not like snow, but I love the ocean, and so did Mom."

Malcolm's eyes preceded the dropping of his head and arms. Of course, Sky would have a story like that. Malcolm felt like crap.

"Do you know how much you've spent on me since we began dating?"

He lifted his head, puzzled. "I have no idea. I don't think about that when we go out."

Eyes serious, if not a little sad, Sky focused on him. "Not once, in the months we've dated, have I paid for one of our dates, including our weekend trip to DC. Even the times I've managed to get my credit card out and pay before you get a chance, I find cash, a day or two later, on my kitchen counter. I've never had a boyfriend who paid me back instead of allowing me to pay my equal share or, heaven forbid, treat him because he deserves it and it makes me happy to make him happy."

"Sky, I just—"

"The earrings you purchased for me weren't cheap. No special occasion, mind you. You told me you saw the earrings and thought of me, so you bought them. I didn't question or complain about the unexpected gift and its price, although I really wanted to. It reminded me too much of how Robert treats our relationship as if he can buy my love and trust with sweet smiles and shiny jewelry."

"That's not why I pay when we go out or why I bought you the earrings. I'm not trying to buy your affection."

"I know, that's why I tamped down my initial annoyance. But you're also not leaving anything for the next level of our relationship. If you're already paying for everything, including random, expensive jewelry, where do we go from here? Clothing sprees? New car? Trip to Bali?"

"What? No. Now who's being dramatic? I simply like being able to take care of you. A little spoiling, if you have to put a label on it."

"That's not what you've been doing, and you know it."

Malcolm thought back to the conversation he'd had with Sean. His brother-in-law and his damn cow anthology.

My point is that Sky isn't your wife yet, but you act as if she is. What's her incentive to move you from the boyfriend column to the husband column? From where I'm sitting, none. She gets all the milk she wants. Sky doesn't have to put in any work. And guess what, that's your fault, not hers.

"We're going to get there, Malcolm, but we aren't there yet. We aren't married, not even engaged. There are things we shouldn't expect from each other or, perhaps, even give each other. We haven't earned them yet."

"Are you saying this trip is about paying me back?" The awful thought had him crossing arms over his chest again.

"You're working hard to ruin this trip and to piss me off. No, I didn't arrange this weekend to pay you back. I brought us here because I wanted to show how much I love and trust you by sharing one of the last special moments I had with my mother. Besides Uncle Kenny, I don't talk about Mom with anyone. I came back here, three years after she died, and couldn't bring myself to walk down to the beach or to stay in a cottage. I thought I could try again, but with you, hoping you'd feel the same way about this tranquil beach as I do. I wanted to get away from Buffalo and our hectic work schedules. Most of all, Malcolm, I wanted to celebrate your birthday in a quiet place where we can get to know each other better."

"Okay, well, now I feel like an ass."

"Why? My motives for this trip were just as self-serving as your efforts to control the pace of our relationship by paying for everything." Sky stood. "In a few years, we'll be forty, which means we've had years to get used to doing and having everything our own way. We're accountable to few people, and we like it that way. There's nothing either of us can buy for the other person we can't purchase for ourselves. We've talked about the possibility of marriage, but we've skirted around the issue of whether we have what it takes to be married to each other. My default, in the face of conflict, is to flee, yours is to hide parts of yourself in order to avoid conflict. Neither approach will take us far, no matter whether we marry each other or someone else."

"You're talking about everything in a relationship that happens before and after mind-blowing sex."

"No, I'm talking about everything that happens that makes a couple want to keep having sex with each other when it's not mind-blowing. No trick, Malcolm, but the best kind of treat. I want that for us."

"To spend every Halloween together."

"To spend every holiday together, and all the uneventful, unnamed days in-between. But let's begin with this first Halloween."

"I'm not used to women paying my way. I didn't realize, until today, how uncomfortable it makes me feel."

"You're going to have to get over that because this weekend is all about you." She stepped closer. "Sweetie, accept my gift. Relax and enjoy yourself. That's what I want. I've never done anything like this for another man. The thought never crossed my mind. With you, I've experienced quite a few firsts."

"You weren't a virgin when we began dating. So not all your firsts were with me."

She smacked his shoulder and laughed. "You really wanted a thirty-five-year-old virgin in your bed?"

"Hell, no. But I wouldn't mind a cheerleader or nurse. Is roleplay on my birthday menu of activities?"

"No."

"Can we add it? I can be the quarterback to your cheerleader."

Sky kissed him, soft and slow. "Or submissive to my dominant."

Their tongues tangled, mouths warm but the wind from the ocean cool.

"Strangers at a bar. I'd pick you up, take you to a sleazy motel and have sex with you on a lumpy bed."

Sky smirked. "We'd need penicillin afterward."

"Most definitely, but it would be worth it."

Sky's hands lowered to his ass and squeezed. "You'd take a penicillin shot here for one night in a dirty motel with a stranger?"

"If that stranger is you and you're dressed as a porn star."

"I have no idea how a porn star dress."

"Let me show you."

Malcolm gave her a quick peck to her lips then escorted Sky inside. She'd put away her clothing, while his clothes were still in his suitcase. He should remove them before they wrinkled even more.

He went to Sky and started to undress her, getting as far as her jacket and shirt before her cell phone rang. By now, he knew the splashing water ringtone belonged to Sky's father, former navy captain and Maryland governor.

They were sprawled on the bed, Malcolm's shoes and shirt on the floor beside his suitcase where'd he'd dropped them before chasing Sky onto the bed. He also knew, when Sky didn't answer her phone Robert had an annoying habit of calling, repeatedly, until she did.

Malcolm rolled off Sky and retrieved her cell phone from the nightstand.

"Sorry," she mouthed to him, before answering the phone.

It was fine. Malcolm knew Sky had promised to call Robert when they landed. Between the car rental and retrieving their luggage, she'd forgotten. Sky may have been thirty-five, but Robert worried about his daughter the way he should've when she was a little girl.

Malcolm grabbed his rolling suitcase and opened it. For Sky's sake, he tried not to dislike her father. Malcolm hadn't even met him but, if everything went the way he hoped, Robert Ellis would become his father-in-law. Still, Robert had not only cheated on his wife but also all but abandoned his daughter, leaving Sade to raise Sky by herself.

His lady wore those cuts on the inside, scar tissue of past hurt and disappointment.

"Yes, we got here safely."

He unpacked his suitcase, listening to Sky's side of the conversation, which wasn't much. She sat against the white headboard, eyes closed, and knees raised to her chest. As usual, her father talked more than she did, and Sky pretended to listen, offering an "Uh-huh" every couple of minutes.

Malcolm's eyes narrowed. How many nights had they talked on the phone, and she'd used the same tactic with him? Probably more than he cared to think about. The woman was unbelievable.

"I still haven't decided yet. Yes, I know it's two months away." She was listening and talking now, the annoyance in her voice unmistakable. "This trip isn't the same as what you're suggesting. Yes. Yes. I am trying, but you're pushing."

For several minutes, Sky didn't speak. Her eyes might still be closed, but she wasn't relaxed. Her right hand tugged at her hair, fingers twisted around wavy locks.

Malcolm stored his empty suitcase under the bed.

"I know what day it is. Do you have any idea what you're asking of me? No, I don't think you do. Because of you, Mom began taking me away for the holiday, so I wouldn't be at home to fixate on not getting a phone call or visit from you."

Not even pretending he wasn't listening to her conversation, Malcolm pushed from the floor and sat on the bed.

"You can't make it up to me. I told you that before. Look, Robert, I don't want to argue about this. I promised to give your invitation serious thought, and I have. I don't think I can do it. If it were just you, maybe, but you also invited your other children. The last thing I want to do is spend Christmas with people who don't know but who dislike me."

Sky went silent again. He wished he could advise her on what to do. Beyond being unsure if she'd take his advice, Malcolm didn't know if spending Christmas in Annapolis with her father and siblings would add more pain to an already tender wound or prove the beginning of a family reconciliation. He hoped the latter but feared the former.

"Let's talk about this when I return home. This weekend is supposed to be about Malcolm and me, not about the two of us. Yes, he's right here. Sure." Sky opened her eyes and handed him her phone. "My father wants to speak with you."

"Why?"

"If I had to guess, he wants to solicit your help in convincing me to visit him this Christmas."

"I'm not going to do that."

"I know, but he doesn't."

Malcolm took the phone from Sky, and she scooted off the bed. He didn't see where she went, but the cottage, while nice, wasn't big. The only other rooms were the kitchen and full bathroom.

"Malcolm?"

"Hey, Robert, I'm here. How are you doing?"

"I'd be better if you married my daughter and moved to Maryland. Any chance that'll happen before I die?"

"The first part, yes, the second part, hell no. Do you play the I'm-going-to-die-soon card with Sky?"

"She doesn't fall for my tricks. My daughter calls me on them every single time. Sky's like Sade, in that respect."

Malcolm detected a hitch in Robert's voice when he spoke of Sky's mother. If Sade Page was anything like Sky, he couldn't imagine Robert not having developed feelings for the woman beyond the physical.

"I won't fall for your tricks either. You've upset Sky."

"I know. I didn't mean to. I was hoping she'd visit."

"There's always spring break. Maybe Sky will change her mind if given more time."

"It won't be the same. I missed so many of her birthdays. I would like to spend as many of them with her as I can, in the time I have left. Not a trick this time, Malcolm, but the truth. I was forty-one when Sky came along."

"What am I missing? I thought you wanted Sky to spend Christmas with you."

"I do."

"So, why are you talking about Sky's birthday?"

Robert paused, and Sky reentered the bedroom, a saucer with a muffin in one hand and a glass of water in the other. She placed both on the nightstand. Breaking off a piece of the carrot cake muffin with cream cheese icing, she offered it to Malcolm. He opened his mouth and let her feed him.

"They're the same. I spent the first four with her but missed the others. I don't want to miss any more of Sky's birthdays."

"On Christmas, you mean?"

"Yes, that's what I said. Sky's birthday is December twenty-fifth."

Malcolm's mouth fell open, and not for another piece of muffin, although Sky promptly filled it. Sky's birthday was on Christmas. Why in the hell hadn't she told him?

"I get the feeling you didn't know."

"I didn't."

"Oh, well, this is awkward. Anyway, if Sky won't come to me, then I'll have to make the trip north to her. Man-to-man, what's my chance of leaving New York with my spine still inside my body if I visit without her permission? By visit, I mean camping outside her overpriced loft until she agrees to speak with me and let me in."

"Not very good."

"That's what I figured. But if Sky doesn't visit, I think I'll risk her wrath and fly to Buffalo."

"I doubt that move will help your cause."

"I know you're right, but Sky is a damn near immovable force. How I handled things in the past is my greatest regret, and I don't mean my affair with her mother. There's so much I want to tell her, that I *need* to tell her. But I don't want to do it over the phone."

Sky finished off the rest of the muffin, which, while good, wasn't as tasty as Sky's desserts or her lips. Malcolm took hold of her waist and pulled her onto his lap.

"It's her decision. Even if you don't like it you need to respect it. People erect boundaries for a reason."

"I'm her father. How do you think she'll feel if I die and we haven't dealt with the gulf between us? I think that's what happened between Sky and Sade. Wait, if you didn't know her birthday, it's safe to assume Sky hasn't told you about her mother's death."

She'd told him her mother and grandmother were dead. What kind of person asked for details? Certainly not him.

"I know enough."

"Which means you don't know anything and Sky is listening to our conversation. When she's ready, she'll tell you. She seems to like and trust you far more than she does me. A bit of advice, don't mess up what

218 · N.D. JONES

you have with her, especially Sky's trust. Once it's gone, it'll be hell to re-earn."

From watching Sean and Angie, Malcolm knew Robert was right.

Sky began a string of kisses, starting at his clavicle and trailing up his neck and to his chin. "I ordered groceries," she whispered. "The delivery arrived before we did, so the kitchen is stocked." More kisses to his cheek and ear. "Unless you intend to speak to my father all day, I suggest you give me the phone. Otherwise, Robert will go on and on." She raised her voice. "Politicians talk more than college professors, and that's saying something, considering how much you like to talk."

"I heard that."

"I meant for you to." Sky claimed her phone from Malcolm and pressed it to her ear. "Robert, we have to go." Pause. "It's none of your business what we're about to do." Pause. "You already have grandchildren. You don't need more."

Whatever Robert said had Sky shaking her head and frowning. The older man went on talking for another three minutes, with Sky paying more attention to Malcolm's neck than her chatty father. She had no right to ever call Malcolm terrible again, not with the way she would "Uh, huh," Robert, all the while kissing and licking his neck, her free hand on his belt and tugging.

Malcolm relaxed onto his back, bringing Sky with him. Straddling his waist and watching him from under long, dark lashes, she licked her lips and said, "Uh, huh," to Robert again.

"Get off the phone," he whispered.

Sky shook her head. A naughty grin spread across her face, and Malcolm knew how a gazelle felt when in the predatory sights of a lioness.

Although he shouldn't have, Malcolm allowed Sky to remove his pants and boxers and climb atop him again after getting as naked as he was.

"Homestead Gardens Annual Fall Festival ended October twenty-ninth, right? That's what I thought. Yes, I assumed you went. How was it?" Sky asked her father.

Off Robert went again, relaying details Sky wasn't listening to. The word wicked came to mind.

Soft, wet southern lips slid over his hard shaft, a slick glide that had Malcolm opening his mouth and closing his eyes. Forward and back Sky went, sliding her clit over the tip of his dick with each steady, slow movement.

"What happened then?"

Damn, this was so wrong. But Sky felt too right for Malcolm to stop her, or himself. He pulled her down for a thorough kiss, her phone fisted in the hand above his head.

Sitting back up, Sky's voice betrayed none of her impishness. "Eastport Yacht Club Lights Parade is next month. Depending on the weather, it may not be too cold to attend."

Robert must've launched into another monologue because Sky winked at Malcolm, lowered the phone and drew him in for another kiss.

Sex rubbed against him, a wonderful friction that had his hands going to Sky's waist and thrusting upward. She bit her lip, and ground more of her sex against him. When Malcolm moaned, Sky covered his mouth with her hand. Neither of them were quiet lovers, but Sky's effort at silence proved effective.

He'd packed condoms in his carry-on bag, which, dammit, was across the room in the closet.

"Wait, I need to get—"

Sky kissed him again. Heavy breasts and erect nipples sank into his chest, a cushion of womanly curves.

"Go on," Sky urged Robert, a little breathless and a lot wet.

The way Sky leaned over Malcolm, low and close, all it would take for him to be inside Sky was for her to move backward or for him to thrust forward.

Malcolm didn't move.

But Sky did. She shifted backward then forward onto him. Sex-to-sex. Skin-to-skin.

Malcolm wore no condom, his mind screamed. "Baby, I'm not—"

"It's fine." A low moan of a response into his ear. "You feel amazing without one. Solid yet soft. Delicious."

Sky felt better than amazing. Twice, he'd entered her without sheathing, but they'd never had full-blown sex without protection, the way they were now. Malcolm had once asked Sky about alternate birth control measures. He'd hoped, since they were monogamous and disease-free, Sky would consider trusting him enough to forego condoms in favor of a female contraceptive.

"Robert, I have to go. Yes, I know we're in the middle of a conversation, but I need to go now. I'll call you later."

Sky ended the call, and Malcolm flipped her over. Her cell phone flew from her hand and hit the headboard.

"Tell me you're on the pill."

"An IUD. Happy birthday." She grinned up at him, more beautiful to Malcolm with each passing day. "I wanted to surprise you. Did I succeed?"

"You know you did." Malcolm thrust, moaning deep in his throat. "A first for both of us. Baby, you're so wet for me. It's like a full-body plunge into heaven. If I didn't know how wicked you could be, I'd swear you were an angel."

"A fallen angel, maybe."

"Mmm, yes, you fell from heaven and straight onto my waiting dick."

CHAPTER SEVENTEEN

At eleven in the morning at Washington Square, Sky and Malcolm stood across the street from the Jane Pickens Theatre & Event Center. The building looked better in person than it did when Sky researched it online. Built in 1834 as a church, the world-class art house showcased films since the 1920s, a time when moviegoers would've never imagined the growth of the film industry, much less sound, color, and 3D movies.

The historic center of Newport bustled with Saturday activity. The windows of stores bore the signature orange and black colors of Halloween. For the more holiday-spirited businesses, spider webs, skeleton pallbearers with coffin, hanging mummies, and a goth vampire lady made for great curb appeal when Malcolm and Sky had strolled down Touros Street and toward JPT.

"What did you do?" Malcolm asked Sky, sounding as surprised and pleased as she'd hoped he would be at this birthday gift.

Malcolm removed his cell phone from his coat, a midnight blue, twill, wool jacket, which looked great with his blue jeans, button-down shirt, and burnished leather ankle boots. Raising his phone, he took several pictures.

"Angie will not believe this, and Sean will be jealous." Malcolm's smile, when he turned to Sky, radiated through her body, warming her with his happy heat. "It's awesome." Malcolm looked at the theater again, and then back to Sky. "My name is on the marquee. Birthday gifts don't get much cooler than this. Miracle of miracles, you got the holiday right for once."

Sky shrugged. "It's your birthday and today is Halloween. I didn't want to confuse the good people of Newport with a marquee that read: Happy Women's International Day, Malcolm Styles."

In truth, Sky had been tempted to use the marquee to tease her holiday-sensitive boyfriend. In the end, she settled on playing it straight with a simple: Have a Ghoulish Halloween and Birthday, Malcolm. After their conversation yesterday, Sky worried Malcolm would brood about everything on her birthday itinerary, spoiling the weekend for them both. Yet, this morning, he'd seemed to come to terms with Sky footing the bill. She wasn't, however, naïve enough to believe the issue of who should pay for what wouldn't resurface as they moved forward in their relationship. Today, though, she loved his reaction to her birthday present.

Malcolm grabbed her hand. "Come on. Let's get closer so you can take a pic of me under the marquee. That's the one I'll post everywhere."

Malcolm was as much a social media junkie as he was a junk food junkie. He used social media as an extension of his class, which EBC faculty and administrators were encouraged to do as a mean of staying connected to students beyond the campus and classroom. From the Desk of President Hicks, weekly updates from EBC's chief executive officer were posted across social media networks, which more college presidents were doing nowadays.

Sky took several pictures of Malcolm under the marquee, making sure to get him and the birthday message in each shot. Until today, she'd thought she'd seen every one of Malcolm's smiles. She hadn't. The way Malcolm grinned had her heart squeezing, his inner child so close to the surface it was hard not to envision the same smile on the faces of their children.

A mother, with a little boy about four and dressed in a ninja costume, stopped when Malcolm flagged her down. "Excuse me. Would you mind taking a picture of us?" Malcolm pointed to his birthday message. "It's my birthday, and my girlfriend had my name added to the marquee."

The little boy poked Malcolm with his plastic sword, just as his mother craned her head to take in the marquee. She smiled. "Seen many names up there on the marquee but never met one of the lucky people. Tourists?"

"Accent gave us away?" Malcolm asked, catching the child's sword before it connected with his side again.

"Well, yes, that, but mainly the fact that you want me to take a picture. Those who live here are so used to JPT we forget how wonderful it is until a tourist reminds us. Sure, I'll be happy to take a picture of you and your girlfriend." A blue eye winked at Sky. "Nice gift for a man who loves movies."

Malcolm liked movies well enough, but he also loved eating popcorn and other snacks while at the theater. Malcolm savored the entire experience, which Sky intended to give him.

After Malcolm showed the mother how to use his phone's camera, he wrapped his arms around Sky's waist and hugged her to him. They smiled for the camera, and the nice lady took several shots, patient, as only a mother of a small child could be, when Malcolm shifted positions for every picture.

"Thanks a lot. I appreciate your time."

"No problem. You two are so cute. Who wouldn't want to take a picture of you both? Here's your phone back, and happy birthday to you."

They watched the mother and son walk down the street, continuing with whatever they planned for the day before being waylaid by Malcolm.

"So, what's next?" He slapped his hands together, endearing in his excitement. "A movie and popcorn?"

"Yes. Come on, let's get inside. The movie starts in twenty minutes."

"Where in the hell is everyone?"

For the third time since entering the auditorium, Malcolm looked at the three hundred seats in the downstairs area where they sat, then up to the one hundred seventy-two seats in the balcony.

"Either we're early, or everyone else will be late. What's going on? What aren't you telling me?"

"Do you have enough to eat and drink?"

"Is that a junk food junkie crack?" Malcolm's infectious smile let Sky know he was playing. "Freshly popped popcorn with real butter, chocolate candy bar, soda, because it's too early for a craft cocktail, and you. I have everything I need. But, um, where are the other people? Are you sure you got the showtime right?"

Sky made a show of looking at the time on her cell phone, her countenance serious. "If I didn't, the rest of the day and my plans will be shot to hell."

"You're saying you got it wrong?"

"Maybe."

"You, who's early for everything and records all appointments on your work calendar, which you linked to your cell phone's calendar, screwed up my birthday itinerary?"

"Maybe. Weren't you the one who just asked if I got the showtime wrong?"

"Sure, but it's unlike you to make that kind of mistake. I just couldn't think of a reason why we're the only people in the auditorium."

Toying with Malcolm was too easy and so much fun.

"Because I'm so anal, is that what you mean?"

"Anal is such a judgmental word. Unless, of course, you're talking about sex then it's the best word in the world. By the way, whenever you want to take our relationship to the next level, I'm all in."

Double entendres like that were the reasons why Sky had no compunction teasing Malcolm.

"All in, huh?"

"Yes. I'm open to moving our relationship forward. Taking it to the next level may hurt in the beginning, but once we get used to it, you know, loosen it up a bit, it'll be great. A tight fit but great."

"You're awful."

"What?" Big, brown eyes blinked at her with a mischievous sexiness that had her shaking her head and smiling. "So, are we staying or leaving?"

Sky settled against the chair cushion, reached her hand into Malcolm's box of popcorn and grabbed a fistful. She'd give him two minutes to figure it out.

He glanced around again as she chomped, enjoying the popcorn. When Malcolm pulled out his phone, she knew what he would do and what he would say once he found the answer to his query.

One minute. Two.

"You've got to be kidding me. The entire auditorium, Sky? Really? Who rents an auditorium for two people?"

"I do, now be quiet. The movie is about to start."

Right on time, lights dimmed, and the movie began. No previews or ads but the opening scene of a movie Malcolm knew well. Her selection was cliché, but she couldn't help it. She blamed Charles and Kimberly Styles for naming Malcolm after Malcolm X and Marcus Garvey.

Two compelling and provocative images appeared first, the beating of African American Rodney King by white police officers and the American flag burning into the shape of an X. These images in 1992 when the film was released, reflected the beliefs, attitudes, and fears of many in the black community about injustice, inequity, and police brutality. More, they indirectly asked viewers to question how far America had come in combating racial oppression and violence since the days of Malcolm X.

The narrative scene took viewers decades into the past. Boston, The War Years, Dudley Street Station appeared on the screen. A train rolled by and the camera panned down to a bustling street with cars and people. _Roll 'em Pete_ by Joe Turner played in the background, drawing viewers into the jazz and ragtime feel of the 1920s.

Sky crunched more popcorn as Spike Lee, zoot suit and big yellow hat with a feather, strolled down the street and into a black-owned barbershop. A smiling, young, and handsome Denzel Washington exited the back room of the barbershop and sat in a barber's chair, his reddish-brown hair natural and about to undergo a drastic change. Anyone who'd read Alex Haley's _The Autobiography of Malcolm X_ knew the Black Nationalist leader once went by the moniker of Big Red. Those were the days when Malcolm X, later El-Hajj Malik El-Shabazz still went by his given name of Malcolm Little.

The narrative scene ended with Malcolm X getting his first-ever conk and dressed as a man of the times in his zoot suit and stylish, flamboyant hat. Over the next few decades, Malcolm's outward appearance would continue to change, reflecting the growth and, at times, the turmoil of the inner man.

"This is my favorite movie, but we've never watched it together."

Malcolm also hadn't told her. His mother and sister were great sources of information.

"You're lucky I like you so much, or we would be watching _The Exorcist_, a true horror classic."

"You and your damn horror movies." Malcolm reached over and hugged Sky, as best he could with an armrest between them. "I love you. I would've been good holed up in the cottage and spending our entire weekend in bed or taking in the beach and resort. But this is much better. You put a lot of thought into everything you do, which I appreciate more than you know."

"You're a sap," Sky muffled against his shoulder.

"So are you, I'm learning, just a closet one. I'm on to your game now, Dr. Ellis."

"Be quiet and watch your movie."

Malcolm hugged Sky tighter and kissed her cheek before letting her go.

Beyond the actors and music, the only other sounds in the auditorium were Malcolm crunching his way through a box of popcorn and washing it down with a large blueberry slushie. Partial to nachos with cheese but not hungry, she'd eaten a third of her food before sliding the boxed container to Malcolm. He frowned at the cheese but finished off the nachos.

Although she knew it was coming, seeing Malcolm X gunned down in the Audubon Ballroom was an emotional punch to the solar plexus. The scene never failed to evoke both sadness and anger within Sky. From the look of Malcolm, Washington's performance had the same effect on him.

When the movie ended with Ossie Davis' eulogy at Malcolm X's funeral, Sky wept, and Malcolm stood, his ovation one of the sweetest things she'd ever seen him do. Between space and time, from one Malcolm to another, from one African American male to another, Sky grasped the pride and sense of empowerment Malcolm felt throughout the movie. Denzel Washington may not have won a Golden Globe Award or Academy Award for his portrayal of the iconic historical figure, but the movie stayed in the hearts and minds of thousands of moviegoers, which, in a way, was a greater barometer of a movie's success.

Malcolm beamed at Sky over his shoulder and whooped. "What's next?"

"Hype much?"

"It's your own fault. You wanted me to get into the spirit of your pricey birthday gift, well, you got it. Let's go, Dr. Ellis, I'm ready for more spoiling."

Pricey birthday gift and spoiling. Sky may have been more like Robert than she thought. Dammit.

"Genie's Hookah Lounge for lunch, sex and a nap back at the cottage, and then Newport Blues Café for dinner and a show. Doors open at seven, but we can get there closer to showtime, which is at ten."

They stepped out of the theater, and Malcolm twined his fingers with Sky's. "Lead the way, my lady."

Malcolm held out Sky's chair and pushed it in when she sat.

"Welcome to Newport Blues Café." The hostess, dressed in a long-sleeved, button-down shirt with blue tie, handed Malcolm and Sky menus."

"Thank you," Malcolm and Sky said in unison.

"Your server will be Katara, who will be right with you to take your drink orders. Enjoy your evening." The hostess walked away, pleasant and professional, but also anxious to help the next customer. The restaurant was busy on this Halloween evening.

Malcolm glanced around the restaurant, taking it all in and grinning when he refocused on Sky. "This is nice. I looked it up. It used to be the Aquidneck National Bank until it was bought and turned into a restaurant and nightclub in 1995. Built in 1892," Malcolm said, remembering the year the bank opened. "This is a great historic district. All the buildings are in tip-top condition."

The multi-storied brownstone might still resemble a bank on the outside, but the inside of the building was all twenty-first century. From the shiny hardwood floors, perfect for dancing, to the mounted flat screen televisions, ideal for watching sports and news, to the stocked bar and local fare listed as "Food for the Soul," on the menu.

Sky had truly outdone herself. Beyond bringing him to a city she'd first experienced with her mother, nothing else about the weekend was about Sky and Sade. He hadn't realized until now how well Sky knew him. She listened, watched, and cataloged everything for later use. Even when they were messing around, Sky on the phone with her father, she'd somehow kept track of Robert's side of the conversation. No detail, no matter how small, slipped past her.

He understood Sky, too. She only took information and people into her space and vault-like memory bank if they mattered to her. He'd seen her smile and nod at a colleague, engage in an entire conversation with that person, and not recall what the person wore, much less what they'd said. She ruthlessly siphoned inconsequential people and facts, which left room in her heart, mind, and life for what most mattered to her.

As the dining and dancing areas swelled with people, many dressed in Halloween costumes, and soulful music gyrated in sultry rhythms around them, Malcolm sensed a shift in their relationship, and in him. For years, he'd felt like the odd Styles out. He hadn't found "the one," settled down, and had children. Everyone else his age had, which left him arriving solo to every family event.

As much as Malcolm wanted a wife and kids, he wasn't ready for marriage if it meant marrying the wrong woman to meet a ridiculous family expectation. When he'd met Sky, however, his body and mind reacted to the woman in a way they never had before, with a jarring recognition of his soulmate. Desperate, Malcolm did all in his power to make Sky his.

But a man couldn't "make" a woman his, and therein lay his fear. He was so ready for marriage, the reality of finally finding "the one," had shocked his heart and frazzled his mind. Fear did odd things to a man, Malcolm had come to learn. But watching Sky observe the crowd, her fingers tapping to the beat of the music against the pink cloth that covered the table, Malcolm's months-long anxiety began to fade.

Patience, for himself and for Sky.

"If it's too crowded down here we can move to the second floor. It overlooks the stage and is more intimate."

Like everything else about this trip, Sky had made decisions based on Malcolm's likes. She had selected the first floor because it put them in the middle of the action, Malcolm's preferred seating. But it wasn't hers.

"I read it's more private upstairs. When Katara arrives to take our drink order, I'll ask about moving."

"Thank you, but I'm fine. You like it down here, right?"

"Yes, but—"

"Good." Sky smiled, her lips glossy and tempting. "I don't want you to miss anything. We came on a great night. You were on the website, so you know who's headlining."

He did. Rick Express. Malcolm watched a couple of videos of them on YouTube, and they were very good. They blended rich flavors of smooth groove R&B, classic Motown, and Top 100 Billboard hits. He couldn't wait for them to come to the stage at ten.

Katara arrived and took their drink orders, and Malcolm refrained from asking the waitress to relocate them upstairs. If Sky said she was fine, then he trusted her to know her limits and mind. It also meant by the end of the evening, when they returned to the beach cottage, she would need a few minutes of silence and alone time. In the small cottage, privacy might be hard to find. However, if Malcolm occupied himself on the bed while Sky read in the sitting area or meditated on the floor, she'd find her peaceful center.

As the night drew on, they ate, laughed, and had an all-around good time.

"So, when's your birthday?"

"We were talking about you wanting to go back to Genie's Hookah Lounge tomorrow night to see the belly dancers."

"We were, now we're talking about your birthday. Tell me when it is."

"You would lose if we played poker for money."

"I don't play poker."

"Good thing because I would own the deed to your house and the title to your truck."

"That's probably true. You went into the wrong career and took me to the wrong city for my birthday. Vegas, baby, with your emotionless stare you'd clean up at the poker table. Then you could use part of your winnings to spring for a Vegas wedding. Without an Elvis impersonator, though." Malcolm snapped his fingers. "I got it, we could have a themed wedding. Like a superhero wedding. I could be Superman and you Wonder Woman. Or, better than that, a Santa's Workshop themed wedding. How does that sound? A wedding with a Christmas theme?"

"It sounds like my father has a big mouth and that I should've never let you speak with him on the phone."

Sky ate the last bite of her Maryland Crab Cake sandwich. Only Sky would travel to another state and eat the same food she would if she were in her home state. She could've at least ordered the New England Clam Chowder.

"By the way, you know way too much about Vegas weddings. The confessional is now open, Dr. Styles."

"You're the one who needs to confess. Why didn't you tell me your birthday is Christmas?"

"You didn't tell me your birthday was on Halloween."

"Don't try to turn the tables, Sky. You know I would've eventually gotten around to telling you. But I get the feeling you never intended to tell me. At the very least, you were going to wait until the last minute to spring the news, leaving me no time to do something special for you beyond the Christmas gifts I've already bought you."

"You've already started your Christmas shopping. Well, aren't you the early bird who got all the worms."

"I'm not falling for your sarcastic diversions. Spill."

On a sigh, Sky claimed a piece of his chocolate lava cake and ice cream. It was Malcolm's dessert, which he hadn't thought he'd be sharing, since, when the waitress had asked if they wanted her to bring two spoons so they could share the mountainous dessert, Sky had assured Katara that she was "stuffed" and didn't have "room for dessert."

"I don't want you to use my birthday as an excuse to propose."

"I wouldn't do that."

Her snort rivaled his sister's. "That's a damn lie. You know it, and so do I." She reached for his dessert again, fork primed.

Malcolm moved his plate. "Get your own. When you prevaricate and bullshit you become a food thief. Good to know. I have no intention of using your birthday as an excuse to propose on Christmas."

"I don't believe you."

"Believe what you want. I'm not trying to push or rush you into marriage."

"Since when?"

"Since right now." Sky didn't believe him, and he didn't blame her. "I mean it. No more talk of marriage, moving in together, or children. No pressure." Malcolm shifted from the seat across from Sky to the chair to her right. He took the hand with the fork reaching for his dessert again. "One day at a time. Like you said yesterday, we'll get there, but we aren't there yet. I can wait to make you my wife."

"When we're both ready?"

"Ready is subjective. If I want it, and you want it, I consider that as ready as two people can be before taking the leap of faith. But you don't see it that way, so we'll wait. No Christmas marriage proposal, I promise."

"You do?"

"I give you my word, and I've never lied to you. Do you trust my word?"

Sky's past with her father meant she didn't give her trust easily or allow emotions to overcome her to the point of making decisions her mind couldn't later accept. Which, when taken together, made Sky a passionate and warm person for those she lowered her drawbridge for and beckoned inside her fortified walls.

She kissed him. Sky tasted of chocolate, trust, and love, a perfect Sky Ellis cocktail.

"I know all men aren't like my father, Malcolm. If I'm hesitant sometimes, it's not because I doubt your sincerity. I've always been afraid to be wrong and to hurt myself in the process. You see, trusting someone else is one thing, but trusting yourself is even more important. My mother graduated from college at sixteen. She earned her MA in marketing and a doctorate in political science by the age of twenty-three. At twenty-four, she organized her first successful political campaign. Six years later, she helped propel a former naval officer into the highest political position in Maryland and gave birth to his child, with no assurance of a future between them, much less a happy one. I've yet to meet anyone as intelligent and as capable as my mother. Yet, when it came to Robert, her eyes were closed and judgment flawed. I may have been a kid, but I wasn't blind. Mom had loved Robert. Much of her anger toward him stemmed from self-criticism and regrets she couldn't fully embrace because of me."

Sky kissed Malcolm again, less than a tongue kiss but more than a peck.

"Robert thinks you and Sade had a falling out before she died, which plagues you."

"My father knows me, as much as I allow him to, but he's ignorant to the type of relationship I had with Mom. She was my best friend, my confidant, my protector and my cheerleader. There was nothing she had that she didn't give me. When we argued, I pouted and acted like the brat I was, giving her the silent treatment. She understood what I didn't because I was too young and self-centered to deconstruct my heart and mind."

Music played, and people talked, the background noise irrelevant to the conversation between Malcolm and Sky.

"You broke Sade's rules and pushed the limits of her patience because you wanted to know if your mother would abandon you the way your father had. You were afraid to trust the love she gave unconditionally. But if Sade still loved you, even when you were a pain in her ass, then you knew your father's abandonment wasn't owing to a deficit in you, but in him."

Sky's eyes went misty, and Malcolm pulled her to him. He hated when she cried. Hated, even more, how deeply her childhood wounds ran.

"Let's dance," he suggested.

Rick Express had taken to the stage, while they'd been talking. Their heads had been pressed together so they could hear each other over the harmonious sounds. People were already on the dancefloor, swaying to Rick Express's version of Barry White's *Can't Get Enough Of Your Love Baby*, a romantic ballad he couldn't pass up.

Malcolm led the way, careful to keep Sky close as he slipped around tables and people to find a good spot for them on the dancefloor. For all they'd shared and done since beginning their relationship, Sky and Malcolm had never danced together. He corrected that oversight at Newport Blues Café.

As the lead male singer crooned, Malcolm held Sky close, his arms around her waist and hers around his neck. They swayed in perfect rhythm as if they'd danced like this for years. The band switched from slow to fast tunes, energizing the crowd with their upbeat tempos then cooling them down with their slow grooves. No matter the pace of the song, Malcolm and Sky existed in their bubble, wrapped around each other and dancing to a song of their own creation.

Well, that was until Rick Express rolled out with Beyoncé's *Love on Top*. That's when Malcolm found out how well Sky moved those sensual hips of hers outside of the bedroom. God, he loved her. Malcolm wouldn't propose to Sky on Christmas, since he'd promised, but that didn't mean he didn't still have a wish for the Christmas present he intended to have come true.

CHAPTER EIGHTEEN

Sitting beside Sky at the dining room table, Malcolm grinned and added more to his story, shameless in the retelling of her birthday weekend gift to him. "Gourmet breakfast, afternoon tea, valet parking, private beach access."

"We heard you the first three times. Shut up about your trip to Newport already. That was a month ago. I saw the pictures more times than I care to recall. We get it." Sean, seated across from Malcolm and Sky, winked at her. "He's a braggart, if you haven't figured it out yet."

"And you aren't?" Angie, still walking with a cane, but more sure-footed than she'd been in October, rolled her eyes at her husband when she retook her seat next to him.

This year was Malcolm's turn to host Thanksgiving dinner at his home. Sky had offered to help him cook, but he'd assured her his family would bring everything. He literally only had to provide a place for the Styles to gather. Sure enough, when they'd arrived, every Styles brought a dish, filling the kitchen, fridge, dining room table, and house with the most delicious foods and scents. She hadn't smelled home cooking like that since the last Thanksgiving dinner she'd spent with her small Page family.

Candied sweet potatoes, collard greens with turkey kielbasa, maca-
roni and cheese, cornbread and oyster dressing, honey baked ham,
potato salad, and the list went on, not counting a mouthwatering array
of desserts. At first glance, Sky thought the Styles had brought too much
food. No way could they consume it all. She'd been wrong.

"I don't see a steak knife in your hand," Sean said to his wife, "but
you still managed to cut me. That's either a talent, Angie, or my curse."

This time, when Sean winked, as charming as ever, he aimed it at
his wife, who, Sky knew, wasn't as unaffected by her husband's flirta-
tion as she pretended.

"Did I mention twice daily housekeeping?"

"Unless you're a slob," Charles began, seated at the head of a table
not his, "why in the hell would anyone need that?"

Malcolm's mother and two of his aunts glanced around. She knew
what they were doing, making sure the children were preoccupied in
case the conversation turned Rated-R. The older kids, like SJ, were in
the backyard, trying to have a snowball fight with two inches of snow.
The younger children, mainly those who couldn't keep up with the teenagers or preferred a warm house to an unseasonably cold, late autumn
in Buffalo, had retreated to the basement when Malcolm's adult cousins
turned on the football game.

The four-thirty match between the Los Angeles Chargers and the
Dallas Cowboys was almost over. Charles had spent the last ninety-
minutes running between the living and dining rooms, committed to
watching the game while also not missing the post-Thanksgiving dinner
conversation around the dining room table.

Sky had no interest in football, although, when the Baltimore Ravens played, she would watch a few minutes of the game, especially
when their opponent was the Pittsburgh Steelers. Malcolm, on the other
hand, loved football and had joined his father in the ridiculous back and
forth, claiming he had to check on her to make sure she didn't wander
away. Where did he think she would go in thirty-degree weather and
her car blocked in?

Damon, Malcolm's twenty-something cousin, looked from Malcolm to Sky and then to Charles. "Come on, Unc, you can't be that old or out of touch. Twice daily housekeeping is perfect for midday sexapades."

"Why is everything with you kids about sex?"

Damon's bark of laughter rippled through the room. "The Styles could fill that Newport resort Malcolm keeps bragging about. That's how much sex and how many children we have. Don't worry, Sky, we won't bombard your home when you and Malcolm marry. Well, we will, but we'll wait at least six weeks before we invite ourselves over and eat you out of house and home."

"He's not lying," Sean said. "After two decades, I'm still recuperating from when the Styles first invaded my home. It was just a one-bedroom apartment back then." He nudged his wife with his broad shoulder. "Remember, Angie, our little loft overflowing with your family? I lost you in the crowd for an entire hour and kept being stopped by your cousins and uncles when I tried to find you."

Angie's soft reply of, "Yes, I remember. That was a long time ago. We aren't that young, idealistic couple anymore," had everyone, except Sean, looking away.

"I know we aren't, but we built the foundation of our marriage in that little loft. You laughed a lot back then."

As much as Sky loved Malcolm's big, close family, there were disadvantages to being a member of the Styles clan. This was one. The adult Styles knew about Sean's infidelity, which had to be hell on both Sean and Angie. From Sky's outsider perspective, she couldn't imagine being Sean and having to face the judgment of people he'd known for years. Yet he did, with a strength of character Sky couldn't help but respect.

Sean Franklin didn't self-flagellate, but he did take responsibility for his actions. In many ways, he reminded Sky of her mother. Both had refused to be defined by their poor choices, unwilling to allow the negative views of others to have them slumping their shoulders and slinking away in shame.

This time, when Angie answered her husband, she pitched her voice to a volume only Sean could hear. After a second, she picked up her fork and began eating what was left of her lemon meringue pie.

Undaunted by whatever she'd said, Sean leaned over and kissed Angie's cheek. He then lifted his eyes to those around the table and smiled. Not just any smile, but the kind that challenged while also offering reassurance.

Sean had earned the love and trust of the Styles. That was clear to see. He didn't want to lose either, Sky could discern that too. More telling, though, was their lack of animosity toward him. Even for a large, close-knit family, the Styles seemed to take a hands-off approach to interfering in each other's marriages, which Sky could appreciate.

"I went to last week's Bills' game," Charles said, his deep voice breaking the uncomfortable silence.

Whether Charles had deliberately changed the subject to a topic the Styles enjoyed and away from one that made the gathered crowd uncomfortable, Sky didn't know. But she didn't miss Sean's smile at the shift in focus from him to Charles.

Kim, seated to the left of her husband, looked at him from under beautifully long lashes and snickered.

"It's not funny."

"You didn't have to go."

"I did. It was a free ticket and a home game."

"Wait. What are you talking about, Dad?" Malcolm asked. "Where did you get free football tickets from and why am I just now hearing about it?"

What Malcolm wanted to know, because he was as much a football fanatic as his father and most every other member of his family, was how come Charles had received a free ticket, and he hadn't.

Men were so predictable.

Kim patted her husband's hand, mirth in her eyes. "The Bills played against the Patriots."

"I know. They kicked our team's butt. But how did Dad get tickets to the game?"

"Not tickets. Just one was mailed to your father, no forwarding address or note inside the envelope." Kim patted Charles's hand again and lowered her head to laugh. "He went by himself and came home mad as hell because the Bills lost. Your father cursed up a storm about Tom Brady." Kim's shoulders shook, and Charles snatched his hand from under hers. "Two days ago, a package with a New England Patriot's jersey arrived at the house. Tom Brady's number twelve is on the back and your dad's name is on the front."

Those gathered around the table laughed, especially Malcolm.

"Dad, you hate the Patriots. Why would you go see the Bills play if you knew they were playing their arch nemesis?"

"David and Goliath," Damon added. "I love my Bills, but damn, they have a five and twenty-nine record against the Pats. What were you thinking, Unc?"

"He thought the ticket was free and that the Bills would break the string of losses." Kim's headshake at her frowning husband only added to the laughter.

"None of you are true fans. If you were, you would've done the same thing."

"Ah, no I wouldn't have." Malcolm pointed to his father. "I bet you sat there for an entire game and watched the Bills take a beating, too stubborn to leave."

"Am I the only one who wants to know who sent Charles the ticket and jersey?"

Sean's question made sense, but the Styles were too busy mocking Charles, so no one answered him.

"Show us the jersey," Damon said. "Did you bring it with you?"

Two uncles and several cousins ambled into the dining room, having overheard part of the conversation.

"What jersey?" Malcolm's Uncle Curtis asked.

"Dad has a Tom Brady jersey."

"Why in the hell would you spend perfectly good money on that?"

"I didn't. It was a gift, just like the ticket to last Sunday's game."

Curtis, as tall as Charles but thinner around his middle and atop his head, frowned at his younger brother. "You saw the Bills play and didn't invite us?"

"It wasn't like that. I just told you, Curtis, I got one ticket for free. Just one. I went by myself."

"Why?" Tiffany asked, a twenty-year-old art student at The Copper Union for the Advancement of Science and Art. "We never watch the Bills when they play the Pats."

"I know but—"

Aunt Debbie, the rare Styles female as petite as Kim, snorted the way Sky had seen Angie do many times. "I knew it. You're an undercover Patriots fan. After all these years, the truth is finally out." She slapped her hand on the table. "Blasphemy, Charles. Traitor."

"It's a damn shame," Uncle Curtis added, "you traded in the majestic blue-and-red of our Bills for the red, blue, and silver of the Patriots."

"Nautical blue, red, and new century silver," Angie supplied, showing she was as much a shit-starter as she'd accused her father of being last month.

Uncle Curtis swore. "Nautical blue and new century silver. They aren't even real colors. Nautical blue, give me a break, Charles. You can't even swim."

"All of you need to calm the hell down. I'm a faithful Bills fan."

"Did you throw the jersey away?" Aunt Debbie challenged.

Kim dropped her forehead to the table, shoulders shaking.

"It was a gift. I couldn't just throw it away."

Malcolm eyed his father. "Why not? You didn't pay for it."

"Maybe not, but someone did. It looks expensive."

"Are you planning on selling it? Is that why you kept it?" Leave it to Malcolm to push, even his own father. "Because, from where I'm sitting, there are only two reasons for you to have kept Brady's jersey. One, you plan on selling it if the Patriots go to the playoffs or win the

Super Bowl again. Two, you've been sucked into the cult of Buffalo fans who secretly love the Pats. Which one is it, Dad? Money or cult?"

Everyone laughed, including Sky.

More and more Styles squeezed into the dining room, adding their thoughts to the growing humor and teasing.

"All of you shut up," Charles raged at his family, but no one listened, not even his wife whose eyes overflowed with laugh tears.

Rodney entered the living room, wearing a rust puffer jacket and a playful grin. "I wondered why there was a big New England Patriots helmet decal on your back window."

"No there isn't."

"Ah, yeah, there is, Uncle Charles. I saw it when I went to my car in search of Brandi's—"

"I've got to see this," Tiffany said, cutting her cousin off and whatever he'd been about to say about his four-month pregnant wife. Tiffany and Curtis ran from the room. A couple of minutes later they were back, shivering from going outside without their coats. "Big and silver, Uncle Charles. Right where Rodney said it was. There's also a decal on the driver's side window, both passenger windows and one on your bumper."

"Super Bowl LI Champions," Curtis scoffed. "I've never seen one Bills' sticker or decal on your car."

Pushing from his chair, Charles stomped from the dining room, followed by a round of laughter.

When he left, presumably to go outside and check his car for himself, every Styles' attention shifted to Sky. It was then she recalled Malcolm telling her no one in the family ever paid Charles back for anything he said or did.

She shrugged. "I sent Charles two gifts. All of you did the rest. And, well, I may have given decals to a couple of the teens to put on his car when they went outside to play."

The family gaped at Sky, and she wondered if she'd gone too far, especially when a growling and cursing Charles stormed back into the dining room.

"Which one of you assholes is messing with me? Curtis? Debbie? Malcolm?" Charles glared down at his hysterically laughing wife. "Kim?"

Methodically, dark eyes traveled from one face to the next, skipping over and dismissing Sky when he reached her and moving on to Faith, Damon's sister. After a circuit, he began again. This time, when he got to Sky, Charles stopped, scrutinized her impassive features, and then cursed.

"You've got to be kidding me. Cute and quiet, but with a devil inside." Charles clapped and laughed, before coming to Sky and lifting her into a bear hug. "You're a keeper." He set Sky back on her feet. "You hear me, son? I said the devil is a keeper."

"Yes, I heard you. As loud as you were, the neighbors heard you, too."

"Do you like rockfish, Sky?"

Why did most people who knew she was from Maryland assumed she loved everything about the panhandle state?

"I like rockfish well enough."

Charles hugged her again, his affection and good humor more than she expected but exactly as Kim had predicted. Sky had gone to the older woman, wanting to make sure her plan wouldn't upset or offend Charles. With much laughter and good cheer, Kim had reassured Sky, squeezing her cheeks and filling her with cherry pie before sending her home to set her plot in motion.

"Well, here we call it bass, and I'm one hell of a griller. Kim will tell you. There's a fish market I like not far from my house. Next time I'm there, I'll pick up a few bass. Malcolm will bring you over, and we'll have a nice dinner. How does that sound?"

"Like you want me to buy you a Bills jersey."

Charles grinned, his smile as boyish and dazzling as Malcolm's. "Christmas is next month, and you already know my shirt size, which means my wife, or my children will be getting coal in their Christmas stocking for helping you punk me."

An hour later, Sky escaped to Malcolm's upstairs bedroom for a private phone call. She would've taken the call in one of his two downstairs bedrooms, but they were filled with Styles. Most had crowded into the living room to watch the New York Giants at Washington. An overflow group of football fans had commandeered the largest of the downstairs bedrooms. The second bedroom, which Sky saw Zuri and Kayla dart into, was for the kids' quiet entertainment. She'd gone with Malcolm when he'd purchased PG-13 and G-rated movies for his young cousins and nieces, knowing they'd retreat into the room when the adults turned on the football game.

The teens not watching the game but uninterested in whatever movie the little kids had on, had claimed the basement. Sky had no idea what they were doing down there, but the basement was fully furnished and had a flat screen television, laptop with Internet access, and a game media cart she'd only seen Malcolm use once. Noticing how everyone, based on age, knew where to go and when, it wasn't hard to conclude they'd done this before, with Malcolm arranging his home with his family in mind.

The thought of her considerate boyfriend had her sitting on his bed and smiling at a framed picture of them on his nightstand. It was one of the pics the nice mother had taken of them under the Jane Pickens Theater's marquee. They were smiling, not at the camera but at each other. Malcolm's hands on her hips, and hers on his cheek, Sky had wanted to kiss him, so tempting were his lips. She'd refrained, of course. Kissing in public and in front of a small child wasn't Sky's idea of an appropriate romantic interlude.

Later that night, their interludes were romantic, but they were still inappropriate for others to see. It had been a great night. Sexapades indeed. Damon had been right.

Unzipping and slipping out of her black riding boots, Sky scooted to the head of Malcolm's bed and propped her back against the headboard, cell phone in hand.

"Did Robert ask you to call and plead his case?"

"I don't take orders from Dad. It's Thanksgiving, you're my baby sister, and we haven't spoken in two months."

Sky hit speaker and placed her phone on the thigh of an outstretched leg. Upstairs and behind a closed door, she no longer had to worry about not hearing or being heard by Carrie.

"Why do you insist on calling me that?"

"Until you came along, I was the youngest. It's nice having a baby sister."

"I'm almost thirty-six, which takes me decades out of the baby category."

"I'm forty-seven and going through my second divorce. If I want to call you baby sister, then dammit, let me."

"Have you been drinking?"

"A little."

"I'm sorry about you and Peter." Although Sky hadn't spent much time with her brother-in-law, she liked the Attorney General. Peter had kind, gray eyes and seemed devoted to Carrie and the children from her first marriage. "Is there anything I can do for you?"

"Don't you want to know what happened between us?"

"Only if you want to tell me. I'm not one to pry."

"Don't I know it. You not only don't pry, but you also don't reach out unless someone does first. You're caring, but don't share without a lot of prompting. You're straightforward when you need to be, but quiet and disengaged to the point of indifference and remoteness. Unlike me, you would make a perfect politician's wife."

"I thought we were talking about Peter, not your first husband."

"Same difference. Peter is considering running for Maryland's third congressional district seat. The boys and I suffered through a grueling senatorial campaign with Jacob, and he didn't even win. I have no desire to return to the political spotlight. But really, Sky, that was your takeaway from all I said?"

"Yes, I chose to ignore the rest. You're drunk."

She could hear ice hitting the side of a glass and the pouring of liquid.

"Tipsy, yes, but far from drunk. Come home for Christmas. Dad misses you, and so do I."

Carrie and Malcolm were of similar personalities. Both outgoing, tenderhearted, and pushy. They wore their hearts on their sleeves, which left them emotionally vulnerable and easily hurt. Yet, they possessed a fortitude matched by few.

Carrie was also the only one of Robert's children who'd befriended Sky. She'd never met her before the day of Sade's funeral. Yet, on the second worst day of her life, the thirty-one-year-old Carrie Ellis had moved to stand beside a weeping Sky at her mother's gravesite. She'd taken her hand and held it through Sky's deluge of tears. Afterward, she'd introduced herself and pulled Sky into a hug.

Motherless at twenty, Sky hadn't known how to respond to the unexpected entry of a sister into her life or to Carrie's kindness. She'd permitted the embrace, but her arms had felt frozen. They were locked in place, with Sky unable to lift them and return Carrie's warm affection. Sky had stood there, a weeping statue of grief and loss, swathed in the warmth of a stranger with her father's eyes.

Sky's eyes.

"Are you still there?" Carrie asked, her speech slow but not slurred.

"Yes."

"Overthinking everything, probably. Come home for your birthday and Christmas. The family wants to see you."

"Your sister and brothers want to see me? I doubt that."

"*Our* sister and brothers. We're a family."

"We've never been a family beyond the technical sense of having a father in common. I now think of you as my sister because you insinuated yourself into my life and wouldn't leave."

Carrie laughed. "You said that as if I'm a disease with no known cure. You're hard to get to know."

Sky knew that about herself. She had her reasons, most of which Carrie knew. It had taken her years to trust her sister and to open her heart to her, but she had.

"I'm grateful you didn't give up on me."

"Yeah, well, that's the family part you keep denying. Now stop being afraid and come home. If not for Dad's sake or yours, then for mine."

Sky stared at the phone before closing her eyes and leaning her head against the headboard. Over the years, she'd made too many decisions based on fear. After her weekend with Malcolm and the obvious effort he'd made this past month not to push the issue of marriage, she had come to an important decision.

If she wanted to free herself from her past, she needed to vanquish the source of her fear. More, if Sky wanted to marry and build a life with Malcolm without tainting it with her toxic past, she needed to face her demons.

Sky hadn't shared her decision with Malcolm and didn't like informing Carrie before him, but her sister had a right to know.

"I've already decided to spend my winter break at home."

"That's why I call you baby sister. Only a brat would put me through all of that instead of telling me your decision when I first asked. Bring Malcolm. I want to meet him. Dad says you're engaged, but I think that's wishful thinking. He wants to throw you a big, fancy Annapolis wedding."

"I would hate that, and I'm not engaged."

"I assumed as much. But Dad wants to stand in a church before God and the community, your hand on his arm as he walks you down the aisle—father and daughter."

When it came to Robert Ellis, he thought too much about his wants and not enough about the desires of others. He wanted to give her away to Malcolm during an extravagant wedding ceremony. Had the irony not occurred to him? He'd given Sky away once before. Was Robert so quick to do it again?

"He's done it twice with you and once with Olivia. I can't see how a fourth time would be different from the other three."

"Parenting doesn't work that way. Before you say Dad wasn't a parent to you, which I damn well know, you get my bigger point. Believe it or not, he's trying."

"I know."

"You can talk to me about anything. You know that intellectually, but I've never felt you believed me."

"You can't possibly want me to talk to you about my mother and your parents. We never have before. Not really."

"Do you want to know what it was like growing up in a household with parents whose silences were broken up only by their arguments? I'm sure at one point, Mom and Dad loved each other. At least that's what I like to think."

Sky had never wanted to know what life was like as a publicly recognized child of Robert Ellis. She'd imagined plenty but never questioned Carrie about her childhood, although she knew her sister would've shared.

"On the other side of pain is forgiveness, Sky."

"I know."

"You keep saying those two words. It's time to stop knowing and start doing. Coming home for Christmas is a good start. What do you want for your birthday? And don't say nothing."

"I haven't given it much thought."

Sky hadn't looked forward to Christmas and her birthday since her mother's passing. The last few years she'd spent the holiday away from home, choosing to hole up in a hotel or a resort in a city she and Sade had never visited.

No decorations or tree.

No presents or family.

She'd done that to herself, wallowing in grief and adding to her misery.

When Sky had moved to Buffalo, she'd pledged not to run away and hide from Christmas this year. What she hadn't counted on was meeting and falling in love with a man who seduced her with his sexy smiles, sensual kisses, and warm heart.

She slid down the bed and moved the phone from her thigh to her chest. "You tell me about Peter and your divorce, and I'll tell you about my trip to Newport with Malcolm and what I want for my birthday."

"Deal."

Cheers and shouting erupted from downstairs, which Sky assumed meant the Giants had scored another touchdown. They weren't the Bills, but they were a New York football team, which, apparently, was good enough for the Styles.

"What was that sound?"

Sky smiled. "The Styles. I can't wait for you to meet Malcolm."

CHAPTER NINETEEN

Annapolis, Maryland
Fifteen Years Earlier

The minute the surgeon walked into the family waiting room, face washed-out and eyes red, Sky knew what he'd say. She didn't rush from her chair over to the doctor the way her grandmother, aunt, and uncle did. She didn't listen to his soft, heartfelt words of apology and regret, the way her two cousins did. Her knees didn't give way at the news. She didn't nearly fall to the floor, the way her grandmother did, her uncle's supportive arms catching his mother but not his own tears.

Sky sat there, weighed down by the crushing knowledge of her mother's death. She couldn't be gone. They were supposed to go out to dinner tonight and take in a movie. She'd arrived home for spring break two days ago. After midterms, she'd been looking forward to sleeping late, hanging out with friends, and catching up with her mother.

"I'm sorry," she heard the doctor say. "I'm so very sorry for your loss."

He was sorry? For her loss? How many times, after failing to save the life of a patient, had the doctor uttered those same words? How many times did he have to walk from an operating room, knowing what he had to say would destroy a stranger's world? How did he sleep at night and get up the next morning, only to do it again and with no assurance another patient wouldn't die under his hands and urgent care?

How did he cope with the loss of life and his powerlessness to defeat death when it neared and challenged him for supremacy?

Sky's heart raced with a sharp pain. Sight blurred. Mouth dried. Body tensed, and head throbbed. People kept talking to her, touching her. Her soul leaked from her body, slithered away from her petrified form and out toward the hallway and light. If she followed, would her soul lead her to Sade's? Or would it find a corner and hide in the darkness of its depleted rays of hope. Her misery was too deep and forbidding, a life without Sade too vast and frightening to contemplate, her soul too puny to cope and her heart in complete distress.

Sky rose, and the hands holding her slipped away. The voice in her ear was familiar but not the one she craved.

"Sky, are you listening to me?" Sade would ask when Sky's mind got lost in a book or fixated on a problem. "Stay on this plane of existence with the rest of us," she'd say. "Don't travel to the stars and forget about me."

"Are you listening to me?" Uncle Kenny asked. "I said wait for me here. I need to get your mother's possessions then I'll drive everyone home."

Not stay there while I get your mother but stay while I claim whatever belongings Sade had on her when she'd been rushed into the emergency room. Uncle Kenny couldn't bring Sade home. They would have to leave her there. By herself in the sterile, cold hospital with people who neither knew nor loved her.

Looking down at her tennis shoes and not at her uncle, aunt, grandmother, and cousins, Sky wished she could travel to the stars, the way her mother had jokingly accused. If she could, if the trek were possible, no doubt she would find Sade waiting for her there. A smile on her beautiful face and a hug all for Sky.

She ran from the room. Sky didn't stop running, couldn't stop running. She ran until her lungs burned and her legs cramped. Then she ran farther, dragging her pain and loss with her. Her tears and grief were batons she passed from one hand to the other, tightfisted and focused. She carried them with her, heavy burdens she bore with a daughter's outrage and bone-deep sorrow.

A few blocks from her house but miles from the hospital that couldn't save her mother, a black sedan pulled alongside a huffing Sky. It stopped, and a man got out.

"You're drenched." The man stepped away from his double-parked car and onto the sidewalk in front of Sky. "Your grandmother is sick with worry. Get in the car and let me drive you home."

Sky lifted her sweaty face to the man she hadn't seen in months. She'd expected, well, she didn't know, but not this. Like the doctor, his eyes bore the distinct signs of stress and grief. Unlike the doctor, this man's eyes were red and puffy from crying.

"I know my way home, Captain, I don't need you to drive me there."

Sky pushed past her father, and he followed, his strides longer than hers. If she weren't so damn exhausted, she'd run and leave him behind. Why in the hell was he there, and how had he found her?

"Sky, it's dark, and you look as if you're going to drop where you are. Please, get in the car."

"I'm not going anywhere with you."

He overtook her and planted himself in her path.

She stopped. "Get out of my way."

"No. I left you once, I won't leave you again. Especially not when you're in so much pain. Jesus, Sky, I'm sorry about Sade. I couldn't believe it when Kenneth called, but he said he thought I needed to know."

"Why? You never cared about my mother, and you damn sure don't care about me."

Robert had reentered her life a few years ago. Why, after so many years, she didn't know.

"That's not true. I can see why you could believe that. But it's not true. I loved Sade, and I love you."

How could Robert Ellis, on the worst day of her life, stand in front of her and utter such cruel lies? If Sky didn't hate him before, she hated him now.

"I came looking for you. Kenneth wanted to do it, but he didn't want to leave Gloria. He never liked me, but he knows, as your father, I would want to make sure you're safe."

"You're *not* my father. You don't know the first thing about me."

"You're right, I don't know as much about you as I should. But I am your father, Sky. The only parent you have left."

Her palms shot out and pushed him—hard—in his chest, forcing the asshole to stumble backward.

"Sade was my parent. She loved and raised me. Wiped away my tears and made me laugh. Sat up with me when I was sick, attended report card and back to school nights. Mom drove me to track meets and theater rehearsals. She taught me how to drive and apply makeup." Sky shoved Robert again, with as much force as the first time. "College applications and essays, science fair projects, and oral reports, Mom helped me with them all." Another push. "Where in the hell were you when she was doing all of that?"

"Sky, please—"

"I'll tell you where you were. You were somewhere *not* being my father. Don't you dare, only hours after Mom's death, talk to me about being my parent. My only real parent is dead, and I wish it had been you instead of her."

Terrible, hurtful words her mother wouldn't approve of, but they were the truth, no matter how awful. If God had to remove someone from Sky's life, why not the man who never wanted to be a part of it? Why take the most important person from her?

"I'm sorry. What I said came out wrong. I just want to help."

"I don't want anything from you." Sky turned away from Robert. "I don't need you. I've never needed you. I've only ever needed her."

Now Sade was gone, leaving Sky alone with a broken heart and a shattered world.

Despite her body's protest, Sky ran toward a house that would never feel like home again and away from a father incapable of being a real parent.

Annapolis, Maryland
Present-Day

"It's nice to finally meet you."

Malcolm shook the extended hand of Dr. Kenneth Page, the sixty-year-old Superintendent of Anne Arundel County Public Schools and Sky's imposing uncle. The man weighed at least two hundred fifty pounds and couldn't have been shorter than six-two. Gray hair mixed with dark-brown, on both his head and full beard, neat and trimmed, as Malcolm would expect from a man of his professional bearing.

"It's nice to meet you, too, Dr. Page."

"Unless you want me to call you Dr. Styles, I suggest you cut out the doctor business and call me Kenneth or, like Sky, Uncle Kenny." The older man looked over Malcolm's shoulder to Sky, who'd retreated to the living room sofa of her childhood home after letting her uncle in. "Come over here, skinny, and give me another hug."

Pouting in a way Malcolm had never seen before, Sky sighed and rolled her eyes but pushed from the sofa. He couldn't see himself calling the man Uncle Kenny. Maybe when he got to know him better he would. For now, Kenneth would do fine.

"You've been away from home too long if you think to act like that and get away with it. Come here, girl." Kenneth wrapped beefy arms around Sky, his suit jacket stretching to within an inch of its life. "You don't call or visit enough."

"We talked yesterday and three days before that."

Could Sky breathe, pressed like that against Kenneth's chest? Was she turning red? Did she need him to rescue her? Shit, what was acceptable protocol when a man's girlfriend might be in danger of being crushed by her bear of an uncle?

"Like I said, you don't call enough. And I haven't seen you since the boys and I helped you get settled in that shoebox you call an apartment." Just when Malcolm thought he'd have to rip Sky away from her Kenneth, lest her uncle suffocated the poor woman, he let her go and stretched out his arms. "Five bedrooms and four full baths. Over fifty-six hundred square feet of house on almost two acres. Your apartment could fit into the three garages with room left over."

Malcolm shouldn't have been floored when Sky had driven the truck rental into an upscale Annapolis neighborhood, then turned onto a cul-de-sac and parked in front of a stucco design house, but he had been.

"You grew up here?" he'd asked, feeling off-balance at the unexpected luxury of Sky's home.

"Mom had the house built when I was ten."

"I thought you said your mother ran political campaigns."

Sky had also told him her mother had graduated from college at sixteen and had a "near-genius IQ."

"She did. Mom had an aptitude in several areas, financial investment being one." Sky had pointed out the SUV's window at the house. "She saw this home as an investment. We didn't need so much space, but she moved my grandmother in, which helped. My cousins visited, and I had friends over as often as Mom would allow."

Malcolm was ashamed to admit he'd unconsciously envisioned Sky's father with wealth but hadn't given Sade Page the same credit. He'd known Sky hadn't grown up in a household that lived paycheck to paycheck, like his. Yet, he'd fallen prey to the racial and gender stereotypes attached to older man, younger woman, and white male, black female relationships. The unequal power dynamics never boded well for the younger woman and black female. When both were put together, as in the case of Sade Page, the double whammy of racism and sexism blinded many, even an African American man who should've known better than to judge a black woman's social, intellectual, and financial worth by skewed and unfair standards.

Malcolm drew himself from the memory and refocused on Sky and Kenneth.

"What is with you and Robert? My apartment is great."

"It's a shoebox."

"It's not," Sky laughed. Going on tiptoe, she kissed her uncle's cheek. "This house is too big for one person. I stumbled around in it for two years after Nana died."

"I know you did. You could've sold it."

"I couldn't have. The house is too big to reside in alone, but it means too much to me to see another family living here."

"You can't have it both ways. A house like this is meant to be lived in, even if only for part of the year." Kenny glanced over his shoulder toward Malcolm. "If you haven't figured it out, Malcolm, that was me lobbing a ball into your court. Why aren't you down on one knee and proposing to my niece? You have my approval."

"He doesn't need your approval." Sky kissed Kenneth's cheek again. "You're terrible. You met Malcolm ten minutes ago, and you're already throwing your only niece at him. What if he's awful and no good for me?"

"Hey, how did I go from approved by uncles the world over to bubblegum on the bottom of your shoe?"

"Oh, yeah, I like this one."

"How many other ones have there been?" Malcolm asked, knowing Sky would hate the question but figuring her fun-loving uncle would love it.

Malcolm enjoyed watching the banter between Sky and Kenneth. He'd never seen her so animated with a family member. Well, he'd never seen Sky interact with a family other than his own. With Malcolm's sister and father, he'd glimpsed snatches of this playful, light-spirited Sky. But nothing on this scale.

"There were always boys calling or stopping by. They drove Sade crazy."

"I didn't date any of those boys."

"That's because your mother scared the holy hell out of them. She didn't need a gun to put the fear of God in those kids. Sade was a fire-breathing dragon momma."

"Mom wasn't that bad."

"Take a good look." Kenneth turned Sky to face Malcolm. "This is what a Page woman looks like when she lies."

"Cut it out. That kind of talk is why I haven't been home to visit. You're supposed to make a good first impression in front of Malcolm, not almost squeeze me to death and call me a liar."

"Have I made a bad first impression, Malcolm?"

"No, sir."

"You see."

"He's being polite. Malcolm only uses *sir* when he's trying to make a good first impression himself."

"I used sir twice with your father, and that was months ago. I can't believe you remember that."

"Sky remembers every damn thing, just like Sade used to. Too smart for her own good, that's what I've always said. But I'm glad Sky is home where she belongs."

"I'm not moving back here."

"Maybe. Maybe not. What are you cooking for dinner?"

"You can't be serious. Where's Aunt Yvette?"

"She'll be here soon enough, so will Brandon and Jeremiah, which means you better get to work."

"I thought we would go out to eat. There's no real food in the house, which means I'll have to go shopping."

"I know. You better leave now." Kenneth patted his extended belly. "I didn't have lunch. Unless you want me to pass out from low blood sugar, I suggest you get a move on."

"This is not how I planned on spending my first evening back. I'm supposed to be on vacation, not catering to your pudgy belly." Sky snatched her purse and keys from an antique gray console table. "Don't think I don't know what you're up to. I came home for Christmas and my birthday, not an engagement party. Malcolm and I have an understanding."

They did. Malcolm had promised not to propose on Sky's birthday. Which also meant no Christmas Eve proposal. He'd promised, and Malcolm would stick to their agreement. That didn't mean, however, he didn't have plans for Dr. Sky Ellis and their future together.

"I'm sure you do have an understanding. Don't forget, I'm on a low-sodium diet."

"You just said I remember everything, and you've made that same claim the last twenty years."

"It doesn't make it untrue. I'm also gluten-free."

"Since when?"

"Since you packed up and left the family. If you were still living here, you would know these things."

Sky glared at her uncle with a cute mix of love and annoyance. Malcolm understood. No one could get under the skin like family. Witnessing how easily Sky allowed her uncle to manage her revealed much about their relationship. She may not have had Robert Ellis growing up, but Kenneth was an admirable example of positive manhood. Every child needed that, not just boys.

Malcolm left the two of them in the living room and went to the closet in the foyer. He grabbed Sky's coat and waited for her by the front door. A couple of minutes later, she joined him, her approach silent without her high heels. When they'd entered the house for the first time, Sky had wasted no time removing her shoes and placing them in one of the shoe baskets near the front door. She was the same way with her Buffalo apartment, so Malcolm knew the routine, and had also removed his shoes.

Sky had to have a service which maintained her house and lawn. Spiderweb and dust-free, everything in Sky's home glistened to an expensive shine. Her lawn, manicured to perfection, had a curb appeal a realtor would die for. Kenneth was right, Sky could sell her home with little effort. Malcolm also knew she wouldn't.

"You're sweet. Thank you."

Malcolm helped Sky into a brown shawl-collar wrap coat and handed her the sexy black pumps she'd deposited earlier.

"You don't have to stay here and put up with Uncle Kenny's interrogation. For all his talk of Mom being a fire-breathing dragon, he was no better. Together, they were the reason I didn't have my first boyfriend until freshman year of college."

Malcolm stepped close and lowered his voice. "Your uncle must be behind me, and you just lied for his benefit because I damn well know you didn't wait until you went off to college to have a boyfriend."

"I'm insulted. What kind of young lady do you think I was?"

"One who wasn't a virgin when she went to college. Is he still watching us?"

"Yes. Is Uncle Kenny making you uncomfortable?"

"He's a big guy. I can see why your boyfriends steered clear of him."

"Not plural. One in this house."

"I don't believe you had only one boyfriend."

"You weren't talking about my high school boyfriends when you used the plural. You were fishing."

True. With Sade gone and a twenty-year-old Sky the sole owner of a high-class house, surely, she'd entertained men there.

Sky pressed a kiss to Malcolm's cheek, her mouth hot and close to his ear. "You've been in my bedroom, how many notches did you see on my bedpost?"

"That's not funny."

"I think it is. Don't worry, sweetie, you won't run into any of my former boyfriends or lovers while we're here."

"Still not funny, and step away from me before your uncle gets the wrong idea."

"Like we're sleeping together? He already knows. You answered my landline at six in the morning one day."

"Who in the hell calls someone so early?"

"An A-type personality superintendent who gets to work at seven and assumes his equally A-type personality niece is also up, which I always am. If you hadn't answered my phone, Uncle Kenny wouldn't now be scowling at you with murder in his eyes."

Malcolm swung around to face the older man, fumbling out apologetic nonsense, only to find an empty foyer.

Sky laughed, and he vowed to pay her back.

"Oh, baby, you have so much coming to you for that one."

Grabbing her by the tied belt of her coat, Malcolm yanked Sky toward him and straight into a kiss. Their mouths melded, and tongues played. Not too long, but enough to generate a buzz of anticipation for when Sky returned. With more members of her family due to arrive, however, he would have to wait to have more of her than a sensual but too short kiss.

Malcolm let her go with a final smack of the lips. "Drive safely."

Ever since Angie's car crash, he'd taken to delivering the same paranoid caution message to Sky. Her response, like his warning, remained unchanged.

"I will. I always do."

Malcolm watched Sky leave the house, get into the rental truck and drive away from the house. He locked the door behind her and then turned… to see Kenneth in the foyer.

Dammit. How much had he seen?

"You can't kiss a woman like that and not put a ring on her finger."

That answered his question.

"I have every intention of marrying your niece. You want to talk to me?"

"Of course. That's why I bullied Sky into going shopping for dinner."

"Good, I want to speak with you, too. You do know Sky let you do that. She doesn't do anything she doesn't want to."

"I've known that girl her entire life. I know her. It's nice to know you do too."

"Her mother was beautiful."

Kenneth followed the direction of Malcolm's gaze to a picture of Sade and an elementary school-aged Sky, which sat on a glass table in the foyer. They wore spring dresses, Sade's floral pink and Sky's light-blue and white. Sky held her mother's hand and smiled at the camera. Sade did more than smile. She laughed, at what Malcolm didn't know. Whatever it was, though, it lit up her face like a thousand shooting stars.

"That picture is from Easter Sunday when Sky was nine, maybe eight. My wife took the picture. She's a wedding photographer, for future reference. Anyway, Sky could always make Sade laugh. It's been too long ago now for me to remember what she said to her mother. But I recall how happy they were together. Even when they argued, they got over their disagreement quickly, and were back to laughing."

"Sky is terrible with jokes. Half the time I have no idea she's teasing."

"You're not wrong about her sense of humor, but the oddity of it was what made her so funny to Sade."

"Are you saying Sky would punk her mother?"

"As much as she could get away with. I'm surprised the girl made it out of childhood in one piece."

When Kenneth looked at the picture again, it was with a younger brother's sadness. The pain of Sade's passing was all too clear in the older man's dark eyes.

As lovely as the picture in the foyer was, the most striking image of Sade Page was on the fireplace mantel in the living room. She appeared a little younger than Sky was now. Whoever had taken the picture, perhaps Kenneth's photographer wife, had captured Sade's radiant joy at the newborn cradled in her arms.

Sky's childhood was displayed, with love and care, on the walls of her home. He'd passed many of the framed pictures when he'd carried their luggage upstairs. Sky, however, had strolled past them as if they were nothing more than paint on an old wall. Malcolm, on the other hand, had marveled at each one.

Too many memories lived on the walls of this house for Sky to ever sell her mother's home. She had misinterpreted Sade's use of the word investment. Sky's mother wasn't investing in the house for later financial gain. The investment was of a more personal nature. She'd used the home to invest in her daughter, offering Sky psychological safety, emotional support, and physical security.

"Sade was beautiful. Inside and out. It hurt like hell when she died. Sky was only a year older than the kid who crossed the median strip and slammed his truck into her mother's car. Booze and—"

Malcolm raised his hand, palm-up and facing Kenneth. "Wait, Sade died in a car crash?"

"Head-on collision. The surgeon did his best, but her injuries were too extensive for him to save her."

His hand dropped, and so did his voice. "I didn't know."

If he had, Malcolm would've never accepted Sky's offer to go with him to visit Angie at the hospital. No wonder she'd looked as if she would toss up her breakfast when she'd gotten there. Being in the hospital under the same circumstances that had claimed the life of her mother had to have been painful as hell.

"A few months ago, my sister was in a pretty bad car crash. By the time the family arrived at the hospital, she was already in surgery."

"Is she fine now?"

"Mostly back to normal, thankfully. But Sky came to the hospital and never uttered a word about her mother's car crash." He raised his head, unsure when he'd lowered it. "Why are you smiling?"

"Come back into the living room."

Malcolm followed Kenneth. Neither sat. Instead, they stood in the middle of the room.

"When Sky told me you would join her, I created a list of questions I wanted to ask you, then I practiced my best intimidation stance and glare."

"Sounds scary. Show them to me."

Kenneth Page must be on a first name basis with Charles Styles because the heavy-handed man brought his bear paw down on Malcolm's shoulder. Shit, with the strength of Hercules coursing through him, Kenneth didn't need an intimidating stance and glare.

"Don't you ever touch me like that again. Damn, your sons are probably three feet tall if you slapped their shoulders when they were growing up like you just did mine."

"What? That hurt?"

"Don't play innocent. I've done this with the best."

"Sky." Kenneth smirked and removed his meaty paw from Malcolm's shoulder "Yeah, my niece is the master. Even Sade found it hard to read her." Kenneth gestured to the sofa where Sky had been seated. "Sit down and let's have our talk."

They did, Malcolm on the sofa and Kenneth on the loveseat to his left.

"After the story about your sister and Sky visiting her at the hospital, I don't have to ask you any of those irrelevant questions I have in my pocket. Do you understand the significance of what she did?"

"I didn't until a few minutes ago."

"How many times have you told Sky you loved her?"

"A lot."

"How many times has she told you?"

"Two or three."

"Take the number of times you've verbalized your love for Sky, multiply it by a thousand and then double that amount. Trust me, whatever the total comes to still won't be greater than Sky's single act of visiting your sister at the hospital."

Not a single act. Sky had visited Angie many times after the first.

"Unless Sky absolutely must, like when her grandmother's cancer returned, and Mom was taken to the hospital, she avoids them. But she didn't with your sister. She pushed back her fear, for you, Malcolm. Sky runs away, not towards what frightens her."

"I know. She told me."

"She's also here to spend Christmas and her birthday with Robert and her siblings for the first time. Sky has never put in the effort to deal with her father and their past. Although I never liked the relationship between Sade and Robert, I respected the fact that Robert was Sky's father. I never tried to be anything more to Sky than her uncle. When she moved to New York, I gave up on them having a true father-daughter relationship. Robert can be a selfish jerk, and Sky holds a grudge like a pitt bull. She took the best and worst of her parents, even if she doesn't realize it. Sky doesn't love easily, but she does love deeply. All my planned questions wouldn't have gotten to any of that, but your story about your sister did. Now, what can I do to get a nephew out of this visit?"

Malcolm grinned and clapped his hands.

"You just realized she's been scamming you with her paltry two or three declarations of love."

Yeah, he would make Sky pay for that too. In the bedroom. Many times.

"Tell me about Sky and Christmas. She told me her mother would take her out of town."

"That's true, but Sade always went all out here before they left on their trip. My sister loved Christmas, even before Sky came along. My niece was almost named Noel."

"Perfect. I already have a couple of things in motion, which I'll tell you about. Do you have Robert's number?"

"I do. Is he part of your plan?"

They would all be part of his plan. Now that Malcolm had met Sky's uncle, he had an ally. Once he spoke with the others, he hoped to have more.

"Up until a month ago, I was positive Sky would turn her father's invitation down." Malcolm leaned forward, forearms going to his knees. "I don't know what changed her mind, but I do know she's apprehensive about spending Christmas with her estranged siblings."

"Sky has two sisters and two brothers, all much older than she is. Oldest to youngest, they are Garrett, Aaron, Olivia, and Carrie. Garrett, I believe, is fifty-four, old enough to be Sky's father instead of her older brother, if he'd had her at eighteen."

"Sky told me about Carrie but doesn't talk about the others."

"She never does. Not that there's much to say. Are they part of your plan, too?"

"Robert told Sky he wanted to spend the holiday season with all of his children. A first, apparently. The reason I asked about you having Robert's phone number is that my brother-in-law and Sky think I treat her as if she's already my wife. I can't say I totally disagree with them."

Kenneth slipped off his black suit jacket and folded it across the back of the loveseat. "I take it you don't have a problem with that."

"Not really. Sky thinks I'm not leaving any room for us to grow, but I disagree. There's plenty of room for growth, but she's also right. I'm not her husband yet."

"What's your dilemma?"

"I think part of Sky's anxiety about spending Christmas with her Ellis family is her lack of control. We're supposed to spend Christmas Eve at Robert's house and stay overnight so we can be there in the morning for Sky's birthday. I'm sure he has everything planned for Christmas and her birthday, down to catered meals and a professionally decorated Christmas tree."

Kenneth's reassuring nod and smile made Malcolm feel better about his idea. "You really do understand my niece. I think I know where you're going, and I like the way your mind works."

"I want Sky to be in full control and not at anyone's mercy. What better way to do that than to have Christmas in the home her mother had built for her? You said Sade loved Christmas and went all out for Sky's birthday."

"She did." Kenneth stood halfway, enough to lean over and shake Malcolm's hand. "I definitely like the way your mind works. The Pages haven't done what you're suggesting in years. Tell you what, I'll talk to Robert."

"I wasn't suggesting—"

"I know you weren't asking me to step in. You were seeking my opinion on the matter before proceeding with your plan. But Sky and your brother-in-law are right. Until you're officially Sky's husband, in certain areas, you must tread carefully. Dealing with her father and siblings is one of those areas. As her uncle, I have a long history with the Ellises, especially Robert. Honestly, I don't see him balking at the change in plans, even at this late date. He wants Sky happy. Even more, Robert wants a strong relationship with his daughter, which they've never had. If he thinks altering his plans will help him achieve his goal, he'll be here with bells on." Kenneth nodded at Malcolm again and grinned. "I mean literal Christmas bells around his neck. That's how much Robert Ellis loves his daughter."

With Kenneth's help, Malcolm felt confident he could pull off his plan and give Sky the best Christmas and birthday. He couldn't wait to get started.

Malcolm jumped to his feet. It was time to get festive.

CHAPTER TWENTY

"Tell me again why you're out with my uncle."

Sky handed Aunt Yvette another bag before returning to the rental truck to retrieve the rest of the groceries, cell phone in hand and pressed to her ear.

"Kenneth had an errand to run. I decided to keep him company."

"Why?"

"Because it would've been impolite to let him go by himself. Besides, you were out. I would've been in that big house of yours by myself."

She snatched another bag from the back of the truck. If she'd known Malcolm and Uncle Kenny wouldn't be there to help when she'd returned with the groceries, she wouldn't have purchased so many supplies.

"Remember the conversation we had about you, lies, and poker?"

"Okay, fine, I lied. Do you want to ruin the surprise? If you do, I can tell you what I'm up to right now and be done with the cloak and dagger stuff."

"Cloak and dagger?" Sky chuckled. "You're hilarious when you're pretending to be indignant. Keep your secrets, Malcolm." Handing her aunt another bag, Sky rushed outside again. Two more bags to go and she'd be finished. "Listen, I need both hands to carry the rest of the groceries into the house."

Lucky for Sky, her Aunt Yvette had used her key to let herself into the house and was waiting in the kitchen when Sky arrived. She could manage the heavy lifting, but it was nice to have someone to help her put the groceries away.

"We won't be long. I'll see you later. By the way, don't think I forgot about that trick from earlier with your uncle. Payback will be sweaty and loud. I hope you took your vitamins today."

Sky stumbled at Malcolm's words. Well, not his words so much but the sensual timbre of his voice when he said them. She licked her lips, her body already anticipating all the wonderfully wicked ways Malcolm could pay her back tonight.

Wherever Malcolm was, her uncle couldn't be close. If Kenny were, Malcolm wouldn't have made that comment. She heard talking in the background, and it sounded like Malcolm was outside. Where, she couldn't begin to guess.

"Promises, promises, Dr. Styles."

Fifteen minutes later, Sky and Yvette had the groceries put away and were sitting at the kitchen table drinking hot chocolate with marshmallows. Good thing both had a long shelf life because they'd been in the cupboard for months.

"What's Uncle Kenny up to?"

Her aunt, thin and tall at five-eleven, grinned at Sky over her eyeglasses. On days she had a wedding shoot, Yvette wore contact lenses. She also wasn't dressed as if she had come from or was planning to go to a wedding. Like Sky, she wore dressy jeans and a warm winter sweater. Unlike Sky, whose hair was pulled back into a twist knot, Yvette's was styled in an attractive side-swept design with bangs and curls. Not a gray hair in sight, despite her sixty-two years.

"Tell me about Buffalo and your new job."

"Come on, you know I don't like when you do that."

Yvette drank more of her hot chocolate, still watching Sky over her glasses.

"If you want to know about my relationship with Malcolm, don't take me around the Chesapeake Bay to get there."

"Okay. Tell me about you and Malcolm."

"No."

"What?"

"You heard me. I said no."

Sky watched Yvette with a straight face, unwavering and serious. She hadn't seen her aunt in too many months. They spoke on the phone, but not as often as Sky and her uncle. Sometimes, like today, her aunt forgot how much Sky enjoyed teasing her family.

"You're such a brat. I almost fell for that."

"You did fall for it, and I'm tired of being called a brat."

"You must've had a recent conversation with Carrie. How is she doing?"

"Carrie claims she and Peter are divorcing, but I'm unconvinced."

"Well, I hope they can work it out." Aunt Yvette placed her cup down, the spoon clanking on the saucer. "Okay, now for you and Malcolm. No one was here when I arrived, so I haven't met him yet. You love him, right?"

"Yes."

"Good. Show me." Yvette tapped a finger next to Sky's cell phone. "I'm sure you have pictures of Malcolm in there."

Of course, she did. Sky pulled up her gallery and scrolled through a dozen pictures, telling her aunt the story behind each one. When Sky finished, she noticed Yvette's eyes were on her and not the phone and the pic of Malcolm she'd taken when she'd found him sleeping on his sofa, head back and research for his latest book scattered around him.

Malcolm had looked so handsome and sweet, Sky couldn't resist taking the pic and then using her lips to awaken him. He'd jerked awake, a hand going to her hair and his hips surging upward.

"I thought I'd never see the day."

"What? It's just a picture of my boyfriend sleeping."

"No, not that. I never thought I'd see the day when you'd let a man win your heart so thoroughly."

"You mean the way Uncle Kenny won yours but the way my mother never let a man win hers after my father. Until Malcolm, I thought I was incapable of loving like this. The thought of giving my heart to someone and loving unconditionally terrified me."

"Oh, sweetheart, we all feel like that. That's when you know your feelings are real and directed at the right person. Loving a man is one-part trust and one-part faith. In yourself and in him. With time, both will grow, but they'll also be tested. That's life, love, and marriage, niece. All three can be terrifying." Yvette reached out and took Sky's hand in hers. "Thirty-seven years of marriage and two children and I'm still afraid sometimes."

"That you'll lose him?"

Not to another woman, Sky knew, but to stress and health issues caused by long work days and lack of exercise.

"Men don't listen, even when you tell them something for their own good. Did Kenneth tell you he's on a gluten-free diet now?"

She nodded.

"It's his new thing, like every weight loss program he's tried. He starts strong then peters out. I support him, the same way you'll support Malcolm when he tries to better himself, even if he's failed a dozen times before. Past failures, mine, Kenneth's, yours, Malcolm's, are the breeding ground for our fears. But your fears don't have to turn into a food desert for your relationship."

"I think I understand."

Food deserts were places, mainly in urban and improvised areas, that had few or no stores that sold healthy foods like fresh fruit and vegetables but contained a disproportionate number of fast food eateries and quickie marts. Sky's past failures and current fears, if left unaddressed, could deny her the healthy emotions every successful relationship required for sustainability and growth. Thus, creating a food desert for her relationship with Malcolm.

"I'm sure you do." Yvette picked up Sky's phone. "He's a good-looking man. The two of you will make beautiful babies."

Sky groaned and reclaimed her phone, placing it back on the kitchen table. "No one says stuff like that anymore."

"I just did."

"Well, don't say it when Malcolm's around. We have an understanding, and I don't want you and Uncle Kenny putting ideas in his head."

"You took a picture of your man sleeping. That's a different kind of intimacy for the watcher and pure vulnerability for the watched. Maybe you should be more concerned with the ideas in your head."

Leave it to her aunt to link Sky's actions to her deepest wish. She stood, went to the refrigerator and began pulling out items for their dinner. "Are you going to help me cook or continue to psychoanalyze me through my pics of Malcolm?"

Yvette picked up Sky's phone again, her thumb swiping to the left as she scrolled through more pics. "I can do both. Cook and—oh my god…"

Too late, Sky remembered the pics she'd taken of Malcolm the night of his birthday. She hadn't forgotten to pack the whipped cream for their trip. When it came to Malcolm, she preferred double chocolate, which was what she'd had when Sky spread chocolate whipped cream all over his… She caught the phone her aunt tossed her, Yvette treating it like a grenade she had to get rid of before it detonated.

Appropriate response because Malcolm had exploded that night, Sky licking every drop of the chocolate cream off him before straddling his waist and riding him to a roaring completion.

"From one woman to another, marry that man and erase those pictures from your phone." Fanning herself with her hand, she got to her feet. "Lord almighty, how do you get any work done with him around?"

"It's really hard," Sky confessed.

"Yeah, I saw. And long."

That wasn't what she'd meant. Sky closed her eyes, mortified on Malcolm's behalf. He'd kill her if he knew her aunt had seen his erect penis. Covered, thankfully, by the whipped cream, but still.

"Let's forget the last three minutes."

"I don't think I can. It's like looking at a solar eclipse directly. Your eyes aren't the same afterward."

They laughed, then set about making dinner. It wasn't long before Sky and Yvette fell into an old rhythm. Her aunt wasn't as good a cook as Sky's mother and grandmother, but she had learned a lot from Kenny, who was a better cook than them all.

Pot roast with baby carrots and chopped onions were in the oven cooking. Yvette prepared garlic mashed potatoes, while Sky skewered a green bean with a fork, tasting it for tenderness. A couple more minutes, they would be ready. Sky lowered the heat on the pan then went about putting together a Caesar salad.

"Do you want me to put the biscuits in the oven now or wait for everyone to arrive?" Yvette asked. "If I wait, they'll be nice and hot when we sit down for dinner."

Oven glove on, Sky removed the roast from the oven and placed it on a trivet mat on the island. "Who's everyone? I haven't heard from Jeremiah and Brandon since I've been back. I assumed it would be the two of us, Malcolm, and Uncle Kenny for dinner."

"Right, right. Do you think we cooked enough food?"

"We cooked enough food to feed—Was that the front door slamming open?"

"It sounded like it. You should go find out."

"I will. Why are you smiling? It could be a home invasion."

"A really loud home invasion. Go, go." Yvette shooed Sky out of the kitchen.

"Okay, okay, I'm going."

The closer she got to the foyer and the front door, the louder the scuffling grew. She heard Malcolm's and Uncle Kenny's voices before she rounded the corner.

"Dammit, I ripped my jacket," Kenny complained.

"That's because you're wearing what my father would call a smedium, which has nothing to do with whether you can literally fit into either of those sizes, but more to do with you squeezing into a too-small suit jacket."

"A small-medium for a big man," a third voice said, deep laughter following the mocking statement. It was Brandon's voice. "Malcolm got you there, Dad. We told you to take the suit jacket off."

"And to start exercising more. Listen to you. You're carrying one little bag, and you're huffing."

Jeremiah too.

Sky stopped at the end of the foyer, mouth agape at the sight down the hall.

Uncle Kenny indeed carried a single bag, but it wasn't small. He had it slung over his shoulder, reminding Sky of Santa Claus before he slipped into his red suit. To Kenny's left was Brandon, his youngest son. Of her cousins, Brandon looked the most like Yvette, although Jeremiah took after his mother, too. They had their father's booming voice and affinity for facial hair, which hid most of their handsome appearances. But their frames were slim cut and long like Yvette's. They weren't as tall as their father but certainly taller than Malcolm, who she didn't see.

Brandon held two plastic storage bins in his arms, as did Jeremiah. She recognized the bins, although she hadn't seen them in a few years. How in the hell had they grabbed those from the garage without Sky and Yvette hearing them?

"Would you giants get out of my way?"

"I told you we'd help carry it," Brandon said, looking over his shoulder and laughing.

"I don't need your help. I just need the three of you to move out of my way."

She heard Malcolm's voice but still didn't see him. Not until he pushed past her cousins and uncle, side swiping them with a few branches protruding from a bound... tree. A Douglas Fir, if she wasn't mistaken.

"It took you forever to find the tree," Kenny complained.

"I wanted the perfect one."

"Then you should've picked one of the pre-cut Frasier Firs. They were nice."

Malcolm, holding what had to be a heavy tree on his shoulder, lowered it to the floor, his back to Sky, the tree upright between his steady hands.

"I wasn't going to buy Sky a tree chosen and cut down by another man. I could've left my good clothes on if that's all I was going to do."

Shocked at seeing Malcolm stroll into her house with a Christmas tree, Sky only then noticed he'd changed from his dress slacks, button-up shirt, and dress shoes into hiking boots, jeans, and an insulated hoody jacket.

Jeremiah plucked fir needles off Malcolm's shoulder. "Sky wouldn't have known the difference."

"I would've known. My gift, my way, for my Sky. Now, will one of you get her so she can tell me where she wants me to put her tree?"

All three Page men nodded toward Sky, who'd inched closer on stockinged feet, while Malcolm spoke to her family as if he'd known them for years.

Brandon and Jeremiah dropped the storage bins they held and enveloped Sky in two breath-stealing hugs. They might not be as large as their father, but they certainly hugged like him.

Brandon picked her up. "It's about time you brought your butt home."

"Put me down, you hairy beast."

"Not a chance."

Brandon ran his scratchy beard over her face, ignoring her squeals of protest. As if Sky weighed nothing and wasn't an actual person but a lifelike doll, Brandon passed her to Jeremiah. At least he kissed her cheek, but his beard was pricklier than his brother's.

"You're not mountain men," Sky griped as Jeremiah placed her on her feet. "I'm getting you all razors for Christmas. I can't believe I'm related to Sasquatch. Two of them." Sky peered around her cousins and to her uncle and amended, "Three of them."

"Yup, that mouth. You're back." Brandon hugged her again, draping his big body over hers and whispering, "Except for the long, girlie hair and earring, Jeremiah and I like him. Malcolm cut down a tree for you."

"I heard."

Sky kept her face and voice neutral. If she didn't, if she permitted her cousins to see how affected she was by Malcolm's unexpected and heartwarming gift, they would harass her mercilessly.

Brandon squeezed her tighter. "I haven't met a woman I'd cut a thorn from a rose for, let alone a big ass tree."

Sky laughed. "I'll make sure to tell your wife when I see her."

"I'll deny it, and she'll believe me. Unlike you, Crystal likes my beard and tight hugs." Brandon let her go. "Where do you want the tree? The old spot?"

"Yes. Thank you."

Jeremiah hefted his crates back into his arms. "I think I have the tree stand in one of these bins. Come on, Brandon, let's take these to the living room and move the furniture aside for the tree. Dad," he called over his shoulder, "put the bag down. I'll come back out and get it."

"I can manage. It's only decorations and lights in here. I'm not that old or out of shape."

"Whatever you say, Dad. Malcolm, give us a few minutes then bring the tree down. Sky, we'll need a knife or scissors to cut off the netting and a big bowl of water for the tree. Okay, men, the quicker we get the tree up, the quicker we can eat whatever Mom and Sky cooked that's got this house smelling so good."

Burdens in hand, the Page men moved to do just that.

Sky's attention shifted to Malcolm. She looked from him to the seven-foot tree in his arms. He held the fir with gentleness and pride, his locs out and down his back, random needles between the twists.

Malcolm looked sexy as hell. If he were a mountain man who lived on a bluff, Sky would become a mountaineer, so much did she want to climb him right now.

"You cut down a tree for me for Christmas."

The evidence of his gesture of love sent a familiar heat to her core... and to her heart. How could one man be this thoughtful?

"Do you like it?"

"More than I can say. Thank you."

Sky had assumed, with it being only a day before Christmas Eve and them spending tomorrow night at Robert's instead of there, it wouldn't make sense for them to buy a tree. She'd resigned herself to going another year without decorating for the holiday. She thought she'd convinced herself she didn't need any of the normal Christmas cheer in her home. Seeing Malcolm, strong of body, as well as spirit, cart in a tree bigger than himself, Sky was woman enough to admit when she was wrong.

For the first time since deciding to return home for Christmas, Sky wasn't plagued with uncertainty. Thanks to Malcolm and whatever plans percolated behind his gorgeous eyes, Sky was beginning to get into the Christmas spirit.

His smile, radiant and self-satisfied, glowed brighter than the lights she would string from the tree he'd cut down for her.

"How many Christmas coupons does this earn me?"

Teary-eyed, she laughed. "A lot."

The coupon book was in the Christmas stocking she'd given Malcolm two days ago, along with a host of sexy items for bedroom play Sky hoped to begin using tonight. Because, if she knew Malcolm, he'd packed the contents of the stocking in his suitcase.

"Twenty kisses not on the lips?" he asked.

"Yes."

"Full body massage?"

"Most definitely."

"Surprise oral sex?"

"I do that already."

"True." He smiled. "Home-cooked chocolates?"

"That's not in the coupon book." She stepped closer and kissed him. "You smell like outside, dirt, and trees."

"Does that I mean I get my home-cooked chocolate?"

"Oh, yes. In bed. Tonight." She'd have to make another run to the grocery store. "You're so sweet." She kissed him again. "And romantic." Another kiss. "And sappy as hell."

The tree fell to the floor when Malcolm took hold of her waist, and Sky stepped over it, so she could press her body against his.

"I thought of a coupon you could redeem now. Get the tree and come with me."

He did.

Sky led Malcolm to the living room, making a detour to the kitchen to grab a pair of scissors. True to his word, Jeremiah had rearranged the furniture in her living room, making space in the far corner of the room and near a window, for the tree.

Malcolm removed the netting and, with Brandon and Jeremiah's help, secured the tree in the stand.

Aunt Yvette brought water for the fir, which led to an awkward introduction to Malcolm who, thank goodness, didn't seem to notice.

Sky grabbed Malcolm's hand. "The food is ready. You guys can get washed up and then sit down for dinner."

Pulling Malcolm along, she began her retreat.

"Where are you going?" Uncle Kenny asked.

"We'll be right back. I'm taking Malcolm to the basement. There are a few of my favorite decorations from Mom I want him to bring up for me." She stopped and held the gaze of her uncle, who seemed as if he wanted to question her more. "You can either begin without us or wait for our return. I'm not exactly sure what box the stuff is in so it may take me a few minutes to find what I'm looking for. If you don't mind waiting to have your dinner, we'll—"

"No, no. With all the crap Sade kept in that basement, who knows how long it'll take you. I'm hungry, and Yvette said something about pot roast."

At the mention of food, Kenny's stomach growled.

"Pot roast sounds good to me." Brandon blew past Sky and Malcolm. "Come on, Jeremiah, let's cut into the roast before Dad gets it."

That was Sky's cue to leave. All but dragging Malcolm behind her, she strolled from the living room, down a short hall and toward a door that led to the basement.

She turned on the light at the top of the stairs. Sky had the basement cleaned and organized years ago. Her mother did have pack-rat tendencies, but Sky knew where everything was, including Sade's old Christmas decorations.

At the bottom of the stairs, Sky pulled Malcolm to her and flicked off the light.

"Quickie coupon redemption," she mouthed against his neck, the vein there jumping, the skin salty from sweat and delicious under her tongue.

"You're crazy. Your family is one floor up."

He said that, but his hand went to the belt and button of her pants, tugging until he had her jeans and panties around her ankles.

Sky wasted no time returning the favor, unable to see Malcolm but knowing exactly where he was and where to touch him.

They moaned into each other's mouths, grinding against each other, her lower half on fire and aching for more contact.

Sky walked them deeper into the basement, their movements slow and cautious with clothing around their ankles. She bumped into a table and stopped. It would do.

Holding Malcolm's hand, she turned, her front facing the table.

278 · N.D. JONES

"Damn, a quickie from behind." One hand on her hip, the other rubbed his hard, thick arousal between her lips and over her ass. "You're so bad, and this quickie is going to be so good."

Malcolm slipped between her wet lips, sliding in, easy and deep.

Sky's head dropped forward, and she moaned. Yes, so good.

Fingers dug into hips and pelvis slammed against her ass. Hard, fast thrusts had the table rocking, Malcolm grunting, and Sky swallowing her moans. At this intense rate, they would beat their quickie record.

"Shit, baby, you hold me just right. Feel so good." A hand left her hip and found her clit. "It's right there waiting for my touch. Enlarged and firm."

He stroked, and she whimpered.

"When everyone's gone home, I'm going to strip you naked, spread you open for me, and suck this into my mouth."

The entirety of his hand palmed Sky's sex, a firm up and down stimulation that had her moaning and bucking against his hand and the rapid thrust of his dick.

They came. Sky first, and then Malcolm.

Forehead against her back, Malcolm rubbed circles on her lower abdomen, his touch soothing, their bodies still joined.

The basement door opened, letting in a stream of intrusive light.

"Sky," Brandon yelled from the top of the stairs, "I hope you're finished fucking Malcolm because your father is here, and he wants to see you."

CHAPTER TWENTY-ONE

A tall, lean white man stood from the dining room table when Sky and Malcolm entered the room. Beyond having seen the seventy-seven-year-old man from newspaper stories and old video clips from his time as Maryland's governor, Malcolm would've recognized Robert Ellis as Sky's father.

They looked nothing alike, and not because of the color of their skin. Sky simply resembled her mother in face and form. He loved Sky's eyes, a magnificent mix of light-brown and green. Her one physical inheritance from her father, who stared at Sky when she approached him, happiness in the orbs that matched his daughter's.

"There you are. I'm so glad you came home for Christmas." Robert reached out, fingers long and thin, and found Sky's shoulder. "I missed you." With a curl of his hand, he pulled her to him, wrapping Sky in a one-arm embrace.

He'd seen the other men in Sky's life give her a welcome home hug, but none like the one from Robert. Kenneth's embrace overwhelmed due to the sheer size of the man, while Brandon's and Jeremiah's were full of fun and humor. Robert's, however, came off as desperate and needy, if not a little nervous and sad.

When Brandon had informed them of Robert's arrival, Sky had gasped her shock then bolted to the basement bathroom to clean herself up, leaving him to grab the first bin he saw marked Xmas Decorations. In retrospect, Malcolm should've told Sky he'd invited her father to her home. Not just her father, her siblings too.

Two blonde women sat at the large dining room table behind Robert. One waved at him, her smile toothy and wide, while the other watched Robert and Sky, her expression as impassive as any he'd seen from Sky. Again, the olive hazel eyes gave the women away. Except for that singular definable feature, Sky didn't resemble a single member of her Ellis family. Then again, she also didn't look like Brandon and Jeremiah.

Sky returned her father's affection with her own. No matter how much the older man drove Sky crazy with his overbearing ways, love was one of the few emotions that could compel a daughter to leave her family behind. Hate could also drive a family apart, but that emotion wouldn't have Sky taking a job in another state and packing her bags for Buffalo.

Sure, Malcolm had no doubt Sky thought her more negative feelings toward her father the motivation for her exodus. But he'd spent three hours with her uncle and cousins. He'd also met her aunt, brief as it was. They were wonderful people who loved Sky. More, she loved them. Her family connection with the Pages was strong and rewarding. Strong enough not to disintegrate if a lamb left the flock.

He'd once read that distance could heal and save relationships doomed to failure with proximity. Seeing them together, Robert overjoyed to have Sky home but also clingy in a way that, if she were there all the time, would drive a deep and permanent wedge between them, Malcolm understood Sky's decision to move away from home.

Whether she knew it or not, her leaving was the best response to her father's need to make amends, which had amounted to smothering. Sky's move to Buffalo may have saved her relationship with Robert. Of course, Malcolm could be wrong, viewing the father-daughter relationship through an uninformed lens and drawing incorrect conclusions.

"Hi, I'm Carrie."

The woman's sudden appearance in front of Malcolm hadn't frightened him, but he certainly hadn't seen her move away from the table and toward him.

Malcolm stared down at Carrie. "Sky's sister."

Carrie beamed at Malcolm as if surprised he knew who she was. Sky may not talk much about her Ellis family or mother, but she'd opened up more to him about her siblings this past month. In her mind, she was preparing him for her family. In his mind, her willingness to share was yet another wall she no longer wanted between them.

Malcolm understood, more than ever before. After the first day of his birthday weekend, he'd stopped waiting for the words and started listening to her actions. In Sky's case, actions truly did speak louder than words.

Carrie extended her hand to him.

Malcolm looked at it, started to lift his hand for the shake, and then dropped it back to his side when he remembered where his hand had been minutes before Brandon had called them upstairs.

Okay, this was awkward. Malcolm couldn't explain, to a seemingly very nice woman, why he couldn't shake her hand.

His eyes skidded to Sky for help, but she was in the middle of a stilted conversation with Olivia, her oldest sister by thirteen years. More than that separated them, though.

"Um, I, um, haven't had time to wash my hands yet. I cut down a tree for Sky's birthday, and my hands are dirty."

He'd worn gloves the entire time he was out. He'd only taken them off after he'd adjusted the tree in the stand.

"Oh, no worries."

"I'm going to, you know, go wash my hands. I'll be right back."

Malcolm turned and sprinted from the room, certain he heard Brandon and Jeremiah laughing. Those guys could've helped him out. They damn well knew what he and Sky had been doing in the basement, even if Kenneth and Yvette didn't.

By the time he'd returned, everyone was seated at the long table. There was only one chair left which, to his annoyance, wasn't next to Sky. He met her gaze from across the table, appearing no happier than he to be squeezed between her father and uncle, both of whom were trying to have separate but simultaneous conversations with her.

His Sky, never one to shrink from a challenge, managed both men the way she did members of the Diversity Progress Committee, with patience and skill. She smiled, nodded, and answered in short responses, which meant she half listened and tossed out the rest of what they said.

Her brothers hadn't arrived, and Malcolm wondered if they would show. He'd been within earshot when Kenneth had called Robert and invited him and his grown children to Sky's home for dinner. Robert had agreed to pass along the invitation. At least two of Sky's siblings had gotten the message and accepted the invitation to the family dinner. Until he knew otherwise, Malcolm wouldn't assume her brothers were MIA because they were assholes who couldn't look past Robert's affair with Sade and treat their youngest sister as an equal and valued member of their family. If they felt that way about Sky, it would be best they stayed away. He hadn't flown to Maryland to get into an altercation with Sky's brothers, which would damn well happen if one of them hurt or disrespected her.

Malcolm was far from an introvert, and his parents hadn't raised him to sit at a table, even among strangers, and not extend himself in conversation. He turned to Carrie. "You chose this seat deliberately, didn't you?"

"I want to know more about the man who's stolen my baby sister's heart." Carrie pointed to Olivia, who sat to his right. "You want to know more about us. That's why we're here, right?"

"Dr. Styles couldn't care less about getting to know us. Tonight is all about Sky. Everything is always about Sky."

Okay, Malcolm had stepped into the middle of a family argument. Olivia, her words rough and raw, eyes jealous flints that watched her father and Sky, wasn't wrong. On a personal level, Malcolm didn't give a damn about Sky's siblings beyond how they treated her. He wasn't looking for more friends and family. He had enough of both. Sky's cousins were awesome, which was great. Even if they weren't but loved and treated Sky well, he would deal because they came with the Sky Ellis package. Robert and Carrie were also part of Sky's family package. The forty-nine-year-old woman who hadn't gotten over whatever shit she felt about her father's affair and Sky's birth wasn't.

"Be nice," Carrie warned Olivia.

"I am. Dad asked, and I'm here. But look at him. He does this every time she's around. He forgets about us and acts as if Sky's his only daughter."

Malcolm listened as the sisters, in low tones, argued, with him stuck between them. He tried, very hard, not to interject, but every word Olivia spoke grated. He couldn't fully enjoy his dinner. Sky and Yvette had cooked a delicious meal. Carrie and Olivia's conversation, however, gave him heartburn.

"You do realize," he whispered to Olivia, in a low, angry voice that stilled whatever she'd been about to say to Carrie and had her eyes shifting to him, "the way you feel, ignored and cast in the background, when Robert is with his youngest daughter, is how Sky's felt most of her life. Your irrational and selfish jealousy doesn't compare to how she felt growing up without an active father and shoved to the margins of Robert's life. None of us asked to be born, and no one has control over the circumstances of their birth. How many Christmases have you spent with your father? How many birthdays? Valentine's Days? Hell, Groundhog Days? High school graduation, did he attend? Prom, did Robert see you in your pretty little dress, meet your pimply-faced date, rent you a limo for the night?"

"You don't know—"

"You? Your life? Maybe not, but I know what it's like to have a dad in the home. I know everything I asked you about my father did with my sister. He was there. For every holiday, big and small, Dad was there. For every scraped knee and embarrassing kid moment, my dad was there for my sister and me. Can you sit here, with a straight face, and tell me Robert wasn't there for you, Carrie, and your MIA brothers?"

Olivia lowered her eyes and didn't answer him. Malcolm didn't like her, neither her arrogance nor her insensitivity. If he had to give Olivia credit for anything, it was for showing up tonight. Beyond that, the woman could go kick rocks.

"Your sister is an amazing woman. I don't say that because I'm trying to convince you to open your arms to Sky and to be a real sister to her. I said it because I want you to know what your closed heart and mind have cost you."

Olivia said nothing, but she did raise her head and meet his eyes. Their gazes held for several seconds before she resumed watching Sky and Robert while she finished her dinner.

Dammit, why in the hell had Malcolm invited Sky's siblings? He knew why, but he'd also been naïve. One Christmas and one meal wouldn't be enough to mend the decades-long rift in the Ellis family.

Carrie's soft hand covered his and squeezed. "You have a good heart. Sweet and kind. Sky told me that about you." She squeezed his hand again. "Does Sky also know how protective you are of her? That, behind your bleeding heart and charming smile, is a lion unafraid to use his fangs and claws in her defense? Should I call and warn my brothers to beware of Sky's lion king?"

"It depends. Do your brothers harbor animosity toward Sky?"

"Not animosity. But they're loyal to Mom."

"Treating Sky as a sister wouldn't make them disloyal to their mother."

"I know, and I've told them the same. I'm surprised Olivia is here. This is a first for her. Despite her attitude, she's not a bad person, Malcolm, and she doesn't dislike Sky. It's just emotionally complicated. For all of us. But you're as sweet as Sky said you were."

"So are you. Thank you for coming." Malcolm claimed the hand on his and shook it the way he hadn't earlier. "It's nice to meet you. I look forward to getting to know you better."

"And I'm looking forward to being Sky's Matron of Honor. Well, Maid of Honor, if I'm divorced by then. Peter and I have a… well, that's complicated too. But you get my point."

Malcolm did. Carrie thought he and Sky would marry, which was his wish, a present he couldn't wait to unwrap.

Brandon pushed from the table, a half-eaten biscuit in his hand. "Are you guys ready?"

"Let me get dessert first," Jeremiah said, "then I'll be right with you guys. Dad, are you having dessert first?"

Kenneth looked at the apple pie in the center of the table with something akin to lust. "No, I'm cutting back." He stood. "Malcolm? Robert?"

"I'm coming." Malcolm also stood. For a second, he thought about excluding Olivia but thought better of it. "We're going to decorate Sky's birthday and Christmas tree," he said to the gathered group. "We're also going to decorate the house, which includes the outside and front lawn. Since it's dark, those of you who can come back tomorrow morning, we can do the front of the house then."

Everyone, except for Sky, stood, even Olivia, which shocked the hell out of Malcolm. They began talking, all at once and loudly. Somehow, they managed to divide themselves into two teams, with Brandon leading the group responsible for decorating the tree and living room and Jeremiah the group who'd assigned themselves the porch and foyer. Before he knew it, everyone had collected their plates, glasses, and utensils and taken them in to the kitchen. Within minutes, the dining room had cleared, leaving only Malcolm and Sky behind.

Sky hadn't moved, except to watch her family evacuate the dining room.

Malcolm walked around the table and sat next to her. "What's wrong? Are you upset with me for inviting your father and sisters without discussing it with you first?"

"No, I—"

"I just thought you'd feel more comfortable if everything took place here. We don't have to stay at Robert's house for Christmas Eve. I know you weren't looking forward to doing that, anyway. So, I thought they could come here, and you'd host."

"Malcolm, I—"

"I know I should've run all of this past you, but I wanted it to be a surprise. A good surprise, I'd hoped. But then your brothers didn't show, and Olivia has a chip on her shoulder. Carrie is nice, though, so that's a plus. Your dad was also happy to see you, another plus. I didn't get a chance to talk to Robert but I'm sure—"

Sky kissed Malcolm, shocking him into silence.

He returned the kiss, hands going to her waist and pulling her onto his lap. "You're not mad?"

"I'm feeling so many emotions right now, but anger isn't one of them." She pinched him.

"Ow. What was that for?"

"I wanted to make sure this is real."

"I think you're supposed to pinch yourself."

"I know I'm real, but sometimes, like today, like now, I'm not sure if you are." She pinched him again. "You definitely are."

"Stop doing that."

"I'm sorry," she laughed, "but you're too good to be true. I think you sprang from a fantasy romance novel and right into my life. An epic hero who slays the dragon, rescues the damsel-in-distress, and wins her heart."

"You're no damsel-in-distress. If you were, you wouldn't be the right woman for me. I like my heroines with backbone and bite." Hand around nape, Malcolm lowered Sky's head for another kiss. "You know how much I enjoy your bites." Sky shivered in his arms, so he kissed her again. "You're happy? Did I get it right?"

"You make me happy."

Not what he'd asked, but she'd answered the more important question.

He kissed her again. "Is that music?"

Sky smiled against his lips. "Nat King Cole's _The Christmas Song_, a favorite of Mom and Uncle Kenny's. He has a CD of Cole's best Christmas hits, so be prepared to get your fill tonight."

"I like Cole's music, but I like your smile better."

"You're giving me Christmas. A present I didn't ask for and didn't know I wanted until today. I... I..."

Malcolm kissed her, knowing Sky didn't have the words. The tongue in his mouth and the hand over his heart were expressions enough.

"Come on, not again." Brandon stood in the doorway between the kitchen and the dining room, arms crossed over his chest. "I told Jeremiah the two of you were in here making out. I should've bet money on it."

"Malcolm's coming." Sky climbed from his lap, embarrassment in the eyes that met her cousin's. "I have to make a quick run to the grocery store."

"Why?" Brandon asked before Malcolm had an opportunity to pose the same question. "It's dark and late."

"It's dark but not that late. I promised Malcolm a special treat. I need to go out to get the ingredients."

"A special treat, huh?"

Malcolm got to his feet. "Yeah, a special treat." He laced his fingers through Sky's. "Brandon's right, though, it's dark. Unless someone goes with you, I'd rather you not drive to the store by yourself. People get extra crazy this time of the year."

"I'll ask Carrie and Olivia to go with me." A hand came to his cheek, soft and warm. "I'll drive safely, Malcolm. Don't look at me with those worried eyes of yours."

Malcolm heard, rather than saw, Brandon retreat.

"Were you ever going to tell me about your mother's death?"

"In the beginning, no. I considered it when Angie got hurt but thought better of telling you when I saw how torn up you were."

"What about after she was released from the hospital and was on the mend?"

Sky's hand stayed on his cheek, thumb stroking back and forth. "In some ways, you're like my father. No matter how many times I tell you not to worry, you do. You're still dealing with almost losing your sister in that awful car crash. I know how long it takes to get over something like that. Telling you how my mother died, even months after Angie's car crash, wouldn't have done anything but increase your anxiety. I see it in your eyes every time I drive away."

Her thumb rose, slid over an eyebrow, down his nose and to his lips, chin, and throat.

He swallowed at the gentle caress and the look of empathy in Sky's eyes.

"I'll never tell you anything I think will hurt you, not if I can help it. It took me a year after she died before I could enter my mother's bedroom. When I finally mustered the courage to go inside, I couldn't go farther than a few steps. I knew she was dead and not coming back, but it was so hard to accept moving on without her. It took me another six months before I could make myself pack her things." Long fingers settled against the pulse point of his neck, soothing and reassuring. "You're still grappling with the realization of your sister's mortality."

"I'm thirty-seven, I know people die."

"I know you do, but you know it differently when it hits you close to home. All your love and worry for Angie was here." Sky's hand touched his face again. "We've talked about it once, but only once because the thought of how close you came to losing your sister hurts you too much."

"You know my pain because you've experienced much worse and at a young age." Malcolm removed the hand on his cheek and placed it over his heart. "I don't want you protecting me at the expense of your own heart. You shouldn't have gone with me to the hospital after Angie's accident. That had to bring up painful memories of your mother."

"It did, and I didn't have to go. But I wanted to be there for you, and for Angie. It's been fifteen years since Mom's death, and there isn't a week that goes by I don't think about the life taken from her. But Mom's gone, Malcolm, and I'm still here. She wouldn't want me using her death as an excuse to avoid emotional commitments, which I've done for too many years. I don't want to live like that anymore."

Malcolm wrapped his arms around Sky. The woman didn't speak her heart often but when she did her words sounded like bells from heaven. "I love you. Happy almost Christmas Eve."

"I love you, too. Happy National Pfeffernüsse Day."

Malcolm set Sky from him. "You had to ruin the moment, didn't you?"

"What? I didn't ruin anything. It's a perfectly valid holiday for December twenty-third."

"If you live in Germany, Denmark, or the Netherlands."

"Come on, tasty small cookies. That's a perfect Malcolm holiday. No chocolate, but cookies. You like cookies."

"Do you know how to make pfeffernüsse or where to buy them?"

"No."

"That's what I thought. You're screwing with me again, and not the way I like."

Malcolm walked away from Sky.

"I could've gone with HumanLight Day. That's also celebrated on December twenty-third. Ah, come on, sweetie, where are you going?"

Malcolm could hear her laughing at him. If he didn't know better, he'd swear Sky researched obscure holidays just to annoy him. He halted in the hallway. Wait, he did know Sky, and that's exactly what she'd do. He'd just been punked.

Again.

CHAPTER TWENTY-TWO

"You came back," Sky had said to Olivia. She'd been surprised to find her elder sister at the door this morning. Carrie, driving Robert, had arrived soon after. Now bundled in a warm coat, hat, and gloves, Sky stood in front of her house with Carrie and Olivia, surveying Malcolm's handiwork.

"Did you mean to say that aloud?"

Olivia reminded Sky too much of her mother, Lois. Olivia was about the same age Lois had been when Sade had taken Sky to see Robert at his home. They shared the same straight blonde hair, downturned eyes, and wide lips. So, too, did Carrie. But Carrie, unlike Olivia and Lois, radiated a warmth that drew people to her. The only warmth she'd detected in Lois was from the hot sting of her hand across the child Sky's face when she'd found Sky alone in the library of her home.

Sky hadn't seen Lois Ellis again after that awful day until she'd become an adult and been publicly acknowledged as Robert's daughter. The few times they'd run into each other, Lois never managed to hold Sky's gaze. To this day, Sky wondered what had happened between Sade and Lois when her mother had gone back to Robert's home after learning of Lois's attack. Sade had never said, and Sky had never been brave enough to broach the topic with her mother.

Olivia would've been about twenty-one then, old enough to know the discord between her parents and the rupture in their marriage. She may have even learned of the affairs, by both her parents. Affairs that had taken place before Sade Page. The difference with Robert's affair with Sade was her unexpected pregnancy and Sky's birth.

It hadn't been Carrie but her uncle who'd told Sky this family gossip. The superintendent knew a lot of people, and not all of them adhered to the idiom of loose lips sink ships. In Annapolis, gossiping was more historic than the state's capital.

Olivia's brow furrowed, her winter trench coat buttoned up to her stiff neck. "Would you like for me to leave?"

"I didn't say that. Until yesterday, you've never visited my home."

"Until yesterday, you never invited me to your home."

Knowing she shouldn't but deciding to poke the grumpy bear that was her eldest sister, she grinned and said, "Technically, I didn't invite you this time. Malcolm did."

"You are unbelievable. I can leave, if I'm not welcome."

Beside Olivia, Carrie laughed, which had Olivia's brow furrowing even more.

"It's not funny."

"You're so uptight, Liv. Relax, Sky is playing with you."

"No, she isn't. She meant what she said."

"Of course, she did, but she's still pulling your leg. You've never been particularly welcoming to Sky yourself, so why would she extend you an invitation to her home? Have you ever invited Sky to your house? Have you introduced her to your husband or children? Have you once called her without being guilted by Dad into doing so?"

"I don't have to—"

"Reach out? No, you don't. But it would be the right thing to do. What has Sky ever done to you, to me, or to our brothers? I mean Sky Ellis, as a person? Not her mother, not our father, but Sky? You hung out with us for the first time ever, yesterday. Three Ellis sisters. That's who we are. You had fun." Carrie craned her head around Olivia and spoke to Sky. "Liv came back because she had fun. She came back because she allowed herself to actually think of you as a real person with feelings and not as a villain who destroyed our family." Carrie faced Olivia again. "Sky's mother didn't break up Mom and Dad's marriage either. They did that all by themselves."

"His affair with Sade Page didn't help."

"No, and neither did Mom's affairs. None of that is our fault, nor is it Sky's. Honestly, I'm tired of this shit. Tired of pretending that Sade's and Sky's race hasn't played a role in how we've reacted to and treated Sky over the years. Not her race, but our attitudes and beliefs about it. I'm surprised she's been as nice to us as she has, all things considered."

Where in the hell had that come from? As close as Carrie and Sky were, they didn't talk directly about race. Sky made sure they didn't, cutting Carrie off whenever she broached the subject. Sky didn't wear blinders and knew no one was colorblind, no matter what many professed. Claiming colorblindness was equivalent to denying the presence of gender or any other obvious form of diversity. No one alleged they didn't see people as a biological male or female, why then did some argue they didn't notice the color of someone's skin?

"Do you really want to talk about that here?"

"You mean in front of our biracial sister? Yeah, I do."

Olivia reddened, and not from the cold. "Well, I don't. You're as pushy as Dad."

"Carrie, leave it alone. You're making Olivia uncomfortable."

"What about your discomfort?"

"You can't browbeat someone into seeing things your way. Race and racism are sensitive topics. There are feelings of anger, shame, and guilt involved, and I don't feel like getting into that today. I deal with it enough at work. People don't know what they don't know. Olivia is here of her own accord. Take her baby step for what it is."

Olivia sucked air between her teeth. "Stop talking about me as if I'm not right here."

"Have I upset you?" Sky asked with a straight face and bland tone.

"I don't think you care if you have." Olivia narrowed her gaze at Sky and crossed arms over her chest. "I'm willing to admit, I may have been unfair to you in the past."

"The past, as in every day since I've met you, up to and including yesterday?"

"Are you serious?" Olivia turned to Carrie. "I can't tell. Is she serious or screwing with my head?"

"Honestly, I can't always tell either. Sky does have an odd sense of humor. But she's also a straight shooter if she chooses to spend words on you. I suggest, if you don't want to know what she's thinking, then don't ask or push her when you should walk away. I think this is the longest conversation the three of us have ever had that didn't involve Dad's health." Carrie smiled at them, lovely and sincere. Sky loved and appreciated her. "We should do this again. This is the funny thing, both you and Sky are the most rigid people I know. Which probably explains why you rub each other the wrong way."

"That's not funny." Olivia shoved her hands into her coat pockets. "I'm not rigid." Carrie's smile broadened, and Olivia swung her gaze to Sky. "You don't have anything to say about being called rigid?"

"I'm not a fan of lying or of being struck by lightning."

Olivia lifted her eyes to the cloudless, winter sky. To Sky's surprise, the older woman smiled. "If lightning comes for me, I'll be sure to move closer to Carrie so she'll be hit too."

"Hey, don't get me involved in your lying lightning strike."

Carrie glanced over her shoulder to Sky's rental parked in the driveway. "How did Malcolm and your cousins manage to get so much stuff in that truck?" She looked back at Malcolm. "And, what is that?"

Olivia and Sky also watched Malcolm, on his hands and knees in Sky's front lawn, but Olivia was the one to answer Carrie. "I think it's a lightshow projector. We'll have to wait until tonight to see the image clearly." With her index finger, Olivia gestured to Sky's house. "If he aims the projector to the right of those windows, toward that big, empty wall space there, it'll make a really nice spotlight. He's been busy. He's already got the porch trees up and the garland around the door. The gold wreath is a nice touch. Altogether, it's beautiful and enough to put anyone in the Christmas spirit."

The colorful additions to the front of Sky's home were lovely, and she would've been fine with only those outside decorations. No one else in the cul-de-sac had more. Although, the Sheckells had two adorable, color-changing snowmen she'd seen lit last night when Sky had made her grocery store run with her sisters.

"Why aren't you engaged to that man?" Olivia asked, and Sky smiled.

The three women focused their attention on Malcolm again, who'd finished installing the projector and had moved on to using an electric air pump to blow up an inflatable green dragon with red-and-green wings and a candy cane in its mouth and between its clawed paws.

"What's with the smile?" For a woman who, until today, hadn't shown any interest in Sky's thoughts or feelings, Olivia had posed two personal questions in less than a minute. "I mean, beyond the fact that your hunky boyfriend is making your home the envy of the neighborhood?"

"Hunky?"

"It's a word, Sky."

"An old word," Carrie said.

"You're only two years younger than me."

"Which makes you seem that much older when you use a word like hunky."

Olivia opened her mouth but shut it before getting into another argument with Carrie. "I only wanted to know the origin of Sky's secret smile, beyond the obvious, which is her very attractive boyfriend, working hard to give her a special Christmas and birthday."

"Yeah, what's with the smile, Sky?"

"The inflatable dragon. I mentioned to Malcolm, just last night, that he reminds me of a hero from a fantasy novel who slays a dragon and wins the heart of the heroine."

"He found you a dragon in less than a day. He wasn't this nice to me last night."

"What do you mean?" It took a lot for Malcolm to be unfriendly, and he hadn't mentioned removing his nice guy hat with Olivia.

"Nothing. Never mind. Malcolm is sweet. I mean sugary-syrup sweet. How can you stand it?"

"Until I met Malcolm, I wouldn't have thought I could. But he's the perfect blend of sweet, sexy, and stubborn. His kind of sweetness doesn't equate to being weak of character or of mind. He's not a push-over, and he calls me on my bullshit. He's sensitive and sappy but only for those who matter the most to him. He can be bullheaded and sexist, but he's also a great listener and caregiver."

Sky didn't know when her sisters had turned to focus on her or how long she'd been going on about Malcolm, but when she peeled her eyes from her hot boyfriend in his stretch jeans that fit his ass to panty-wetting perfection, Olivia and Carrie were staring at her. In much the same way Aunt Yvette had yesterday when she'd shared her pics and stories of Malcolm.

"What?"

Olivia smiled again and, for the first time, didn't remind Sky of Lois. "I've never heard you string so many words together at once. You're normally quiet and reserved. Until yesterday, I thought that's just how you were. I mean, you are quiet and reserved, I can see that. But you're also not. Your Page family brings out a different side of you." She nodded in Malcolm's direction. "So does he. You should see yourself when you speak about him. How animated you become and how your eyes light up."

"Liv's right. I saw it yesterday, too. But your feelings for Malcolm are even clearer today. I've never seen you this happy, or so at peace with yourself. I know it's not all due to Malcolm. I think the move and new job helped. But falling in love can do wonders for a woman's spirit."

When had Sky become so transparent? She didn't mind people knowing how much she loved Malcolm. She did, however, take issue with her inability to keep from gushing over him like a schoolgirl.

"So, back to my original question. Why aren't you engaged to that man?" Olivia asked for the second time.

"He hasn't proposed."

"Because you told him not to, I bet."

"I didn't say that exactly."

"Then what did you say?" Olivia asked, sounding like the older sister she'd never been to Sky.

"I told Malcolm not to use my birthday as an excuse to propose. As you can see, he's romantic in the extreme. I have no idea how he found that dragon inflatable or how he had time to get it. Yet there it is, and he still has more decorations in the truck."

"So, you don't want Malcolm to propose?" Olivia appeared confused.

"It's not that. I don't want Malcolm to propose because he thinks it would be the ultimate romantic gesture to ask me to marry him on the most commercialized holiday of the year and oh, by the way, it's also his girlfriend's birthday, so win-win."

"I get it," Carrie said, snapping her fingers. "You think the proposal would be more about the romantic atmosphere of the holiday and less about the two of you as a couple." They watched Malcolm move from the inflatable dragon to a big box on the side of the house with God only knew what inside. "I can kind of see your point. He gets off on this stuff. I think doing all of this for you makes him happy. He loves Christmas, doesn't he?"

"It's his favorite holiday. I don't want him to confuse his feelings for Christmas with his desire to marry me."

Olivia smirked at Sky before shaking her head. "I've always thought you were older than your years. I still think that. There's no shortage of gray matter between your ears."

"But?"

"When it comes to this, love and relationships, you're a babe. Not immature but inexperienced. There's an important difference. A difference I can see. I'm sure Carrie can too, but she's too nice to say. I'm not, though."

"Too nice to say what?"

"That you're an idiot with three advanced degrees, none of which is in the sociology of relationships. Carrie should've told you. Then again, she's having an affair with her own husband. I don't begin to understand what's going on with them."

"I can sleep with my husband if I want."

"No, you can't. Not if you're supposed to be getting a divorce. Which, let me be honest with you, I have no idea why you are, other than you're both too sensitive to have an argument then make-up like a reasonable couple. But no, you take everything that's said in the heat of the moment so damn personally."

Sky began to walk away from Olivia, while she was preoccupied with Carrie.

"No, you don't." Olivia grabbed Sky's hand before she took more than two steps. "Carrie wants us to be real sisters, this is what sisters do."

"I didn't ask you to be my real sister."

"Too bad. You and Carrie opened Pandora's Box, now deal with the aftermath. No man likes Christmas this much, not even one as romantic and sappy as your Malcolm Styles. I guarantee you, if your birthday were October twelfth, June eighth, August first, or any day other than December twenty-fifth, he would still be out here surrounded by Christmas decorations. Malcolm isn't doing all of this because of the romanticism of Christmas. He's doing this because he loves you and wants you to be his wife. The over-the-top part is the sap in him. But everything else is all him and all you."

"I know."

"You do?" Olivia gaped at Sky, confusion returning to her face. "But you acted as if you hadn't a clue."

Sky did something she thought she'd never do, she reached out and pulled Olivia in to a hug. The woman must've been just as shocked as Sky was herself, but she recovered quickly and returned the embrace. "Thank you for your concern."

"Wait. What?"

She released her sister and stepped back. "I have to go. I told Robert I'd be in to speak with him after I checked on you all out here."

"What am I missing?"

"Nothing," Sky said. "Everything," Carrie answered at the same time.

Sky and Carrie smiled at each other. Breaking Olivia in would be so much fun. It really was unfair of them to team up against her. But, as Olivia had said, they'd opened Pandora's Box, and the Ellis sisters would have to deal with what came out of it.

Sky wasn't surprised to find her father in her office. The room had been Sade's lair, the only place in the house she'd spent more time in than her bedroom. Over the years, Sky had updated the room. Fresh paint and new furniture, different books on the shelves and hardwood instead of carpeting. When this was Sade's office, she'd favored gray, gold, and Peacock blue. Sky, on the other hand, preferred moody blues and browns. The office faced the back of the house, a picturesque scene of wide open space and tall trees.

Between two of the trees used to hang a hammock Sade loved to relax in, reading and napping during the warm months. While Sade slept below, Sky had played in the treehouse above. She remembered when Uncle Kenny built the structure, calling it her "little slice of Sky heaven." Whenever Sade couldn't find Sky in her bedroom, she would exit the house through the backdoor and head straight for the tree and Sky's make-believe castle home.

Other times, Sade would sit behind her desk and keep an eye on Sky from her office window. Every now and then, Sky would climb down and press her face against the window pane, smearing it with her little fingerprints and forehead. Sade would smile and blow Sky a kiss before shooing her away from the window and resuming whatever Sky had interrupted with her silliness.

She closed the door behind her. Robert didn't stir, although she knew he'd heard her. He stood, back to Sky, looking out Sade's window. Seeing him again, after ten months, hit Sky like a bolt. He was grayer than she remembered and thinner. He'd be eighty in three years. Most of his life was behind him. While Sky had grown up, her father had grown old. She wished this wasn't the beginning of the twilight years of Robert's life, but a stab of grief told her they were.

"Before the day of Sade's death, when I followed you home and came inside, I'd never been in this house. I knew where the two of you had moved to, of course, but I'd never been here." Robert turned to face Sky, handsome and distinguished in black dress slacks, white shirt with black tie and an unbuttoned burgundy-and-black cardigan. "Sade always made sure I knew where you were."

"I didn't think you guys talked casually."

"We didn't. Not really. Mostly, we argued, about you, about us."

He pointed to a wooden keepsake box in the center of Sky's desk. An abstract design swirled around letters that looked like... Sky moved closer to the desk and the box. Reaching out, she ran her index finger over the grooved letters.

"Sade gave it to me, and I had it engraved with your name and birth date. It's about six months older than you are. Solid cedar. You can't find craftsmanship like that anymore. Come sit with me, Sky. We need to talk."

With care, Robert took hold of the box.

He sat on the beige and chocolate sofa. Sky joined him, leaving a cushion between them, where her father placed his keepsake box.

"Except for you, this box was the last gift Sade gave me." His smile, sad and nostalgic, twisted something inside Sky. "Actually, that's not true. Sade gave me more gifts than I deserved." A weathered hand caressed the top of the keepsake box, where her name was inscribed in calligraphy letters. "Did you know we spent the first four birthdays and Christmases of your life together as a family?"

"Mom told me."

"But you don't remember, do you?"

"No."

"I didn't think so. You were so small back then. Sade granted me visitation rights, and I took advantage of them when I could."

Sade had never badmouthed Robert in front of Sky, other than when Sky overheard Sade's side of their heated arguments on the phone. Sade wasn't that kind of woman or mother. No matter what transpired between her parents, or even between Sky and Robert, she knew her mother didn't want to negatively influence her opinion of her father.

"I did nothing to earn the privileges Sade gave me, not even the first four years of your life. The only thing she'd ever asked of me was to be a real father to you. She never nagged me to leave Lois for her, although I told Sade, many times, I would. She never demanded child support to help raise you. I sent her checks anyway, more to assuage my guilt than to provide anything you might have wanted or needed. The first two checks, she returned. But I kept sending them anyway, once a month, sometimes twice."

"Mom set up a savings account for me."

"Sounds like Sade. Smart woman. Always thinking about the future and your security. She didn't spend a drop of my money, did she?"

Sky shook her head.

"Figures. Sade was proud, but I suppose she also wanted to make a point, even if only to herself. Our relationship," his eyes lowered to the keepsake box, which his hand rested on, "our affair, wasn't about money or power, not even lust." Robert reddened into a rosy blush. "Well, a little about lust, mainly on my part."

"TMI, Robert. I'll never be ready for you to go there, so please don't."

"Right, sorry. I got lost in memories. I want you to know I loved Sade."

"You were married. You shouldn't have loved a woman who wasn't your wife."

"I know, but I did. Lois and I hadn't been happy for a long time. In my day, men and women didn't divorce as quickly as they do now."

"But you told my mother you would divorce your wife for her."

"I did."

"I can't believe Mom would swallow such a blatant lie."

"But I didn't lie, Sky. Not really. My marriage with Lois was over. We didn't share the same room or bed. We had an understanding, for the sake of the children and my political career. And Sade didn't believe me. Not completely, anyway. I think it was more a case of her wanting to believe, so she talked herself into accepting my declarations."

Sky felt a migraine building. As close as Sky and Sade had been, her mother had drawn a line. Robert and Sade's affair was on the other side of that line that neither woman crossed, which suited them just fine. Sky didn't want to have this conversation with Robert. In fact, her legs shook with the urge to get up and run.

Sky stayed seated.

"I didn't inquire how Lois spent her days and with whom, and she didn't ask where I went late at night."

"Affairs were fine, as long as you both were discreet. I get it, but there's nothing discreet about a pregnant lover."

"Sade was more than a lover to me. We were more than that to each other. I wanted Sade but was too much of a coward to have her."

Robert's body sank into the back cushions as if the admission had drained him. Perhaps it had, but his confession wasn't any different from the conclusion Sky had drawn. The same one, no doubt, her mother had reached years ago. Probably before Sky's birth. If not before, then soon afterward.

"For god's sake, Robert, it wasn't the 1800s. Loving versus Virginia took care of anti-miscegenation laws, and that was in nineteen sixty-seven."

"You're thinking about the wrong kind of laws, Sky. You know what I'm talking about. You grew up here, just as I did. Just as Sade had. My career would've been ruined if I'd left my white wife for my black lover." Defeated, ashamed eyes met hers. "I've never said that aloud before, not even when Sade accused me of it. I never said it, didn't even want to admit it. Not to anyone. Not even to myself."

With each confession, her father grew paler. Shoulders slumped, and eyes dimmed, but he kept talking. His resolve to unburden himself must've been stronger than whatever had kept his secret shame inside for so long. Mortality, guilt, she didn't know.

This was the conversation Sky had avoided having with every member of her Ellis family, especially Robert. But it was also the conversation they should've had years ago. The unspoken, invisible barrier between them.

"When Sade told me she was pregnant, I didn't know what to do. We weren't as careful as we should've been, so the news shouldn't have surprised me, but it did."

"You wanted Mom to have an abortion."

"Did she tell you that?"

"No, but it's what most married men would want."

"It would've made my life easier, true, but I never suggested the procedure. Not that Sade would've listened."

"You didn't ask Mom to have an abortion?"

"You sound so shocked. I'm not a total ass, Sky. I wanted you, as much as your mother did. I wanted all my children, including you. You're a part of me."

"A part you cut from your life like a malignant tumor. You can't have it both ways. You can't claim to have wanted me, then ignore me for the first half of my life."

Robert's hand found the keepsake box again. He lifted it and handed the box to Sky. "Open it."

Taking the box from her father, she placed it on her lap. "What's inside?"

"My greatest treasures and deepest regrets."

"That makes me not want to open it." She did anyway, lifting the gold clasp and pushing up the cedar top. A pile of papers met her eyes. "What's all of this?"

"See for yourself."

Sky picked up the folded paper on top, a little yellow from age but in good condition. Unfolding it, she scanned the paper. She'd seen the document before. She had an identical copy in her lockbox in her Buffalo apartment, along with her other important documents.

"My birth certificate." Sky raised her eyes to her father's, who watched her with an emotion she couldn't name. "You have a copy of my birth certificate."

"An original. As your father, I could request a copy, which I did."

Robert Joseph Ellis III was listed as father, age forty-one.

"Look at the rest."

Sky handed Robert the three-decade-old birth certificate before lifting out the stack of papers inside the wooden box. Like the certificate, Sky recognized most of the items—pictures mainly, but also report cards, certificates of achievement, playbills from her high school and college performances. Snapshots of the first twenty years of her life were in Robert's keepsake box.

"What in the hell is all of this?"

"I told you. My greatest treasures and my biggest regrets."

"Did you take these from the house? When did you go through Mom's things? I can't believe you would—"

"Sade sent them to me. Everything in the box, except for the birth certificate, came from your mother."

Frowning, Sky flipped through the pictures. Seventh-grade dance recital. Second grade trip to Smithsonian's National Zoo. Nine-year-old Sky in bed asleep, an open book on her stomach. A skinny and awkward thirteen-year-old Sky on the boardwalk at Ocean City. Her junior ring dance with Khalil Bryant. Her dorm room at Harvard. Sky's smile after passing her driving test.

She dropped everything back into the box, closed the lid and handed it to Robert. All the while, trying to control her trembling hands. "Why would Mom send you all of that stuff?"

"At first, I thought Sade was being spiteful. She would mail me a picture or a copy of a report card or something else from your life. No note, just an item that had to do with you. At first, I thought they were her way of reminding me of what an awful father I was to you. But they weren't. Sometimes, Sky, when your heart is full of guilt and regret, you see ulterior motives where there are none."

Robert held the box in his lap, his hand, once more, going to the abstract design and Sky's name. His fingers followed the indentations of the design, mindless yet methodical.

"She wasn't being spiteful, but thoughtful. Sade wanted me to know you, despite myself. Instead of hating me and raising you to feel the same way, Sade shared you with me. I didn't deserve her kindness, but I looked forward to every envelope she sent. I found myself craving them. An addict with a sole supplier for my fix."

"This is sick. You could've been a part of my life whenever you wanted. You said it yourself, Mom didn't deny you parental rights. Just tell me already. Tell me why you couldn't or wouldn't be a real father to me back then."

Unable to stay seated and still any longer, Sky jumped from the sofa and began to pace. Her parents, when it came to each other, had been out of their damn minds. Sade may not have sent Robert a chest of Sky's childhood moments out of spite, but she damn sure hadn't done it out of magnanimity either. Sade Page was a master of telling people to go fuck themselves in a hundred subtle ways.

Spiteful, not quite. Passive aggressive, most definitely. For all Sade and Robert loved each other, they hadn't understand the other person as well as they thought they did. Some people should never procreate together. Her parents were two of them.

"Don't get mad."

"Too late. Tell me what I already know."

"What you already know?"

"Olivia called me an idiot earlier. Despite her normal nastiness, she didn't mean it. You, on the other hand, must think I'm stupid, blind, or both."

"I don't think you're either. I just... well," Robert slid to the edge of the sofa, his keepsake box cradled in his hands, "I didn't want to hurt you. I knew if I helped raise you, if I brought you into my world, you would get hurt."

"Because I'm biracial and your family, colleagues, neighbors, and most of your friends are white."

"You say that as if it's a small fact. It's not. I know how they think and what they say when not in mixed company. Not all of them, of course, but enough where I didn't want you anywhere near them."

"The way they think. What they say. What about you, Robert? Do you think like the people you didn't want me around? Do you speak like them, when you're not in mixed company?"

His eyes dropped, and so did his keepsake box. Twenty years of her life slipped from his careless fingers and spilled onto the hardwood floor at his feet, a thudding symbolism of their relationship.

"People say things they shouldn't. Think in a way that's not challenged. We lie to ourselves, blame others and make excuses. We call others out on their paternalism and supremacist ideas and actions, while

blind to our own. We have friends and lovers of color, people we gen-
uinely care about and who care about us in return. But, at the end of the
day, I had a brown-skinned child I wanted to protect from well-meaning
and not so well-meaning people. I didn't want you to grow up questioning yourself because of everyday microaggressions."

"I grew up like that anyway, despite Mom's best efforts. But it was
worse because everyone knew I had a white father who didn't care
enough about me to stick around. I'm not the first biracial person in
existence, Robert. Not in this neighborhood, my schools, Annapolis or
this entire damn country. Your white privilege allowed you to run
away."

"I know. I'm sorry." He got to his feet. "I'm sorry. I know my apology changes nothing. Racism is a rough reality of life."

"My reality of life, Robert, not yours." Sky shook her head, angry at
a truth she'd known for years.

"I love you. Please know I always have, even when I wasn't around
to show it."

Sky knew Robert did, which made his confession even more fucked
up.

Robert took her hands in his and raised them between their bodies.
His white and hers brown. "I don't want this to separate us. The color
of our skin shouldn't have so much power over us."

"The amount of melanin in peoples' bodies has never been the problem, not even during times of enslavement." Sky lifted a finger to her
father's temple and tapped. "It's what we carry around in there that's
the problem. Color has no meaning outside of what we ascribe to it. The
same with race. Race doesn't exist beyond being a social construct. But
that social construct impacts our lives so much, even when we wish it
didn't or pretend it doesn't."

"Sky, I—"

She kissed his cheek. "I'm going to go upstairs, change, and then go
for a jog."

"Don't do that. Don't run away from me again."

"There's a difference between jogging to clear my head and running away. I'm done with running away. You haven't said anything I didn't know in my heart, which doesn't make this conversation any less painful. I don't know how other interracial families handle this issue. Maybe they ignore it like we did. Maybe it's part of their natural dialogue and interactions. Or maybe, for some, they simply don't view it as an issue."

Sky moved around Robert and to the mess he'd made on the floor. Kneeling, she righted the keepsake box and, with care, returned each item to the box and closed the lid.

"Here you are."

With a grateful, albeit watery smile, Robert claimed his box, hugging it to his chest. "You're more than a box of pictures and papers to me. For a long time, though, they were all I had of you. They were never enough. I've wasted so much time. I see you with Malcolm and know he'll give you the security and family I never did. All I've ever wanted was your happiness. I didn't think I could give that to you, so I walked away when you were too young to miss me from your life. But I couldn't stay away. Not completely."

Sky had no response, although his pleading eyes begged for a reassuring reply. She didn't have that to give him either. But she granted her father what she could, which was another kiss to his cheek. "I need to go."

"When will you return?"

"Don't wait for me, Robert. I'm going to be awhile."

"You want me to go home?"

Damn, could he sound any more dejected?

"I'm not running away. I need time and a little space, which means you should let Carrie or Olivia drive you home. If you want, I'll pick you up tomorrow morning and bring you here."

"You still want to spend Christmas and your birthday with me?"

"That's why I came home."

His relieved smile hurt almost as much as his crestfallen frown had. They had so far to go in their relationship, and time wasn't guaranteed to anyone.

"Have Malcolm pick me up."

"Why?"

His look turned mulish, and Sky knew Malcolm had gotten to her father.

"Et tu, Brute? Whatever you and Malcolm are up to, please don't go overboard."

Robert's smile revealed everything. He'd already gone overboard, and there was no coaxing him or Malcolm back from the edge.

"See you tomorrow, Robert."

"I'm looking forward to spending your birthday with you. You coming home means more to me than you'll ever know."

Sky fled her office before more words could be exchanged. Her head pounded, the pain increasing even as she threw on sweats and sneakers and ran down the stairs and toward the front door.

When the door opened, she skidded to a halt, almost slamming into Malcolm, who caught her by the arms.

"Whoa, where are you off to so fast? You nearly mowed me over, Sky." Dark-brown eyes fell to her body, taking in her athletic attire, then rose back to her face. "I guess you and Robert talked and it didn't go well."

"It went exactly as I thought it would."

"Meaning what?"

"Meaning, I have a stress headache I need to get rid of."

"By running?"

"I'm not running."

Malcolm's eyebrow quirked up, and he took in her clothing again.

She sighed. "I am, but not in the way you and Robert think. I'm not running away. I'm just... running."

She thought Malcolm would argue and remind Sky of her pattern of running away from her pain. Of shutting down and shutting people out, instead of dealing with her issues head-on like an emotionally stable and responsible adult. Instead, he hugged her and kissed the neck that pulsed with tension. Thick, strong arms held her close. Malcolm's subtle rocking was a blanket of muscular security that had Sky melting into his embrace.

Eyes closed, and tears fell. In that moment, Sky wasn't certain if she cried for the child she'd been, for the woman she was, or for the wife she wanted to become.

"Be careful."

"I will."

"Be back before it gets dark, please."

"Promise. I'm not running. Trust me. I'm not running."

"I know you aren't, and I do trust you to come back to me."

Sky had no intention of running away from Malcolm, her life, or anything else ever again. Those days were over.

"Have a good run."

Sky left the house and jogged past a large SUV pulling into her driveway. She waved at the occupants but didn't stop to greet them properly. Smiling to herself, Sky pulled the lightweight, run skullcap over her ears. Her Christmas gift for Malcolm had finally arrived.

CHAPTER TWENTY-THREE

Malcolm stood in the foyer of Sky's home watching as his mother examined the picture of Sky and Sade on the foyer table, marveling at their resemblance, as if her own daughter didn't look as much like her as Sky did Sade. He'd been surprised when a seven-passenger SUV pulled into the driveway and his family piled out. That had been five minutes ago, and Malcolm's father hadn't come into the house yet. Charles had taken one look at Jeremiah's purple, Baltimore Ravens, heavyweight jacket and had gone straight up to the man to talk football, uncaring he didn't know Sky's cousin from Adam and that Jeremiah was on a ladder stringing lights on the tree beside the house.

The voices of children had drawn Carrie from the kitchen where she'd been baking. With a plate of hot sugar cookies with colored sprinkles, Carrie had new friends in Kayla and Zuri, who followed the blonde Pied Piper of Christmas Sweets back into the kitchen.

Malcolm had introduced his parents to Olivia and Robert before they'd left. Robert had shaken his hand, a strong grip for a man his age. Robert had appeared sadder than when he'd arrived but also lighter somehow. "I'm looking forward to tomorrow," he'd said. "Thirty-two years, an inexcusable truth I wish I could take back, but I can't. Thank you for returning Sky to me."

"She decided to come home on her own. Sky doesn't like to be pushed, so I try not to."

"You underestimate the power of love, son." Robert had shaken his hand again. "Except for my sweet Carrie, all of my children are pig-headed." He'd smiled at Olivia, who stood beside him. "Present company definitely included. I have two sons and two sons-in-law. I'd love to add you to that count. No pressure, Malcolm. But three sons-in-law would be great. More grandchildren would also be wonderful. Again, no pressure."

"Dad thinks by saying 'no pressure' it minimizes the impact of everything he said before. I'm going to drive Dad home then pick up a few last-minute items for tomorrow."

"Olivia means she waited until today to think of getting a present for Sky."

"Actually, I bought Sky a gift two months ago. I planned to mail it to her because I didn't think she would accept your invitation to an Ellis Christmas."

"You bought Sky a birthday gift two months ago?" Malcolm hadn't meant to sound incredulous, but nothing he'd seen from Olivia would've led him to believe she cared enough about Sky to purchase her anything, much less a Christmas or birthday present.

"I never have before. I thought I should this year."

Olivia had raised her chin when she'd spoken, neither defiant in her belated kindness to Sky nor challenging Malcolm to judge her thoughtlessness of past years, but from ingrained self-righteousness. He was glad Olivia had decided to befriend Sky. For his part, Malcolm still didn't like the woman.

Angie hugged him. Small arms went around his waist and head to his chest, drawing him back to the present.

He kissed the top of his sister's head. They'd seen each other only a few days ago, but he'd still missed her.

"Did we surprise you?"

"I had no idea you guys were coming."

Malcolm stretched out one of his arms so his mother could join the family hug. He looked over their heads to make sure Kim had returned Sky's picture to the table. She may have walked around her house seemingly oblivious to the pictures of herself and Sade, but Malcolm knew his lady. The saying, a place for everything and everything in its place, could've been coined by Sky.

"Sky knows how to keep a secret." Kim kissed his cheek, with Malcolm's help. His mother and sister really were short. If he didn't bend down, they'd never reach him. "Where was she off to in such a hurry?"

They released each other.

The door was wide open, and Malcolm could hear his father's loud voice and critique of the Ravens' offensive line.

"I introduced you to her father and sisters."

His mother nodded, her sage eyes on his. "Did she face her demons?"

Two weeks ago, Sky had shocked Malcolm when she'd brought up her own childhood during a dinner with Kim, Charles, and Angie's family at his parents' house. While Sky hadn't provided gritty details of Sade and Robert's affair, she did share a little about her mother being a single parent and Sky's years-long estrangement from her father. In retrospect, Malcolm understood Sky's motivation. At that point, she must've already invited his family to Maryland. Her "casual" dinner conversation had, in fact, been a well-designed laying of groundwork for this visit. They'd never played chess against each other. After today, he resolved they never would.

"I think so. We haven't had time to talk yet. Sky runs when she's stressed. The physical exertion helps her relax. You're right about demons, though. I think Sky and Robert did a bit of exorcizing, which is why they were upset."

"What kind of man ups and leaves his child?" Charles, a bag of wrapped gifts in his hand, walked into the house. "I'll never understand someone like that. I know it's not my place to say and I won't when Sky's around. Ellis seemed like a decent enough man if I forget what he did to his daughter."

"I'm sure Sky didn't invite you here to judge her family. They're a work in progress. We need to respect the family they are trying to become and not judge them on the family we think they should've been. Not to be rude, but why are you guys here?"

"That's the last of it." Sean closed the door and set down a black rolling suitcase, his son right beside him.

While everyone else found something to do other than unload the SUV, Sean and SJ had taken it upon themselves to bring in the luggage.

Malcolm pointed behind him. "SJ, if you go down the hall and turn right, you'll run into the kitchen. Zuri and Kayla are in there with Sky's sister, Mrs. Carrie, and there are homemade cookies. Mrs. Carrie won't mind if you help yourself."

"Thanks, Uncle Malcolm." SJ extended his fist, and Malcolm bumped it with his. "This house is straight fire. I saw a covered pool in the backyard."

"Yeah, when he was supposed to be helping me bring the bags in." With a gentle shove to his shoulder, Sean pushed his son. "Go to the kitchen, introduce yourself to Sky's sister, wash your hands, and don't tell Zuri about the pool."

"What about the cookies?"

"Add that to your To Do list. Now go."

The fifteen-year-old, long-limbed and grinning, jogged down the hall and disappeared around the corner.

Sean ran a hand over his face. "That boy." His eyes scanned the shiny hardwood floor, high ceiling, cornice molding, and the crystal and metal orb chandelier that, while off now, lit the entryway to Sky's home with a bright, sensual glow. "SJ's not wrong. This is a great house. A million-dollar home would be my guess." Sean whistled. "Her father must be a piece of work if she left all of this behind to move to Buffalo. Your girl's rich, who knew?"

Not Malcolm.

"Let me say it again, keep discussion of Sky's family situation to a minimum. By minimum, I mean shut up about it. Back to my previous question, why are you here, not that I'm unhappy to see everyone."

"I think," his mother began, "Sky felt bad about taking you away from home for Christmas. In fact, I'm sure of it. She invited us here as a Christmas gift to you so you wouldn't spend the holiday without your family while surrounded by hers and people you only just met. Sky's a sweet girl."

"I told her it wasn't necessary." Charles picked up the same picture of Sade and Sky that Kim had. "She offered to fly us out, but we chose to drive."

"Speak for yourself, Dad. You wanted to drive, the rest of us would've been fine on a plane, as well as paying for the round-trip flight."

"Seven hours on the road didn't kill you. It made for quality family time."

"We get enough quality family time." Angie snorted. "On that note, Malcolm, Sky sent me a text message this morning. It has our room assignments. I'd love to take a shower and a nap."

"She sent you room assignments?" His eyes lowered to his sister.

"And a map of her house."

"A map? You can't be serious."

Angie showed him her cell phone. Sure enough, Sky had included a three-level, computer-generated map of her home.

"I thought it was a joke until I remembered who'd sent the text. Is Sky ever not prepared?"

"Not that I've yet to experience. From what Sky has here, you and Sean are in the room at the end of the hall. The girls are next to the two of you and SJ across from them. Mom and Dad are…"

Sky had a nice sized bedroom. But he'd known, when she'd showed him where to put their luggage, it wasn't the master suite. He'd assumed, after all these years, Sky would've claimed her mother's room for her own. If for no other reason than to feel closer to Sade. But she hadn't. She'd kept her childhood bedroom and had left her mother's room vacant for fifteen years.

The family room had a sofa bed, as did the basement. SJ would've been fine staying in one of those places, leaving the guest room she'd given him to Malcolm's parents. But no. His Sky had decided to keep the Styles together, even if that meant permitting his parents to sleep in her deceased mother's bedroom.

Malcolm wondered what the decision had cost Sky emotionally. He knew how much her gesture meant to him. Yesterday, he'd told Olivia that Sky was an amazing woman. As true as he knew his statement to be, Sky had still managed to floor him with her generosity and thoughtfulness.

He'd spent most of the morning working with Brandon and Jeremiah decorating Sky's home. He was sweaty and hungry and in need of a break. Malcolm had gone overboard but didn't care. Everyone thought him a self-indulgent romantic and an irredeemable sap, which wasn't true. He'd never treated any woman he'd dated the way he did Sky. The reason was clear. No other woman had treated Malcolm and his family the way Sky did. She demonstrated, time and again, how much she loved and respected him. Not by words or even grand physical gestures, but through refined acts of emotional surrender.

"We're where, Malcolm?" his mother asked. "A shower and a nap do sound like a good idea."

"Sky put you and Dad in the room across from the two of us. Sean, I'll help you carry the luggage upstairs and show everyone their room. I haven't been in them, but I'm sure they're as nice as the rest of the house."

Belatedly, Malcolm recalled Sky's no shoes rule. She'd overlooked it yesterday when Malcolm and the Page men brought in the tree and Christmas decorations. He didn't miss, however, how Sky couldn't go up to bed until she'd vacuumed the living room floor and swept and mopped the foyer. He'd offered to help, but she'd frowned at Malcolm and called him a "guest."

"Wait, you guys need to remove your shoes and put them in one of the baskets or on that burgundy shoe rug over there."

Charles's eyes lowered to the shoe baskets. "You want us to do what?"

"Take off your shoes. There are also non-slip shoe covers next to the shoe baskets."

The sound Angie made came out as a strange amalgam of a snort and a laugh. "Yes, prepared for every eventuality, including people who don't want to walk around the house in their socks. I forgot. Sky did put something in the text about shoe baskets. Dad, that rug didn't do anything to you. Stop staring at it as if it's your mortal enemy. Sky's house, Sky's rules. Take off your shoes already so Malcolm can relax and breathe again."

"I am relaxed."

Sean slapped him on the back, his laughter ringing in Malcolm's ear. "You should see yourself, bro. Following a woman's rule, even when she isn't around. That's a sure sign."

"A sign of what?"

His family laughed. At least when they finished, their shoes were on Sky's shoe rug.

When Malcolm carried a bag into the room assigned to Sean and Angie, neither complained about the accommodations. While Malcolm couldn't be certain, he didn't think Angie had let Sean move back into their bedroom. Sean's satisfied grin revealed more about his hopes for the next few nights than Malcolm cared to think about. Angie, on the other hand, glanced from the queen-sized bed and then to her grinning husband.

She rolled her eyes, grabbed her toiletry bag and fresh outfit from her suitcase, and then escaped into the en suite bath.

"I could kiss Sky."

"Keep your lips away from my future wife."

"Future wife, huh? Got something planned for Christmas? A ring that's been burning a hole in your pocket?"

"I didn't expect you guys, but you all being here balances everything out. Page, Ellis, Styles, three families but one family if Sky marries me."

"You have plans for tomorrow you need our help with? If you do, I'm in."

"Thanks, but I need to talk to Mom and Dad. They're the key, but the rest of you will be back-up."

Charles and Kim represented the Styles, while Robert represented the Ellisses and Kenneth and Yvette the Pages. Malcolm's plan was a Christmas-inspired one. Robert Ellis, as Sky's father, was Sky's wish of Christmas past. Kenneth and Yvette, Sky's surrogate mother and father, were her wish of Christmas present. As Malcolm's parents, he hoped Sky would see Charles and Kim as her wish of Christmas future.

"Sounds like you've got it all figured out."

"Sky's uncle and aunt are here, and so is her father. Since Mom and Dad weren't here, I was going to wing their part. Now I don't have to. I know Mom and Angie want to rest, but we need to have a family talk before Sky gets back from her run."

"How long will she be gone?"

"I don't know. Sky promised to be back before it got dark, which should be around five o'clock."

Sean tossed his coat on the bed. "Okay, it's almost one now. Give your mother and sister at least two hours to freshen up and rest. Even if Sky gets back a little earlier than sunset, she'll shower and change before she comes looking for us, which will give you more time if you need it."

"Makes sense. Want to help me and Jeremiah decorate the big tree next to the house?"

Sean pulled his sweatshirt over his head, leaving him in a short-sleeve shirt. "Ahh, no. I have other plans."

"What other…?" The sound of running water filtered out to the bedroom. "Never mind."

"Sex plans."

"I said never mind."

"We've made progress in counseling, so now may be the perfect time to make my move."

"What part of never mind, don't you get?"

Off came Sean's T-shirt. "I've been working out." He slapped the palm of his right hand over his six-pack abs. "I can't entice my wife into having sex if I've got love handles."

"You've never had love handles."

What in the hell was he saying? Malcolm didn't want to have this conversation with Sean.

"Twenty years of marriage means Angie's seen it all. So, I need to go the extra mile to attract her to my bed. If I'm lucky, Sky's guest bed. Hell, it's been so long, I don't need a bed. The floor, wall, dresser—"

Malcolm got the hell out of there before Sean listed all the places he wanted to have sex with Angie. He didn't want to know Sean's sex plans for his sister. But he did need to get his nephew and nieces shoes off them and into a basket before Sky returned.

"What did Sky say?"

Malcolm plopped into a chair at the kitchen table. Instead of answering Angie's question right away, he stared at his focused girlfriend and her family. How could so many A-type personalities co-exist in a single family and not murder each other?

"She said we're guests and that her mother didn't raise her to put guests to work."

"But you helped her cousins decorate the house."

"She views that as an exception because it was a Christmas and birthday present from me to her. Other than that, Sky doesn't want me doing anything in 'her kitchen.'"

Angie and Kim nodded, unspoken female solidarity he knew better than to comment on. The women sat across from Malcolm at the six-person table. Charles, Sean, and SJ were in the family room watching the Hawaii Bowl, Fresno State Bulldogs versus the Houston Cougars. Apparently, Zuri and Kayla didn't count as guests, since Sky had offered to show them how to make her grandmother's triple layer chocolate cake and sweet potato pie. At the thought of the twin desserts, Malcolm's mouth watered.

"She's getting better."

Malcolm didn't have to ask his mother to qualify her statement. He knew what she meant. Ever since Sky had joined the Styles for their annual October-Halloween and birthday celebration and Zuri claimed Sky's lap as hers, she'd become more comfortable in her interactions with the girls. Even now, Sky had Zuri sitting on a barstool in front of her, stirring a delicious-smelling confection while Sky nodded and whispered directions into her ear. She'd given Kayla the task of mashing the baked sweet potatoes, which his niece executed with a self-satisfied grin. Malcolm was pretty sure, before today, he hadn't seen Kayla prepare anything beyond a PB&J sandwich.

"We could never do anything like that." Like Malcolm and Kim, Angie watched the scene on the other side of the kitchen. "Two Styles in a kitchen is company, three is competition, four or more is all-out culinary combat."

"And they're quiet." Kim rested her elbows on the table and leaned forward, conspiratorially. "It's unnatural to be so quiet in the kitchen."

"They aren't quiet, Mom, they just aren't Styles loud."

He understood his mother's point but the Pages, like the Styles, had their own way of doing things. For them, they worked together like a well-oiled Page-Ellis cooking machine. Kenneth, Yvette, and Sky, when she wasn't working with Zuri and Kayla, oversaw tomorrow's main courses. Brandon and Jeremiah prepared appetizers and soup, while Brandon's wife, Crystal, was on salad duty. Carrie and Olivia were deep in cookies, pies, and cakes, which Malcolm hoped to sample before they put them away.

If he asked nicely and pretended he was happy Olivia had returned, maybe she'd let him try her cheesecake truffles.

"It's impressive, actually. I wish my executive leadership team worked so well together. They've gotten worse since I've been on medical leave."

"That's because a couple of them were probably hoping you wouldn't return and they'd have a shot at the presidency. I may not have a doctorate like the two of you, but I know people. They saw a potential open door and hoped to walk through it."

"As Dad would say, 'You ain't never lied.' " Malcolm's sister and mother smirked at him before laughing, louder than the ten-people preparing Christmas dinner. "At the rate their working, they're going to have a six-course meal done tonight."

He looked at Sky again. She really was beautiful and not just physically. When she'd returned from her run, sweaty and breathing hard, she'd kissed him before darting into the bathroom for a shower.

"I'm fine," she'd said when she exited the bathroom, a towel wrapped around her body, hair damp and curly.

"Are you sure?" Malcolm had asked. "We can talk about it if you want."

"I'm relaxed and headache-free. Let's leave my discussion with Robert for another day. Did your family settle in okay? I'll have to apologize for not stopping to say hello. I should've."

"If you had, they would've talked your ear off, and you would've never gotten to your run. No apology is necessary. Come here."

"Why?"

Sky had backed away, a sultry retreat that had Malcolm following. The leash on his heart and body was invisible but more potent than Wonder Woman's Lasso of Truth. *Wonder Woman* was one of the few flicks Sky selected for movie date night, along with *Black Panther*, that wasn't a horror movie. Feminism had Sky wanting to see Gal Gadot portray the iconic superheroine, while Chadwick Boseman in a body-hugging catsuit made Sky an instant Black Panther fan. She'd even worn a "Wakanda Forever" sleep shirt to bed that night. Those two DVDs were next to her favorite horror movie: *The Exorcist*.

No offense to Boseman's acting ability, but how could the same person who played Jackie Robinson also play James Brown, Thurgood Marshall, and an Afrofuturistic king from a fictitious African country? Sky had shaken her head when Malcolm had offered his opinion of Boseman and his monopoly on quality African American male roles in Hollywood.

Malcolm had made sure to thank Sky for inviting his family there for Christmas. "I would've been fine, not seeing them tomorrow, but I'm grateful I get to spend Christmas with you and with them." He'd nipped her jaw, unable to resist the feel and taste of her. She smelled of lavender body soap, which had him nuzzling her neck and getting as close to her as possible. "Take off that towel and let me give you a proper thank you."

"We can't."

"Why not?"

"I have too much to do, beginning with checking in on your family. Besides, your parents are across the hall."

"Where you put them. Please don't tell me you're going to get weird about sex now that my parents are here."

"If we were in their home, I wouldn't feel comfortable having sex with you. But we're in mine, and I have no interest in a celibate Christmas."

He'd removed her towel, an early unwrapping of a present he desperately wanted.

"I don't have time."

Malcolm had chased Sky onto the bed, and she offered no further protest when he wedged himself between her thighs. "I'm redeeming another naughty Christmas coupon."

"Spontaneous sex?"

"You got it, and I got you." Lips pressed to her neck and kissed. "Now show me the perks of having an extreme jogger as my lover."

Sky had.

Two hours later, three families were gathered in Sky's kitchen.

Malcolm blinked when a small hand waved in front of his face. Zuri, the pixie-cherub.

"Uncle Malcolm, is it time to see the Christmas lights?"

He'd waited, not daring to interrupt Sky again once she and her family began cooking. From the look of them, now seemed like a good time to take everyone outside.

"Sure, squirt. Go get your dad, granddad, and brother."

Angie and Kim stood from the table. "Mom and I will grab coats. If we don't, SJ and Zuri will run outside without them."

So would Malcolm, but he kept that to himself.

It didn't take the group long to bundle up, Annapolis at nine-thirty was a crisp thirty degrees. No one seemed to mind the chill in the air, though.

As awed as Zuri, who ran around the lawn decorations squealing, Sky's mouth hung open in a very unlike Sky way.

Before everyone converged on the front lawn, Malcolm had exited the house to make sure everything was plugged in and working. The projector displayed falling snow off the front right wall of Sky's house. The tall tree blinked white and multi-colored lights. An assortment of shatterproof ornaments, glittery, dot and lines, striped, and plaid, hung on the outside tree. There'd been no rhyme or reason to the ornamental selections beyond Malcolm's desire to give Sky her splash of color.

White lights were suspended from the edge of the roof, and green-and-red gift box statues with color-changing lights lined both sides of the driveway.

Zuri and Kayla poked the Christmas dragon, cracking silly smiles when their father pulled out his cell phone and took pictures of them.

Taking Sky's hand in his, Malcolm showed her all the little touches he'd planted in her front lawn. A metal bobble Santa, a wooden pre-lit gift box Santa and snowman, a silver glitter doe, a crystal cone tree with lights, and a toy shop with revolving train garden. Independently, the outdoor decorations were cute. Together, they created a Christmas feast for the eyes. If he didn't think the neighbors would mind, Malcolm would've added holiday music to the Christmas scene.

In silence, Sky took everything in, her hand in his and her eyes suspiciously wet. When they reached the outside Christmas tree, Malcolm reached inside a box he'd placed at the base of the tree earlier. He handed Sky a tree topper with an African American female figurine decked-out in a gold dress with halo, the palms of her hands pressed together, as if in prayer, and her white wings feathers of serenity.

The tree topper had been the last Christmas gift he'd purchased for Sky. Malcolm had seen it on an Instagram ad and thought of Sky's mother, unaware, at the time, of the details of her tragic death. He'd packed the gift in his carry-on bag, unsure of the unshakable impulse he'd had to purchase the angel. Of everything he'd bought Sky, the topper was the least expensive of his gifts. Yet, when he'd snooped in Sky's lockbox in search of her birth certificate and her mother's full name, the unexplainable urge to buy the topper for Sky fell into place, and a sense of rightness had washed over him.

Sky gripped the angel topper with such ferocity, he thought she'd snap the figurine in two. She remained silent, but tears fell, and lips trembled.

Malcolm gathered her to him, stroking her hair and back. "Your cousins and I left the top of your birthday Christmas tree bare, so you could do the honors."

If Sky looked closely, she'd see her mother's name stitched into the gold dress. He'd asked his own mother to take care of the embroidery, which she'd done with a warm smile and a "You're a good man, Malcolm. You make me so proud."

Today, he'd been proud of Sky and the way she'd handled her emotions and relationships with her family, particularly Robert. She'd returned from her jog happy and refreshed and not dwelling on the past but settled in the present and looking forward to Christmas and her birthday. In Sky's quiet, resilient way, Malcolm believed she had come to terms with her rocky familial past. Her brothers hadn't visited or called, neither of which seemed to bother her. She and Olivia were feeling each other out, but both seemed willing to lay aside past hurt and work on building an Ellis sisterhood, with Carrie smack in the middle as the happy glue.

"Do you want to go inside and put your mother's topper on the tree?"

She shook her head.

"What do you want to do then? Stay out here a little longer?" Their family had returned to the house, soft retreats meant to give them privacy and Sky time to compose herself. "Or do you want to return to the kitchen and finish cooking?"

"I want to stand here for a while and soak in your heat, smell, and the Christmas joy you've brought to my heart and home. I haven't felt like this since Mom's death. I thought the wonder of the season lost to me, never to return." Sky moved out of his embrace and, with one hand clutched around the figurine, she gestured to the house and front lawn with the other. "But you've brought it back, Malcolm."

"Not just me. Brandon and Jeremiah helped a lot. So did your uncle."

"I know, but you reminded us all of the meaning of Christmas. Family, fun, and laughter."

"Don't forget food."

She chuckled, a sweet sound he wanted to hear for the rest of their lives. "Of course, how could I forget my junk food junkie's stomach?" Sky's gaze fell to the angel topper. "I love this. It's beautiful, and gold was one of Mom's favorite colors. Thank you very much. I'll treasure the gift always." She lifted her eyes, gorgeous and wet from happy tears. "I don't think you'll be able to outdo yourself next year."

"I'm not finished with this year."

"You don't need to do anything else for me. You've gone above and beyond for Christmas and for my birthday. You're spoiling me."

The way Sky had said that Malcolm knew, this once, she didn't mind being spoiled by him. If anything, his spoiling touched her more deeply than she had words to express. He could tell, in the way she held the figurine and in the way she held his gaze, with love and gratitude.

"At this point, I think it's safe to say we spoil each other. We need to own it, and then get over it."

"True. What will Santa bring me tomorrow?"

"You'll have to wait and see, my Christmas belle. But I can tell you what Santa will bring you tonight."

Malcolm pulled an item from his pocket, lifted it over Sky's head and waited for her to look up.

"You're a Santa of many surprises. Where did you find a sprig of mistletoe with white berries?"

It was plastic, and he'd ordered it two weeks ago. But why ruin the romantic moment with unromantic truths?

Before Malcolm could proffer an answer, Sky slipped her arms around his waist and pressed her lips to his. "Happy Christmas Eve."

CHAPTER TWENTY-FOUR

Long limbs and hair surrounded Sky, a cocoon of muscles, heat, and man. She opened her eyes and smiled at the sight before her. Sky had seen Malcolm like this before, handsome face in repose, locs splayed down his back and on both of their pillows, light stubble on his jaw and body curled against hers. Yes, she'd seen it all before, but the sight of Malcolm, first thing in the morning, never failed to awaken her possessive side.

He was hers, in most ways that mattered. But not in every way possible. Malcolm had worked his way into her life and heart, making her his through the subtle art of Malcolm Styles Seduction. Every kiss, touch, and laugh drew her in deeper. Every kind word, thoughtful gesture, and selfless act bound her to him. Every difference and disagreement strengthened them. Every tear and fear brought them closer. Sky knew, with absolute certainty, no matter the holiday or state, she wanted to awaken in the arms of the man she loved. The man she adored.

She did nothing to disturb Malcolm's well-earned rest. The sun wasn't yet up, and they'd gone to bed late. Later than normal since they'd snuggled on the living room sofa, marveling at the Christmas tree and talking. Sky hadn't added the topper to the tree. She couldn't bring herself to part with the gift, so she'd brought it upstairs and into her room.

Glancing over Malcolm's shoulder to the nightstand, where she'd placed the figurine, Sky couldn't help the lump that formed in her chest. The angel tree topper, fourteen inches and typical of most of its kind, wasn't special in and of itself. She'd seen angel figurines before. She'd also seen African American-inspired tree toppers, mainly Santa Claus but also angels. While all were very nice, nothing about them had brought tears or set her heart pounding.

The same would've been true for the angel in her lovely gold dress, if Sky had seen it any place other than in Malcolm's hand, in front of her mother's home, and on Christmas Eve. She'd had no emotional defense against the combination. Under different circumstances and in front of anyone but Malcolm, Sky would've shoved her emotions into a secret hole until she was alone. Only then would she have allowed them their freedom and the consumption of her heart.

With Malcolm, however, his openness and vulnerability were modeled encouragement for Sky to offer him the same. His love may have been unconditional, but he expected Sky to put in the emotional work to reinforce and build upon the foundation they'd started months ago. The thought had once frightened her. Now, she couldn't imagine living any other way. If they broke up tomorrow, Sky wouldn't return to her old, emotionally-distant ways. Not that she had any intention of letting her real-life hero go.

So, she watched him sleep, as she'd done many mornings before. Sky could envision the tracks of time on Malcolm's body. Each gray hair and every fine line and wrinkle. She could see an elderly Malcolm Styles, in her mind's eye, still charming, sweet, and romantic. He was surrounded by his children, their children, a broad smile for them and a warm hug for her.

Sky didn't ascribe to the concept of fate, any more than she believed in love at first sight. She looked at the angel topper again, her mother's name stitched above the red, green, and gold trim of the dress. She'd never told Malcolm her mother's middle name, but there it was: Sade Angel Page.

She turned back to Malcolm... and smiled. "You're awake. Merry Christmas."

An arm tightened around Sky's waist and pulled her flush against a bare, hard chest. "Happy birthday."

For all her early morning musings, Sky had forgotten today was her birthday. This time last year, she was at a spa resort in Cancun, Mexico, waking up with one hell of a hangover. Why a resort needed six bars and lounges, Sky would never know. Why she went bar hopping to each of them was an even better question. She'd gone to bed alone, avoiding the temptation to drown her melancholy in anything other than strong spirits and fine dining. Sky had spent her birthday among strangers. At the time, she'd savored the anonymity and solitude. Now, after the last couple of days, with family and friends, she grieved for the lonely woman of only a year ago.

"Thirty-six."

"Don't remind me."

"I can't wait until you're sixty-six."

"Why?"

"Because we would've been together for thirty years."

That was the first marriage statement Malcolm had made since promising not to propose on Christmas or to push Sky on the issue. Being a man of his word, Malcolm wouldn't break his promise, no matter the temptation. Hearing him speak of marriage again did all kinds of wonderful things to Sky's body.

She kissed him, a slow, wet, morning kiss with tongue and roaming hands.

The rays of the sun battled with draperies covering the room's three windows. Voices in the hallway slipped under the bedroom door, excited children anxious to open presents.

"My family's up."

Sky hooked a leg over Malcolm's waist and pushed him onto his back. He wore only boxers, his erection poking her in the stomach.

"You're also up."

"It's morning, baby. I don't have to work for this hard-on." His hands skated down her back and settled over her ass. "With you, getting like this doesn't take much effort."

"What about in thirty years?"

"I may need a little more help when I'm sixty-seven, but we'll manage. I'll still be able to make you come for me, even if I can only keep my erection going for half the time I do now."

They were talking about a long-term relationship again, and it felt right. Better than right.

Fate, maybe. Their destiny...?

He nibbled her neck. The hands on her bottom pushed up her nightgown, and he shifted her up and over his erection.

The door across the hall closed and more voices, Charles's and Kimberly's, drifted to ears but had no effect on bodies.

Sky didn't know if the Styles would begin opening gifts without them. What she did know, however, was neither Malcolm nor she intended to leave this bedroom until they were boneless and sated.

A wiggle and shift of the hips had Malcolm's boxers off, buried under the covers at the foot of the bed.

Malcolm's hands skimmed over the silk of Sky's red shorty nightgown, up her waist and over breasts aching for his tender, and not-so-tender, touch.

"Leave this on for me. I love the way you look in it. It gives me ideas."

She whimpered at his words and the fingers pinching nipples through the thin silk.

"It's even better because you have nothing else on. I can get used to this."

"Me going to bed in lingerie and no underwear. I just bet you can."

"Hell, yes, that, but I meant spending your birthday morning in bed making love to you."

"We haven't made love yet."

"An easy fix." Malcolm's tongue came out and ran over his lips, eyes locked on Sky's.

His desire was a flickering flame of heat and lust that scorched Sky, her skin on fire and wanting everything he silently promised.

"We're not sixty-six yet, but that's no reason we can't do sixty-nine. Come here." Malcolm repositioned them, flinging the covers off the bed first then sprawling his sexy ass, dick up, across the mattress.

She crawled over him, straddling his head while facing his erection, pre-cum already leaking from the tip. It was Sky's turn to lick her lips.

Malcolm's arms rose and trapped her hips between them. Then Malcolm was there, not waiting for Sky to take him into her mouth before kissing and licking her. Hands held her open for his exploration, and she rocked against his hot, wet mouth.

Her head lowered and licked his length over and again before taking him into her mouth and sucking. His moans blew warm air into her sex, so she did it again, hollowing her cheeks and fucking Malcolm with her mouth.

One of them should be the resting partner. When they started, it was Sky. But she wanted them to peak together, so she fought the craving to sink into the pleasure he gave her. Malcolm was so good at oral sex. His mouth and tongue were inspiring, and his fingers were masterful mediators.

Yessss, his tongue was in constant motion, flat then pointy, soft then firm, fast then slow.

His dick fell from her mouth, her ragged breathing making it impossible to continue the mutual pleasure. Sky's head dropped to his leg, and she accepted everything he gave her. Malcolm would see her drenched and his face covered in her release before giving in to his own. She knew that about him and, today of all days, he would guarantee her pleasure first.

She came, body wracked with euphoria. Malcolm kept going and Sky continued to tremble her orgasm and keen with the gratifying carnality of having Malcolm between her legs, his tongue doing worshipful laps into her overflowing channel.

"Happy birthday," he mumbled against her lips.

Happy birthday indeed. Damn.

She took Malcolm in her mouth again, and his hands tightened around her hips. Raising his knees, Malcolm thrust upward, a short movement which sent him even deeper. She took all of him, the way he had her. No man had ever tasted so good in her mouth. It was Sky's birthday, Malcolm was close, and she would have all of him.

She sped up, and he tensed.

He tapped her lower back, a warning he was close, and she needed to stop. They always stopped before he came in her mouth. She didn't know if Malcolm thought it was the gentlemanly thing to do or whether he assumed she wouldn't allow him to finish that way.

Until today, she wouldn't have permitted him to come in her mouth. Sky sucked the head of his dick, drawing his pre-cum into her mouth and swallowing.

"Fuck. If you keep doing that—"

She did it again, relentless to take Malcolm to the edge and to push him over.

He came, and Sky didn't pull away. She held Malcolm in her mouth and let him ride out his orgasm, her hand around his dick and stroking him to completion. The sounds he made, behind her, were rewarding and erotic as hell.

Sky slipped from the bed and into the bathroom. She may have enjoyed giving Malcolm that level of freedom and pleasure, but she didn't think she'd ever get used to having sperm in her mouth.

When she finished brushing her teeth and turned to exit the bathroom, it was to meet Malcolm at the threshold, chest heaving and lips grinning. She'd never seen Malcolm like this, a primitive edge to the modern intellectual man. His irises were blown wide, nostrils flared, and dick phenomenally hard.

Her body responded to his. Sex throbbed with a strength that sent frissons of reawakened need through her.

"We're not done yet."

Oh, god.

The next thing Sky knew, Malcolm had her on the bathroom counter, with him between her legs and driving into her.

Oh, god, oh, god.

"I'm not close to being done with you."

She had no idea what to say to that, but a random thought sprang to mind and flew out of her mouth.

"Happy National Pumpkin Pie Day."

What Sky did to a red dress should be a crime. She was all soft curves, long legs, and cute bare feet covered by ballerina slippers, and Malcolm couldn't keep his eyes off her. Which explained, when Sky had come to an abrupt stop, why Malcolm ran into her back, his eyes on her toned legs and tight ass and not on where he was going.

She spun around, grabbed him by his hand and yanked him away from the kitchen and back into the hallway. "What in the hell are all those people doing in my kitchen?" A quick glance into the kitchen had Sky frowning. "And with their shoes on. I have shoe baskets in the foyer for a reason."

Malcolm peeked around Sky and into the kitchen. There had to be at least twelve people in there, half of them sitting at the kitchen table, while the others milled about her kitchen, talking and eating. Breakfast pastries were on her island, next to an assortment of juices. He smelled coffee, which meant someone had messed around in Sky's kitchen and had turned on her expensive-ass coffee maker. When he saw Yvette, he

334 · N.D. JONES

understood. Only Sky's aunt or uncle could get away with letting people into her home without her permission and not suffer her wrath.

Malcolm moved before anyone in the kitchen saw him. "Why are so many white people in your kitchen?" He frowned, as if he had a problem with the racial composition of her guests.

"Very funny."

"I'm serious. There are a lot of white people in your kitchen, none of whom I recognize."

Untrue. Malcolm recognized Robert, Olivia, and Carrie. Sky, who was rarely caught off guard, was so flustered at seeing her family there, he couldn't help but tease her.

"They're Robert's family. Oh, shit, Robert. I was supposed to have you pick him up and bring him here."

"It seems he got his own ride or drove himself. By the way, they're your family too."

"Robert's an awful driver, which is why he normally gets the chauffeur treatment. And I know they're my family, but I don't know who half of them are."

"It's about time the two of you decided to come downstairs and join the rest of us."

From the time he was a kid, and his mother always caught him doing something he shouldn't have, Malcolm knew Kimberly Styles had ninja skills. He and Sky turned to face his mother. Next to her was Charles and behind his parents were Angie and Sean. His brother-in-law stood close to Angie, his hands on her shoulders. Malcolm didn't want to think about what might have taken place between them after he'd left the guest room or last night after they'd turned in. Angie's smile-free face gave nothing away, which made it easier for Malcolm to push his sister's sex life from his mind.

Sean smirked at Malcolm and he knew what came next would have Sky blushing and him wanting to punch his brother-in-law in the face.

"So, it's noon on Christmas Day, and we've all been down, eaten, then showered, dressed, and came back downstairs. The Pages arrived, all of them looking for the birthday girl. Happy birthday, by the way, Sky. You don't look a day over twenty-five. Then the Ellises came, also looking for the birthday girl. And, guess what, no Sky or Malcolm until now. So, Sky, how's your birthday been so far? Any complaints you'd like to file with Counselor Franklin or a prenup you'd like me to draw up?"

Malcolm reached over his mother toward Sean's face.

The tall man laughed and dodged. "So sensitive. It's Christmas, bro, lighten up."

Malcolm swung at Sean again, another half-hearted attempt to shut his brother-in-law up. They hadn't played like this in months. Maybe it was the spirit of Christmas, the morning of amazing sex or maybe, just maybe, it was the glimmer of happiness returned to his sister's eyes. Slight but there.

But noon? Damn, he hadn't realized how long they'd been. After making love in the bathroom, they'd fallen back asleep, with Malcolm spooned around Sky. He'd awoken first the second time. They'd made love again, unrushed and playful. They'd kissed a lot and touched each other everywhere. He'd licked his way from her wiggling toes to her shivering shoulders and back down to her jiggling ass and quivering sex.

"You play too much. I'm going to knock that grin off your fa—"

"My birthday Sky."

Robert's voice halted Malcolm's playful "assault." He would pay Sean back later.

Taking Sky's hand in his, Robert escorted her into the kitchen, and Malcolm followed. Aunt Yvette gestured for him to join her by the island. He understood and left Sky to her father and her Ellis family.

"Merry Christmas," she said as soon as Malcolm approached, her arms going around his neck and hugging him as if they'd known each other for years and not simply two days.

"Merry Christmas."

336 · N.D. JONES

He hoped she wouldn't mention the obvious. With how late they'd joined the family, everyone had to know what Sky and he had been doing most of the morning. Thankfully, Sky's aunt had more tact than Malcolm's brother-in-law.

Yvette fixed Malcolm a plate of food and made him sit at the island and eat. He could get used to this treatment. The Pages exemplified southern hospitality.

"Orange, apple, or cranberry? Or would you rather have coffee?"

"Apple, please."

Yvette poured him a glass of juice, which he used to wash down the best scrambled eggs he'd ever had. Was that Old Bay seasoning and crab meat he tasted, mixed with sautéed onions and spinach? Yum. He added the salsa she'd placed on the side of his plate on top of a bite of omelet, which had him moaning at the deliciousness of the flavor. It was a sound he shouldn't make outside of the bedroom, but one he often did when eating great food.

"With noises like that, you and Sky will be expecting by this time next year."

"Sorry, I didn't mean to—"

"Don't be sorry, Malcolm. It's flattering. I'm sure Sky thinks so, too. She's cooked for you, right?"

"Sometimes. Mainly desserts. But we've also cooked together, the way you all did last night."

Yvette added more eggs and bacon to his plate. "That's good. A couple who cooks together stays together. Sky knows how to cook far more than desserts. Gloria, her grandmother, owned a restaurant. For a while, we thought Sky would take over the business, but she decided to go into higher education. My boys and Crystal run the restaurant. Sky will bring you there before you return to Buffalo. You look like you'd enjoy southern soul food. Try Brandon's slow baked turkey wings with rice and gravy. Jeremiah makes tasty pork ribs, so you'll have to come back for another night. How does that sound?"

"Like I'd be as wide as this island if I stayed here too long."

She laughed. "All in moderation. So, a pregnancy by next Christmas, which means a spring wedding. This house would be perfect for a spring wedding."

It would, but Yvette was putting the cart before the horse. He hadn't proposed, and while every instinct told him Sky would accept, the overweight kid who lived inside him feared she wouldn't.

Malcolm looked at Sky and her Ellis family.

So did Yvette. "How can a man have five children and not one of them look like him?"

Malcolm wondered the same. At least Robert's daughters had his olive hazel eyes. The two men, standing closest to Sky, who he assumed were her brothers Garrett and Aaron, didn't even have that Ellis feature, from what he could tell from there. The men did share their father's tall, lean frame and brown hair, although most of Robert's had turned white.

Olivia introduced Sky to people who were probably her husband and young adult children. Carrie sat at the kitchen table beside a blond man in glasses, who watched Carrie and not the awkward interplay between Sky and her no longer MIA brothers.

Other people sat at the table with Carrie, likely wives and children of Sky's brothers. When he'd invited her siblings, he hadn't envisioned all of this. He couldn't tell how Sky was handling having so many people in her house. Technically, they were her family. But family was more than biology. Still, the Ellises had to start building their bridge sometime. Why not on Christmas and Sky's birthday?

"There're more of them."

A glass of apple juice halfway to his mouth, Malcolm stopped and peered at Yvette who nodded in the direction of the archway that led to the dining room.

"Carrie's three children are here. All boys. A high school sophomore and a senior and a college junior. The last I saw of them, they were in the backyard with your nephew and a football. There're also a few little ones running around somewhere. Garrett's and Aaron's grandchildren.

I believe there may be more Ellises in the dining room, but after the fourth carload of them arrived, I stopped counting."

"Are you telling me Sky's entire Ellis family is somewhere in her house?"

He set the glass down. Malcolm didn't know whether to feel embarrassed for making love to Sky upstairs while her family was waiting for her downstairs or pissed-off at Robert for taking a simple invite for five and turning it into a damn Ellis family reunion.

"As far as I know. All four siblings, their spouses, and children. In the case of her brothers, their children's spouses and their grandchildren. Fun fact, Garrett's oldest daughter is only five years younger than Sky. I think he has the hardest time accepting Sky because, when he sees her, he's reminded of everything he dislikes about his father and himself. Garrett may not look like Robert, but the woman next to him is his third wife. Unlike Garrett's mother, his wives didn't put up with his cheating."

With a grin so Yvette would know he was teasing, Malcolm shook his head and tsked, "You're full of tea this morning."

"They're going to be your family, too. You might as well go into it with your eyes open."

He'd never understood the wide-eyed expressions people got when meeting the Styles. Sure, they could be loud and often lacked tact, but they were a fun-loving family with good hearts. Sitting across from Sky's complex family and, let's be honest, what family wasn't complex, Malcolm experienced his first wide-eyed moment.

"Does Robert know his daughter at all?"

"I've asked myself the same, over the years." Yvette plucked a cheese Danish from a dessert plate and put it on the saucer in front of her. Between sharing Ellis gossip, she'd sipped from her coffee cup. "Robert doesn't know Sky nearly as well as he wants to or should. Most of that is his fault, but some of it is also Sky's. She doesn't trust him fully, so she's found it difficult to be totally open with him. But Robert does know his daughter. He knows she would've never approved of him inviting over a dozen people, who she doesn't know, into her home. He knows, if left to her own devices, Sky would never make herself available to any of the people here today. He also knows, if he doesn't pull Sky into the Ellis family now, when he passes away, Carrie alone won't be enough to make it happen. In his stumbling, overbearing way, Robert is trying to give Sky the Ellis family his absence in her life denied her."

"They're strangers."

"They're also her family. Now that she's met them, and they've met her, it's up to them to determine how they'd like to move forward. It's Robert's birthday gift to his daughter. I doubt Sky sees it that way now. One day, however, I think she will. Now finish your meal."

Malcolm polished off the rest of his brunch, a full belly and a pleased smile from Yvette were his reward.

Sky glanced over her shoulder at Malcolm. He knew that look. It was the same one she'd worn when his family had cornered her in the hallway outside of Angie's recovery room. Back then, she'd sent him a text message asking for help. They'd left their cell phones in the bedroom, not that Sky would've texted him an SOS in front of her family.

"She needs you."

"Yeah, time for me to rescue my Christmas belle."

CHAPTER TWENTY-FIVE

Sky plastered on a smile. The same one she pulled out for members of EBC's Board of Trustees, for upset parents, for arrogant professors, for biased community members. Hell, for the president of EBC and for anyone she knew she could neither walk away from nor speak to the way she wanted without there being consequences she'd rather not face.

Robert patted her hand and beamed down at Sky with a smile that wasn't fake, but his joviality was damn sure forced. The man knew she hated being blindsided, which was exactly what he'd done by bringing all these people to her home without asking. Okay, not random people, but members of her extended Ellis family. That truth made Robert's actions marginally better.

Garrett and Aaron, whom she hadn't seen in two years, greeted Sky with self-conscious hugs. They'd never even touched her before today, much less hugged. Why in the hell were they doing so now?

"You're as beautiful as ever." Garrett, at fifty-four and dressed in a V-neck, black sweater with a collared white shirt underneath, had also never paid Sky a compliment. She wished he hadn't because now she had to say something kind in return.

"It's good to see you, Garrett. You too, Aaron. Merry Christmas to you both and to your families."

Three years younger than Garrett, Aaron had treated Sky with indifferent kindness, which she found worse than Olivia's mean barbs and Garrett's haughty attitude. Today, however, his blue eyes took in Sky with a level of sincerity she'd never seen from him before. It unsettled her because the sudden change placed her on an unsure footing. These were the brothers she'd grown to know and to distrust. But they weren't acting according to their established script.

An excruciating amount of time was spent on introductions. Sky met her brothers' wives, children, and grandchildren. Olivia had also returned for a third day, her family in tow. Her husband, Jared, as large and friendly as Uncle Kenny, wasn't what she'd expected. She'd assumed any man married to Olivia wouldn't be in possession of either a heart or a spine. An awful way to view her sister, but Olivia had earned Sky's harsh opinion of her. Although, as she'd begun to know the less hostile version of Olivia, Sky had to update her analysis of her sister. Perhaps she'd have to do the same for her brothers.

She watched people move between the kitchen and the dining room. Sky tried to tamp down her annoyance at having virtual strangers traipsing through a home built by a woman many of them had despised. Part of her conflict with her brothers was their obvious hostility toward her mother. She got it. Sky really did. At the same time, she wouldn't tolerate any anti-Sade language in front of her. They could hate Sade all they wanted, that was their right, but Sky would be damned if she stayed silent while they maligned her mother.

So, they rarely saw each other or spoke. If not for Robert's heart attack, which brought them together at the hospital, then at his home after his release, Olivia, Garrett, and Aaron wouldn't have tried to include Sky in the family at all.

Her discomfiture and low-grade anger were precisely how she thought she'd feel if she spent the holiday with her Ellis family. Thanks to Malcolm, the degree of both wasn't as intense as they could've been if this family reunion had occurred at Robert's home instead of hers.

Sky searched for and found Malcolm. Lucky man, Aunt Yvette had steered him clear of the Ellises and had fed him. She would thank her aunt later. She also needed to eat. Malcolm was an exhausting lover. With him around, Sky wouldn't need to jog so much to burn calories.

"This is a great house."

Letting Aaron know Sade had paid to have the house built was on the tip of her tongue. She looked over her shoulder to Malcolm again. She'd die a thousand deaths if she were forced to endure small talk with her brothers.

"Thank you."

Their wives and children had drifted away, after introductions. Olivia and her husband sat with Carrie and Peter at the kitchen table. Sky waved at Peter, who appeared as besotted with Carrie as ever. Like Olivia, she had no idea why Carrie claimed they were divorcing. Who in the hell invited their soon-to-be ex-husband to a family Christmas gathering? From the look of Carrie, she hid something under the red-and-white candy cane scarf around her neck. Olivia was right, Carrie was having an affair with her husband.

"Tell your brothers about Buffalo and your new job."

Curse Robert. What had he expected would happen, when he brought them together? They were worse than strangers. With strangers, when they met, they started from scratch. They didn't come into the situation with preconceived notions. For Sky and her siblings, all they had were fixed beliefs and intolerance. To change the direction of their dysfunctional relationship would take a lot of effort on everyone's part. Sky didn't think her brothers were committed to putting forth that kind of effort. She didn't know if she was either.

Like a wish on a shooting star, Malcolm appeared by her side and laced their fingers. As soon as they touched, his hand steady and solid, Sky exhaled. His silent strength buoyed. For so long, Sky had relied only on herself, too afraid to depend on anyone the way she had Sade. With Malcolm, she had a partner and a wall of support.

Before she could introduce Malcolm to her brothers, Robert stepped in.

"This is Dr. Malcolm Styles. Malcolm, I hope you don't mind, but I told Aaron and Garrett a little about you. The tall guy in front of you is Garrett, Sky's oldest brother. And this is Aaron, my youngest son."

The men shook hands, Malcolm as friendly and charming as ever.

"It's nice to meet you both. I'm glad you could fit us into your holiday plans."

"It's Sky's birthday," Aaron said. "As an Ellis family, we don't get together nearly enough. We're all so busy, heads in the sand, we forget to look up every once and a while to see what's going on around us." Aaron's gaze moved from Malcolm to her. "Happy birthday, Sky. I've never said that before, which makes me a shit brother."

Garrett, taller than Sky at six-one, reached out and touched her shoulder, but quickly withdrew his hand, as if she would shrug him away if he left it there too long. "Mom told us what she did to you when you were a kid."

Robert stiffened at her side. "What are you talking about? What did Lois do to Sky?"

She hadn't seen her father angry in a long time. Sky had forgotten, with Robert's heart attack and health issues, how formidable the former captain and governor could be.

Garrett didn't flinch at Robert's hard tone, but he did look to his brother for support before responding to their father. "We thought you knew. We assumed, since it happened so long ago, Sky or her mother would've told you. I know Mom never did but I ..."

Twenty-eight years ago, to be precise. Like Garrett, Sky had also assumed Sade had told Robert. When her father never mentioned his ex-wife having slapped a seven-year-old Sky, she hadn't questioned the omission. She'd wanted to forget the ugly scene had ever happened. For once, Sky thought she and Robert had drawn the same conclusion about the past. Some instances were best left in the past. But Robert hadn't known, and heat radiated from him in waves of anger.

"Mom told Aaron and me yesterday. I haven't seen Mom cry in years."

"I'll ask again, what did Lois do to Sky?"

Sky shook her head at Garrett when his questioning eyes fell to her. She would not get into this today. To hell with Lois and her guilty conscience. She should've kept her mouth shut. No wonder her brothers had shown up on her doorstep. Lois had passed along her guilt to her sons.

She didn't want their sympathy or Robert's belated anger. From the look of the men, she had them anyway. Dammit.

Malcolm raised the back of her hand to his mouth and planted a sweet kiss there. He then kissed her cheek, his actions characteristic of hime, but in stark contrast to the rising tension.

With two chaste kisses, he'd calmed Sky and deescalated what could've been a terrible family argument.

"Listen, Ellises, it's Christmas and Sky's birthday, as we all know. I know you are family, but you don't know each other well. You also don't know me. But this is what's not going to happen. No one, not her brothers or even her father, will ruin her day. Garrett and Aaron, I don't care why you're here, as long as you're nice and respectful to your sister. I also don't care what happened between your mother and Sky. She clearly doesn't want to talk about it so no one will have that conversation in her home. If you must have it, Garrett, then you and Robert can take it outside and beyond earshot of Sky and everyone else. Final point, there are shoe baskets in the foyer, use them or your sister will continue to obsess about the dirt you already tracked into her home." Malcolm squeezed Sky's hand and asked, "Anything else?"

"No."

"The lady has spoken. But she hasn't eaten yet. Have the two of you?"

Like Olivia, Garrett didn't have the warmest of smiles, but he offered it to Sky and Malcolm. "Aaron and I can always eat." He looked down at his feet. "Um, we'll join Sky after we take care of our shoes."

Like the naval officers they were, Aaron and Garrett ordered everyone back to the foyer. Robert went with them, assuring Sky he would "make sure they got it right."

Sky didn't know how they could get it wrong, but for a blessed three minutes, her kitchen was quiet.

She kissed Malcolm. "You're sexy when you're acting like an alpha male. I brought two Christmas-themed lingerie with me. I'll wear one for you tonight. Or we could sneak back upstairs and—"

A throat cleared from the direction of the kitchen table. Carrie. "Happy birthday, baby sister."

A quiet kitchen, but not an empty one.

Even though she'd eaten a late breakfast, Sky had plenty of room for Christmas dinner. To her surprise, her Ellis family not only stayed for dinner but also for the opening of presents. Garrett, Olivia, and Aaron must've made a pact forged in Hell because they were pleasant, even friendly.

She needed to stop thinking of them as three escaped demons from the hot and fiery place. If she didn't, they would never move beyond the cold animosity which defined their relationship. Sky couldn't deny the olive branch they'd extended her, especially Olivia. The least she could do was accept theirs and offer her own.

"Why are you frowning?"

Malcolm whispered the question in her ear. They sat on the loveseat. If not for the fact this was Sky's home and birthday, with so many people visiting, they may have found themselves seated on the floor with most everyone else. Charles, Kim, Robert, Yvette, and Kenny shared the chaise sectional sofa. Her brothers' wives and Olivia claimed the second sofa, while Garrett, Aaron, and Jared sat on the floor in front of the women.

Sean had commandeered the two single chairs in the room for Angie and Carrie. He'd pulled up the ottoman and sat beside his wife, which was typical of Sean. Following the other lawyer's lead, Peter had grabbed the ottoman in front of Carrie and sat. She'd seen Peter and Sean talking earlier, Maryland's Attorney General and a respected civil rights lawyer.

Everyone else either stood or sat on the floor. With so many people in attendance and the tree and presents taking up an entire corner, it made for a tight fit. No one complained, though.

No one except Sky.

She turned and whispered to Malcolm. "There are too many people in my home. Stop laughing, I'm serious."

"I know you're serious. That's why I'm laughing." He kissed the tip of her nose, as if humoring an irrational child. "You're adorable when you've exhausted your social interactions meter."

"I don't have a social interactions meter. What I have are over two dozen people in my house who are very close to having overstayed their welcome."

"Yeah, I don't know where I got the idea you have a social interactions meter. Nope, not you. You're the life of the party. A true social butterfly."

"Oh, be quiet. Maybe I do have a meter that's perilously close to the top. Even you can't deny there are too many people in this room."

"It's kind of tight, true. But once the presents are opened, people will spread to other parts of the house."

"They've been here for hours already. I've sheltered and fed them. What else do I need to do before they get bored and leave?"

"You're awful. I would call you a mean introvert, but I'm afraid you'll add me to the list of people you want to kick out of your house."

"You're cute, but not funny."

Sky trailed her hand down Malcolm's tie. After dinner, he'd gone upstairs and changed clothes. His intelligence, stylish suits, long dreadlocks, and overall good looks had drawn her to him even when he'd asked her out and she'd turned him down.

He wore a black pinstriped suit with a white shirt and a green, red, and white striped holiday tie. He'd left the suit jacket upstairs, but she had no idea why he'd changed. When she'd asked, he told her his khakis and sweater didn't match her red dress. That was true, his clothing had been more casual than hers. But he'd known that when they'd dressed together.

Sky didn't mind. Malcolm had exquisite taste in clothing. He'd also pulled his hair up into a bun. She'd seen him do it before, but it still amazed her how he managed to wrap so much hair into such a tidy bun that stayed put.

"You also know you're the last person I'd kick out."

"You wouldn't kick anyone out. You're too polite."

"Not Angie and her children."

"Oh, only those four? You'd kick out your father and my parents?"

"Maybe."

"Your aunt and uncle?"

"Probably."

He laughed and hugged her to him. "Just admit it. You're enjoying yourself, even with a house full of people."

"Perhaps."

"Another one-word response. Your meter really is full. On another note, Robert hasn't done anything over the top for your birthday."

"You mean other than inviting every Ellis in Maryland to my home without telling me?"

"Yeah, other than that."

Malcolm had a point. She'd expected Robert to breeze in with caterers and an ostentatious birthday cake made by a French pastry chef.

Other than the entourage of Ellises, Robert had been low-key in his celebration of Sky's birthday. It was a nice change of pace. For once, her father had made a decision based on her needs instead of on his.

"The no-frills birthday is his present to you."

"I'm just now realizing that. It's the best gift Robert has ever given me. Yesterday, when he asked me to have you pick him up, I was sure the two of you had something up your sleeves."

"Something over-the-top, you mean?"

"It would be like the two of you. I don't need grand gestures. Simplistic and thoughtful are the best gifts. It's why I love the angel topper so much."

With Jeremiah's help, Sky had added the topper to her Christmas tree. When the Pages had seen Sade's name stitched into the hem of the gold dress, as if compelled, their gazes had shifted to the framed picture on the mantel of Sade holding a newborn Sky.

She swore her mother had smiled at them but knew it had to be the play of the tree lights and her curtain of tears.

They stopped talking when people began exchanging presents. While Malcolm and Sky were otherwise preoccupied upstairs, Sean and Angie had permitted their children to open gifts from them and their grandparents. Sky didn't blame the couple. SJ, Kayla, and Zuri were already away from home on Christmas. They shouldn't also have to wait until the evening to open their presents.

The kids tore through the gifts from their uncle and Sky. Everyone watched, in silence and with smiles. Most of the adults were parents, so they'd seen this scene many times before. Who didn't love watching happy children? Even without presents, the Franklin-Styles children were happy. That didn't happen accidentally. Angie and Sean were wonderful parents.

"Thank you, Uncle Malcolm." SJ held up a logo backpack and a virtual reality headset.

"You're a sneaky woman. I dropped off everyone's gifts before we left so they would have them on Christmas, even with me here."

"It's all part of my Christmas gift to you. I like to be thorough. If the children opened your gifts at home, you would've missed how happy you'd made them."

Sky nodded to Kayla, who pulled out one item after another from a new fuchsia ballerina duffle bag Malcolm had purchased the eleven-year-old. She squealed as she unwrapped each gift. A ballerina treasure music box, an emoji dancing girl soft toy, a personalized water bottle, a dance bag tag, and a ballet dancer beaded bracelet.

"I've never missed a Christmas with them or a birthday. I know I won't be able to make every one of them, especially when they grow up. But now, when they're still young, I do love to see them like this."

Half of Zuri's body disappeared into her large gift bag, as she removed one present after another. Of the gifts Malcolm had purchased for his youngest niece, Sky's favorite was the Princess Shuri action figure. "She's brilliant and can kick ass," Malcolm had told Sky. "An overrated Black Panther aside, his sister Shuri is a great role model for a little girl." He'd laughed and amended, "The action figure may be redundant, though, considering Zuri has a brilliant, kickass mother at home."

Zuri opened her second gift from Sky. Technically, the season passes to New York City's The New Victory Theater, a nonprofit, specializing in shows for kids and families, were for the entire family. Zuri handed the red envelope and tickets to Angie who explained the gift to her daughter.

Malcolm squeezed her tight to him. "Thank you for knowing how much I would've missed seeing my family today, especially the kids."

Zuri, Kayla, and SJ made their way to their uncle. He accepted their hugs, as he always did, with a big grin and watery eyes. They also hugged Sky, thanking her for their presents. Unlike Malcolm, she had no idea what they would like. A gift card and money, easy go-to-gifts, seemed lazy and impersonal. They should really thank their mother, who'd supplied Sky with a couple of gift ideas from the children's Christmas lists. However, Sky could take credit for The New Victory

Theater idea. She understood the importance of integrating the arts into the lives of children, and so did Sean and Angie.

"Robert," Charles's voice boomed, "I know Sky's your daughter, but I'm going to take her from you."

"You can't have my Sky. Although I may be willing to make a gift trade. What did she get you in that gift basket? Anything navy related?"

"Sorry to disappoint, but Sky knows what I like, and it isn't the water. Buffalo Bills all the way. She even got the jersey right this time."

Malcolm's warm breath rimmed her ear. "I hope you got me one too, or I'm stealing Dad's."

She had, but he'd have to wait until tomorrow night. She planned to wear it to bed. If he wanted the jersey, he'd have to peel it from her nude body. The thought had Sky squeezing Malcolm's thigh and kissing his jaw.

Her aunt and uncle exchanged gifts and received presents from their sons, daughter-in-law, and Sky. Angie and Sean didn't open gifts from each other. Sky didn't know whether they'd done that earlier, when Malcolm and Sky were upstairs, or if they'd decided to forego exchanging gifts this year.

"You should give your father his gift now," Malcolm suggested.

Sky went to the mantel and grabbed the nine by twelve manila envelope she'd put there yesterday and handed it to Robert. Her father was a difficult man to buy for because he was picky and had a lot of material possessions. She rarely thought Robert and her were alike but, in some ways, they were.

Like Sky, Robert needed to feel loved and wanted.

He opened the envelope and pulled out the papers. Three were receipts and the others Sky's work calendar.

"The days marked in blue are when EBC is closed, and I don't have to work. Green represents my busy weeks, but I'm not so overloaded I can't take a Friday off for a long weekend. Red is when I'm swamped so those won't be good times."

"These are receipts for two open-ended airline tickets to Buffalo."

"For spring break and summer vacation. Carrie agreed to travel with you so Olivia, Garrett, and Aaron won't worry."

"What's this other receipt?"

"Father's Day weekend. I'll be back then, but without Malcolm."

She hadn't spoken loudly. In fact, her voice was pitched so only Robert could hear. But the room had gone silent, and Sky felt everyone's eyes on the two of them.

A daughter's olive branch and public forgiveness. Sky couldn't do this anymore. Her last boyfriend told her to "fish or cut bait." He was the first to put her inability to commit so bluntly, but her other boyfriends had made similar comments. Each time, she'd cut bait. Sky looked back at Malcolm, who still sat on the loveseat, and then back to Robert. No, Sky was done with cutting bait.

This time, with Robert and with Malcolm, she would fish.

Robert's embrace didn't surprise Sky, but his tears did. They'd hugged before but never like this. "I'm sorry. If I could do it over, I would be a better father to you."

"I know." She'd told him that before, but this was the first time she'd meant it. The first time Sky believed Robert had meant what he'd said. "Consider this new beginning as a Christmas present for us both."

"I haven't given you my gift yet." He kissed her cheek. "I used to keep it in my keepsake box, but I took it out yesterday and left it on the windowsill in your office."

"I didn't see it."

"I wanted to give it to you yesterday, but you were too upset. You don't have to open it now or even today. It's yours. I hope, one day, you'll find a use for it."

He kissed her cheek again and held Sky for a long while before letting her go and returning to the sofa. Uncle Kenny patted Robert on the back and shook his hand.

After the moment with Robert, she'd walked past a waiting Malcolm, down the hall, and into her office.

He'd followed, closing the office door after them.

"Are you okay?" Malcolm asked.

She didn't know. "Robert said he left my Christmas present in here."

On the windowsill was a box. Small, dark-red, velvet. Sky trembled, but her hand managed to keep hold of the ring box when she picked it up and turned back to Malcolm. She opened her palm to reveal the box to him.

"Are you proposing, Dr. Ellis?"

"No, but I think my father did."

"You mean to your mother? I thought you said he was married when you were a kid."

"He was, but Robert and Lois divorced. I don't know when. By the time Robert reentered my life, he and Lois were no longer married. I never cared enough to want to know details. When we talked on the sofa last night, I told you about Robert's keepsake box."

"His greatest treasures and biggest regrets."

"Right. Apparently, this was also in there."

Sky inhaled deeply, held it, then released the breath. With Malcolm's reassuring presence in front of her, she opened the box.

Simple and sophisticated. No colored stones or artsy settings just a classic design. It was a traditional diamond engagement ring.

Malcolm whistled. "Beautiful."

An understatement. Sky removed the ring from the case, examining every inch of it. "I think there's writing on the band. Can you read what it says?"

They moved to the desk, and Malcolm clicked on the lamp. Better.

"Sade Ellis," they read aloud.

"Your father proposed to your mother."

"Apparently."

"And she turned him down."

"She must've. Mom never told me about the proposal."

"Makes sense she didn't. You knowing wouldn't have changed anything. Your father got a divorce then came crawling back to your mother after abandoning her and you for years."

"Mom couldn't forgive him, I suppose."

"Either that or she no longer loved Robert. Probably both."

"Why would he give me this now?"

"Because you never believed he loved your mother, and he probably couldn't think of another way to prove to you that he had. For Sade, Robert's proposal was probably a case of too little too late. For him, it was his final play of the game, fourth down with no timeouts and an entire football field to traverse. It was his Hail Mary into the end zone. One shot. Win or lose." Malcolm took the ring from Sky's hand and returned it to the box, snapping the top closed. "He lost."

The way he said those two words had Sky placing the box on her desk and looking at him. "What's wrong?"

"Nothing."

A lie.

"Malcolm, tell me what's wrong."

"It's nothing. I was just thinking how deflated Robert must've been when your mother turned him down. Don't get me wrong, Sade should've sent his ass packing. What were you, like sixteen, when he found his balls and decided to do the right thing by you and Sade?"

She nodded.

"Robert didn't deserve a second chance, which doesn't mean I still don't feel sorry for him. He had to know the chances of Sade accepting his proposal were slim to none. But he went for it anyway. Maybe to prove to himself he could. Likely, though, he wanted to prove to your mother he'd stopped being a coward and was finally ready to put the two of you first in his life."

"Not exactly a romantic proposal."

"Guilt and a broken heart don't make for a good foundation of a marriage. Thankfully, your mother knew that."

Malcolm was right, but Sky sensed a deeper emotion coming from him. The only thing she could liken it to was the night he'd shared stories of his childhood obesity.

"We should be getting back. Besides Robert, no one has had a chance to give you gifts." She said nothing, and he shook his head at her. "You forgot, didn't you?"

"I didn't forget. I just wasn't expecting anything."

"Which is worse than forgetting. Come on, time for you to open birthday and Christmas presents."

CHAPTER TWENTY-SIX

"Sky looks happy." Sean bumped Malcolm's shoulder with his. "You don't. Cold feet?"

From the threshold of the living room, Malcolm watched Sky. She sat at the loveseat with Robert, who played Santa Claus, handing Sky one gift after another from her family. There were many, each of which Sky took her time opening, reading birthday and Christmas cards first before unwrapping each present. No doubt, Sade Page had instilled that bit of polite protocol into her daughter.

Malcolm walked away from the gathering and toward the kitchen. As he hoped he would, Sean followed. They sat across from each other at the table, which, like the island, was covered with containers of leftovers. When Sky had realized the Ellises planned on staying for Christmas dinner, she'd ordered food from the Page family restaurant—Soulful Cravings. The last-minute holiday takeout order pushed Christmas dinner back two hours and filled in more of Sky's social interactions meter.

"What's going on with you? All things considered, this turned out to be a pretty good Christmas. By the way, thanks for the gifts. You always know the right presents to buy for the kids. They all love Uncle Malcolm."

"I love them, too."

"Put a ring on Sky's finger, and you can have your own Styles of Love trilogy. You're kind of long in the tooth, though," Sean joked. "If you and Sky start right after you marry, you could have three ankle biters of your own before you turn forty-two."

Malcolm knew he wanted children. He had for a long time. But he didn't want to have a child for the sake of becoming a father. The right woman needed to come first.

"Now that we're alone. There's something that's been bothering me." Sean sounded serious, but his eyes twinkled with humor. "There are pictures of Sky's mother in the foyer and living room. The woman was JET Beauty of the Week gorgeous. This is my question. How in the hell did Robert Ellis score a woman like her? Don't get me wrong, he's not fugly, but Sade Page was way out of his league. Kind of like Sky is way out of yours."

"You're an ass." Malcolm couldn't help it, he laughed. "I had the same thought, though."

"About Sky being way out of your league?"

"No, you, punk, about Robert and Sade. Honestly, I think they had a lot in common. Don't underestimate the power of cerebral attraction."

"I know all about cerebral attraction. Only a stupid or shallow man looks for a woman with more body than brains. Your sister has both."

"So why did you cheat?" Shit, he hadn't meant to ask that. Sean and him were beginning to find their old rhythm. Malcolm missed their friendship. Yet, he couldn't forget what Sean had done. "Sorry, that was out of line. I didn't mean it."

"You meant it. It's the question everyone wants to know. If I love and desire my wife, how could I fuck around on her? Men cheat for many reasons. While Sky didn't come right out and tell the family the complete deal with her parents, having met her father and siblings, it was easy enough to fill in the blanks. I don't know why Robert screwed around on his wife with Sade, other than the fact the woman was hot. For some guys, that alone is enough. If the woman is attractive, interested, and low-maintenance, he's there. If she's a challenge but digs him, he's there. If he's lonely and she makes time for him, he's there. If he's tired of perfunctory sex with the missus and thinks a different woman will spice up his sex life, he's there."

"Which category did you fall into?"

Sean's eyes dropped from Malcolm's to the wooden kitchen table. He remained quiet for several minutes. Soul searching, perhaps, or figuring out the best words to explain his infidelity, or maybe hoping Malcolm would move on to another topic. Which, yeah, was fair. They hadn't escaped the living room for the privacy of the kitchen to talk about Sean's marriage.

"Listen, skip my question. It's none of my business. Angie is the only person entitled to the answer, anyway. I guess that's part of the marriage counseling."

"It is. We covered the why of my cheating early on in therapy. Every time I go, it's like being under a goddamn microscope. I can't lie, because lying is what got me in this shit in the first place. I can't tell my wife I enjoyed the sex but felt like dirt afterward. But I kept going back, so what the fuck does that say about me? A part of Angie thinks she did something wrong, that there's a deficiency in her that drove me to another woman. How messed up is that? I do something wrong, and Angie blames herself. Sometimes, Malcolm, a man is just weak. I know it's not what you want to hear, especially since you plan on proposing to Sky. But it's the truth. I'm not saying you'll be like Robert and me and creep out on your wife or that Sky will let some other guy—"

"Don't go there."

"Right. Sorry, man. My point is that most men go into marriage with the best intentions. Unless he's a piece of shit to begin with, he doesn't see himself betraying the woman he loves. But it happens all the time. Some women forgive, while others can't. Real talk, bro, Sky will walk away from your ass if you hurt her the way I did Angie. If any part of you thinks you can't go the rest of your life having sex with one woman, don't you dare propose. I mean it. I'm not talking about only Sky's feelings. I'm also talking about yours. You'd break your own heart if you did something to cause Sky to run fast and far from you. You don't want to do that to yourself. I was this close" —Sean raised his index finger and thumb, the two almost touching— "to Angie putting my ass out the house permanently and being done with me. I swear, if it weren't for our children, I think she would've. Besides her car crash, I've never been so afraid of losing my wife."

The conversation had taken an unexpected turn. Sean and Malcolm used to confide in each other. Since learning of his brother-in-law's infidelity, their friendship, like Sean's marriage, had taken a serious hit. Watching his friend, he could see the toll the past year had taken on him and how much he'd lost. While Angie had countless people she could confide in, including Sky, Sean wasn't the type of man to share his family issues, not even with his friends. Malcolm had been the exception. In this situation, however, he didn't have Malcolm's ear or even his heart. Those belonged to Angie. He would always have his sister's back. But no one had had Sean's.

"I'm sorry. I didn't mean to unload like that. You're my brother, and I love you. Sky is amazing, and you are perfect for each other. The two of you are every corny love song."

Malcolm liked that idea. "*Baby Love*, The Supremes."

"*Endless Love*, Diana Ross and Lionel Richie."

"I'll raise you a duet with a quartet. Boyz II Men's *I'll Make Love to You*."

"Bet. Rihanna featuring Calvin Harris. *We Found Love*. The song was on Billboard's hot one hundred chart for ten weeks." Sean grabbed a brownie from a container in front of him, devouring it in two bites. "Don't ask me why I know that bit of worthless information."

"Was the song before or after the Chris Brown incident?"

"I have no idea, but Brown's image hasn't been the same since he was arrested for abusing Rihanna. Are you folding?"

"No, but I have a song for you. Al Green's _Let's Stay Together_."

"Just because we're alone in the kitchen, it doesn't mean I won't tell your sister you hit on me."

They slapped hands, laughing loudly.

"What I've learned from counseling is that staying together is only one step. An important step, don't get me wrong, but still only one. For months, I thought if I could just convince my wife to stay then everything would be fine. But it wasn't. Staying is just that. I stayed. She stayed. But we were stuck. Staying together isn't enough."

"So write the rest of the lyrics to Green's song."

"That's what I've been trying to do."

"Don't try. Do."

"Are you going to take your own advice?"

"I found out tonight, after his divorce, Robert proposed to Sade and she rejected him."

"I get it now. That's what's bothering you." Sean devoured another cheesecake brownie. "Sky's not her mother, and you're damn sure not her father. Your lady won't turn you down."

"How do you know? Sky literally told me not to use her birthday as an excuse to propose on Christmas."

"Look, I won't pretend I know what in the hell goes on in a woman's mind. This is what I do know because I have eyes, ears, and a highly functioning brain. Sky told Robert she'd visit him for Father's Day, but that you wouldn't be with her."

"So?"

"As smart as you are, you can be dense sometimes. A few months ago, I accused you of treating Sky like your wife. I was right, by the way, but moving on. This trip, however, was the first time I witnessed Sky treat you like her husband. She gave you full run of her expensive house, allowing you to make decisions she could've made herself. Angie told me what Sky said to you about accepting your work around her house because it was a present to her. A gift from me to you: that was pure bull. If she had a problem with you treating her home as if it were

360 · N.D. JONES

your personal DIY project, she would've shut you down. Sky didn't say anything because she couldn't care less if you wanted to turn her home into a case of neighbors on Christmas crack. She let you do it, not for her own sake but for yours."

The fist that had taken hold of his heart and squeezed when he'd seen Robert's love, manifested in an elegant diamond ring and engraved with the last name Sade Page had never claimed, began to ease. Malcolm had almost allowed fear and self-doubt to take him off his fated path.

"Sky's already thinking about how the two of you will divvy-up your time with family and between two states. She knows you'll want to celebrate Father's Day with Charles, while Robert will want to do the same with her. She didn't want to put you in the position of having to choose between staying in Buffalo or traveling here with her, so she made the decision for you. If that's not a wife move, I don't know what is. She's ready. The best part is Sky knows she's ready. You know it too. You just got twisted around for a minute. It happens to the best of us. Wait until the day of your wedding. Your brain will turn to complete mush, especially when you see your wife-to-be standing at the altar, beautiful and waiting to take you as her husband."

"You cried at your wedding."

"No, I didn't."

"Big tears and with snot running from your nose. You were disgusting, but Angie married you anyway."

"I didn't snot on my wife. I may have cried a tear or two." Sean smiled. "That was the happiest day of my life. Then Angie gave me SJ and that became my happiest day. Then Kayla and Zuri came along, and I felt blessed even more."

"You also cried at their births."

"Trust me, so will you. I won't even pretend I didn't. It's the best feeling in the world to see the woman you love give birth to a child you created together. It's humbling but also empowering. You and Sky will have all of that, and so much more."

He believed Sean because he trusted himself and had faith in the love he and Sky shared. But his past, present, and future family plan, based on a statement Sky had made today, needed a bit of alteration. *I don't need grand gestures. Simplistic and thoughtful are the best gifts.*

"Do me a favor, let everyone know I no longer need their help. I'm taking Sky out, so I also need you to make sure anyone who's not staying here is long gone by the time I get back with Sky. The Styles have rooms, make sure you're in them, so I can have the downstairs."

"Because you got this, right?"

Hell, yes, Malcolm had this.

"Here, Aunt Sky."

She smiled down at Zuri, adorable in her red Mary Jane Christmas dress with long sleeves, Peter Pan collar, and a ruffled tutu skirt. A red and white Elf's hat covered most of her braids, as well as her eyes. Sky pulled the pom-pom embellishment, so she could better see the little girl.

"Where did you get this?"

Sky took her cell phone from Zuri and glanced around. Most of the Styles, as well as her father and brothers, had retreated to the family room to watch Monday Night Football. Apparently, since Christmas fell on Monday this year, the National Football League had scheduled a doubleheader. She had no idea which teams had to spend their holiday chasing a ball and being hit by other men, but she'd been grateful when eight-thirty had rolled around. The beginning of the game didn't lower the volume of voices in her home, but it had reduced the number of people in her living room.

"Uncle Malcolm gave it to me."

"Thank you." Sky bent and kissed Zuri's forehead. She was a sweetheart.

As only a five-year-old could, Zuri skipped away, humming the tune to *Jingle Bells*.

Malcolm had disappeared with Sean, about an hour ago. While Sean had returned, Malcolm had not. It wasn't like him to leave without saying anything to her. True, he may not have wanted to interrupt since she was opening gifts. None of her presents had been from Malcolm, though, which was fine. Sky hadn't given him his either. She assumed they would exchange gifts once everyone had gone home.

Still, his unexplained absence worried Sky, more than her irrational sting of disappointment did. She'd asked Malcolm not to propose on her birthday. It was what Sky had wanted. So why, after all presents had been given and received, did she feel a sense of loss? Malcolm was a man of his word, so he hadn't broken his vow.

Her smile of gratitude for the kind gifts masked the crushing weight of her letdown. It had hit her, an unexpected tsunami. The earthquake in her heart caused the high sea wave, fissures of delusion and desire exploding upon impact. She was a damn fool. Pride and trepidation were inadequate roots for sound decision-making.

The cell phone in her hand buzzed. Bringing the screen to life, Sky hit the message icon and read the text.

Your sleigh awaits. Meet me in the foyer.

Above Malcolm's message was an emoji of a red-nosed reindeer.

Sky's heart picked up, and so did her feet, as she ran from the living room and toward the entryway. She slid to a stop. Malcolm, suit jacket on and dressed to impress, stood in front of the front door. In one hand, he held her coat and purse. In the other a pair of high-heeled boots she'd bought before moving to Buffalo. Sky's second closet was full of clothing she hadn't taken with her, including over a dozen pairs of shoes.

She didn't know what possessed her to buy the pair he held, other than she loved the ruby color. The four-inch-high, red sequined, thigh-high boots matched her red dress to perfection.

Sky snatched off her ballerina slippers and dropped them into a shoe basket.

"Been digging through my closet, I see." She took the shoes from Malcolm. The boots were as gorgeous as she remembered, and the sequins felt like liquid. "When I put these on, I'm going to be taller than you by two inches."

"I don't care."

Malcolm watched her pull down the side-zipper closure and put the boots on. Sky hadn't worn heels this high in a while, so it took her a second to steady herself.

"I knew they would look sexy on you. You're gorgeous. I'm a lucky man."

He made her feel like a lucky woman. With a single text message, Malcolm had pushed back her raging tsunami. His good looks and secretive smile were a pot of gold at the end of a Christmas rainbow.

"Where are we going?" Malcolm helped Sky into her coat and handed her her purse, into which she dropped her cell phone. "I didn't think you knew any places in Annapolis."

"I don't. I'm the chauffeur, but you're the GPS. Let's go."

Route fifty took them to Sandy Point State Park, seven hundred eighty-six acres of protected land. Swimming, fishing, crabbing, boating, and hiking, Sandy Point drew thousands of people a year, mainly locals but also tourists like Malcolm.

He slowed at the tunnel leading to the Chesapeake Bay Bridge, and the sight took Sky's breath away. Archways of white light crossed overhead, from one side of the road to the other. A stunning light display Sky hadn't seen in years.

"Lights on the Bay." The words came out on a whispered sigh of pleasure. "How did you know about this place?"

"How else? Google. I searched Christmas in Annapolis. Lights on the Bay at Sandy Point State Park popped up. I vaguely remember you mentioning the park another time. You've seen this before, right?"

"A long time ago. I didn't remember it being this lovely, though."

Malcolm drove through the park, as awed by the holiday displays as Sky. They pointed out each light display on their side of the truck, making sure the other didn't miss anything.

"Angie's kids would love it here, especially Zuri."

"I know. I've already sent your sister pics. She told me to get off the phone and enjoy my birthday outing."

Santa and his sleigh, pulled by nine reindeers, reminded Sky of Malcolm's reindeer emoji. Five Victorian carolers and a giant holiday train had Malcolm slowing even more. But it was the ice castle display, with polar bears and flags coming from steeples that had Malcolm stopping.

"Come on, I want to take a pic of us in front of this one."

Before she got out of the truck, Malcolm was on the passenger side, his hand helping her down. He didn't have on his coat, so she took hers off, which made for the quickest round of picture-taking ever. But Malcolm had gotten his pictures of them outside the wrought-iron gate, which enclosed the ice castle, their nice clothing not covered by winter coats.

"Is that a juggling snowman?" Malcolm asked, when they were back in the truck and moving again.

"It is. I have one on my side, too, except the snowman is juggling candy canes and not..." Sky stared at the snowman on Malcolm's side. He wore a green hat and red scarf, but she couldn't make out what he juggled. "They look like lit circles."

"I'm going with marshmallows."

"Marshmallows? Wouldn't snowballs make more sense?"

"Not to me. When I think of marshmallows, hot chocolate with real chocolate comes to mind. Do we have any back at the house?"

"Maybe."

"Maybe, huh? I'll take that as a yes."

"I suppose you want me to fix you a cup of homemade hot chocolate, when we get back."

"If it's no bother. It is your birthday, after all."

"Which means you should be the one to fix me the hot cocoa."

"Maybe."

"That's an awful imitation. I don't sound like that."

"Whatever you say. Look at the snowman playing hockey."

She'd rather look at Malcolm. Whatever had taken him out of the Christmas spirit, while in Sky's office, thankfully, hadn't lasted long. Her romantic and smiling Malcolm was back.

She took a picture of him.

"Hey, watch the flash. I'm driving."

"Barely. Do you think those other drivers have gone around you for the fun of it?"

"I'll drive two miles per hour if it means you don't miss anything. They're lucky I kept my hands in the car when they blew past me."

"New York driver," she accused with a laugh.

"And proud of it. That's why my middle finger is in such good shape." His pointed look had Sky crossing her legs, trying to ignore the sudden ache. "You can testify to the strength of my middle finger, especially when combined with my index finger." His hand rose to her face and caressed. "You're blushing."

"If I am, it's your fault."

They exited the park, and Malcolm got back on Route fifty. She thought he would drive straight home.

"Where are we going?"

"Nowhere, really. It's after ten and Christmas night, which means everything in this cute little Naval Academy town is closed. I thought I would drive for a while before taking you home. Lean the seat back, if you want, and relax. You've had a heavy day, although it was better than you thought it would be."

Sky wasn't physically tired, but she was emotionally exhausted. She reached for Malcolm's thigh, resting her hand there while he drove. Eyes closed, but not asleep, she allowed the events of the day to settle into place. She'd come home and had spent Christmas with her Ellis family, and it hadn't turned into a disaster.

She'd reconciled with her father, which removed tons of unhealthy weight from her heart and soul. For once, she felt connected to a sibling other than Carrie. In time, Sky thought Olivia and her could become friends. She didn't think they would ever be as close as she was with Carrie, but she wouldn't erect barriers to the possibility.

Her brothers were still an unknown. Them coming to her home and celebrating Christmas and her birthday was a huge step for Aaron and Garrett. When she came home for the Fourth of July weekend, she'd invite them to the Page's annual BBQ. Brandon and Jeremiah killed on the grill.

Sky smiled. "This is nice."

"The music?"

A few minutes into their drive, Malcolm had found a station that played instrumental Christmas music, which, admittedly, was nice.

"I meant this. Us. The night, soft music, and you beside me. It's nice. I didn't realize how much I needed this." But Malcolm had. "I figured I'd have to wait until the football game ended before I could politely suggest people leave."

"How desperately did you want to hide away in your bedroom?"

"More than I should admit. But I also didn't want to scurry away. You were right, I was enjoying myself. I'm glad I came home. I'm even happier you came with me."

"So am I."

Sky closed her eyes and listened to the Christmas music while Malcolm drove, not opening them again until he pulled onto the cul-de-sac, then drove past the Styles' rental and into a vacant garage. This wasn't right. When they'd left, all three of her garages were full, and her family's cars occupied the driveway and more than their share of the circle.

Where had everyone gone?

She repeated the question, but aloud, when they entered a silent house. No television. No voices. No people. The shoes in the baskets and on the rug were gone, except for those belonging to the Styles.

"Umm, Malcolm, did you hire a hit team to dispose of my family while we were out?"

He took her coat from her and hung it in the hall closet with his own.

"Nope. A lawyer, which is ten times more effective at hiding dead bodies than a hit team."

She laughed, knowing, if Sean had heard the quip, it would be on between the men.

Malcolm placed his hand on Sky's arm, as she reached for the zipper of her right boot. "No, leave them on, unless your feet hurt."

They didn't, so, when Malcolm held her hand and led her into the living room, she let him.

The tree lights were still on and the room spotless. Even the opened gifts that had littered the base of the tree were gone. Sky supposed Sean was also responsible for organizing the clean-up party.

Malcolm turned off the overhead light, which left them in a room illuminated only by the Christmas tree and the glow from the Sade angel topper.

"What are you up to?"

He didn't answer. Instead, Malcolm retrieved his cell phone from his pants pocket and propped it on the fireplace mantel. "I made a playlist for you." A slow groove ballad began. "May I have this dance?" Malcolm held out his hand to Sky.

With the romantic atmosphere of the room, Malcolm's outfit change had a different meaning. He hadn't switched clothes only to match Sky's dressy outfit. He'd dressed up for her.

Sky's stomach began to do flip-flops and Malcolm hadn't even pulled her into his arms yet.

She accepted his offered hand.

"Do you remember the first time I danced for you?"

How could she forget? He'd stripped to Ginuwine's _Pony_, ending the song with a lap dance that had left her panting and wet.

"It was the first time we made love." She wrapped her arms around Malcolm's neck.

His hands, like the man, were bold, sliding from her waist down to her backside. Face settled in the crook of her neck, lips soft, full, and warm. He kissed her there, singing the words to Major's *Why I Love You*. Their bodies swayed, Sky heady from the music and the man.

Malcolm didn't have the best singing voice. But what he lacked in vocals, he made up for in passion.

Sky held him tighter.

Malcolm continued to serenade her, every chosen love song a gold nugget of their relationship. By the fourth song, Sky's stomach had plummeted to her toes, and her heart had stuttered with giddy anticipation.

When Demetria McKinney's *Happy* ended, and the next song on Malcolm's playlist began, he lowered to one knee, his upturned face adoring.

She gasped, and he smiled, which had the effect of filling her eyes with tears.

Malcolm held Sky's hands through the first chorus of Eric Benet's *Spend My Life With You*. When Benet asked if he could spend his life with the woman he wanted to open his eyes to every morning, Malcolm slipped a ring on Sky's finger.

She had no idea when he'd let go of her hands, or where he'd pulled the ring from, but it appeared, like a Christmas miracle, on her finger.

Malcolm kissed the hand with the ring.

Sky cried.

And Eric Benet faded into the background. No other man mattered, in that moment. Only Malcolm.

From what she could see, through her tears, it wasn't a classic or traditional engagement ring like the one Sade hadn't accepted from Robert. Malcolm's ring was better because it was from him and meant for her.

"You're the splash of color in my life. Will you marry me, Sky El-lis?"

She sobbed, choking on a response stuck in her pounding heart, tightening throat, and drying mouth. Through it all, Malcolm remained on his knee, the hand around hers firm, eyes hopeful and wet.

"A one-word reply. That's all I need. I would prefer the three-letter word. The ring is already on your finger. You can't give it back."

"I don't want to give it back. It's mine." Sky tugged on Malcolm's hand, and he stood. "So are you. All mine."

"Say it, Sky. I want to hear the word."

She pressed her lips to his and whispered, "Yes."

Sky thought Malcolm would clap or whoop, the way he did when happy. He didn't. Her tenderhearted man embraced her. Not fiercely, as if relieved she'd accepted, despite asking him not to propose today. Not sensually, his mind on consummating their engagement with mind-blowing sex. But with infinite love and affection.

"You've made me so happy. Do you like the ring?"

She did, for all Sky could see of it in the dimly lit room and through her tears. Malcolm must've realized the same because he left her to turn on the light.

"Better?"

She had no idea.

"You're not looking at it."

No, her eyes were on Malcolm. The sexy, sweet man who would be her husband.

"You still haven't gotten a good look. Do you know how long it took me to select the perfect ring for you?"

"No."

"Well, a hell of a long time. A lot longer than it would take you to look at the ring properly."

Sky would examine every inch of her engagement ring. Malcolm had excellent taste and knew her style. She had every confidence he'd agonized for nothing and had chosen, as he'd said, the perfect ring for her. Right now, she wanted to mess with her fiancée.

Fiancée. The word sounded wonderful in her head. It would taste like a fine wine when she said it aloud.

"You gave me your word."

Malcolm frowned. "My word? What are you talking about?"

"You promised not to propose on my birthday. You broke your promise."

Malcolm's comeback was quick and lethal. "I'm going to strip that dress off you and fuck you while you wear those kickass heels. Your long legs will be over my shoulders so I can rub up and down the sequins while you take all of me. Then we're going to do it from behind and in front of your full-length mirror. You'll get to see everything I do to you. My hands on your breasts, your hair, your hips. My mouth kissing your neck, my lips sucking your shoulder, my tongue telling you how good you feel around my dick."

She gulped. Damn Malcolm. His form of retaliation was so much better than hers.

Malcolm's strong arm wrapped around her waist and pulled Sky flush against him. "FYI, Dr. Ellis, I proposed precisely five minutes after midnight. I kept my promise. No Christmas or birthday proposal. That was the deal, and I stuck to it. You said nothing about not proposing during the winter holiday season." Mouth lowered to collarbone and nipped. "Happy Kwanzaa, baby."

Kwanzaa, December twenty-sixth through January first. Sky dropped her head to Malcolm's shoulder and laughed. Caught in her own holiday trap. She was so focused on Christmas and harassing Malcolm with obscure holidays, she'd forgotten about Kwanzaa.

Malcolm raised her left hand for her inspection. "Umoja is the first principle of Kwanzaa, and it's celebrated on the first day of the holiday."

"Unity." Sky's eyes drifted away from Malcolm and down to her hand. A unity engagement ring sparkled on her finger. A pear-cut wrap diamond ring with a ruby in the center. Red, like her birthday dress. Red, like her sequin boots. Sky's splash of color.

"It's magnificent. Thank you."

"And a perfect fit. Speaking of that, remind me to return your birthstone ring."

She smacked his shoulder. "I've been looking for that ring for over a month. I thought I'd lost it."

"It's at my house. You can get it back, when you move in or when we move into our new home. It doesn't matter to me, as long as we're together and you're my wife."

Wife. A better word than fiancée.

"The wedding and summers here? How does that sound?"

"Wonderful."

"A late spring wedding?"

"Lovely."

"A baby by the following summer?"

"Possibly."

"Another a year after that?"

"Now you're pushing."

"I was hoping you'd do the pushing. I push, and you're pregnant. You push, and we have a baby. It seems fair to me."

"Only in a man's mind is that fair."

He held her close, pressing the lower half of his body into hers. She got his point.

"I already have names picked out."

"I just bet you do. Martin after MLK? William after WEB DuBois? Or, if we have a girl, Assata after Assata Shakur?"

"No, but those are good, especially Assata."

"What then?"

"Aria, Solstice, Cypress."

Sky groaned. "No nature names."

"Yes, nature names. Everest, Ginger, Chase."

"Chase?"

"Like that one? Remind you of something?"

"You didn't have to chase me."

"The hell if I didn't. When will it be my turn?"

Sky smiled, and then chased Malcolm's lips into their bright, sappy future. What started out as an office romance, a delicious perk of higher education, had morphed into a happily-ever-after holiday trope, which no one minded, least of all Sky and Malcolm.

THE END

 If you enjoyed the novel, the author invites you to leave a review.

EXCLUSIVE SNEAK PEEK: THE GIFT OF SECOND CHANCES

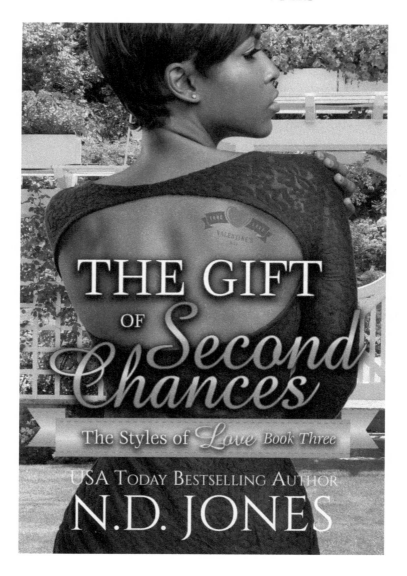

Angie stood in the doorway of her bedroom, a bottle of cold water in each hand. A naked Sean sat on the side of the bed, head down and cell phone in hand. She watched him read what she assumed were the text messages that had interrupted their lovemaking. He'd ignored them earlier, the same way he had when they were at the mall.

She'd also ignored her phone while they were out, knowing each ding was a work-related email. Like Sean, Angie had waited until they weren't together to check her messages, which she'd taken care of while downstairs.

Angie hadn't enjoyed the sense of dishonesty and guilt that had swept over her when she'd deliberately checked her emails when her husband wasn't around. She'd felt sneaky. Angie wondered if Sean felt the same.

"Who are all the texts from?"

Sean's head snapped up. "I didn't hear you come back."

"Obviously." She threw him one of the bottles of water but didn't move to join him in their bedroom. "So, who are they from?"

Sean had good reflexes. He'd caught the bottle with the hand not holding his phone. The feat was especially impressive considering the force she'd used to lob the bottle at his head.

"Darryl. I gave him the Cavanaugh racial profiling case, and he had a few questions he needed me to answer."

Darryl O'Neal was one of three lawyers at Franklin & Associates. He was the first attorney her husband had hired, a fifty-year-old Georgian native who ate too much peace cobbler and all but bathed in cologne. She liked Darryl. The man was compassionate and open-minded, and his Atlanta-Buffalo accent a cute mix of Southern and Eastern urban.

For as long as she'd known Darryl, she didn't recall him ever blowing up Sean's phone the way he'd done today. Although, it was possible all the texts were from Darryl. "Why didn't he call? It would've been quicker if he needed the information right away."

"He knows weekends are off limits. I know I can't put every case on the backburner during the weekends. As much as possible, though, that's my goal. When I said I wanted us to spend more time together, I meant I had to adjust my work schedule, too. By the way, why are you standing over there?"

She didn't know. No, that wasn't true. Angie needed to ask Sean a question, and the distance helped force the words out her mouth and into the marital air between them. "Is there something you want to tell me?"

"Like what?"

"I don't know. Something."

"Something like what? Am I supposed to know what you're talking about?"

Sean dropped his cell phone and bottle of water onto the bed. She thought he would get up and put on a robe, like she had, or slip into a pair of boxers. Instead, he stared at her, his luscious brown eyes pools of confusion.

"If you have something you'd like to tell me, I wish you would."

"I have no idea what you're talking about. You aren't making sense. Come over here."

"No. Just tell me. Be honest." Her grip on the water bottle tightened, and her heart pounded with anxiety. "Be. Honest." The two words escaped on a whispered, angry plea. "Was that really Darryl who'd texted you?"

"Come here and find out for yourself."

Her legs were like marble columns planted at the threshold of her bedroom. For the last two months, she couldn't have asked for a more loving and attentive husband. Not that Sean wasn't before, but lately, he'd taken notice of Angie the way he hadn't in years. He brought her flowers and gifts more often. He'd taken to surprising her at work with lunch. Sean prepared her breakfast, so she'd have a decent meal to begin her day. And yes, he'd reduced his workload, coming home earlier and taking the weekends off.

The changes were sweet, but Angie couldn't help but wonder at the unexpected behavior and attitude shift.

As naked as the day he was born, Sean got to his feet and grabbed his cell phone. His long legs brought him to stand in front of her in mere seconds.

"Here, look for yourself." She stared down at the offered cell phone. "Take it. I don't have anything to hide. Check whatever you want. My texts, emails, call logs, Facebook page, whatever."

Angie had never been one of those women who searched her man's wallet, pants pockets, cell phone, or social media accounts. She didn't pull up the search history on his laptop when he wasn't around, looking for porno addiction and god knows what else that would give a woman a reason for concern.

She wasn't that kind of female. Angie had assumed, if a woman felt a need to go through all of that, then she might as well let the man go. Whether he was loyal or not, her actions proved she didn't trust him enough not to spy.

Angie trusted her husband, but she found it difficult to ignore her instincts. She snatched the phone from Sean's hand but didn't waste her time scrolling through the device. Even if her suspicions were correct, Sean wouldn't be so stupid as to leave evidence around for her to find. And he certainly wouldn't offer up his confession on an electronic platter.

ABOUT N.D. JONES

N. D. Jones, USA Today Bestselling author, lives in Maryland with her husband and two children. A desire to see more novels with positive, sexy, and three-dimensional African American characters as soul mates, friends, and lovers, inspired the author to take on the challenge of penning such romantic reads. She is the author of two paranormal romance series: Winged Warriors and Death and Destiny. She's also embarked on a science fiction romance series, Forever Yours. N.D. likes to read historical and paranormal romance novels, as well as comics and manga.

OTHER BOOKS BY N.D. JONES

Winged Warriors Novella Series (Angels and Demons)
Fire, Fury, Faith (Book 1)
Heat, Hunt, Hope (Book 2)

Death and Destiny Trilogy (Witches and Were-Cat Shifters)
Of Fear and Faith (Book 1)
Of Beasts and Bonds (Book 2)
Of Deception and Divinity (Book 3)

Forever Yours Series (Fantasy Romance)
Bound Souls (Book 1)

Dragon Shifter Romance (Standalone Novels)
Stones of Dracontias: The Bloodstone Dragon
Dragon Lore and Love: Isis and Osiris

The Styles of Love Trilogy (Contemporary Romance)
The Perks of Higher Ed (Book 1)
The Wish of Xmas Present (Book 2)
The Gift of Second Chances (Book 3)

NEWSLETTER

JOIN N.D.'s NEWSLETTER FOR:

- Advanced Reader Copies
- Sales
- Freebies
- Giveaways
- Exclusive Excerpts
- Cover Reveals
- New Releases

All <u>newsletter</u> **subscribers will receive a FREE audiobook copy of *Fire, Fury, Faith*.**